BETRAYAL AT KOSSEIR

Everywhere men ran to the boats, the seamen first to man the oars and haul in the anchors. In a wavering line the marines retreated, holding the advancing French just far enough away to permit the embarkation of the British.

In the dark confusion Morris found it a matter of ease to spin the wounded Drinkwater round as they waded into the water, to bring his knee up into Drinkwater's groin and to drop him as though shot. In falling Drinkwater had cut his leg upon the blade of his sword . . .

Morris was smiling as he scrambled over the bow of his boat. In the final surge of the sea as it washed the beach of Kosseir Bay lay the body of Nathaniel Drinkwater . . .

BOOKS BY RICHARD WOODMAN

For Christine

"I shall believe that they are going on with their scheme of possessing Alexandria, and getting troops to India—a plan concerted with Tipoo Sahib, by no means so difficult as might at first be imagined."

NELSON, 1798

Contents

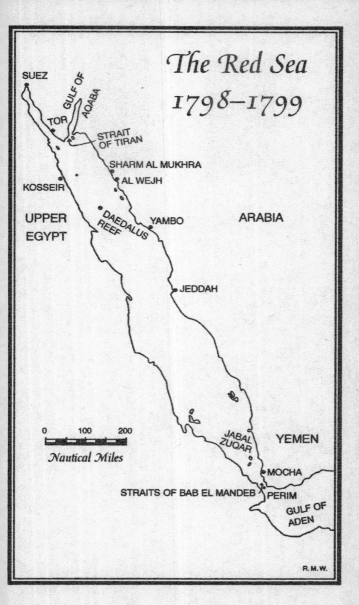

The Red Sea
1798–1799

SUEZ

TOR

GULF OF AQABA

STRAIT OF TIRAN

SHARM AL MUKHRA

AL WEJH

KOSSEIR

UPPER EGYPT

DAEDALUS REEF

YAMBO

ARABIA

JEDDAH

0   100   200
Nautical Miles

JABAL ZUQAR

YEMEN

MOCHA

STRAITS OF BAB EL MANDEB

PERIM

GULF OF ADEN

R. M. W.

Paris

February 1798

Rain beat upon the rattling window and beyond the courtyard the naval captain watched the tricolour stiff with wind, bright against the grey scud sweeping over Paris. In his mind's eye he conjured the effect of the gale upon the green waters of the Channel and the dismal, rain-sodden shore of the English coast beyond.

Behind him the two secretaries bent over their desks. The rustle of papers was reverently hushed. An air of expectancy filled the room, emphasised by the open door. Presently rapid footsteps sounded in the corridor and the secretaries bent with more diligence over their work. The naval officer half turned from the window, then resumed his survey of the sky.

The footsteps sounded louder and into the room swept a short, thin, pale young man whose long hair fell over the high collar of his over-large general's coat. He was accompanied by an hussar, whose elaborate pelisse dangled negligently from his left shoulder.

"Ah, Bourienne!" said the general abruptly in a voice that reflected the same energy as the restless pacing he had fallen into. "Have you the dispatches for Generals Dommartin and

Cafarelli, eh? Good, good." He took the papers and glanced at them, nodding with satisfaction. "You see Androche," he remarked to the hussar, "it goes well, very well and the project of England is dead." He turned towards the window. "Whom have we here, Bourienne?"

"This is Capitaine de Frégate Santhonax, General Bonaparte."

"Ah!"

Hearing his name the naval officer turned from the window. He was much taller than the general, his handsome features severely disfigured by a recent scar that ran upwards from the corner of his mouth into his left cheek. He made a slight bow and met General Bonaparte's appraising grey eyes.

"So, Captain, you contrived to escape from the English, eh?"

"Yes, Citizen General, I arrived in Paris three weeks ago."

"And have already married, eh?" Santhonax nodded, aware that the Corsican knew all about him. The general resumed his pacing, head sunk in thought. "I have just come from an inspection of the Channel Ports and the arrangements in hand for an invasion of England . . ." he stopped abruptly in front of Santhonax. "What are your views of the practicality of such an enterprise?"

"Impossible without complete command of the Channel, any attempt without local superiority would be doomed, Citizen General. Conditions in the Channel can change rapidly, we should have to hold it for a week at least. The British fleet, if it cannot be overwhelmed, *must* be dissipated by ruse and threat . . ."

"Exactly! That is what I have informed the Directory . . . but do we have the capability to achieve such a local superiority?"

"No, Citizen General." Santhonax lowered his eyes before

the penetrating stare of Bonaparte. While this young man had been trouncing the Austrians out of Italy he had been working to achieve such a combination by bringing the Dutch fleet to Brest. The attempt had been shattered by the British at Camperdown four months earlier.

"Huh!" exclaimed Bonaparte, "then we agree at all points, Captain. That is excellent, excellent. The Army of England is to have employment in a different quarter, eh Androche?" He turned to the hussar, "This is Androche Junot, Captain, an old friend of the Bonapartes." The two men bowed. "But the Army of England will lay the axe to the root of England's wealth. What is your opinion of the English, Captain?"

Santhonax sighed. "They are the implacable enemies of the Revolution, General Bonaparte, and of France. They possess qualities of great doggedness and should not be underestimated."

Bonaparte sniffed in disagreement. "Yet you escaped from them, no? How did you accomplish that, eh?"

"Following my capture I was taken to Maidstone Gaol. After a few weeks I was transferred to the hulks at Portsmouth. However my uniform was so damaged in the action off Camperdown that I managed to secure a civilian coat from my gaolers. When the equipage in which I was travelling changed horses at a place called Guildford, I made my escape."

"And?"

Santhonax shrugged. "I turned into an adjacent alleyway and then the first tavern where I took a corner seat. I speak English without an accent, Citizen General."

"And this?" Bonaparte pointed to his own cheek.

"The escort were looking for a man with a bandage. I removed it and occupied an obscure corner. I was not discovered." He paused, then added, "I am used to subterfuge."

"Yes, yes, Captain, I know of your services to the Republic, you have a reputation for intrepidity and audacity. Admiral Bruix speaks highly of you and as you are not at present quite persona grata with the Directors," Bonaparte paused while Santhonax flushed at the allusion to his failure, "he recommends you to this especial command." The general stopped again in front of Santhonax and looked directly up at him. "You are appointed to a frigate I understand, Captain?"

"The *Antigone*, Citizen General, now preparing for a distant cruise at Rochefort. I am also to have the corvettes *La Torride* and *Annette* with me. I am directed to take command as commodore on receipt of your final orders."

"Good, very good." Bonaparte held out his hand to Bourienne and the secretary handed him a sealed packet. "The British have a small squadron in the Red Sea. They should cause you no fear. As you have been told the Army under my command is bound for Egypt. When my veterans reach the shore of the Red Sea I anticipate you will have secured a sufficiency of transport, local craft of course, and a port of embarkation for a division. You will convey it to India, Captain Santhonax. You are familiar with those waters?"

"I served under Suffren, Citizen General. So we are to harrass the British in India." Santhonax's eyes glowed with a new enthusiasm.

"You will carry but the advance guard. Paris burns the soles of my feet, Captain. In India may be found the empire left by Alexander. There greatness awaits us." It was not the speech of a fanatic, Santhonax had heard enough of them during the Revolution. But Bonaparte's enthusiasm was infectious. After the defeat of Camperdown and his capture, Santhonax's ambition had seemed exhausted. But now, in a few words, this dynamic little Corsican had swept the past aside, like the Revolution itself. New visions of glory were opened to the imagination by a man to whom all things seemed possible.

Abruptly Bonaparte held out the sealed packet to Santhonax. Junot bent forward to whisper in his ear. "Ah! Yes, Androche reminds me that your wife is a celebrated beauty. Good, good. Marriage is what binds a man to his country and beauty is the inspiration of ambition, eh? You shall bring Madame Santhonax to the Rue Victoire this evening, Captain, my wife is holding a soirée. You may proceed to Rochefort tomorrow. That is all, Captain."

As Santhonax left the room General Bonaparte was already dictating to his secretaries.

CHAPTER ONE

The Convoy Escort

February–June 1798

A low mist hung in the valley of the Meon where the pale winter sunshine had yet to reach. Beneath the dripping branches of the apple trees Lieutenant Nathaniel Drinkwater paced slowly up and down, shivering slightly in the frosty air. He had not slept well, waking from a dream that had been full of fitful images of faces he had done with now that he had come home. The nocturnal silence of the cottage was still disturbingly unfamiliar even after two months leave of absence from the creaking hull of the cutter *Kestrel*. It compelled him to rise early lest his restlessness woke his wife beside him. Now, pacing the path of the tiny garden, the chill made the wound in his right arm ache, bringing his mind full circle to where the dream had dislodged it from repose.

It had been Edouard Santhonax who had inflicted the wound and of whom he had dreamed. But as he came to his senses he recollected that Santhonax was now safely mewed up, a prisoner. As for his paramour, the bewitching Hortense Montholon, she was in France begging for her bread, devil take her! He felt the sun penetrate the mist, warm upon his back, finally dispelling the fears of the night. The recent gales had gone, giving way to sharp frosty mornings of bright sunshine. The click of a door latch reminded him he was in happier circumstances.

The dark hair fell about Elizabeth's face and her brown eyes were full of concern. "Are you not well, my dear?" she asked gently, putting a hand on his arm. "Did you not hear the knock at the street door?"

"I am quite well, Bess. Who was at the door?"

"Mr. Jackson at the Post Office sent young Will up from Petersfield with letters for you. They are on the table."

"I am indebted to Mr. Jackson's kindness." He moved to pass inside the cottage but she stopped him. "Nathaniel, what troubles you?" Then, in a lower voice, "You have not been disappointed in me?"

He caught her up and kissed her, then they went in to read the letters. He broke the one with the Admiralty seal first: *Sir, you are required and directed that upon receipt of these instructions you proceed* . . . He was appointed first lieutenant of the brig-sloop *Hellebore* under Commander Griffiths. In silence he handed the letter to Elizabeth who caught her lower lip in her teeth as she read. Drinkwater picked up the second letter, recognising the shaky but still bravely flowing script.

My Dear Nathaniel,

You will doubtless be in receipt of their L'dships' Instructions to join the Brig under my Command. She is a new Vesfel and lying at Deptford. Do not hasten. I am already on board and doing duty for you, the end of the month will suffice. Our Complement is almost augmented as I was able to draft the Kestrels entire. We sail upon Convoy duty. Convey my felicitations to your wife,

I remain, etc.

Madoc Griffiths

P.S. I received News but yesterday that M. Santhonax Escaped Custody and has been at Liberty for a month now.

Drinkwater stood stunned, the oppression of the night returned to him. Elizabeth was watching, her eyes large with tears. "So soon, my darling . . ."

He smiled ruefully at her. "Madoc has extended my leave a little." He passed the second letter over. "Dear Madoc," she said, brushing her eyes.

"Aye, he does duty for me now. He has nowhere else to go." He slipped his arm around her waist and they kissed again.

"Come, we have time to complete the purchase of the house at Petersfield and your cook should arrive by the end of the week. You will be quite the *grande dame*."

"Will you take Tregembo with you?"

He laughed. "I doubt that I have the power to stop him."

They fell silent, Elizabeth thinking of the coming months of loneliness, Drinkwater disloyally of the new brig. "*Hellebore,*" he said aloud, "ain't that a flower or something? Elizabeth? What the devil are you laughing at?"

Lieutenant Richard White had the morning watch aboard *Victory*. Flying the flag of Earl St. Vincent the great three decker stood north west under easy sail, the rest of the blockading squadron in line ahead and astern of her. To the east the mole and lighthouse of Cadiz were pale in the sunshine but White's glass was trained ahead to where a cutter was flying the signal for sails in sight to the north.

A small midshipman ran up to him. "Looks like the convoy, sir."

"Thank you, Mr. Lee. Have the kindness to inform His Lordship and the Captain." Mr. Lee was ten years old and had

endeared himself to Lieutenant White by being the only officer aboard *Victory* shorter than himself. Instinctively White
looked round the deck, checking that every rope was in its
place, every man at his station and every sail drawing to perfection before St. Vincent's eagle eye drew his attention to it.

"Good morning, my lord," said White, vacating the windward side of the deck and doffing his hat as the admiral ascended to the poop for a better view of the newcomers. "Good
morning, sir," responded the admiral with the unfailing courtesy that made his blasts of admonition the more terrible.

Captain Grey and Sir Robert Calder, Captain of the Fleet,
also came on deck, followed by *Victory*'s first lieutenant and
several other officers, for any arrival from England brought
news, letters and gossip to break the tedium of blockade.

They could see the convoy now, six storeships under the
escort of a brig from whose masthead a string of bunting
broke out. In White's ear Mr. Lee squeaked the numerals followed by a pause while he hunted in the lists. "Brig-sloop
Hellebore, sir, but newly commissioned under Commander
Griffiths."

"Thank you, Mr. Lee. Brig *Hellebore*, Captain Griffiths,
my lord, with convoy."

"Thank you, Mr. White, have the goodness to desire him to
send a boat with an officer."

"Aye, aye, my lord." He turned to Lee who was already
chalking the signal on his slate and calling the flag numbers
to his yeoman.

White, who had given the commander his courtesy title
when addressing the punctilious St. Vincent, was wondering
where he had heard the name before. It was not long before
he had his answer.

When the brig's boat hooked onto *Victory*'s chains he
recognised the figure who came in at the entry.

"Nathaniel! My dear fellow, so you're still with Griffiths, eh? How capital to see you! And you've been made." White indicated the gilt-buttoned lieutenant's cuff that he was vigorously pumping up and down in welcome. "Damn me but I'm delighted, delighted, but come, St. Vincent will not tolerate our gossiping."

Drinkwater followed his old friend apprehensively. It was many years since he had trod such a flagship's deck and the ordered precision of *Victory* combined with her size to show Admiral Duncan's smaller, weathered and worn-out *Venerable* in a poor light. Drinkwater uncovered and made a small and, he hoped, elegant bow as White introduced him to the earl. He felt himself under the keenest scrutiny by a pair of shrewd old eyes that shone from a face that any moment might slip from approbation to castigation. Lord St. Vincent studied the man before him. Drinkwater's intelligent gaze met that of the admiral. He was thirty-four, lean and of middle height. His face was weathered and creased about the grey eyes and mouth, with the thin line of an old scar puckering down the left cheek. There were some small blue powder burns about the eyes, like random inkspots. Drinkwater's hair, uncovered by the doffed hat, was still a rich brown, clubbed in a long queue behind the head. Not, the admiral concluded, a flagship officer, but well enough, judging by the firm, full mouth and steady eyes. The mouth was not unlike Nelson's, St. Vincent thought with wry affection, and Nelson had been a damned pain until he had hoisted his own flag.

"Are you married sir?" St. Vincent asked sharply.

"Er, yes, my lord," replied Drinkwater, taken aback.

"A pity, sir, a pity. A married officer is frequently lost to the service. Come let us descend to my cabin and arrange for the disposition of your convoy. Sir Robert, a moment of your time . . ."

When the business of the fleet had been attended to Drinkwater had a few minutes for an exchange of news with White while *Victory* backed her maintopsail and summoned *Hellebore*'s boat.

"How is Elizabeth, my dear fellow?"

"She goes along famously, Richard, and would have asked to be remembered to you had she known we might meet."

"When were you gazetted, Nat?"

"After Camperdown."

"Ah, so you were there. Damn! That still gives you the advantage of one fleet action to boast of ahead of me," he grinned. "D'you have many other old Kestrels besides Griffiths on your brig?"

"Aye, Tregembo you remember, and old Appleby . . ."

"What? That old windbag Harry Appleby? Well I'm damned. She looks a long-legged little ship, Nat," he nodded at the brig.

"She's well enough, but you still have the important advantages," replied Drinkwater, a sweep of his hand including *Victory*, the puissant personages upon her deck and alluding to White's rapid rise by comparison with his own. "Convoy work ain't quite the way to be made post."

"No, Nat, but my bet is you're ordered up the Mediterranean, eh?" Drinkwater nodded and White went on, "That's where Nelson is, before Toulon, Nat, and wherever Nelson is there's action and glory." White's eyes gleamed. "D'you know St. Vincent sent him back into the Med after we evacuated it last year and a month ago he reinforced Nelson with Troubridge's inshore squadron. Sent the whole lot of 'em off from the harbour mouth before Curtis's reinforcements had come up with the fleet. And the blasted Dons didn't even know the inshore squadron had been changed! What d'you think of that, eh? No," he patted Drinkwater's arm condescendingly, "the Med's the place, Nat, there's bound to be action with Nelson."

"I'm only escorting a convoy in a brig, Richard," said Drinkwater deprecatingly.

White laughed again and held out his hand. "Good fortune then Nat, for we're all hostage to it, d'you know."

They shook hands and Drinkwater descended to the boat where Mr. Quilhampton, two years older than Mr. Lee, but with a fraction of the latter's experience, overawed by the mass of *Victory* lumbering alongside his cockleshell cutter, made a hash of getting off the battleship's side.

"Steady now, Mr. Q. Bear off forward, put the helm over and *then* lower your oars. 'Tis the only way, d'you see," Drinkwater said patiently, looking back at *Victory*. Already her main topsail was filled and White's grin was clearly visible. Drinkwater looked ahead towards the tiny, fragile *Helle-bore*. The cutter rose over the long, low Atlantic swells, the sea danced blue and gold in the sunshine where the light westerly wind rippled its surface. He felt the warmth in the muscles of his right arm.

"*Hecuba* and *Molly* to accompany us into the Med, sir, to Nelson, off Toulon. We're to proceed as soon as possible." Drinkwater looked at Griffiths who lent heavily against the rail, gazing at the stately line of the British fleet to the eastward. "*Prydferth, bach*, beautiful," he muttered. Drinkwater stared astern at the convoy, their topsails aback in an untidy gaggle as they waited to hear their fate. Boats were bobbing towards the brig. "I've sent for their masters," Griffiths explained.

"How's the leg today, sir?" Drinkwater asked while they waited for the boats to arrive. The old, white-haired Welshman looked with disgust at the twisted and puffy limb stretched stiffly out on the gun carriage before him.

"Ah, devil take it, it's a damned nuisance. And now Appleby tells me it's gouty. And before you raise the matter of my bottle," he hurried on with mock severity, "I'll have you know that without it I'd be intolerable, see." They grinned at each other, their relationship a stark contrast with the formality of *Victory*'s quarterdeck. They had sailed together for six years, first in the twelve-gun cutter *Kestrel*, and their intimacy was established upon a mutually understood basis of friendship and professional distance. For Griffiths was an infirm man, subject to recurring malarial fevers, whose command had been bestowed for services rendered to British intelligence. Without *Hellebore* Griffiths would have rotted ashore, a lonely and embittered bachelor in anonymous lodgings. He had requested Drinkwater as his first lieutenant partly out of gratitude, partly out of friendship. And if Griffiths sought to protect his own career by delegating with perfect confidence to Drinkwater, he could console himself with the thought that he did the younger man a service.

"You forget, Mr. Drinkwater, that if I had not broke my leg last year you'd not have been in command of *Kestrel* at Camperdown."

Drinkwater agreed, but any further rejoinder was cut short by the arrival of the storeship commanders.

To starboard the dun-coloured foothills of the Atlas Mountains shone rose-red in the sunset. To larboard the hills of southern Spain fell to the low promontory of Tarifa. Far ahead of her elongated shadow the Mediterranean opened before the bowsprit of the brig. From her deck the horizontal light threw into sharp relief every detail of her fabric: the taut lines of her rigging, the beads of her blocks, her reddened canvas and an unnatural brilliance in her paintwork. Astern on either quarter, in dark silhouette, *Hecuba* and *Molly* followed them.

Drinkwater ceased pacing as the skinny midshipman barred his way.

"Yes, Mr. Q?" The gunroom officers of H.M. Brig *Hellebore* had long since ceased to wrap their tongues round Quilhampton. It was far too grand a name for an animal as insignificant as a volunteer. Once again Drinkwater experienced that curious reminder of Elizabeth that the boy engendered, for Drinkwater had obtained a place for him on the supplication of his wife. Mrs. Quilhampton was a pretty widow who occasionally assisted Elizabeth with her school, and Drinkwater had been both flattered and amused that anyone should consider him a person of sufficient influence from whom to solicit "interest". And there was sufficient resemblance to his own introduction to naval life to arouse his natural sympathy. He had acquiesced with only a show of misgivings and been rewarded by a quite shameless embrace from the boy's mother. Now the son's eager-to-please expression irritated him with its power to awaken memories.

"Well," he snapped, "come, come, what the devil d'you want?"

"Begging your pardon, sir, but Mr. Appleby's compliments and where are we bound, sir?"

"Don't you know, Mr. Q?" said Drinkwater, mellowing.

"N . . . no, sir."

"Come now, what d'you see to starboard?"

"To starboard, sir? Why that's land, sir."

"And to larboard?"

"That's land too, sir."

"Aye, Mr. Q. To starboard is Africa, to larboard is Europe. Now what d'you suppose lies between, eh? What did Mrs. Drinkwater instruct you in the matter, eh?"

"Be it the M . . . Mediterranean, sir?"

"It be indeed, Mr. Q," replied Drinkwater with a smile, "and d'you know who commands in the Mediterranean?"

"Why sir, I know that. Sir Horatio Nelson, K.B., sir," said the boy eagerly.

"Very well, Mr. Q. Now do you repair directly to the surgeon and acquaint him with those facts and tell him that we are directed by Earl St. Vincent to deliver the contents of those two hoys astern to Rear Admiral Nelson off Toulon."

"Aye, aye, sir."

"And Mr. Q . . ."

"Sir?"

"Do you also direct Mr. Appleby to have a tankard of blackstrap ready for me when I come below at eight bells."

Drinkwater watched the excited Quilhampton race below. Like the midshipman he was curious about Nelson, a man whose name was known to every schoolboy in England since his daring manoeuvre at the battle of Cape St. Vincent. Not that his conduct had been put at risk by the enemy so much as by those in high places at the Admiralty. Drinkwater knew there were those who considered he would be shot for disobedience before long, just as there were those who complained he was no seaman. Certainly he did not possess the abilities of a Pellew or a Keats, and although he enjoyed the confidence of St. Vincent he had been involved in the fiasco at Santa Cruz. Perhaps, thought Drinkwater, he was a man like the restless Smith, with whom he had served briefly in the Channel, a man of dynamic force whose deficiencies could be forgiven in a kind of emulative love. But, he concluded, pacing the deck in the gathering darkness, whatever White said on the subject, it did not alter the fact that *Hellebore* was but a brig and fitted for little more than her present duties.

CHAPTER TWO

Nelson

July 1798

"She hasn't acknowledged, sir. Shall I fire a gun to loo'ard?"

Griffiths stared astern to where *Hecuba*, her jury rigged foremast a mute testimony to the violence of the weather, was struggling into the bay.

"No, Mr. Drinkwater. Don't forget she's a merchantman with a quarter of our complement and right now, *bach*, every man-jack aboard her will be busy."

Drinkwater felt irritated by the mild rebuke, but he held his tongue. The week of anxiety must surely soon be over. South of Minorca, beating up for Toulon the northerly mistral had hit the little convoy with unusual violence. *Hecuba*'s foremast had gone by the board and they had been obliged to run off to the eastward and the shelter of Corsica. Drinkwater stared ahead at the looming coastline of the island, the sharp peaked mountains reaching up dark against the glow of dawn. To larboard Cape Morsetta slowly extended its shelter as they limped eastward into Crovani Bay.

"Deck there! Sail dead ahead, sir!"

The cry from the masthead brought the glasses of the two men up simultaneously. In the shadows of the shoreline lay a three-masted vessel, her spars bare of canvas as she lay wind-rode at anchor.

"A polaccra," muttered Griffiths. "We'll investigate her when we've brought this lame duck to her anchor," he jerked his head over his shoulder.

The convoy stood on into the bay. Soon they were able to discern the individual pine trees that grew straight and tall enough to furnish fine masts.

"Bring the ship to the wind Mr. Lestock," Griffiths addressed the master, a small, fussy little man with a permanent air of being put upon. "You may fire your gun when we let the bower go, Mr. Drinkwater."

"Aye, aye, sir." Lestock was shouting through the speaking trumpet as men ran to the braces, thankful to be in the lee of land where *Hellebore*'s deck approximated the horizontal. The main topsail slapped back against the mast and redistributed its thrust through the standing rigging to the hull below. *Hellebore* lost forward motion and began to gather sternway.

"Let go!"

The carpenter's topmaul swung once, then the brig's bow kicked slightly, as the bower anchor's weight was released. The splash was lost in the bark of the six pounder. While Lestock and his mates had the canvas taken off the ship, Drinkwater swung his glass round the bay. *Molly* was making sternway and he saw the splash under her bluff, north-country bow where her anchor was let go. But *Hecuba* still stood inshore while her hands struggled to clew up her fore-course. Unable to manoeuvre under her topsails due to her damaged foremast, her master had been obliged to hold on to the big sail until the last moment, now something had fouled.

"Why don't he back the damned thing." Drinkwater muttered to himself while beside him Lestock roared "Aloft and stow!" through the speaking trumpet. The Hellebores eagerly leapt into the rigging to pummel the brig's topsails into the gaskets, anxious to get secured, the galley stove relit and some steaming skillygolee and molasses into their empty, contracted bellies.

Then he saw *Hecuba* begin her turn into the wind, saw the big course gather itself into folds like a washerwoman tucking up her skirts, the main topsail flatten itself against the top and the splash from her bow where the anchor was let go.

"Convoy's anchored, sir," he reported to Griffiths.

The commander nodded. "Looks like your gun had another effect." Griffiths pointed his glass at the polaccra anchored inshore of them. Drinkwater studied the unfamiliar colours that had been hoisted to her masthead.

"Ragusan ensign, Mr. Drinkwater, and I'll warrant you didn't know 'em from the Grand Turk's."

Drinkwater felt the tension ebbing from him. "You'd be right, sir."

Lestock touched his hat to Griffiths. "She's brought up, sir, and secured."

"Very well, Mr. Lestock, pipe the hands to breakfast after which I want a working party under Mr. Rogers ready to assist the re-rigging of *Hecuba*. Send both your mates over. Oh, and Mr. Dalziell can go too, I'd very much like to know if that young man is to be of any service to us."

"Aye, aye, sir. What about Mr. Quilhampton, sir? He is also inexperienced."

Griffiths eyed Lestock with something approaching distaste.

"Mr. Quilhampton can take a working party ashore with the carpenter. I think a couple of those pines would come in useful, eh? What d'you think Mr. Drinkwater?"

"A good idea, sir. And the Ragusan?"

"Mr. Q's first task will be to desire her master to wait upon me. Now, Mr. Drinkwater, you have been up all night, will you take breakfast with me before you turn in?"

Half an hour later, his belly full, Drinkwater stretched luxuriously, too comfortable to make his way to his cabin. Griffiths dabbed his mouth with a stained napkin.

"I think Rogers can take care of that business aboard *Hecuba*."

"I hope so sir," yawned Drinkwater, "he's not backward in forwarding opinions as to his own merit."

"Or of criticising others, Nathaniel," said Griffiths solemnly. Drinkwater nodded. The second lieutenant was a trifle overconfident and it was impossible to pull the wool over the eyes of an officer as experienced and shrewd as Griffiths. "That's no bad thing," continued the commander in his deep, mellifluous Welsh voice, "if there's substance beneath the facade." Drinkwater agreed sleepily, his lids closing of their own accord.

"But I'm less happy about Mr. Dalziell."

Drinkwater forced himself awake. "No sir, it's nothing one can lay one's finger upon but . . ." he trailed off, his brain refusing to work any further.

"Pass word for my servant," Griffiths called, and Meyrick came into the tiny cubby hole that served the brig's officers for a common mess. "Assist Mr. Drinkwater to his cot, Meyrick."

"I'm all right, sir." Drinkwater rose slowly to his feet and made for the door of his own cabin, cannoning into the portly figure of the surgeon.

Griffiths smiled to himself as he watched the two manoeuvre round one another, the one sleepily indignant, the other wakefully apologetic. Appleby seated himself at the table. "Morning sir, dreadful night . . ." The surgeon fell to a dissertation about the movement of brigs as opposed to ships of the line, to whether or not their respective motions had an adverse effect on the human frame, and to what degree in each case. Griffiths had long since learned to disregard the surgeon's ramblings which increased with age. Griffiths remembered the mutual animosity that had characterised their early relationship. But that had all changed. After Griffiths had been left ashore at Great Yarmouth in the autumn of the previous year it had been Appleby who had come in search of him when the *Kestrel* decommissioned. It had been Appleby too who had not merely sworn at the incompetence of the physicians there, but who had nearly fought a duel with a certain Dr. Spriggs over the manner in which the latter had set Griffiths's femur. Appleby had wished to break and reset it, but was prevailed upon to desist by Griffiths himself, who had felt that matters were passing a little out of his own control.

Still raging inwardly, Appleby had written off to Lord Dungarth to remind the earl of the invaluable services performed by Griffiths during his tenure of command of the cutter *Kestrel*. Thus the half-pay commander with the game leg had found himself commissioning the new brig-sloop *Hellebore*. Appleby's appointment to surgeon of the ship was the least Griffiths could do in return and they had become close in the succeeding weeks.

Lord Dungarth had pleaded his own cause and requested that a Mr. Dalziell be found a place as midshipman. It was soon apparent why the earl had not sent the youth to a crack frigate, whatever the obligation he owed the Dalziell family. Griffiths sighed; Mr. Dalziell was fortunately small beer and unlikely to cause him great loss of sleep, but he could not escape a sense of exasperation at having been saddled with such a make-weight. He poured more coffee as Appleby drew to his conclusion.

"And so you see, sir, I am persuaded that the lively motion

of such a vessel as this, though the buffetting one receives
below decks is apt to give one a greater number of minor con-
tusions than enough, is, however, likely to exercise more
muscles in the body and invigorate the humours more than the
leisurely motion of, say, a first rate. In the latter case the som-
nolent rhythms may induce a langour, and when coupled to
the likelihood of the vessel being employed on blockade,
hove to and so forth, actually contribute to that malaise and
boredom that are the inevitable concomitants of that unenviable employment. Do you not agree sir?"

"Eh? Oh, undoubtedly you are right, Mr. Appleby. But
frankly I am driven to wonder to what purpose you men of
science address your speculations."

Appleby expelled his breath in an eloquent sigh. "Ah well,
sir, 'tis no great matter . . . how long d'you intend to stay
here?"

"Just as long as it takes Mr. Rogers to assist the people of
Hecuba to get up a new foremast. Under the circumstances
they did a wonderful job themselves, for in that sea there was
no question of them securing a tow."

"Ah! I was thinking about that, sir. Nathaniel was talking
about using a rocket to convey a line. Now, if we could
but . . ." Appleby broke off as Mr. Q popped his head round
the door.

"Beg pardon sir, but the captain of the Ra . . . Rag . . ."

"Ragusan," prompted Griffiths.

"Yes, sir . . . well he's here sir."

"Then show him in, boy, show him in."

Griffiths summoned Drinkwater from sleep at noon. The tiny
cabin that accommodated the brig's commander was strewn
with charts and Lestock was in fussy attendance.

"Ah, Mr. Drinkwater, please help yourself to a glass." Griffiths indicated the decanter which contained his favourite *sercial*. As the lieutenant poured Griffiths outlined the events of the morning.

"This mistral that prevented our getting up to Toulon has been a blessing in disguise . . ." Drinkwater saw Lestock nodding in sage agreement with his captain. "The fact that we have had to run for shelter has likely saved us from falling into the hands of the French."

Still tired, Drinkwater frowned with incomprehension. Nelson was blockading Toulon; what the devil was Griffiths driving at?

"The French are out, somewhere it is believed, in the eastern Mediterranean. That polaccra spoke with Admiral Nelson off Cape Passaro on June the twenty-second . . . two weeks ago. He's bound to Barcelona and was quizzed by the admiral about the whereabouts of the French armada."

"Armada, sir? You mean an invasion force?"

Griffiths nodded. "I do indeed, *bach. Myndiawl*, they've given Nelson the slip, see."

"And did this Ragusan offer Sir Horatio any intelligence?"

"Indeed he did. The polaccra passed the entire force, heading east . . ."

"East? And Nelson's gone in pursuit?"

"Yes indeed. And we must follow." Drinkwater digested the news, trying to make sense of it. East? All his professional life the Royal Navy had guarded against a combination of naval forces in the Channel. His entire service aboard *Kestrel* had been devoted to that end. Indeed his motives for entering the service in the first place had had their inspiration in the Franco-Spanish attempt of 1779 which, to the shame of the navy, had so nearly succeeded. East? It did not make sense unless it was an elaborate feint, the French buying time to exercise in the eastern Mediterranean. If that were the case they might draw Nelson after them—such an impetuous officer would not hold back—and then they might turn west, slip through the Straits, clear St. Vincent from before Cadiz and join forces with the Spanish fleet.

"Did our informant say who commanded them, sir?" he asked.

"No less a person than Bonaparte," said Lestock solemnly.

"Bonaparte? But we read in the newspapers that Bonaparte commanded the Army of England . . . I remember Appleby jesting that the English Army had long wanted a general officer of his talent."

"Mr. Appleby's joke seems to have curdled, Mr. Drinkwater," said Lestock without a smile. Drinkwater turned to Griffiths.

"You say you'll follow Nelson, sir, to what rendezvous?"

"What do you suggest, Mr. Drinkwater? Mr. Lestock?"

Lestock fidgetted. "Well, sir, I er, I think that in the absence of a rendezvous with the admiral we ought to proceed to, er . . ."

"Malta, sir," said Drinkwater abruptly, "then if the French double for the Atlantic we might be placed there with advantage, on the other hand there will doubtless be some general orders for us there."

"No, Mr. Drinkwater. Your reasoning is sound but the Ragusan also told us that Malta had fallen to the French." Griffiths put down his glass and bent over the charts, picking up the dividers to point with.

"We will proceed south and run through the Bonifacio Strait for Naples, there will likely be news there, or here at Messina, or here, at Syracuse."

There was no news at Naples beyond that of Nelson's fleet having stopped there on 17th June, intelligence older than that from the polaccra. Griffiths would not anchor and all hands eyed the legendary port wistfully. The ochre colours of its palazzi and its tenements were lent a common and ethereal appeal by distance, and the onshore breeze enhanced a view given a haunting beauty beyond the blue waters of the bay by the backdrop of Vesuvius.

"God, but I'd dearly love a night of sport there," mused Rogers, who had acquitted himself in re-rigging the *Hecuba* and now seemed of the opinion that he had earned at least one night of debauchery in the Neapolitan stews. Appleby, standing within earshot and aware of the three seamen grinning close by said, "Then thank the lord you've a sane man to command your instincts, Mr. Rogers. The Neapolitan pox is a virulent disease well-known for its intractability."

Rogers paled at the sally and the three men coiled the falls of the royal halliards with uncommon haste.

Hellebore worked her way slowly south, past the islands of the Tyrrhenian Sea and through the narrow Straits of Messina; but there was no further news of Nelson or the French.

On 16th July the convoy stood into the Bay of Syracuse to wood and water and to find a welcome for British ships. Through the good offices of the British Ambassador to the Court of the Two Sicilies, Sir William Hamilton, facilities were available to expedite the reprovisioning of units of the Royal Navy.

"It seems," Griffiths said to his assembled officers, "that Sir Horatio has considered the possibility of using Syracuse as a base. We must simply wait."

They waited three days. Shortly before noon on the 19th the British fleet was in the offing and with the *Leander* in the van, came into Syracuse Harbour. By three minutes past three in the afternoon the fourteen ships of the line under the command of Rear Admiral Sir Horatio Nelson had anchored.

Within an hour their boats swarmed over the blue waters of the bay, their crews carrying off wood and water, their pursers haggling in the market place for vegetables and beef.

Hellebore's boat pulled steadily through the throng of craft, augmented by local bumboats which traded hopefully with the fleet. Officers' servants were buying chickens for their masters' tables while a surreptitious trade in rot-gut liquor was being conducted through lower deck ports. The apparent confusion and bustle had an air of charged purpose about it and Drinkwater suppressed a feeling of almost childish excitement. Beside him Griffiths wore a stony expression, his leathery old face hanging in sad folds, the wisps of white hair escaping untidily from below the new, glazed cocked hat. Drinkwater felt a wave of sympathy for the old man with his one glittering epaulette. Griffiths had been at sea half a century; he had served in slavers as a mate before being pressed as a naval seaman. He was old enough, experienced enough and able enough to have commanded this entire fleet, reflected Nathaniel, but the man who did so was only a few years older than Drinkwater himself.

"You had better attend on me," Griffiths had said, giving his first lieutenant permission to accompany him aboard *Vanguard*, "seeing that you are so damned eager to clap eyes on this Admiral Nelson."

Drinkwater looked at Quilhampton who shared his curiosity. Mr. Q's hand rested nervously on the boat's tiller. The boy was concentrating, not daring to look round at the splendours of British naval might surrounding him. Drinkwater approved of his single-mindedness; Mr. Q was developing into an asset.

"Boat ahoy!" The hail came from the flagship looming ahead of them, her spars and rigging black against the brilliant sky, the blue rear-admiral's flag at her mizen masthead.

Drinkwater was about to prompt Quilhampton but the boy rose, cleared his throat and in a resonant treble called out *"Hellebore!"* The indication of his commander's presence thus conveyed to *Vanguard*, Quilhampton felt with pleasure the half smile bestowed on him by Mr. Drinkwater.

At the entry port four white gloved side-boys and a bosun's mate greeted *Hellebore*'s captain and his lieutenant. The officer of the watch left them briefly on the quarterdeck while he reported their arrival to the demi-god who resided beneath the poop. Curiously Drinkwater looked round. *Vanguard* was smaller than *Victory*, a mere 74-gun two decker, but there was that same neatness about her, mixed with something else. He sensed it intuitively from the way her people went about their business. From the seamen amidships, rolling empty water casks to the gangway and from a quarter gunner changing the flints in the after carronades emanated a sense of single-minded purpose. He was always to remember this drive that superimposed their efforts as the "Nelson touch", far more than the much publicised manoeuvre at Trafalgar that brought Nelson his apotheosis seven years later.

"Sir Horatio will see you now sir," said the lieutenant, re-emerging. Drinkwater followed Griffiths, ignoring the gesture of restraint from the duty officer. They passed under the row of ciphered leather fire-buckets into the shade of the poop, passing the master's cabin and the rigid marine sentry. Uncovering, Drinkwater followed his commander into the admiral's cabin.

Sir Horatio Nelson rose from his desk as Griffiths presented Drinkwater and the latter bowed. Nelson's smallness of stature was at first a disappointment to Nathaniel who expected something altogether different. Disappointing too were the worn uniform coat and the untidy mop of greying hair, but Drinkwater began to lose his sense of anti-climax as the admiral quizzed Griffiths about the stores contained in *Hecuba* and *Molly*. There was in his address an absence of formality, an eager confidence which was at once infectious. There was a delicacy about the little man. He looked far older than his thirty-nine years, his skin fine drawn, almost transparent over the bones. His large nose and wide, mobile mouth were at odd variance with his body size. But the one good blue eye was sharply attentive, a window on some inner motivation, and the empty sleeve bore witness to his reckless courage.

"Do you know the whereabouts of my frigates, Captain?" he asked Griffiths, "I am driven desperate for want of frigates. The French have escaped me, sire, and I have one brig at my disposal to reconnoitre for a fleet."

Drinkwater sensed the consuming frustration felt by this most diligent of flag officers, sensed his mortification at being deprived of his eyes in the gale that had dismasted *Vanguard*. Yet *Vanguard* had been refitted without delay and the battle line was impressive enough to strike terror in the French if only this one-armed dynamo could catch them.

"There is *Hellebore*, Sir Horatio," volunteered Griffiths.

"Yes, Captain. Would that the whereabouts of the French squadron was my only consideration. But I know that their fleet, besides sail of the line, frigates, bomb vessels and so forth, also comprises three hundred troop transports; an armada that left Sicily with a fair wind from the west. It is clear their destination is to the eastward. I think their object is to possess themselves of some port in Egypt, to fix themselves at the head of the Red Sea in order to get a formidable army into India, to act in concert with Tipoo Sahib. No, Captain, I may not permit myself the luxury of retaining *Hellebore* . . ." The admiral paused and Drinkwater felt apprehensive. Nelson made up his mind. "I must sacrifice perhaps my reputation but that must always subordinate itself to my zeal for the King's service which demands I acquaint the officer on the station of the danger he may be in. I have already written to Mr. Baldwin, our consul at Alexandria, to determine whether the French have any vessels prepared in the Red Sea. As yet I have had no reply. Therefore, my dear Griffiths, I desire that you wood and water without delay and send a boat for your written orders the instant you are ready to proceed to the Red Sea."

Drinkwater felt his mouth go dry. The Red Sea meant a year's voyage at the least. And Elizabeth had given him expectation of a child in the summer.

CHAPTER THREE

A Brig of War

July–August 1798

Lieutenant Drinkwater stared astern watching the seas run up under the brig's larboard quarter, lifting her stern and impelling her forward, adding a trifle to her speed until they passed ahead of her and she dragged, slowly, into the succeeding trough. *Hellebore* carried sail to her topgallants as she raced south west before the trade wind, the coast of Mauretania twenty-five leagues to the east.

Drinkwater had been watching Mr. Quilhampton heave the log and had acknowledged the boy's report, prompted by the quartermaster, that they were running at seven knots. Something would not let him turn forward again but kept him watching the wake as it bubbled green-white under the stern and trailed away behind them in an irregular ribbon, twisted by the yaw of the ship and the oncoming waves. Here and there a following seabird dipped into its disturbance.

He had felt wretched as they passed the Straits of Gibraltar and took their departure from Cape Espartel, for he had been unable to send letters back to Elizabeth, so swift had been *Hellebore*'s passage from Syracuse, so explicit the admiral's orders. Now it was certain he would be separated from her until after the birth of their child, he regretted his inability to soften the blow of his apparent desertion.

He was aware of someone at his elbow and resented the intrusion upon his private thoughts.

"Beg pardon, zur." It was Tregembo. Ten years older than Drinkwater, the able seaman had long ago attached himself to him with a touching and unsolicited loyalty. He had cemented the relationship by supplying Elizabeth with a cook in the person of his wife Susan, certain that service with the Drinkwaters represented security. The personal link between them both gratified and, at that moment, annoyed Drinkwater. He snapped irritably, "What is it?"

"Your sword, zur, 'tis now but half a glass before quarters, zur." Drinkwater looked guiltily at the half-hour sand-glass in the binnacle and took his sword. Since they left the Mediterranean Griffiths had adopted the three watch system. It was kinder on the men and more suited to the long passage ahead of them. There were no dog watches now but at five hours after noon, ship's time, they went to general quarters to remind them all of the serious nature of their business.

Drinkwater turned forward and looked along the deck of the *Hellebore*. She was a trim ship, one of a new class of brig-sloop designed for general duties, a maid of all work, tender, dispatch vessel, convoy escort and commerce raider. He stood on a tiny raised poop which protected the head of the rudder stock and tiller. Immediately forward of the poop the tiller lines ran through blocks to the wheel with hits binnacle, forward of which were the skylight and companionway to the officers' accommodation. Beneath the skylight lay the lobby which served her two lieutenants, master, surgeon, gunner and purser as a gunroom, their cabins leading off it. Griffiths messed there too, unless he dined alone in his cabin, set right aft and entered via the gunroom. Forward of the companionway to this accommodation rose the mainmast, surrounded by its pin rails and coils of manila rigging, its pump handles and trunks. Between the main and foremast, gratings covered the waist, giving poor ventilation to the berth space below, covered by tarpaulins at the first sign of bad weather. Here too was the capstan. Just beyond the foremast the galley chimney rose from the deck next to the companionway that led below to the berth space where the hundred men of *Hellebore*'s company swung their hammocks in an overcrowded fug. The remaining warrant officers and their stores were tucked under the triangular foredeck. A tiny raised platform served as a fo'c's'le, providing just enough foothold to handle the head-sail sheets and tend the catheads.

She was pierced with twenty gunports but so cluttered did she become in the eyes that the foremost was unoccupied. The remaining eighteen each sported an iron six-pounder. These guns were still a subject of frequent debate amongst her officers. Many vessels of similar size carried the snub barrelled carronades, short-ranged but devastating weapons that gave a small sloop a weight of metal heavy enough at close quarters to rival frigates of the sixth rate. But *Hellebore* had been armed by a traditionalist, retaining long guns each with its little canvas covered flintlock firing device. The only carronade she carried was her twelve-pounder boat gun which lay lashed under the fo'c's'le.

Drinkwater descended from the poop as Griffiths came on deck. The glass was turned and the people piped to general quarters. The hands tumbled up willingly enough, the bosun's mates flicking the occasional backside with their starters more for form than necessity. But Drinkwater was not watching that: he was seeing his laboriously drawn up quarter-bill come to life. The gun crews ran to their pieces to slip the breechings and lower the muzzles off the lintels of the gunports. The port lids were lifted as the coloured tompions were knocked out and the men threw their weight on the train tackles. Irregularly, but not unpleasantly discordant, the trucks rumbled over the deck. One by one the gun captains raised their right arms as their crews knelt at the ready position. It was not quite like a frigate. There were no bulkheads to come down since *Hellebore* carried her artillery on her upper deck, there was no marine drummer to beat the *rafale*; not many officers to go round once the gunner had disappeared into his magazine and Lestock and Drinkwater had come aft to the quarterdeck. There was a quarter gunner to each section and a master's mate at either battery. Second Lieutenant Rogers was in overall command of the engaged side with Mr. Quilhampton (nominally a "servant" on the ship's books, but fulfilling the function of a midshipman) as his messenger. Dalziell, the only midshipman officially allowed the brig, commanded the firemen, two men from each gun who assisted each other to extinguish any fires started by an enemy. Drinkwater himself commanded the boarders while Lestock attended to the sails. Under the first lieutenant's command were the men in the tops, sail trimming topmen and a detail of sharpshooters, seamen picked from a competition held weeks earlier in the Downs, and mostly landsmen whose past included either service in the sea fencibles, the volunteers or in a longer feud with their local gamekeepers.

Drinkwater glanced aloft to where Tregembo as captain of the maintop touched his forehead and a man named Kellet acknowledged his section alert in the foretop. He uncovered to Griffiths. "Main battery made ready, sir. I'll check below."

"Very good."

It was only a formality. Below her upper deck *Hellebore*'s accommodation, stores and hold consisted of "platforms" set at various levels according to the breadth of the hull available at each given point. Her berth space, above the main hold, was no more than five feet deep. In the gloom of the hammock space he found the carpenter with his two mates, their tools and a bag of shot plugs. "All correct Mr. Johnson?" The man grinned. His creased features and his Liverpool accent reminded Drinkwater of *Kestrel* and the same Johnson hacking the anchor warp as they beat off the French coast one desperate night two years earlier. "All correct, Mr. Drinkwater."

He passed on, descending a further ladder to where, whistling quietly to himself Mr. Appleby presided over his opened case of gruesome instruments, the lantern light gleaming dully on his crowbills, saws, daviers and demi-lunes. His two mates sat on the upturned tubs provided for the amputated limbs honing surgical knives. A casual air prevailed that annoyed Drinkwater when compared to the deck above. He raised an eyebrow at Appleby who nodded curtly back conveying all his professional hostility to the rival profession of arms that made his presence in the septic stink of the hold necessary. Drinkwater proceeded aft, beneath the officers' quarters where, in less than four feet of headroom, lay the magazine. Trussel's face peered at him through the slit in the felt curtain.

"Ready Mr. Trussel?"

"Aye, sir, ready when you are." His ugly face was illuminated by fiercely gleaming yellow eyes that caught the light from the protected lanterns and Drinkwater was reminded of a remark of Appleby's when he was dissecting the physiognomy of his messmates. "Yon's arse spends so much time six inches from powdered eternity that it's bound to have an effect on the features." The gunner's bizarre head, disembodied by the felt, was reflected in the awesome apprehension of the quartet of powder monkeys, boys of eight or nine who crouched ready to bear the cartridges, hot-potato like, to the guns above.

Drinkwater returned to the hammock space, passing the cook and his assistant in the galley standing amid the stream generated by the extinguishing of the fire and the purser at his post by the washdeck pump. He blinked at the brightness of the daylight after the gloom of the brig's nether regions.

"Ship cleared for action, sir," he reported.

"Very well. Mr. Rogers, larboard broadside, run in and load. Three rounds rapid fire, single ball."

"Aye, aye, sir."

Drinkwater watched Rogers draw his sword with a flourish, watched little Quilhampton run to the after grating and call for powder. In a small ship on such a long passage Griffiths refused to keep his guns loaded, considering the morning discharge practised on so many ships to rid the guns of damp powder as a quite unnecessary extravagance. The two powder monkeys serving the larboard battery emerged to scamper across to the nine six-pounders trundled inboard. The charges, wads and balls were rammed home and the gun captains inserted their priming quills as Rogers barked out the ordered steps. "Cock your locks!" The crews moved back from the guns as the captains stretched their lanyards. Each raised his free hand.

"Larboard battery made ready, sir!" reported Rogers.

"You may open fire," ordered Griffiths.

"Fire!"

The rolling roar that erupted in a line of flame and smoke along the brig's side was matched inboard by the recoil of the squealing trucks. Daily practice had made of the broadside a thing of near unanimity.

"Fire as you will!"

For the next two minutes the larbowlines, watched critically by the idlers on the starboard side, sponged and rammed and hauled up their pieces in a frenzy of activity.

"Numbers two and eight are good, sir," shouted Drinkwater above the din.

"Let's wait until we are becalmed and try them at a target Mr. Drinkwater, then I'll be looking for accuracy not speed."

Number eight gun was already secured, its crew kneeling smartly rigid but for the panting of their bare torsos.

There was a scream from forward. In their haste not to be last, Number Four gun had been fired too early. The recoiling truck had run over the foot of the after train tackle man. He lay whimpering on the deck, blood running from his bitten tongue, his right foot a bloody mess. Drinkwater ran forward.

"Mr. Q, warn the surgeon to make ready, you there, Stokeley, bear a hand there." They dragged the injured man clear of the gun and Drinkwater whipped his headband off, twisting it swiftly round his ankle. He had fainted by the time the stretcher bearers came up.

"Secure all guns! Secure there!" Rogers was bawling, turning the men back to their task. As Drinkwater saw the casualty carried below, the guns were fully elevated and run up with their muzzles hard against the port lintels. The lids were shut and the breechings passed.

"Both batteries secured, sir," reported Rogers, "bloody fool had his damned foot in the way . . ."

"That will do, Mr. Rogers," snapped Griffiths, colour mounting to his cheeks and his bushy white eyebrows coming together in imperious menace across the bridge of his big nose.

"Secure from general quarters, Mr. Drinkwater." The commander turned angrily below and Rogers looked ruefully at Drinkwater for consolation.

"Stupid old bastard," he said.

Drinkwater regarded the young lieutenant and for the first time realised he did not like him. "Carry on Mr. Rogers," he said coldly, "I have the deck." Drinkwater walked forward and Rogers turned aft to where Midshipman Dalziell was gathering up his signal book and slate. "I have the deck," mimicked Rogers and found Dalziell smiling conspiratorially at him.

The sun went down in a blaze of glory. As it set Drinkwater had the deck watch check the two boats that hung in the new-fangled davits on either quarter in case they were needed during the night. They also checked the lashings on the four long pine trunks that were secured outboard between the channels, as there was no stowage elsewhere. Briefly he recalled the depression he had suffered earlier and found its weight had lightened. He tried to divine the source of the relief. Guiltily he concluded that the injured man and Rogers' lack of compassion had awoken him to his duty. He recalled the words of Earl St. Vincent: "A married officer is frequently lost to the service . . ."

That must not be the case with himself. He had a duty to the ship, to Griffiths and the men, and especially to Elizabeth and the child growing within her. That duty would best be served by anticipation and diligence. They had a long way to go, and even further to come back.

At eight bells Drinkwater went below to where Appleby, fresh washed but still smelling of gore, ate his biscuit and sipped his wine.

"How is the patient?" asked Drinkwater, hanging his coat and hat in his cabin and joining the surgeon in the gunroom. "It was Tyson, wasn't it?"

"Yes. He's well enough," spluttered Appleby, crumbs exploding from his lips, "as we were not in action I was able to take my time." He paused, emptied his glass and dabbed at his mouth with a stained napkin. "I saved the heel, if it does not rot he will walk on his own leg though he'll limp and find balance a trouble."

"The devil you did! Well done, Harry, well done." Appleby looked pleased at his friend's approval and his puffy cheeks flushed.

"I must amend my books," said Drinkwater, reaching to the shelf that contained the half-dozen manuscript ledgers without which the conduct of no King's ship, irrespective of size, could be regulated.

He opened the appropriate volume and turned up his carefully worked muster list. "Damn it, the man's a boarder . . . when will he be fit again?"

Appleby shrugged. "Given that he avoids gangrene, say a month, but the sooner he has something to occupy his mind the better."

"I wonder if he can write?"

"I doubt it but I'll ask."

Mr. Trussel came in for his glass of madeira. "I hear the captain is not stopping at the Canaries, is that so, sir?"

"We stop only of necessity for water, Mr. Trussel, otherwise Admiral Nelson's orders were explicit," explained Drinkwater, "and we are to limit ourselves to one glass each of wine per evening to conserve stocks."

Trussel made a face. "Did you not know that powder draws the moisture from a man, Mr. Drinkwater?"

"I don't doubt it, Mr. Trussel, but needs must when the devil drives, eh?"

"I shall savour the single glass the more then," answered the old gunner wryly.

Drinkwater bent over his ledger and re-wrote the watch and

quarter bills, pulling his chair sideways as Lestock joined them from the deck to stow his quadrant and books.

"I can't make it out, can't make it out," he was muttering. Drinkwater snapped the inkwell closed. "What can't you make out, Mr. Lestock?"

"Our longitude, Mr. Drinkwater, it seems that if our departure from Espartel was truly three leagues west . . ." Drinkwater listened to Lestock's long exposition on the longitude problem. *Hellebore* carried no chronometer, did not need to for the coastal convoy work to which she had been assigned. Recent events, however, revealed the need for them to know their longitude as they traversed the vast wastes of the Atlantic. Lestock had been dallying with lunar observations, a long and complicated matter involving several sets of near simultaneous sights and upon which the navigational abilities of many officers, including not a few sailing masters, foundered. The method was theoretically simple. But on the plunging deck of the brig, with the horizon frequently interrupted by a wave crest and the sky by rigging and sails, the matter assumed a complexity which was clearly beyond the abilities of Lestock.

As he listened Drinkwater appreciated the fussy man's problems. He knew he could do little better but he kicked himself for not having thought of the problem in Syracuse. With a chronometer the matter would have been different and Nelson had offered them whatever they wanted from the fleet. He had had to. In the matter of charts alone *Hellebore* was deficient south of the Canaries. They had scraped together the bare minimum, but the chart of the Red Sea was so sparse of detail that its very appearance sent a shudder of apprehension down Lestock's none too confident spine.

". . . And if the captain does not intend to stop we'll have further difficulties," he concluded.

"We will be able to observe the longitude of known capes and islands," said Drinkwater, "we should manage. Ah, and that reminds me, during the morning watch tomorrow I'll have a jackstay rigged over the waist and spread and furl a spare topsail on it to use as an awning and catchwater . . . keep two casks on deck during your watch, Mr. Lestock, and fill 'em if you get the opportunity. Captain Griffiths intends only to stop if it becomes necessary, otherwise we'll by-pass the Cape of Good Hope to avoid the Agulhas current and take wood and water somewhere on the Madagascan coast. In the meantime direct your attention to the catchwater if you please." Lestock returned to the deck, the worried look still on his face.

"It would seem that an excess of salt spray also draws the moisture from a man," observed Appleby archly.

"Aye Mr. Appleby, and over-early pickles the brain," retorted Trussel.

Day succeeded day as the trades blew and the internal life of the brig followed its routine as well as its daily variations. Daily, after quarters, the hands skylarked for an hour before the hammocks were piped down. The flying fish leapt from their track and fanned out on either bow. Breakfasts were often spiced by their flesh, fried trout-like and delicious. During the day dolphins played under the bowsprit defying efforts to catch them. The sea at night was phosphorescent and mysterious, the dolphins' tracks sub-aqueous rocket trails of pale fire, the brig's wake a magical bubbling of light. They reeled off the knots, hoisting royals and studding sails when the wind fell light. Even as they reached the latitude of the Cape Verdes and the trades left them, the fluky wind kept a chuckle of water under the forefoot.

It was utterly delightful. Drinkwater threw off the last of his depression and wallowed in the satisfying comfort of naval routine. There was always enough to occupy a sea-officer, yet there was time to read and write his journal, and the problems that came inevitably to a first lieutenant were all sweetly soluble. But he knew it could not last, it never did. The very fact of their passage through the trade-wind belt was an indication of that. At last the winds died away and the rain fell. They filled their water casks while Griffiths had the sweeps out for two hours a daylight watch and *Hellebore* was hauled manually across the ocean in search of wind.

"*Du*, I cannot abide a calm hereabouts," Griffiths growled at Drinkwater staring eastward to where, unseen below the horizon, the Gambia coast lay.

"I remember the smell, *bach*. Terrible, terrible." For a second Drinkwater could not understand, then he remembered Griffiths's slaving past. "The Gambia, sir?" he asked quietly.

"Indeed yes . . . the rivers, green and slow, and the stockadoes full of them; the chiefs and half-breed traders and the Arabs . . . and us," he ended on a lower note. "Christ, but it was terrible . . ." It was the first time he had ever disclosed more than the slightest detail of that time of his life. They had often discussed the technicalities of slaving ships, their speed and their distant loveliness, but though there was a growing revulsion to the trade in Britain neither he nor Griffiths had ever voiced the matter as a moral problem. He was tempted to wonder why Griffiths had remained to become chief mate of a slaver when the old man answered his unasked question.

"And yet I stayed to become mate. You are asking yourself that now, aren't you?" He did not wait for a reply but plunged on, like a man in the confessional, too far to regret his repentance. "But I was young, *du*, I was young. There was money there, money and private trading and women, *bach*, such women the like of which you'd never dream of, coal black and lissom, pliant and young, opening like green leaves in spring," he sighed, "they would do anything to get out of that stinking 'tween deck . . . anything."

Drinkwater left the old man to his silence and his memories. He was still at the rail when Lestock came on deck at eight bells.

In the morning a breeze had sprung up.

CHAPTER FOUR

Shadows of Clouds

September 1798

"I want him flogged, Drinkwater!"

Drinkwater looked up from his breakfast of burgoo at the angry face of Lieutenant Rogers. "It is not for you to decide the punishment," he said coldly.

"I know Tregembo's your damned toady, Drinkwater, and that you and the captain are close, but damn it, I threatened him with a flogging and a flogging he shall have!"

"I shall present the facts to the captain and . . ."

"Oh, devil take the facts man, and devil take your sanctimonious cant . . ."

"Have a care what you say, *Mr*. Rogers." Drinkwater stressed the title and resisted the impulse to stand and swing his hand across Roger's choleric face. The restraint was not appreciated.

"Flog him, Drinkwater, or by Christ I'll bring charges against you for failure to maintain good order . . ."

"You'll do no such damned thing, sir," snapped Drinkwater. "You will sit down and be silent while we examine precisely what happened. And, by God, you'll address me as *mister*."

"You fail to intimidate me *Mister* Drinkwater. Your commission predates mine by two weeks. That ain't seniority enough to cut much ice in the right quarters . . ."

Drinkwater sprang to his feet and leaned across the intervening table. "Another word, sir, and I'll clap you in irons upon the instant, d'you hear? By God you've gone too far! Two weeks is sufficient to hang you!"

Their faces were inches apart and for a long moment they remained so; then Rogers subsided, answering Drinkwater's questions in resentful monosyllables.

It appeared that during the middle watch Midshipman Dalziell, proceeding forward on routine rounds had stumbled over the feet of Tregembo. The Cornishman had been sleeping on deck. With the three watch system in operation and the brig in the tropics the berth space became intolerable and a number of men slept on deck. There had been an exchange between the midshipman and the able seaman which had resulted in Dalziell bringing Tregembo aft to Rogers. From what Drinkwater had seen of Dalziell he was not surprised at Tregembo's reaction. Drinkwater did not entirely support Earl St. Vincent's contention that the men should be made to respect a midshipman's coat. He qualified it by requiring that the midshipman within was at least partially deserving of that respect. He doubted that Mr. Dalziell answered the case at all. Besides Drinkwater was damned if Tregembo, or anyone else for that matter, was going to have his back laid open for such a trivial matter.

"Thank you, Mr. Rogers."

"I want the whoreson flogged, d'you hear?" Rogers flung over his shoulder as he withdrew to his cabin. Drinkwater sat in the gunroom alone, sunlight from the skylight sliding in six parallelograms back and forth across the table. He knew Griffiths would not hesitate to flog if necessary. Insolence was not to be tolerated. But had Tregembo been insolent? Drinkwater was by no means certain and he had seen the man flogged before. Griffiths, who had slung his hammock above the guns on the lower deck of a seventy-four understood the mentality of the men. There were always those who would challenge authority if they thought they could get away with it, and he knew many seamen who approved of flogging. Life below decks was foul enough without suffering the molestations of the petty thieves, the queers, the cheats and liars, never mind the drunks who could knock you from a yard in the middle of the night. No, swift retribution was welcomed by both sides.

But only if it was just.

"Mr. Lestock, Mr. Appleby, you are sitting on a tribunal to determine the precise nature of an incident occurring in the middle watch last night during which the captain of the main top, Able seaman Tregembo, is alleged to have used abuse against Mr. Midshipman Dalziell."

The two warrant officers nodded, Lestock fidgetting since he had had to be relieved on deck by Trussel and was anxious about observing the meridian altitude of the sun at noon. Appleby was splendidly portentous but, for the moment, silent.

"Lieutenant Rogers," Drinkwater inclined his head to the second lieutenant sitting opposite with one leg dangling over the arm of his chair, contemptuously examining his nails, "is in the nature of the accusing officer." He raised his voice, "Mr. Q!"

The door opened. "Sir?"

"Pass word for Mr. Dalziell and then have Tregembo wait outside to be called."

"Aye, aye, sir," replied the boy, casting a frightened look round the interior of the gunroom which had changed its normal prefectural atmosphere to one of chilly formality.

Dalziell knocked and entered. He had not had the sense to put on full uniform.

"Now Mr. Dalziell, this is an inquiry to establish the facts of the incident that occurred this morning . . ." Drinkwater went laboriously through the formal processes and listened to Dalziell's carefully stated account.

He had gone forward on the rounds that were performed by either a master's mate or a midshipman at hourly intervals. He had found the man Tregembo asleep under the fo'c's'le with his legs obstructing the ladder and had stumbled over them. The man had woken and there had been an exchange. As a consequence Dalziell had ordered him below. There had been a further exchange after which Dalziell had brought Tregembo aft to the officer of the watch. "And Lieutenant Rogers said he would see the man flogged for his insolence, sir." It was all very plausible, almost too plausible, and the malice in that last sentence set a query against the whole.

They called Tregembo. "What did you say to Mr. Dalziell when he stumbled against you?" asked Drinkwater, careful to keep his voice and expression rigidly formal.

Tregembo shrugged. "I'd been awakened zur, I thought it was one of my mates," he growled.

"Were you abusive?" butted in Lestock, "come man, we want the truth."

Tregembo shot a glance at Drinkwater. "Happen I was short with him, zur," he conceded but repeated, "I thought it was one of my mates, zur . . . I didn't know it was Mr. Dalziell, zur."

"A storm in a tea cup," muttered Appleby and Rogers flushed. Drinkwater was tempted to leave the matter there, but Lestock persisted to fuss.

"What *exactly* did you say, man?" he asked testily.

Drinkwater sighed, both Rogers and Dalziell were only

holding their peace with difficulty. "Come Tregembo," he said resignedly, "what did you say?"

Tregembo frowned. He knew Drinkwater could not protect him and his head came forward belligerently. "Why zur, what I'd say to a mess-mate, that he was a clumsy fucker . . . zur."

Drinkwater stifled a grin and he saw both Dalziell and Rogers relax, as though their case was proved.

"That seems to be clear abuse," said Lestock and Drinkwater suddenly felt angry about the whole stupid business. Without Lestock's tactless interjections he might have ended it then and there, but now had to take the offensive.

"Now think carefully, Tregembo. What was then said to you? Remember we want the truth, as Mr. Lestock says." Tregembo looked at Dalziell, opening his mouth then closing it again before he caught the intense expression in Drinkwater's eyes. He had known the lieutenant long enough to take encouragement from it.

"He called me an insolent whoreson bastard, zur, and told me to get my pox-ridden arse below decks where it belonged."

Drinkwater swung his glance swiftly to Dalziell. There was no denial from the midshipman, only a slight flushing of the cheeks. Dalziell blurted "And he called me a cocky puppy, damn it!"

"Silence, Mister!" snapped Drinkwater. "Tregembo, do you mind your tongue in future when you address an officer." The two exchanged glances and Drinkwater dismissed him. He turned to his two colleagues, suddenly aware that he had closed the case without consultation. "I am sure you agree with me, gentlemen, that Tregembo's initial remarks were made by mistake under the false assumption that another hand had tripped over him. The manner of Mr. Dalziell's subsequent ordering of him below was of such a nature as to disqualify him from receiving the manner of address expected from an able seaman to a midshipman." There was a sharp indrawn breath from Rogers but Drinkwater was undeterred. "The midshipmen aboard any ship of which I am first lieutenant will be obliged to behave properly. I will not tolerate the apeing of bloods out whoring which seems the current fashion. It would not be in the interests of the ship to flog Tregembo."

"Damn you, Drinkwater, damn you to hell." Rogers leapt from the chair.

"Be silent, sir!" stormed Drinkwater, suddenly furious at Rogers. Then, in a quieter tone he turned to the master and surgeon. "Well gentlemen, d'you agree?"

"Of course, Nathaniel, damned stupid business if you ask me." Appleby eyed Rogers disapprovingly.

"Is my character to be disputed by an apology for a poxdoctor . . . ?" he got no further. Emerging from his cabin Commander Griffiths appeared. The five men in the gunroom rose to their feet. He had clearly heard every word through the flimsy bulkhead.

"I approve of your decision, Mr. Drinkwater, just as I disapprove of your conduct, Mr. Rogers." Griffiths spoke slowly then paused, turning his lugubrious face on Dalziell. His bushy white eyebrows drew together. "As for you, sir, I can think of only one place where your presence will not infect us all. Proceed to the fore t'gallant masthead."

The commander passed between Rogers and the scarlet midshipman with ponderous contempt and made for the upper deck.

They had rolled Polaris and the constellations of the far north below the horizon without ceremony. To the south blazed Canopus, Rigel Kentaurus and the Southern Cross, whilst

Orion wheeled overhead, astride the equinoctial. They had picked up the south-east Trades in five degrees south latitude and romped southwards. The matter of Dalziell faded from Drinkwater's mind almost as soon as the boy had descended from the mastheading. Ruling all their lives, burying their petty quarrels with its stern and soothing rhythm, the routine of a King's ship proceeded remorselessly. They had avoided all ships in case any were French cruisers. It was unlikely, but only a single mischance could disrupt the delicate strategy of empire. Even a ship of equal force might jeopardise their mission and it was likely that a French cruiser in the South Atlantic would be one of their fast, well-found frigates.

On a morning of alternating sunshine and shadow as an endless stream of fair-weather cumulus scudded before the fresh wind and the large dark petrels and bizarre red-footed boobies swooped about the ship, the matter of Dalziell was revived.

Appearing to take his meridian altitude, Mr. Quilhampton was found to possess a black eye.

"Where the deuce did you get that from, young shaver?" asked Drinkwater who had of late made a practice of joining Lestock on the tiny poop to help determine the brig's latitude.

"Oh, I banged into my cabin door, sir." The boy was nearly sobbing and the excuse was clearly fabricated. He failed to catch the sun successfully and it was Dalziell's smirking "I made my altitude seventy degrees fifty-four minutes, Mr. Lestock," that formed the suspicion in Drinkwater's mind that he might be the cause of Mr. Quilhampton's misery. It seemed confirmed by the muffled grunt from the young midshipman as the first lieutenant agreed his own altitude within a minute of Dalziell's. Lestock pursed his lips in disapproval when Quilhampton announced his failure.

"Mr. Q has a contused eye, Mr. Lestock. Cut along to the

surgeon, cully, and get him to look at it." He watched the boy move away and turned to Mr. Dalziell. "Now what d'you make our latitude?" He knew he was displacing Lestock but noted that Dalziell was suddenly less confident. The sun was chasing them south, would cross the equator in a day or so and the calculation was elementary. A mere matter of addition and subtraction but Dalziell baulked at it. Drinkwater suspected he cribbed frequently from the younger boy who showed a certain aptitude for the mysteries of astronomical navigation.

"Er, sixteen degrees, er . . . about sixteen degrees south, sir, er . . ." he frowned over his slate while Lestock tut-tutted and nodded agreement at Drinkwater's figures.

"Perhaps you would be better studying Robinson, Mr. Dalziell, than thrashing your messmate."

Dalziell's open-mouthed stare as he descended the ladder made him chuckle inwardly. He remembered wondering as a midshipman how the first lieutenant always seemed so omniscient. Experience was a wonderful teacher and there was little new under the sun. The reference to the late object of their observations further amused him and he was in a high good humour as he returned his quadrant to its carefully lashed mahogany box. It was only on straightening up from the task that his eye was caught by the little watercolour of the American privateer *Algonquin*, wearing British over Yankee colours. She had been his first command. It was a trifle stained by damp now and had been done for him by Elizabeth before they were married. The thought of Elizabeth scudded like one of those cumulus clouds over his good humour. In the oddly circuitous way the mind works it made him think of Quilhampton and the misery that could be a midshipman's lot. He called the mess-man. "Pass word for Mr. Quilhampton, Meyrick."

When the boy came he had clearly been crying. He was fortunate, Drinkwater thought. The brig had no cockpit and the two midshipmen each had a tiny cabin, mere hutches set on the ship's plans as accommodation for stewards. At least they did not have to live in the festering stink of the orlop as he had had to aboard *Cyclops*. But the atmosphere of Quilhampton's environment was a relative thing. It might be easier than Drinkwater's had been, but it was no less unpleasant for the boy.

"Come now, Mr. Q, dry those eyes and tell me what happened."

"Nothing, sir."

"Come, sir, do not make honour a sticking point, what happened?"

"N . . . nothing, sir."

Drinkwater sighed. "Mr. Q. If I were to instruct you to lead a party of boarders onto the deck of a French frigate, would you obey?"

"Of course, sir!" A spark of indignant spirit was rekindled in the boy.

"Then come, Mr. Q. Do not, I beg you, disobey me now."

The muscles along Quilhampton's jaw hardened. "Mr. Dalziell, sir, struck me, sir. It was in a fair fight, sir," he added hurriedly.

"Fights are seldom fair, Mr. Q. What was this over?"

"Nothing, sir."

"Mr. Quilhampton," Drinkwater said sharply, "I shall not remind you again that you are in the King's service, not the schoolroom."

"Well, sir, he was insulting you, sir . . . said something about you and the captain, sir . . . something not proper, sir."

Drinkwater frowned. "Go on."

"I er, I thought it unjust sir, and I er, demurred, sir . . ." The boy's powers of self-expression had improved immeasurably but the thought of what the boy was implying sickened Drinkwater.

"Did he suggest that the captain and I enjoyed a certain intimacy, Mr. Q?" he asked softly. Relief was written large on the boy's face.

"Yes sir."

"Very well, Mr. Q. Thank you. Now then, for fighting and for not obeying my order promptly I require from you a dissertation on the origin of the brig-sloop, written during your watch below this afternoon and brought to me when you report on deck at eight bells."

The boy left the cabin happier in spite of his task. But for Drinkwater a cloud had come permanently over the day and a dark suspicion was forming in his mind.

He spoke to Dalziell when he relieved Rogers at the conclusion of the afternoon watch. Quilhampton had delivered into his hand an ink-spattered paper which he folded carefully and held behind his back.

"For fighting, Mr. Dalziell, I require an essay on the brig-sloop. I desire that you submit it to me when I am relieved this evening."

Dalziell muttered his acknowledgement and turned away. Drinkwater recalled him.

"Tell me, Mr. Dalziell, what is the nature of your acquaintanceship with Lord Dungarth?" Dalziell's face relaxed into a half-concealed smirk. Drinkwater hoped the midshipman thought him a trifle scared of too flagrantly punishing an earl's élève. That feline look seemed to indicate that he was right.

"I am related to his late wife . . . sir."

"I see. What was the nature of your kinship?"

"I was second cousin to the countess." He preened himself,

as if being second cousin to a dead countess absolved him from the formalities of naval courtesy. Drinkwater did not labour the point; Mr. Dalziell did not need to know that Lord Dungarth had been the director of the clandestine operations of the cutter *Kestrel*. "You are most fortunate in your connections, Mr. Dalziell," he said as the boy smirked again.

He was about to turn away and give his attention to the ship when Dalziell volunteered, "I have a cousin on my mother's side who knows you, Mr. Drinkwater."

"Really?" said Drinkwater without interest, aware that Rogers had neglected to overhaul the topgallant buntlines which were taut and probably chafing. "And who might that be?"

"Lieutenant Morris."

Drinkwater froze. Slowly he turned and fixed Dalziell with a frigid stare.

"And what of that, Mr. Dalziell?"

Suddenly it occurred to Dalziell that he might be mistaken in securing an advantage over the first lieutenant so soon after the tribunal. He realised Mr. Drinkwater would not cringe from mere innuendo, or could he employ the crudities that had upset Quilhampton. "Oh, n . . . nothing sir."

"Then get below and compose your essay." Drinkwater turned away and fell to pacing the deck, forgetting about the topgallant buntlines. He hated the precocity of Dalziell and his ilk. The day was ruined for him, the whole voyage of the *Hellebore* poisoned by Dalziell, a living reminder of the horrors of the frigate *Cyclops* and Morris, the sodomite tyrant of the midshipman's mess. Many years before, during the American war, Drinkwater had been instrumental in having Morris turned out of the frigate. Morris was lucky to have escaped with his life: an Article of War punished his crime with the noose. Now a drunken threat, uttered by Morris before he left

—

the frigate, was recalled to mind. It seemed Morris had kept in touch with his career, might have been behind Dungarth's request that Dalziell be found a place, though it was certain the earl knew nothing of it. Something about Dalziell's demeanour seemed to confirm this suspicion. For half an hour Drinkwater paced furiously from the poop ladder to the mainmast and back. His mind was filled with dark and irrational fears, fears for Elizabeth and her unborn child far behind in England, for long ago Morris had discovered his love for her and had threatened her. Gradually he calmed himself, forced his mind into a more logical track. Despite the influence he once appeared to wield at the Admiralty through the carnal talents of his sister, he had risen no further than lieutenant and many years had passed since that encounter in New York. Perhaps, whatever Dalziell knew of the events aboard *Cyclops*, it would be no more than that he and Morris were enemies. Surely Morris would have concealed the reason for their enmity. Strange that he had planted in the midshipman's mind the notion that Drinkwater indulged in the practices that had come close to breaking Morris himself. Or perhaps it was not so strange. Evil was rightly represented as a serpent and the twists of the human mind to justify its most outrageous conduct were, when viewed objectively, almost past belief.

Nevertheless, two hours passed before Drinkwater remembered the topgallant buntlines. He found Mr. Quilhampton had already attended to them.

CHAPTER FIVE

The *Mistress Shore*

September–October 1798

The following morning Drinkwater found a moment to study the literary efforts of the two midshipmen. It was clear that Mr. Dalziell's essay had suffered from being written after that by Mr. Quilhampton. True the penmanship was neater and better formed than the awkward, blotchy script of Mr. Q, but the information contained in the composition was a crib from Falconer's *Marine Dictionary* with a few embellishments in what Mr. Dalziell clearly considered was literary style.

. . . And so the Brig-Sloop, so named to indicate that she was commanded by a Commander or Sloop-Captain, as opposed to a Gun-Brig, merely the command of a Lieutenant, arrived to take its place in the lists of the Fleet and perform the duties of a small Cruizer to the no small satisfaction of Admiralty . . . Was there a sneer within the lengthy sentence? Or was Drinkwater unduly prejudiced? Certainly there was little information.

By contrast Mr. Quilhampton's erratic, speckled contribution, untidy though it was, demonstrated his enthusiasm.

. . . The naval Brig was developed from the merchant Snow and Brig, both two-masted vessels. In the former the main-

*mast carried both a square course and a fore and aft spanker
which was usually loose footed. Its luff was secured to a small
mast, or horse, set close abaft the lower main-mast. The merchant Brig did not carry the maincourse, the maintopsail
sheeting to a lower yard of smaller dimensions, not unlike the
cross-jack yard. The mainsail was usually designated to be
the fore and aft spanker which was larger than that of the
snow and furnished with a boom, extending its parts well aft
and making it an effective driver for a vessel on the wind . . .*

Drinkwater nodded, well satisfied with the clarity of Mr.
Quilhampton's drift, but the boy was in full flood now and did
not baulk at attempting to untangle that other piece of etymo-
logical and naval confusion.

*The naval brig is divided into two classes, the gun-vessel,
usually of shallow draft and commanded by a Lieutenant, and
the brig-sloop, under a Commander. The term "sloop" in this
context (as with the ship-sloop or corvette) indicates its status as the command of Captain or Commander, the ship-sloop
of twenty guns being the smallest vessel commanded by a
Post-Captain. The Captain of a brig-sloop (sometimes
known, more particularly in foreign navies, as a brig-
corvette) is always addressed as "Captain" by courtesy but is
in reality called Master and Commander since at one time no
master was carried to attend to the vessel's navigation. The
term "sloop" used in these contexts, should not be confused
with the one-masted vessel that has the superficial* [there were
several attempts to spell this word] *appearance of a cutter.
These type of sloops are rarely used now in naval service,
having been replaced by the faster cutter. They differ from the
cutter in having less sail area, a standing bowsprit and a
beakhead . . .*

Drinkwater lowered this formidable document in admiration. Young Mr. Q had hit upon some interesting points, par-

ticularly that of Masters and Commanders. He knew that many young and ambitious lieutenants had objected to submitting themselves for the navigational examination at the Trinity House to give them the full claim to the title, and that the many promotions on foreign stations that answered the exigencies of war had made the system impracticable. The regulation of having a midshipman pass for master's mate before he could be sent away in a prize was also one observed more in the breach than otherwise. As a result the Admiralty had seen fit to appoint masters or acting masters to most brigs to avoid losses by faulty navigation. In Mr. Lestock's case Drinkwater was apt to think the appointment more of a burden to the ship than a safeguard.

Quilhampton's essay echoed the gunroom debate as to the armament of brigs, repeating the carronade versus long gun argument and concluding in didactic vein, . . . *whatever the main armament of the deck, the eighteen-gun brig-of-war is, under the regulation of 1795, the smallest class of vessel to carry a boat carronade.*

Drinkwater was folding the papers away when a cry sent him hurrying on deck.

"Deck there! Sail on the weather bow!"

He drew back from the ladder to allow Griffiths, limping painfully but in obvious haste, to precede him up the ladder. As the two men emerged on deck the pipes were shrieking at the hatchways. Lestock jumped down from the weather rail and offered his glass to Griffiths. "French cruiser, by my judgement."

Griffiths swore while Drinkwater reached in his pocket for his own glass. It was a frigate beyond doubt and a fast one judging by the speed with which her image grew. She was certainly French built and here, south of Ascension Island in the path of homecoming Indiamen, probably still in French hands.

"All hands have been called, sir," said Lestock primly.

"Then put the ship before the wind and set everything she'll carry." It was clear Griffiths was taking no chances. The importance of their mission was too great to jeopardise it by the slightest hesitation.

"Mr. Drinkwater, have the mast wedges knocked out and I want preventer backstays rigged to t'gallant mast caps!"

"Aye, aye, sir!" Lestock was already bawling orders through the speaking trumpet and the topmen were racing aloft to rig out the stunsail booms. Drinkwater slipped forward to where Johnson, the carpenter, was tending the headsails, hoisting a flying jib and tending its sheet to catch any wind left in the lee of the foresails as their yards were braced square across the hull.

"Mr. Johnson, get your mates and knock the mast wedges out, give the masts some play: we want every fraction of a knot out of her. Then have the bilges pumped dry and kept dry for as long as this goes on." Drinkwater jerked his head astern.

Johnson acknowledged the order and sung out for his two mates in inimitable crudity. Drinkwater turned away and sought out Grey, the bosun.

"Mr. Grey, I want two four-inch ropes rigged as preventer backstays. Use the cable springs out of an after port. Get 'em up to the t'gallant mastcaps and secured. We'll bowse 'em tight with a gun tackle at the rail."

"Aye, aye, sir."

"And Mr. Grey . . ."

"Sir?"

"I don't want any chafing at the port. See to it if you please." It was stating the obvious to an experienced man, but in the excitement of the moment it was no good relying on experience that could be lost in distraction.

As he went aft again Drinkwater was aware of the lessening of the wind noise in the rigging. Running free cut it to a minimum, while the hull sat more upright in the sea and it was necessary to look to the horizon to see the wave caps still tumbling before the strong breeze to convince oneself that the weather had not suddenly moderated. Already the stunsails were being hoisted from their stowage in the tops, billowing forward and bowing their thin booms. Lestock was bawling abuse at the foretopmen who had failed in the delicate business of seeing one of them clear of the spider's web of ropes between the top and its upper and lower booms. A man was scrambling out along the topgallant yard and leaning outwards at the peril of his life to clear the tangle.

Lestock's voice rose to a shrill squeal and Drinkwater knew that on many ships men would be flogged for such clumsiness. Lestock's vitriolic diatribe vexed him.

"Belay that, Mr. Lestock, you'll only fluster the man, 'twill not set the sail a whit faster."

Lestock turned, white with anger. "I'll trouble you to hold your tongue, damn it, I still have the deck and that whoreson captain of the foretop'll have a checked shirt at the gangway, by God!"

Drinkwater ignored the master. The distraction had silenced Lestock for long enough to ensure the stunsail was set and he was far too eager to get aft and study the chase.

He joined Griffiths by the taffrail, saying nothing but levelling his glass.

"He's gaining on us, *bach*. I dare not sacrifice water, nor guns . . . not yet . . ."

"We could haul the forward guns aft, sir. Lift her bow a little, she's burying it at the moment . . ." Both men spoke without removing the glasses from their eyes.

"Indeed, yes. See to it, and drop the sterns of the quarterboats to catch a little wind." Drinkwater snapped the glass shut and caught Quilhampton's eye.

"Mr. Q, do you see to lowering the after falls on each of the quarter boats. Not far enough to scoop up water but to act as sails." He left Quilhampton in puzzled acknowledgement and noted with satisfaction the speed with which Grey's party had hauled the four inch manila hemp springs aloft. The gun tackles were already rigged and being sweated tight.

"Mr. Rogers!"

"Yes? What is it?"

Drinkwater explained about the guns. "We'll start with the forward two and get a log reading at intervals of half an hour to check her best performance."

Rogers nodded. "She's gaining, is she?"

"Yes."

"D'you think the old bastard's lost his nerve," he paused then saw the anger in Drinkwater's face. "I mean she might be British . . ."

"And she might not! You may wish to rot in a French fortress but I do not. I suggest we attend to our order."

Drinkwater turned away from Rogers, contempt flooding through him that a man could allow himself the liberty of such petty considerations. Although the stranger was still well out of gunshot it would need only one lucky ball to halt their flight. And the fortress of Bitche waited impassively for them. Drinkwater stopped his mind from wandering and began to organise the hauling aft of the forward guns.

In the waist the noise of the sea hissing alongside was soon augmented by the orchestrated grunts of men laying on tackles and gingerly hauling the brig's unwieldy artillery aft. Two heavy sets of blocks led forward and two aft, to control the progress of the guns as the ship moved under them. From time to time Grey's party of men with handspikes eased the awkward carriage wheels over a ringbolt. After four hours of labour they had four guns abaft the mainmast and successive streaming of the log indicated an increase of speed of one and a half knots. But that movement of guns aft had not only deprived *Hellebore* of four of her teeth, it had seriously impeded the working of her after cannon since the forward guns now occupied their recoil space.

When the fourth gun had been lashed the two lieutenants straightened up from their exertions. Drinkwater had long forgotten Rogers's earlier attitude.

"I hope the bastard does not catch us now or it'll be abject bloody surrender, superior goddam force or not," Rogers muttered morosely.

"Stow it, Rogers, it's well past noon, we might yet hang on until dark."

"You're a bloody optimist, Drinkwater."

"I've little choice; besides faith is said to move mountains."

"Shit!"

Drinkwater shrugged and went aft again. Despite the work of the past hours it was as if he had left Griffiths a few moments earlier. The old Welshman appeared not to have moved, to have shrunk in on himself, almost half-asleep until one saw those hawkish eyes, staring relentlessly astern.

There was no doubt that they were losing the race. The big frigate was clearly visible, hull-up from the deck and already trying ranging shots. As yet these fell harmlessly astern. Drinkwater expressed surprise as a white plume showed in their wake eight cables away.

"He's been doing that for the past half hour," said Griffiths. "I think we have about two hours before we will feel the spray

of those fountains upon our face and perhaps a further hour
before they are striking splinters from the rail." His hands
clenched the taffrail tighter as if they could protect the timber
from the inevitable.

"We could swing one of the bow chasers directly astern,
sir," volunteered Drinkwater. Griffiths nodded.

"Like that *cythral* Santhonax did the day he shot *Kestrel*'s
topmast out of her, is it?"

"Aye."

"We'll see. It will be no use for a while. Did Lestock in his
zeal douse the galley fire?"

"I've really no idea, sir." At the mention of the galley
Drinkwater was suddenly reminded of how hungry he was.

"Well see what you can do, *bach*. Get some dinner into the
hands. Whatever the outcome it will be the better faced on full
bellies."

Half an hour later Drinkwater was wolfing a bowl of burgoo. There was an unreal atmosphere prevailing in the gunroom where he, Lestock and Appleby were having a
makeshift meal. Throughout the ship men moved with a quiet
expectancy, both fearful of capture and hopeful of escape. To
what degree they inclined to the one or to the other depended
greatly upon temperament, and there were those lugubrious
souls who had already given up all hope of the latter.

Drinkwater could not allow himself to dwell over much on
defeat. Both his private fears and his professional pride demanded that he appeared confident of ultimate salvation.

"I tell you, Appleby, if those blackguards had not fouled up
the starboard fore t'gallant stunsail we'd have been half a
mile ahead of ourselves," spluttered Lestock through the por-
ridge, his nerves showing badly.

"That's rubbish, Mr. Lestock," Drinkwater said soothingly,
unwilling to revive the matter. "On occasions like this small

things frequently go wrong, if it had not been the stunsail it would likely have been some other matter. Perhaps something has gone wrong on the chase to delay him a minute or two. Either way 'tis no good fretting over it."

"It could be the horseshoe nail, nevertheless, Nat, eh?" put in Appleby, further irritating Drinkwater.

"What are you driving at?"

"On account of which the battle was lost, I paraphrase . . ."

"I'm well acquainted with the nursery rhyme . . ."

"And so you should be, my dear fellow, you are closer to 'em than I myself . . ."

"Oh, for heaven's sake, Harry, don't you start. There's Mr. Lestock here like Job on a dung heap, Rogers on deck with a face as long as the galley funnel . . ."

"Then what do we do, dear boy?"

"Hope we can hold on until darkness," said Drinkwater rising.

"Ah," Appleby raised his hands in a gesture of mock revelation, "the crepuscular hour . . ."

"And have a little faith in Madoc Griffiths, for God's sake," snapped Drinkwater angrily.

"Ah, the Welsh wizard."

Drinkwater left the gunroom with Lestock's jittery cackling in his ears. There were moments when Harry Appleby was infuriatingly facetious. Drinkwater knew it stemmed from Appleby's inherent disapproval of bloodshed and the illusions of glory. But at the moment he felt no tolerance for the surgeon's high-flown sentiments and realised that he shared with Rogers an abhorrence of abject surrender.

He returned to the deck to find the chasing frigate perceptibly nearer. He swore under his breath and approached Griffiths.

"Have you eaten, sir?"

"I've no stomach for food, *bach*." Griffiths swivelled round, a look of pain crossing his face as the movement restored circulation to his limbs. His gouty foot struck the deck harder than he intended as he caught his balance and a torrent of Welsh invective flowed from him. Drinkwater lent him some support.

"I'm all right. *Du*, but 'tis a dreadful thing, old age. Take the deck for a while, I've need to clasp the neck of a little green friend."

He was on deck ten minutes later, smelling of sercial but with more colour in his cheeks. He cast a critical eye over the sails and nodded his satisfaction.

"It may be that the wind will drop towards sunset. That could confer a slight advantage upon us."

It could, thought Drinkwater, but it was by no means certain. An hour later they could feel the spray upon their faces from the ranging shots that plummetted in their wake.

And the wind showed no sign of dropping.

Appleby's crepuscular hour approached at last and with it the first sign that perhaps all was not yet lost. Sunset was accompanied by rolls of cloud from the west that promised to shorten the twilight period and foretold a worsening of the weather. The brig still raced on under a press of canvas and Lestock, earlier so anxious to hoist the stunsails, was now worried about furling them, rightly concluding that such an operation carried out in the dark was fraught with dreadful possibilities. The fouling of ropes at such a moment could spell disaster and Lestock voiced his misgivings to Griffiths.

"I agree with you, Mr. Lestock, but I'm not concerned with stunsails." Griffiths called Drinkwater and Rogers to him. The two lieutenants and the master joined him in staring astern.

"He will see us against the afterglow of sunset for a while

yet. He'll also be expecting us to do something. I'm going back on him . . ." He paused, letting the import sink in. Rogers whistled quietly, Drinkwater smiled, partly out of relief that the hours of passivity were over and partly at the look of horror just visible on Lestock's face.

"Mr. Lestock is quite correct about the stunsails. With the preventer backstays I've no fear for the masts. If the booms part or the sails blow out, to the devil with them, at least we've all our water and all our guns . . . As to the latter, Mr. Rogers, I want whatever waist guns we can work double shotted at maximum elevation. You will not fire without my order upon pain of death. That will be only, I repeat only, if I suspect we have been seen. Mr. Drinkwater, I want absolute silence throughout the ship. I shall flog any man who so much as breaks wind. And the topmen are to have their knives handy to cut loose anything that goes adrift or fouls aloft. Is that understood, gentlemen?"

The three officers muttered their acknowledgement. A ball struck the quarter and sent up a shower of splinters. "Very well," said Griffiths impassively, "let us hope that in forty minutes he will not be able to see us. Make your preparations, please."

"Down helm!"

The brig began to turn to larboard, the yards swinging round as she came on the wind. The strength of the wind was immediately apparent and sheets of stinging spray began to whip over the weather bow as she drove to windward.

"Full an' bye, larboard tack, sir," Lestock reported, steadying himself in the darkness as *Hellebore* lay over under a press of canvas.

Drinkwater joined Griffiths at the rail, staring into the dark-

ness broad on the larboard bow where the frigate must soon
be visible.

"There she is, sir," he hissed after a moment's pause, "and
by God she's turning . . ."

"Myndiawl!" Drinkwater was aware of the electric tension
in the commander as Griffiths peered into the gloom. "She's
coming onto the wind too; d'you think she's tumbled us?"

Drinkwater did not answer. It was impossible to tell,
though it seemed likely that the stranger had anticipated Griffith's manoeuvre even if he was unable to see them.

"He must see us . . ."

The two vessels surged along some nine cables apart, running on near parallel courses. Drinkwater was studying the
enemy, for he was now convinced the frigate was a Frenchman. Two things were apparent from the inverted image in
the night glass. *Hellebore* had the advantage in speed, for the
other was taking in his stunsails. The confusion inherent in
the operation had, for the moment, slowed her. She was also
growing larger, indicating she did not lie as close to the wind
as her quarry. If *Hellebore* could cross her bow she might yet
escape and such a course seemed to indicate the French captain was cautious. And then several ideas occurred to
Drinkwater simultaneously. He could imagine the scene on
the French cruiser's deck. The stunsails would be handled
with care, men's attention would be inboard for perhaps ten
minutes. And the Frenchman was going to reach across the
wind and reduce sail until daylight, reckoning that whatever
Hellebore did she would still be visible at daylight with hours
to complete what had been started today.

He muttered his conclusions to Griffiths who pondered
them for what seemed an age. "If that is the case we would do
best to wear round his stern . . ."

"But that means we might still encounter him tomorrow

since we will be making northing," added Drinkwater, "whereas if we hold on we might slip to windward of him and escape."

He heard Griffiths exhale. "Very well," he said at last.

There was half a mile between the two ships and still the distance lessened. At any moment they *must* be observed. Drinkwater looked anxiously aloft and he caught sight of a white blur that was Lestock's face. Nearby stood Dalziell and Mr. Q.

Hellebore's mainmast was drawing ahead of the frigate's stem and Drinkwater could see her topgallants bunching up where the sheets were started and the bunt-lines gathered them up prior to furling. He was certain that his assumption was correct. But another thought struck him: one of the top-men out on those yards could not fail to see the brig close to leeward of them.

A minute later the cry of alarm was clearly heard across the three hundred yards of water that separated the two ships. Drinkwater tried to see if her lee ports were open and waited with beating heart for a wild broadside. He doubted that any of their own guns would bear. He could see Rogers looking aft, itching to give the order to fire. Lestock's fidgetting was growing unbearable while all along the deck the hands peered silently at the ghostly black and grey shape that was the enemy.

There were several shouts from the stranger and they were unmistakably French. A low murmur ran along *Hellebore*'s deck.

"Silence there!" Drinkwater called in a low voice, trusting in their leeward position not to carry his words to the frigate. "Mr. Q. See to the hoisting of a Dutch ensign."

A hail came over the water followed by a gunshot that

whistled overhead, putting a hole in the leeward lower stunsail. A second later it tore and blew out of the bolt ropes.

The horizontal stripes of the Dutch colour caused a small delay, a moment of indecision on the enemy quarterdeck, but it was not for long. The unmistakable vertical bands of the French tricolour jerked to her peak and her forward guns barked from her starboard bow. Three of the balls struck home, tearing into the hull beneath the quarterdeck making a shambles of Rogers's cabin, but no one was hit and then the brig had driven too far ahead so the enemy guns no longer bore. Eighty yards on the beam *Hellebore* drove past the cruiser's bowsprit.

"He's luffing, sir . . ."

"To give us a broadside, the bastard." Griffiths looked along his own deck. "Keep her full and bye Mr. Lestock, I'll not lose a fathom, see."

Drinkwater watched the French ship turn towards the wind and saw the ragged line of flashes where she fired her starboard battery. Above his head ropes parted and holes appeared in several sails, but not a spar had been hit.

"Ha!" roared Griffiths in jubilation, "look at him, by damn!"

Drinkwater turned his attention from the fabric of *Hellebore* to the frigate. He could hear faint cries of alarm or anger as she luffed too far and lost way, saw her sails shiver and the flashes of a second broadside. They never remarked the fall of shot. Griffiths was grinning broadly at Drinkwater.

"Keep those stunsails aloft, mister, even if they are all blown to hell by dawn, we'll not have another chance like this."

"Indeed not, sir. May I secure the guns and send the watch below?"

Griffiths nodded and Drinkwater heard him muttering "Lucky by damn," to himself.

"Mr. Rogers! Secure the guns and pipe the watch below. Mr. Lestock, relieve the wheel and lookout, keep her full and bye until further orders."

Lestock acknowledged the order and Drinkwater could not resist baiting the man.

"It seems, Mr. Lestock, that our opponent appeared to be the one with the lack of horseshoe nails."

"A matter of luck, Drinkwater, nothing more."

Drinkwater laughed, catching Rogers's eye as he came aft from securing his guns. "Or of faith moving mountains, eh Samuel?"

When he looked astern again two miles separated the two ships. The French ship was again in pursuit but five minutes later she had disappeared in the first rain shower.

Daylight found them alone on an empty ocean and as the hours passed it became apparent that they had eluded their pursuer. They resumed their course, dragged the cannon back to their positions and continued their voyage. The stunsail gear needed overhauling for three booms had sprung during that night and several of the sails needed attention. A week later the even tenor of their routine had all but effaced the memory of the chase.

And then the South Atlantic surprised them a second time. At four bells in the forenoon eight days after their escape from the French cruiser a cry from the masthead summoned Drinkwater on deck.

"Deck there! Boat, sir, broad on the weather bow!"

He joined Lestock by the rail, steadying his glass against a shroud. A minute later Griffiths limped over to them.

"Well?" he growled, "can you see it?" Both officers answered in the negative.

Patiently they scanned the tumbling waves until suddenly something held briefly in clear silhouette against the sky. It was undoubtedly a boat and for the smallest fraction of a second they could see the jagged outline of waving arms and a strip of red held up in the wind.

"On the beam, sir, there! Passing fast!" The boat was no more than half a mile from them and had already disappeared in the trough of a wave.

"Watch to wear ship, Mr. Lestock. Call all hands."

The cry was taken up as Lestock turned to pass orders through the speaking trumpet. "I'll get up and keep an eye on 'em sir." Without waiting for acknowledgement Drinkwater leapt into the main rigging and raced for the top. The sudden excitement lent energy to his muscles and he climbed as eagerly as any midshipman. Over on his back he went, scrambling outboard over the futtocks and up the topmast shrouds to cock his leg over the doublings at the topmasthead. Below him, her spanker brailed, *Hellebore* had begun her turn to starboard, the watch squaring the yards until she had the wind aft. Drinkwater looked out on the starboard beam. At first he could see nothing. The occupants of the boat might have subsided in despair and he could think of no greater agony than being passed so close by a vessel that did not sight them. Then he saw the flicker of red. Despair had turned to joy as the castaways watched the brig manoeuvre. *Hellebore* was still turning, the red patch nearly ahead now. Around him the yards groaned slightly in their parrels as the braces kept them trimmed.

"Keep her off the wind, sir, they are fine on the weather bow," he yelled down.

Hellebore steadied with the wind on her beam. The

watches below, summoned for whatever eventuality that might arise, were crowding excitedly forward. Drinkwater saw an arm outstretched, someone down there had spotted the boat. Mindful of his dignity he descended to the deck.

"Afterguard! Main Braces! Leggo and haul!" *Hellebore* was hove to as the main topsail and topgallant cracked back against the mast, reining her onward rush and laying her quiet on the starboard tack some eighty yards from the boat.

They could see it clearly now as its occupants got out a couple of oars and awkwardly pulled the boat to leeward.

" 'Ere, there's bleeding women in it!" came a shout from forward as the Hellebores crowded the starboard rail. A number of whistles came from the men, accompanied by excited grins and the occasional obscene gesture. " 'Cor ain't we lucky bastards."

"Don't count yer luck too early, one of 'em's pulling an oar."

"An 'hore on an oar, eh lads?"

"If thems whores the officers'll 'ave 'em!" The ribald jests were cut short by Drinkwater's "Silence! Silence there! Belay that nonsense forward!"

He and Griffiths exchanged knowing glances. Griffiths had refused to sanction celebrations on the equator for a good reason. "They'll dress them powder monkeys up like trollops, Nathaniel, and all manner of ideas will take root . . . forget it." They had forgotten it then but now they were confronted with a worse problem. There seemed to be three women in the boat, one of whom was a large creature whose broad back lay on an oar like a regular lighterman on his sweep. She had a wisp of scarlet stuff about her shoulders and it was the waving of this that had saved their lives. Exciting less interest, there were also six scarecrows of men in the boat which bumped alongside the *Hellebore*. The brig's people crowded into the chains and reached down to assist. There was much eager heaving and good natured chaffing as the unfortunate survivors were hoisted aboard. " 'Ere, there's a wounded hofficer 'ere." A topman jumped down into the boat and the limp body of a red-coated infantry captain was dragged over the rail.

Appleby was called and immediately took charge of the unconscious man; in the meantime the other nine persons were lined up awkwardly on deck. They drank avidly from the beakers brought from the scuttlebutt by the solicitous seamen. The six bedraggled men consisted of two seamen and four private soldiers. The soldiers' red coats were faded by exposure to the sun and they wore no cross-belts. They were bleareyed, the skin of their faces raw and peeled. The two seamen were in slightly better shape, their already tanned skins saving them the worst of the burning. But it was the women who received the attention of the Hellebores.

The big woman was in her forties, red-faced and tough, with forearms like hams and a tangled mass of black hair about her shoulders. She tossed her head and planted her bare feet wide on the planking. Next to her was a strikingly similar younger version, a stocky well-made girl whose ample figure was revealed by rents in the remains of a cotton dress. Her face was burnt about the bridge of her nose and slightly pockmarked.

Beside him Drinkwater heard Griffiths relieve himself of a long sigh. "Convicts," he muttered, and for the first time Drinkwater noted the fetter marks on their ankles. The third woman was a sharp faced shrew whose features fell away from a prominent nose. She was about thirty-five and already her dark eyes were roving over the admiring circle of men.

"Which of our men is the tailor, Mr. Drinkwater?"

"Hobson, sir."

"Then get him to cobble something up this very day to cover their nakedness; he can use flag bunting if there's nothing else, but if I see more than an ankle or a bare neck tomorrow I'll have the hide off him."

"Aye, aye, sir."

"And turn the two midshipmen out of their cabins. They can sling their hammocks in the gunroom. I want the women accommodated in their cabins," he raised his voice, "now you have had something to drink which of you will speak? Who are you and whence do you come from?"

"We come from His Majesty's Transport *Mistress Shore*, captain," replied the big woman, clearing her throat by spitting on the spotless deck. The officers started at this act of gross impropriety for which a seaman would have had three dozen lashes. Griffiths merely raised his voice to send the off-duty watches below and to get the gobbet swabbed off His Majesty's planking.

"Do not do that again," he said quietly, "or I'll flog you. Now why were you adrift?"

"Ask the sojers, captain, they're the blackguards who . . ."

"Shut your mouth, woman," snapped one of the soldiers, appearing to come out of a trance. Drinkwater guessed the poor devils had been sick as dogs in the boat while the indomitable spirit of this big woman had kept them all alive. The woman shrugged and the soldier took up the tale, shambling to a position of attention.

"Beggin' your honour's pardon, sir, but I'm Anton, sir, private soldier in the New South Wales Corps. Forming part of a detachment drafted to Botany Bay, sir. The officer wot's wounded is Captain Torrington, sir. We was aboard the *Mistress Shore*, sir, twenty men under the Cap'n. The main guard consisted of French emigré soldiers and some pardoned prisoners of war, sir, who had volunteered for service with the colours," Anton turned his head to express his disapproval of such an improvident arrangement and caught himself from spitting contemptuously at the last moment. He wiped the back of his hand across his mouth.

"Beg pardon, sir . . . these dogs rose one night and under a French gent called Minchin they overpowered the guard, murdered the officers of the ship and took her over."

"You mean they overpowered the whole crew?"

"It were a surprise, sir," Anton said defensively, "they put twenty-nine off in the longboat and twelve of us away in the cutter . . . two of 'em died, sir."

"How many days were you adrift?"

"Well, sir, I don't rightly . . ."

"Twenty-two, Captain," said the big woman, "with a small bag of biscuit and a small keg o' water."

Griffiths turned to Drinkwater. "Have the men berthed with the people, the soldiers to be quartered in the tops, the two seamen into the gun crews. As to the women I'll decide what to do with them tomorrow when they are presentable. In the meantime, Mr. Lestock, we will now be compelled to call at the Cape."

Drinkwater and Lestock touched their hats and moved away to attend their orders.

Manifold and strange are the duties that may befall a lieutenant in His Majesty's service, Drinkwater wrote in the long letter he was preparing for Elizabeth and that he could send now from the Cape of Good Hope. It was two days after the rescue of the survivors of the *Mistress Shore.* Already they had been absorbed in the routine of the ship. Drinkwater had learned something of their history. The big woman and her daughter were being transported for receiving stolen goods, offenders against the public morality who had yet though their own virtue sacrosanct enough to have denied it to the treacherous Frenchmen. So spirited had been their resistance that Monsieur Minchin had wisely had them consigned to a boat before they tore his new found liberty to pieces. The woman was known as Big Meg and her daughter's name was Mary. They were decked out in bizarre costume by Hobson since when Big Meg was also known as "Number Four", the greater part of her costume having been made from the black and yellow of the numeral flag.

Both Meg and her daughter adapted cheerfully to the tasks that Drinkwater gave them to keep them occupied. They chaffed cheerfully with the men and appeared to maintain their independence from any casual liaisons as Griffiths intended. This the men took in good part. There were women aboard big ships of the line, legitimate wives borne on the ship's books and of inestimable use in tending the sick. They became mothers to the men, confessors but not lovers, and stood to receive a flogging if they transgressed the iron rules that prevailed between decks. But on *Hellebore* a more delicate situation existed. While the women might be thought to be everybody's without actually being anybody's, while they were willing to banter with the men, their effect was salutary. Even, despite the roughness of their condition, the nature of their convictions and their intended destinations, improving both the manners and the language of the officers. Rogers paid a distant court to Miss Mary who was much improved by some crimson stuff Hobson had laid his hands on which had been tastefully piped with sunbleached codline. Opinion was apt to be kind to them: there were, after all, kindred spirits on the lower deck. If they were guilty in law there was in them no trace of flagitiousness.

Big Meg and her daughter picked oakum and scrubbed canvas, scoured mess kids, mended and washed clothes, while the third woman assisted Appleby. Her crimes were less easy to discover. A sinister air lay about her and it was darkly hinted by her companions that abortion or murder might have been at the root of her sentence of seven years transportation, rather than the procuring commonly held to be her offence. Certainly she claimed to have been a midwife and Appleby was compelled to report she had a certain aptitude in the medical field.

Knowing Appleby's distrust of the sex in general, Drinkwater was amused at his initial discomfiture at having Catherine Best as his assistant. His mates found their unenviable work lightened considerably and that in the almost constant presence of a woman. Catherine Best made sure that her presence was indispensible and whatever her lack of beauty she had a figure good enough to taunt the two men, to play one off against the other and secure for herself the attentions of both. But this was not known to the inhabitants of the gunroom.

"Ha, Harry, it is time you damned quacks had a little inconvenience in your lives," laughed Drinkwater as he directed a thunderstruck Appleby to find employment for the woman.

"I emphatically refuse to have a damned jade among my business . . . if it's true she's a midwife then I don't want her on several accounts."

"Why the devil not?"

"Perceive, my dear Nathaniel," began Appleby as though explaining rainfall to a child, "midwives know very little, but that little knowledge being of a fundamental nature, they are apt to regard it as a cornerstone of science and themselves as the high priestesses of arcane knowledge. Being women, and part of that great freemasonry that seeks to exclude all men from more than a passing knowledge of their privy parts, they dislike the sex for the labour they are put to on their behalf and can never tolerate a man evincing the slightest interest in the subject without prejudice."

Drinkwater failed to follow Appleby's argument but sensed that within its reasoning lay the cause of his misogyny. He was thinking of Elizabeth and her imminent accouchement. He did not relish the thought of Elizabeth in the hands of someone like Catherine Best and hoped Mrs. Quilhampton would prove a good friend to his wife when her time came. But he could not allow such private thoughts to intrude upon his day. He was impotent to alter their fates and must surrender the outcome to Providence. For her part the woman Catherine Best attended to Captain Torrington and earned from Appleby a grudging approval.

The men who had been rescued were soon indistinguishable from *Hellebore*'s crew, the soldiers as marines under Anton, hastily promoted to corporal. Captain Torrington emerged from his fever after a week. He had been thrust twice with a sword, in the arm and thigh. By great good fortune the hasty binding of his wounds in their own gore had saved them from putrefaction, despite the loss of blood he had suffered.

The sun continued to chase the brig into southerly latitudes so that they enjoyed an October of spring sunshine. The beautiful and unfamiliar albatrosses joined them, like giant fulmars, elegant and graceful on their huge wings. Here too they found the shearwaters last seen in the Channel, and the black and white Pintada petrels the seamen called "Cape pigeons."

They sighted land on the second Sunday in October, Griffiths's sonorous reading of Divine Service being rent by the cry from the masthead. At noon Lestock wrote on the slate for later transfer to his log: *Fresh gales and cloudy, in second reefs, saw the Table land of the Cape of Good Hope, East an half North eight or nine leagues distant.* In the afternoon they knocked the plugs out of the hawse holes and dragged the cables through to bend them onto the anchors. The following morning they closed the land, sounding as they approached, but it was the next afternoon before they let go the bowers and finally fetched an open moor in twenty-two fathoms with a sandy bottom. To the north of them reared the spectacular flat-topped massif of Table Mountain. Beneath it the white huddle of the Dutch-built township. Drinkwater reported the brig secure. The captain's leg was obviously giving him great pain.

"Very good, Mr. Drinkwater. Tomorrow we will purchase what fresh vegetables we may and water ship. If any citrus fruits are available we will take them too. Do you let the purser know. As for our guests we will land them all except the seamen. They will stay. I wish the gig to be ready for me tomorrow at eight of the clock. I will call upon the Governor then; in the meantime do you direct Rogers to salute the fort."

"Aye, aye, sir." He turned away.

"Mr. Drinkwater."

"Sir?" Griffiths was lowering himself onto his chair, his leg stiffly extended before him. An ominous perspiration stood out on his forehead and his flesh had a greyish pallor.

"There are Indiamen inshore there, three of them. I am sure one of them will carry our mails to England."

"Yes sir. Thank you."

As he sat to finish the long letter to Elizabeth the first report of the salute boomed out overhead.

CHAPTER SIX

The Cape of Storms

October–November 1798

Drinkwater woke with a start, instantly alert. He stared into the inky blackness while his ears strained to hear the sound that had woken him. The ship creaked and groaned as the following sea rolled up astern and passed under her. It had been blowing a near gale from the south west when he had come below two hours earlier and now something had woken him from the deepest sleep. Whatever the cause of his disturbance it had not alerted those on deck, for there were no shouts of alarm, no strident bellows of "All Hands!" He thought of the ten cannon they had struck down into the hold before leaving the Cape a week ago. There had been barely room for them and they were too well lashed and tommed to move. It might have been the boats. They had both been taken out of the davits and turned keels up either side of the capstan, partially sheltering the canvas covered gratings amidships, in the room made by the absent six-pounders. He doubted they would have sent such a tremble through the hull as he was now persuading himself he had felt.

Then it came again, a slight jar that nevertheless seemed to pass through the entire hull. It had a remorseless quality that fully alarmed Drinkwater. He swung his legs over his cot and reached for his breeches and boots. The source of that judder was not below decks but above. Something had carried away aloft. In the howling blackness of the night with the roar and hiss of the sea and the wind piping in the rigging, those on deck would not be aware of it. He pulled on his tarpaulin and turned the lengths of spunyarn round his wrists. The bump came again, more insistent now but Drinkwater was almost ready. Jamming his hat on his head he left the cabin.

He was doubly anxious, for effective command of the brig was his. Griffiths had been afflicted with malarial fever, contracted long ago in the Gambia, which returned to incapacitate him from time to time. He had been free of it for over a year but as *Hellebore* reached into the great Southern Ocean, down to forty south to avoid the Agulhas current, and made to double the Cape before the favourable westerlies, it had laid him delirious in his cot.

The wind hit Drinkwater as he emerged on deck and pulled the companionway cover over after him. Holding his hat on he cast his eyes aloft, staggered over to the foot of the mainmast and placed his hand upon it. He could feel the natural tremble of the mast but nothing more.

A figure loomed alongside. "Is that you, Mr. Drinkwater?"

"Yes Mr. Lestock," he shouted back, "there's something loose somewhere, but I'm damned if I know where." He turned forward as a sea foamed up alongside and sluiced over the rail. The first dousing after a dry spell was always the worst. Drinkwater shuddered under the sudden chilling deluge. He was cursing foully as he reached the foremast and looked up. The topgallant masts had been sent down and he saw the topmast sway against the sky. The racing scud made it impossible to determine details but the pale rectangle of the triple-reefed topsail was plain. The instant he put his hand upon the mast he felt the impact, a mighty tremble that shook the spar silently, transmitting a quiver to the keelson below. He looked up again, spray stinging his eyes. It crossed his mind that Lestock had furled the forecourse since the change of watch. Drinkwater would have doused the topsail to keep the centre of effort low. Lestock seemed to do things by some kind of rote, an old-fashioned, ill-schooled officer. He felt the shudder again and then he saw its cause.

Above him the bunt of the fore topsail lifted curiously, the foot forming a sharp hyperbola rather than an elliptical arc. The foreyard below it looked odd, not straight but bending upwards.

"Mr. Lestock!" Drinkwater turned aft. Somewhere in the vicinity of the jeers the big yard had broken, only the fore-course furled along it was preventing it from breaking loose. "Mr. Lestock!" Drinkwater struggled aft again, tripping over the watch huddling abaft the boats.

"I think the foreyard has carried away near the slings. One end seems to be fast under the jeers but t'other is loose and butting the mast. You can feel it below. We must get the fore topsail off her. Don't for God's sake start the braces; the whole thing will be down round our ears. Let the ship run off dead before the wind under the fore topmast staysail and rouse up all hands." He was shouting in Lestock's ear but someone heard the cry for all hands and in a second the duty bosun's mate was bellowing down the companionway. Drinkwater grabbed one of the seamen.

"Ah, Stokeley, get everybody mustered abaft the boats, if that lot comes down it'll likely take someone with it. Who's on the fo'c's'le?"

"Davies, sir."

"Right, Mr. Lestock, Mr. Lestock!"

"What is it?"

"Pass me the speaking trumpet." He took the trumpet and held it up. "Fo'c's'le there! Davies! Come aft here at once!" The wind carried his voice and the man came aft. Drinkwater left the explanations to Stokeley and joined the men assembling at the mainmast.

"Listen carefully, my lads. The foreyard has broken. We must start the sheets and clew up the topsail as quickly as possible. Then I want four volunteers to come aloft with me and pass a rope round the broken end of the yard, to lash it against the top until daylight."

The men moved forward. Rogers emerged from the after companionway, he could see the two midshipmen. "Be ready to tail on as required." He gave his orders to have the man stationed to take in the topsail but as soon as they eased the sheets he could see it would not work. The eagerness with which the men sought to quell the flogging topsail by heaving on the clew and buntlines only added to the weight of wind in the sail, forcing it upwards like washing on a clothesline. The topsail sheets tugged the foreyardarms upwards, twisting the furled course below. Perhaps the broken wood severed the first gasket that restrained the huge sail but suddenly three or four gaskets parted and the forecourse blew out in a vast pale billow. There was a crack like a gun and it disintegrated into a thousand streaming ribbons fluttering along the broken yard. The sail had blown clean out of the bolt ropes and the extent of the wounded yard could not be seen. It was a view that all hands contemplated for a split second. Then with a juddering crash the whole starboard half of the yard came down, the topsail stretched flat before splitting and tearing loose then blew off to leeward in an instant. The larboard half of the yard trailed its outboard extremity in the water, crashing downwards parting lifts, halliards and buntlines which fell in entangling coils, snaking across the deck to be torn overside by the wind then dragged aft past *Hellebore*'s onrushing hull. What Drinkwater had intended to be the ordered application of manpower turned into a confused bedlam of shouts, curses and orders.

Drinkwater swore deeply and began to shout. At all costs those spars should be saved, not for their own sake, but for the iron fittings that they would be unable to replace. "Mr. Lestock! Keep the ship off before the wind! Mr. Rogers! A party to secure that starboard yardarm before we lose it!"

Rogers gathered men about him. He was not argumentative, thought Nathaniel, terrible circumstances and the assertion of discipline drove the men in their common necessity. Drinkwater turned forward with his volunteers.

Gathering up a long length of manila hemp that had previously been part of the yard lifts, he dragged it into the rigging, the men assisting. The inner broken end of the larboard half of the yard had come up under the forward edge of the top, the wooden platform round the join of the lower and topmasts. Beneath the top the jeers, a big tackle that held the yard aloft by its slings, was chafed as the whole thing twisted and turned, its splintered end grinding and splitting the top so that the structure bucked under the forces playing on it.

The outboard edges of the top supported the shrouds of the topmast. If it was weakened the whole topmast was in jeopardy and at present the only thing that kept *Hellebore* manageable was the foretopmast staysail below them, its stay secured round the mast just above the damaged jeers. That too was in imminent danger of parting under the relentless grinding of the broken yard.

Drinkwater leant over the forward edge of the top, his tarpaulin blowing up over his head. The men crouched close by awaiting his orders. Beneath his belly he could feel the heavy timbers of the platform bucking and straining. The kick of the butt end of the yard was enormous close to. Even in the dark he could see the chafe in the jeers and his extended fingers confirmed his worst fears.

He wriggled round and looked at the men. Tregembo was there, and Stokeley and Kellet. Mr. Quilhampton too, his small face a blur with two dark patches where his eyes were wide with the wild excitement of the night. It crossed Drinkwater's mind inconsequentially to wonder if the boy knew the danger they were in: that to broach in such a sea meant death for them all. Mr. Quilhampton had a very pretty mother, Drinkwater remembered, she would weep for the loss of her son. He shook his head clear of such irrelevant thoughts, aware that they were a symptom of his indecision.

"Mr. Q!"

"Sir?"

"Descend to the deck and have Mr. Lestock get a turn of something strong round the yard in the vicinity of the rail, get one of the loose gun tackles on it and bowse it tight. Then lash it to the chess tree. Tell him to let me know when he's done it and that the yard must come down to the deck but the jeers are enfeebled. Do you understand?"

Quilhampton repeated the instruction. "Good. Off you go."

"D'you wish me to return to the top, sir?"

"No." He could do that much for a pretty widow. The midshipman's acknowledgement was crestfallen. "Oh damn it, yes. But hurry; and find out how Mr. Rogers is doing." Quilhampton disappeared over the futtocks and Drinkwater turned his attention to the yard.

"We will have to pass the bight of this rope," he indicated the manila, "round the yard so that it will render. Tregembo get that lead block up there," he pointed to one of the blocks, vacated by the broken lift, banging against the upper ironwork of the doubling. Pulling his spike out, Tregembo scrambled up to loosen the shackle.

"Stokeley, cut off a couple of fathoms and make up a strop."

"Aye, aye, sir."

Drinkwater looked over the forward edge of the top as he waited for the men to finish their tasks. The chafing was worse. They had very little time before the heavy yard crashed below. He looked down. Roger's party was a confused huddle of men pulling, cutting and struggling but he could see the dull line of the starboard yard arm. He wondered what damage it had done in its descent, at least it was the smaller section and devoid of the heavy gear attached to the slings.

"Here, sir," Stokeley had the strop and Tregembo the block. Drinkwater began to ease himself over the rim of the platform. "Here zur, I'll do that," said Tregembo indignantly. Drinkwater ignored him. It was his job. Maybe if he had joined the ship weeks before she sailed, as a good first lieutenant should, he would have spotted the defect in the spar. It had not been fair to suppose that Griffiths could do the work as efficiently as himself. Tonight he would pay Providence the debt he owned for that extra time with Elizabeth.

He lowered his weight gently onto the moving spar, gradually transferring his grip. He had hold of the lower jeers block and the movement of the whole thing was alarming now that his life depended on it. Reaching up he took the end of the strop and began to crouch, easing himself down until he was astride the yard, his legs wrapped round it. He let go of the jeers block to have both hands for the strop. His whole body was now transferred to the yard at its alarmingly cockbilled angle. Now the movement was exaggerated, swinging him from side to side with a twitch at the end of each oscillation that threatened to throw him off.

It gave a sudden violent jerk. Drinkwater flung his arms about the spar, retaining sufficient presence of mind not to let go of the strop. For a second the absence of further movement convinced him he was in wild descent.

Then from the deck came a hail: "End's secure, sir!" The jerk had been Lestock's men bowsing the lower end down, unable to see their first lieutenant clinging to its upper extremity. Drinkwater passed the strop round the spar, pulled it tight through its own part and held it up. Stokeley grabbed it and, as Drinkwater scrambled back into the top, secured the block to it. Tregembo had rove the rope through the block and secured one end round the topmast. All that remained to do was to reeve the hauling part through another vacant block. Tregembo had brought a buntline block and shackled it to give a clear lead to the deck and it was the work of only a few minutes to prepare their extempore double whip.

Mr. Quilhampton reappeared. "Mr. Rogers has secured the starboard piece, sir."

"Right. All go below. I'll remain here. Have Mr. Lestock man the jeers and be to lower handsomely on them. Desire him also to take the weight on this manila inch. Make sure he has caught a turn with it."

"Aye, aye, sir."

Drinkwater watched them go, leaning back against the topmast doubling, feeling hot and mad as the gale howled about him. His mouth was dry and he knew he would start shaking from the reaction from his exertions. Thank God they had a good man at the helm, the ship had not slewed from her course once. He must remember to find out who it was; the fellow was deserving of praise.

"Ready masthead there!" came the shout from below.

"Set tight the whip!" he bawled back, lowering himself onto his belly to watch progress. The strop drew tight.

"Ee-ease the jeers!"

The platform beneath him trembled. As *Hellebore* pitched forward and scended the yard moved down a foot, forward six inches. As the wave passed under her the bowsprit stabbed at the sky and the spar swung aft, hitting the mast with a judder. Damn! He should have thought of that! They needed a down-haul.

"Belay there! 'Vast lowering!" He peered down while the yard swung forward and back. Again the jarring thump shot through his body. Then he had it. He reached down. One of the clew garnet lead blocks had a trailing rope through it. If he could just reach it . . .

His fingers missed it by an inch. He thought of getting the hands to haul upon the whip but that might put too great a load on it. He wriggled over the top, turning so that his legs dangled over the edge. With one leg he hooked a trailing end of the line over his foot, bent his leg and, reaching down with one hand grabbed it, heaving himself back into the top. Quickly he fashioned a figure of eight knot in its end and let it go.

"Mr. Lestock! Get the starboard clew garnet, it's trailing round the fiferail, pull it tight and lead it forward to the cat-head. Use it as a downhaul to keep the yard off the mast!"

"Aye, aye!"

There was an interminable pause while Lestock sorted out the tangle of ropes. Then a shout that all was ready. Drinkwater peered once more over the edge of the top. His knot had drawn tight against the block and the rope led downwards.

"Lower away handsomely and keep the downhaul tight!"

The yard began its descent. The jeers parted, whirling to leeward in a cloud of dust causing confusion as the men on

deck, suddenly relieved of the weight, fell over. The oscilla-
tions of the yard grew greater as it was lowered but the clew
garnet, stretched like a thread, prevented its contact with the
mast. As the yard's angle lessened the men at the chess tree
slackened their lashings and there was a dull thud as the broken yard's second part finally lay across the deck. As if angry
with a wild beast the men leapt upon it and threw lashings
round it. Drinkwater climbed wearily down. Scrambling aft,
he joined the master. "Well done Mr. Lestock. Whom did you
have on the wheel?"

"Gregory, sir."

"Give him my compliments for keeping the ship so steady.
When all the gear is secure you may send the watches below.
What time is it?"

"Two bells in the middle watch."

"Good God, I'd no idea . . ."

Their exertions had taken three hours. If he had been asked
Drinkwater would have imagined no more than an hour had
elapsed. Wearily he went below to find Appleby sitting in the
gunroom, a baleful look upon his face and a jug of blackstrap
before him.

"Couldn't you sleep, Harry? Did we poor jacks make too
much noise banging about aloft?" His tone was ironic for he
was too tired for sarcasm. "If that's blackstrap for God's sake
give me some. Harry? What's the matter?"

Appleby looked up at Drinkwater as though seeing him for
the first time.

"Women," he said in a low voice. "We've got a festering
bitch of a woman on board."

CHAPTER SEVEN

Vanderdecken's Curse

November 1798

Closing his mind to one problem Drinkwater was unwilling to face another. He was very tired and the implications of Appleby's remark took several seconds to penetrate his brain. The blackstrap coiled round his belly and radiated its warmth through him so that stiff muscles relaxed. But it stimulated his mind and he turned to Appleby. "Woman? What the devil d'you mean? We landed 'em all at the Cape."

Appleby shook his head, his jowls flapping lugubriously. "You thought you did."

Drinkwater swung his legs round and put both elbows on the table. "Look man, I saw the bloody boat away from the ship's side. Big Meg actually smiled at me and I footed a bow at Miss Mary. Your wench was already in the boat when I reached the rail."

"Exactly! Did she look up?"

"No. Why should she? She wasn't exactly undergoing a pleasure cruise, I daresay they put gyves on 'em as soon as they got ashore."

"I don't doubt it, cully, but that is not the point. Who wrote out the receipt?"

"I did," said Drinkwater, rising to reach down the ship's letter book. He flicked over the pages. "There!" He spun the book to face Appleby. The pasted in receipt bore the words "Three convicts, ex *Mistress Shore*, Government Transport, female."

"So?"

"Oh, for God's sake Harry, quit hazing me. If you've a woman on board let's see her." But Appleby, angry and dismayed by the turn of events would not yet produce his evidence.

"That proves nothing, any fool can squiggle a signature and pretend it's that of a garrison subaltern. All one does is draw up a second one and throw it overboard on the way back to the ship."

"But that indicates a conspiracy. Damn it, Griffiths would have reported three female convicts to the Governor; Torrington or his men knew there were three of 'em. Come on, bring the woman in, I'm tired of fencing with words." He swallowed the blackstrap.

"Look, Nat, I don't suppose Torrington gave it a second thought and I daresay the soldiers were a party to it. As for the Governor, who knows what our captain said to him? The Old Man was already feverish and we know His Excellency was annoyed that Griffiths had not called immediately upon arrival . . . who knows what either of them remembered to say during or after their interview? I daresay H.E. was obsessed with Griffiths's lack of protocol before worrying about whether he had reported two or three convicts. We sailed the following day . . . but one last question. Who took the boat ashore to see those trollops off?"

Drinkwater's argument was merely a symptom of his fatigue. Both of them knew Appleby was not lying but

Drinkwater was trying to delay the inevitable with logic. It was a spurious argument. "Rogers," he said resignedly.

"Huh! Now, to reward your exemplary patience I will produce the evidence." Appleby rose and left the gunroom. Drinkwater emptied the jug of blackstrap into his mug. The door opened and Appleby returned. Drinkwater looked up. Leaning against the closed door was Catherine Best. Her pinched face was almost attractive, half shadowed in the swaying lantern light. An insolent half-smile curled her mouth while a provocative hip was thrust out in allurement.

Drinkwater closed his mouth, aware that he had flushed. He was aware too that she knew well the hold she had over them all. It was not difficult to imagine a conspiracy among the hands, an easy woman amongst them would seem like the answer to a seaman's prayer.

"Where have you been living?"

"She's been in the cable tier," volunteered Appleby.

"That is Lestock's province."

"He delegates his rounds of the hold to one of his mates."

"But I myself was there yesterday . . . no, no, the day before . . ."

"Efficient though you are, Nathaniel, you are an officer of regular habits. It is easy enough to give warning of your coming."

Drinkwater nodded. It was all too true, a dreadful nightmare. He looked again at the woman and was suddenly furious. "I shall have you flogged!" he snapped vindictively. "Turn Dalziell out of his cabin again and lock this trollop in for the night!" Appleby turned to take the woman out. She remained for a moment, resisting the hand upon her arm, looking fixedly at Drinkwater. He felt again the colour mounting to his cheeks.

"Get out, damn you!" he roared, angry at his own weakness. As usual Drinkwater had the morning watch, from four until eight a.m. He woke with the realisation that something was very wrong and the bare two hours sleep that he had enjoyed left him in a foul temper when he reached the deck and realised the nature of his problems. Quilhampton brought him coffee but it did nothing to lighten his mood. The men avoided him, all knowing the mad scheme to carry their own doxy had been discovered by the surgeon and Mr. Drinkwater.

Whilst the watch below melted away and the unhappy culprits in Mr. Drinkwater's watch busied themselves about the decks, the first lieutenant paced up and down. An hour passed before he realised that daylight was upon them, that the sun was above the horizon, revealing a grey-white sea, furrowed and torn by the ferocity of the gale the night before. The wave crests, half a mile apart, were already losing their anger as the gale abated, to turn them slowly from breaking seas to crested swells.

He swept his glance over the shambles of the deck. Luck had been with them again last night. Later he hoped he would find Griffiths surfacing for a lucid moment and could tell him what they had been through. But then he would also have to tell him about the woman Catherine Best, and he was not looking forward to that. He swore to himself. He could not flog the woman alone since all were guilty, all these sheepish seamen who crept round the deck pretending to check the lashings on the pieces of yard. Tregembo passed him and Drinkwater was struck by a feeling of abandonment.

"Tregembo!"

"Zur?"

"Did you know about this woman?" he asked in a low voice.

"Aye zur."

"And you didn't tell me?"

Tregembo looked up agonised. "I couldn't zur, couldn't welsh on my mates . . . besides, zur, there was officers involved."

Drinkwater bit his lip. Tregembo could no more pass tittletattle than he could have favoured Tregembo over the ridiculous flogging business. Nevertheless the apparent disloyalty hurt. "Have you lain with her?"

"No, zur!" Tregembo answered indignantly. "I've my Susan, zur."

"Of course . . . I'm sorry."

"It's all right, zur . . . you've a right to be angry, zur, if you'll pardon me for so saying." He made to move away. Drinkwater detained him.

"Just tell me by whom I was deceived?"

"Zur?"

"Who dressed as the jade in the boat at the Cape?"

"Why Mr. Dalziell, zur."

Drinkwater closed his gaping mouth. "How very interesting," he said at last in an icy tone that brought an inner joy to Tregembo. "Thank you Tregembo, you may carry on."

Tregembo touched his forehead and moved aft, passing the wheel.

"What was he asking you?" growled the quartermaster apprehensively.

"Only who was tarted up like the woman at the Cape, Josh. And I reckon the buggers'll see the sparks fly now. He's got his dander up."

Drinkwater took two more turns up and down the deck then he spun on his heel. "Mr. Quilhampton! Pipe all hands!"

That would do for a start. The middle watch would be deeply asleep now, damn them, and the members of the first watch had been a-bed too long. If they thought they could pull the wool over the eyes of Nathaniel Drinkwater they were going to have to learn a lesson; and if he could not flog them all then he would work them until sunset.

The men emerged sleepily. Lestock came up, followed by Rogers. "Ah, Mr. Lestock, I do not require your presence, thank you." The elderly man turned away muttering. "Mr. Rogers, I desire that you take command of the hands and unrig the broken yard, clear all that raffle away and then get one of those Corsican pines inboard and rig it as a jury yard to reset the spare topsail without delay. Wind's easing all the time. When you have completed that bring in a second tree and get a party of men under the direction of Mr. Johnson to start work with draw knives in shaping up a new yard, better let Johnson choose the spars. We'll transfer the iron work after that and paint the whole thing before swaying it aloft. Your experience on *Hecuba* should stand you in good stead."

Still fuddled with sleep, Rogers could not at first understand what was happening. It dawned on him that it was not much past five a.m. and that he had had hardly any sleep. It was doubtful if he yet knew of Drinkwater's discovery of Mistress Best or of his part in the conspiracy. "Look, damn you Drinkwater, if you think . . ."

Drinkwater took a step quickly and thrust his face close to Rogers's. "It used to be said that every debt was paid when the main topsail halliards were belayed, Rogers, but it ain't so. Newton's third law states that every action has an equal and opposite reaction. Now you are about to have that demonstrated to you. You have had your pleasure, you poisonous blackguard, and by God, sir, now you are going to pay for it! Carry on!" Drinkwater turned contemptuously away and called Mr. Quilhampton to his side.

"Fetch my quadrant and the time-keeper from my cabin

take your time, Mr. Q. Make two trips. If you drop that chronometer it will be the worse for you."

The boy hurried off. Drinkwater was beginning, just beginning, to feel better. He would take a series of sun altitudes in a while and calculate their longitude by chronometer. He was very proud of the chronometer. The convalescing Captain Torrington had been landed with his men at the Cape. The army officer had been most grateful to the commander and gunroom officers of the *Hellebore* and asked if there was any service he could perform for them. By chance his brother, a civil officer in the service of the East India Company, was taking passage home in one of the Indiamen in Table Bay and Torrington intended to return with him to England. His brother had advanced the Captain a considerable sum of money to defray his expenses whilst the Indiamen were at the Cape and he was willing to do his best to purchase some comforts for his benefactors.

Drinkwater, having missed his opportunity to obtain a timekeeper at Syracuse, knew that John Company's ships carried them. "Sir, if I could prevail upon you to beg a chronometer from the commander of one of the Indiamen we should be eternally obliged to you. You are aware of the nature of our mission and that we were sent on it somewhat precipitately; a chronometer would be of great use."

"I should regard myself an ingrate if I were not to purchase you one my dear Drinkwater, a few wounds and a clock are a small price to pay to avoid Botany Bay." They had laughed heartily at the noble captain as they lowered him into the boat.

"You know I used to deplore the sale of army commissions but when you have a generous and wealthy fellow like that to deal with it don't seem so bad a system," Griffiths had said ironically.

The following morning the instrument arrived in an exotically smelling teak case. Drinkwater had taken it in charge, not trusting Lestock to wind it daily at the appointed hour. He had confirmed the longitude of Table Bay to within seven minutes of arc and this morning would be the first time they had seen the sun since leaving to run their easting down in the Roaring Forties. The result would make a nice matter for debate when Lestock came below for dinner.

After Lestock relieved him at eight bells and Drinkwater permitted the hands to cease their labour for half an hour to break their fasts, the first lieutenant sent for the woman. He sat himself down at the gunroom table and made her sit opposite while Appleby passed through into Griffith's cabin to tend the commander.

The door hardly closed on the surgeon when Drinkwater felt his calf receive a gentle and seductive caress from her leg. Last night, tired and a little drunk, he had been in danger of succumbing. The lure of even Catherine's used body had sent a yearning through him. But this morning was different. His position would not tolerate such licence as the men toiled in expiation above his head. Besides, despite his fatigue, his spirit was repaired and his body no longer craved the solace of poor, plain and desperate Catherine. Daylight did not help her case.

"Last night I threatened to have you flogged. I have decided against that, but if you attempt the seduction of me or a single one of the men I will visit the cat upon your back." He saw the initiative fade from her eyes. "Have you ever seen a flogging, Catherine?" he asked coldly.

She nodded. Drinkwater opened the ship's muster book, snapped open the inkwell and took up his pen. "I am entering you on the ship's books as a surgeon's assistant. You will be fed and clothed. If you prove by adhering to the regulations of the ship that you can carry out your duties, I will use my best endeavours to have your sentence remitted by whatever time you serve aboard this ship. I have a little influence through a peer of the realm and it may prove possible, if your services are of a sufficiently meritorous nature, that the remission of the whole of your sentence is not beyond the bounds of possibility."

He did not know if such a course was remotely possible but it kindled hope in Catherine's eyes. She was a creature of the jungle, an opportunist, amoral rather than immoral and yet possessed of sufficient character to have hazed a whole ship's company. That showed a certain laudable determination, Drinkwater thought. His plan might just work. "Will you agree to my conditions? The alternative is to be put in irons indefinitely."

"Yes, yer honour." She lowered her face.

"Look at me Catherine. You must understand that *any* infringement of the ship's rules will destroy our agreement." She looked up at him, then at Appleby, who had come from Griffiths's cabin shaking his head over the captain's condition. "Mr. Appleby here will witness your undertaking."

"I understand yer honour, but . . ."

"But what?"

"Well sir," she said ingenuously, "it's Mr. Jeavons and Mr. Davey, sir."

"The surgeon's mates?"

She nodded.

"They're my regulars, like, sir, they've come to expect . . . you know . . ." She looked down again while Drinkwater looked at an Appleby empurpling with rage. "Why the damned, festering . . ." Drinkwater held his hand up.

"I will deal with them Catherine. They will not trouble you

again." He turned the book round and held the pen out. "Make your mark there," he pointed to the place but she said indignantly, "I know, sir, I can read and write."

She signed her name with some confidence. "Very well, Catherine, now while I read out the men's names do you tell me with whom you have slept." He began to read. She did not know all their names but the percentage of the crew who had visited her was large. But neither was it surprising. It was even possible that this bedraggled creature possessed a gentleness absent from the lives of the seamen and that it was for more than lust that they came to her.

"It must stop now, Catherine." She nodded, while Appleby, with a hideous implication said, "I will look into this matter."

Drinkwater dismissed Catherine and sent for Appleby's mates. It was certain that they had been instrumental in suggesting Catherine dupe the brig's officers to their own advantage. Their plan had misfired when they discovered that many more of the hands would have to be a party to it and that those men would soon come calling for their share of the trophy. Besides, Catherine had to be found employment under supervision. Appleby was the only trustworthy person who did not have to keep a watch, and as the woman showed an aptitude for medical work she would be best employed with him.

It was the work of a moment to disrate the surgeon's mates. They protested they held their warrants from the College of Surgeons, that they were gentlemen unused to the labour of seamen. But being alone in the Southern Ocean had its advantages. There was neither court of appeal nor College of Surgeons south of the equator and they were soon turned to on deck where the starters of the bosun's mates were stinging their backsides with a venom spurred by a gradual realisation that the hands were being worked like dogs because of a certain lady of easy morals between decks. That her two pimps had been turned among them was a matter for some satisfaction.

Drinkwater concluded his morning's work by also appointing Tyson surgeon's assistant. He too could write, they had discovered, and Drinkwater was amused to find Appleby growling over the radical alterations to his department. "My dear fellow," said Drinkwater, summoning Meyrick from the pantry with some blackstrap, "you have always fancied your chances as a philosopher, now you have the most literate department in the ship. You will be able to plead the benefit of clergy for all of 'em. Now do be a good fellow and allow me to compute this longitude before Lestock comes below."

At noon Drinkwater called the hands aft. His announcement to them was brief and to the point. The woman, Catherine Best, he told them, had been apprehended. The deception against the Regulations for the Good Order of His Majesty's Navy on board His Britannic Majesty's Brig of War *Hellebore* was at an end. Although it verged upon the mutinous by virtue of its very nature as "a combination", in the effective absence of the captain, he had decided that he could not flog the woman without inflicting the penalty upon them all. He held them all culpable, however, and would punish all of them by a stoppage of grog, to be indefinite against their good behaviour. The groan that met this announcement convinced Drinkwater that it was the correct measure. The deprivation of jack's grog was a punishment incomprehensible to landsmen. As for the woman, he continued, she was now part of the ship's company. Any man found lying with her would receive the same punishment as that prescribed by the Articles of War for that unnatural act whereby one man had knowledge of another. He did not need to remind them that the punishment for sodomy was death.

When he had finished he sent them to their dinner. "By heaven, Nathaniel, that was a rare device," muttered Appleby admiringly, "what a splendid pettifogging notion. Worthy of Lincoln's Inn."

Drinkwater smiled thinly. He was thinking how far they had yet to travel and how little of their task they had yet accomplished.

"What d'you intend to do about Dalziell and Rogers?"

"Let them stew a little, Harry, let them stew."

In longitude forty-five east they hauled to the northward, the wind quartering them until it gradually eased and died away from the west. They entered the great belt of variables south of Madagascar and worked north by frequent yard trimming. Twice they sighted sails but on both occasions they did not seek to close the other. The men began to mutter. The deprivation of their grog continued days after they had toiled to get first the jury foreyard up, then its permanent replacement. The lack of it was beginning to rankle. As the weather continued to improve Drinkwater had sent up the topgallant masts. On their first day of light winds they had hoisted the boats out and hauled them up to the davit heads on either quarter. Griffiths had recovered sufficiently to be told of the events of the last fortnight. He had been so choleric that Appleby feared for a recurrence of his fever, but the old man had subsided to order that Drinkwater continue the ban on grog just at the point when Drinkwater was considering reinstating it.

"No indeed! The weather is improving, the men do not need it to drive them aloft, see; let them feel the want of it a little longer."

Catherine Best appeared a reformed character and Appleby was the butt of jokes about the reclamation of fallen women. Although he resisted at first, Griffiths had finally allowed her to attend him. Reporting to the commander one morning Drinkwater had commented on her as she left the cabin. "There is a little good in the worst of us," Griffiths quoted with more than a trace of Welsh piety, Drinkwater thought wryly. "*Du,* but she's a sight better than those gin-soaked mountains of lard at Haslar . . . or for that matter the herring gutters they had in the hospital at Yarmouth . . ." Griffiths was beginning to enjoy his convalescence and if the men thought their commander had adopted their bawd then let them, he thought. They would be of that opinion anyway and Drinkwater was at last able to wring the issue of grog from Griffiths.

It was whilst observing Venus after sunset that he first heard the rumour. Beneath the poop two men sat in the gloom of dusk while *Hellebore* ran north north east under easy sail.

"We be a cursed ship with a woman on board," he heard one voice.

"Ah, bull's piss. They Indiamen carry women *and* chaplains, they seem to manage. Anyway you tried hard enough to have her."

"No I didn't."

"You bloody well did, you said yerself that if you'd been below before that slimy rat Jenkins you'd'ave slipped her what she had coming to her. I heard you."

"We still be accursed. You heard o'the Flying Dutchman? Him what inhabits these waters? You heard of him then?"

Drinkwater brought the planet down to the fast fading horizon, twisting the quadrant gently and smoothly. Satisfied, he rocked it slightly from side to side so that the gleaming disc just cut the horizon, all the time adjusting the index to follow the planet's setting. "Now!" he called to Quilhampton who was taking the time on the chronometer. He paid no more attention to the rubbish he had overheard. Lestock came up shortly afterwards to relieve him and looked suspiciously at the longitude Quilhampton had chalked on the slate.

"Come, come, Mr. Lestock, the Board of Longitude thought the problem worth twenty thousand sterling. All I ask is that you have a little faith in their investment." But he did not wish to get involved in an argument and he went on, "It's high time we had those guns out of the hold. We're coming up with Ile de France, even you latitude sailors must know that, and it's time we mounted a full broadside before we meet a Frenchman. If it is calm tomorrow we'll hoist 'em out. In the meantime she's full and bye, nor'nor'east, all plain sail and nothing reported. Logged six knots five fathoms at one bell, wheel and lookouts relieved. Good night, Mr. Lestock."

"Good night, Mr. Drinkwater."

As he broke his fast the following morning, when a dying wind held every prospect of their being able to remount the guns, he heard again the words "Flying Dutchman". He called Meyrick from the pantry. "Come now what's all this about?"

Meyrick was shamefaced but clearly confused. He told how a tale was going round the brig about them being condemned to everlasting drifting about, like the Flying Dutchman. It was all on account of the woman. "It's nothing but scuttlebutt, sir, but . . . well I . . ." Drinkwater smiled. It sounded ridiculous but he knew the grip a superstition could have over the minds of these men. It was not that they were simple but that their understanding was circumscribed. They had no idea where they were, they endured hours of remorseless labour to no apparent purpose. The best of them was paid twenty-nine shillings and sixpence gross, less deductions for the Chatham Chest, medical treatment, slops and whatever remaining delights, like tobacco, the purser sold them. Their lives were forfeit if they broke the iron-bound rules of conduct, and ruled by an arbitrary authority which was a yoke, no matter how enlightened. Recent events had conspired to make it the more irksome and there would be those among them with sufficient theology to assure their more credulous messmates that they were being punished for their carnal misdemeanours. It was not surprising therefore that their minds should react to a story as vivid as that of Vanderdecken, the legendary Flying Dutchman. The question was who had started its circulation?

"Where did you first hear the story, Meyrick?"

The man pondered. "It was here in the gunroom, sir. Begging your pardon sir, I wasn't listening deliberately, sir, but I heard . . ."

"Well who was telling it, man?" said Drinkwater impatiently, well knowing Meyrick eavesdropped and passed the conversation of the officers to the cook who, from his centrally situated galley where all came during the day, fed out to the hands the gossip he saw fit.

"I think it were Mr. Quilhampton, sir."

"Mr. Q, eh? Thank you, Meyrick. By the way you did not concern yourself over such things on *Kestrel* did you?"

"Lord love you no, sir. But we was never far from home, sir. Ushant, Texel, them's home for British jacks sir, but up there now," he pointed to the deckhead, "why nobody knows the stars, sir, even the bleeding sun's north of us at noon, sir. One of the men says there's islands of ice not many leagues to the south. It just don't seem right sir, kind of alarming . . ."

Drinkwater sent for Mr. Quilhampton. "Meyrick tells me he heard you spinning the yarn of the Flying Dutchman, is this true?"

"Well no, sir. Actually I was listening. I mean I had heard it before, but I didn't like to say so, sir."

"Who was telling the tale then?"

"Oh it was just by way of entertainment, sir. I was listening with Dalziell."

"But who was telling it?"

"Why Mr. Rogers, sir."

"No wind, Mr. Lestock."

"None, Mr. Drinkwater."

"Very well, clew up all sails and square the yards. A tackle at each of the lower yard arms, one on the main topmast stay and a bull rope to the capstan. The watch can rig those then turn up all hands."

He fell to pondering the problem. Since the discovery of Catherine Best, Rogers had been very quiet. Whether or not he had had a relationship with the woman Drinkwater did not know. Neither did he care. Appleby told him the woman believed herself barren and there seemed no evidence of other complications. Nevertheless Rogers had been a party to the conspiracy. More, Drinkwater hoped, out of a misplaced, schoolboy prankishness than a calculated act. But Drinkwater was not sure. Rogers might have been evening the score, proving himself smarter than the first lieutenant. But that did not ring quite true. Rogers was an impetuous, fiery officer, spirited if low in moral character, certainly able and probably brave. The service was full of his type; they were indispensable in action. But Rogers was not a dissembler. His weakness lay in his impetuous temper. When Dalziell had brought Tregembo for a flogging Rogers had acted without a second thought. So was Dalziell behind this silly rumour? There was an inescapable logic about it. Not that the yarn was in itself sinister, but the persistence of its power to unsettle and subvert was real; very real. The sooner they had the guns remounted the better. Now that they were in temperate latitudes once again they could resume their routine of general quarters, suspended since the Cape in the heavy weather of the Roaring Forties. Drinkwater knew it was not sufficient to read the Articles of War once a month to keep the people on their toes. Only the satisfying roar and thunder of their brutish artillery could do that.

"All ready, Mr. Drinkwater. Hands at the tackles, the hatches off and the toms off the guns."

"Very well, Mr. Lestock, then let us turn to."

The first to emerge was the foremost starboard waist gun. The tackles of the starboard fore and main yardarms were overhauled and married to the big stay tackle. The three purchases thus joined were lowered into the hold. There they were hooked onto the gun, ready slung by a strop around its trunnions.

A bosun's mate commanded the hauling part of each tackle and at the gratings the bosun, Mr. Grey, his silver chained whistle suspended about his neck, stood poised.

"Set tight all!" The slack in the three tackles were taken up.

"Stay tackle heave! Handsomely there now . . . yard tackles up slack!"

The black doubled hemp of the main topmast stay assumed a shallow angle and the mainmast creaked gently. The six pounder weighed eighteen hundredweights. Below in the hold six men tallied on a bull-rope round the gun's cascabel, steadying the black barrel. The next order came as the gun rose level with the deck: "Yard tackles heave!" The men grunted away in concerted effort. There were no merchant ship's shanties but a rhythmic grunt as fifty men, barefoot and sweating in the sunshine, strained at their work. "Walk back the stay tackle handsomely!"

The gun, suspended now from all three tackles, began to move horizontally across the deck. The bull-rope trailed slack and was pulled onto the deck by one of the topmen who ran forward to reeve it through a train tackle block.

"Vast heaving main yard!" As the stay tackle party lowered slowly back and the mainyard party ceased work, the gun slewed forward under the pull of the foreyard tackle. It began to move across the deck diagonally.

"Capstan party heave tight!" Twenty men walked round the capstan and tightened the bull-rope. Theirs was a job of adjustment, as was that of the gunner's party that stood by the waiting gun carriage.

"Walk back the mainyard!" The gun moved forward now, almost over the carriage.

" 'Vast all!"

"Walk back handsomely!" Slowly, almost imperceptibly, the gun began to descend. Trussel made some furious signals while Mr. Grey held first the foreyard party, then the main. The gun stopped while Trussel's men shoved the carriage a little. A minute later the gun rested on its trunnions. The capsquares were shut. The carriage was slewed into position and run up against its port linel, then the breechings were passed.

"Overhaul all . . ." The three tackles were passed down into the hold for the second gun.

They finished by mid-afternoon and were piped to dinner after which they were piped up again and went to general quarters. The broadsides were ragged and from his cot Griffiths expressed his disappointment.

"Tell the people," he muttered crossly, "that if that is the best they can do I will stop their grog again."

It was not an order Drinkwater made haste to obey. The mood of the ship was too delicate and Appleby had told him the fever had aggravated Griffiths's leg and he was likely to be irritable and a semi-invalid for some time.

"God knows what will become of him," the surgeon said worriedly, "but his powers of recovery are greatly diminished since last year's attack."

The silence of exhaustion fell upon the brig as the sun set. It was mixed with discontent for, despite reprovisioning at the Cape, some of the salt junk had been found bad and there had been no more that day to replace it. "It is likely to be a long voyage," Drinkwater had reluctantly told the purser, "we must adhere to the rationing."

He came below at eight p.m., his shirt sticking to his back, too tired for sleep. Not that sleep was to be had in the airless cabin. In the gunroom Appleby dozed over his madeira. Drinkwater slumped in a chair as the door to Griffiths's cabin opened and Catherine Best emerged. She held a finger to her lips, the very picture of solicitude.

As she passed Drinkwater she gave a little curtsey. He could scarcely believe his eyes and his mind was just forming a quite unjustified suspicion that she must have ulterior motives when a piercing cry of alarm came from the deck.

A silence followed, brief but oppressive with the most awful horror. Then, in that stunned hiatus, clearly heard through the open skylights and companionways: "It's him, boys! It's the Dutchman!"

So potent had been the cry that the senses seemed devoid of reason. Drinkwater felt his intelligence replaced by fear, then with a curse he rose and rushed on deck. He ran forward to where Kellett, captain of the foretop, his arm outstretched, was openmouthed in terror.

Others arrived and they too pointed, muttering fearfully, a papist or two crossing themselves, a good Protestant on his knees confessing his sins direct to his maker. "Oh God forgive me that I did indeed have carnal knowledge of Mistress Best when that vessel of uncleanness was a greater whore than all the . . ." Next to him Drinkwater saw Dalziell. The midshipman was shaking as though palsied.

Drinkwater stared ahead at the dull, greenish glow. The night had become cloudy and dark, there was just a breath of wind and the glow grew larger. If his theory about Dalziell having initiated the silly rumours was correct the youth was paying for it now in a paroxysm of fear.

"Whisht, listen boys! Listen!" The hubbub faded and they could hear the screams, the screams of souls in torment. "Holy Mary, Mother of God, blessed is the fruit of thy womb . . ."

"Jesus Christ, what the hell is it?"

" 'Tis the Dutchman, boys . . . the Dutchman . . ."

Drinkwater pushed his way aft, unceremoniously grabbing Lestock's glass from the master's paralysed hand. He swung himself into the mainchains.

It was the hull of a galleon all right, with a high poop. But the vessel had been dismasted. He thought he could see movement, pale shapes flitting about on it. The hair on the nape of his neck crawled. He dismissed the superstition with an effort. But perhaps an old wreck, like those supposedly trapped in the weed of the Sargasso . . . ?

No, there was something familiar about those screams. "Mr. Lestock!"

"Eh? What?"

"Do we have steerage way?"

"Steerage way? Eh, oh, er we did, sir, just. Come you lubbers back to the wheel, damn it, what d'ye think this is?"

"A point to starboard if you please."

A gasp of incredulity greeted this order. Cries of supplication and threats floated aft. "The devil may take you, Mr. Drinkwater, but not us, hold your course mates."

"Belay that forward! What's the matter my bully boys? Have you lost your stomachs? Come now, I don't believe it. A point to starboard there . . ."

"What the deuce is it Drinkwater?" muttered Rogers below him, "lend me the glass." Drinkwater handed it down. "Let me see after you," said Appleby. "Damn your eyes, it's my bloody glass." Lestock snatched it peevishly from Rogers's eye.

"You can see for yourself, Harry," said Drinkwater, suppressing laughter.

They were closing the apparition fast now. The supposition that it was a galleon had made a fantasy of distance. In fact it was quite close and as they passed it there was a surge backwards from the rails, cries of revulsion as the stink of the dead whale assailed their noses.

"Well it stinks like hell for sure!" There was the laughter of relief up and down the deck as they realised what huge fools they had been.

The decomposing whale had swelled up and glowed from the millions of tiny organisms that fed upon it. Shrieking and screaming above it a thousand seabirds enjoyed the funeral feast of the enormous mammal while the water about it was thrashed to a frenzy by a score of sharks.

They watched it fade astern. Laughing at themselves, the men drifted below. It seemed the atmosphere about the ship had been washed clean by that appalling smell. Drinkwater wished his companions good night when a party was seen coming from forward. Four men were carrying the inert white-shirted and breeched body of a midshipman. "Is that Mr. Q?"

"Lord no, sir. I'm here."

"It's Mr. Dalziell, zur," said Tregembo, lowering the midshipman. "Fainted he did, zur, in a swoon."

"Well, well, well," said Drinkwater ironically, "it seems that vengeance is still the Lord's."

CHAPTER EIGHT

A John Company Man

November–December 1798

Drinkwater was bent over his books, alarmed at the high expenditure of cordage due to the loss of the foreyard, when he heard the cry from the masthead.

"Deck there! Sail Ho! A point of starboard!" He gratefully accepted the excuse to rush on deck, feeling the welcome breeze ruffling his open shirt. They had sighted the high land of Ras Hafun three days earlier and doubled Cape Guardafui under the strong katabatic winds that blew down from the Somali plateau. Now they romped westward into the Gulf of Aden carrying sail to the mastheads. It was the forenoon and the watches below were preparing for dinner so that at the cry most of her hands crowded *Hellebore*'s waist. They were eagerly awaiting a sight of the stranger from the deck. Drinkwater saw Quilhampton at the rail.

"Up you go, Mr. Q, and see what you make of her." The boy grabbed a glass and leapt into the rigging. The sight of anything would be welcome. They had seen several dhows inshore of them as they closed the coast but the stranger might be a square-rigged ship, a friend, or, just possibly, an enemy.

Hellebore had had her fill of the wonders of the Indian

Ocean. Flying fish, whales and dolphins had been seen in abundance, turtles and birds of many descriptions, petrels, long-tailed tropic birds and the brown boobies that reminded them of the immature gannets of Europe. Little sketches filled the margins of Drinkwater's journal together with a description of a milk sea, an eruption of foaming phosphorescence of ethereal beauty. This phenomenon had prompted Quilhampton to essay his hand at poetry. The scorn of Mr. Dalziell ended the endeavour, though Mr. Quilhampton was quick to refute the assertion that poets were milksops by pointing out they were not the only persons to be sent into a swoon at the sight of the world's natural wonders. But none of these observations thrilled them as much as the two white topgallants that were soon visible from the deck.

"She's a brig sir, like us ... or she might be a snow, sir," reported Quilhampton with uncertain precision.

"Colours?"

"Not showing 'em, sir," he answered, unconsciously aping Mr. Drinkwater's abbreviated style.

"No colours, eh?" said Griffiths, hobbling up on his swollen foot.

"No, sir."

"Waiting for us to declare ourselves, eh? Clear for action Mr. Drinkwater, Mr. Lestock! Take the t'gallants off her, square away to intercept this fellow."

The pipes squealed at the hatchways and the men lost their dinner as the cook doused his stove. All was hurrying urgency. They had improved their gunnery coming up from the south, shot at casks with the "great guns" and shattered bottles at the yard arms from the tops. Their grog had long ago been reinstated and Catherine Best had assumed the demeanour of a nun. Never was a meal more cheerfully forgotten. This was no lurking French cruiser of overwhelming force. The sun was shining, the breeze was blowing and the shadows of the sails and rigging were sharp across the deck as it was sprinkled with sand.

"Cleared for action, sir."

The two ships were three miles apart when the chase freed off, altering to the north so that she presented her broadside to them. "She's a snow," muttered Quilhampton, pacing up and down the starboard battery in the wake of Lieutenant Rogers.

"She's an odd looking craft," said Drinkwater. She was like a small sloop but with a long poop, painted green with enormous gun ports in it.

"Hoist the colours!"

"Or the god-damned topgallants, you bloody old goat," muttered Rogers who thought the chase would escape his eager gunners.

Hellebore's ensign snapped out and jerked to the spanker peak, streaming out on the starboard beam. Griffiths watched the snow respond, heaving to with her main topsail against the mast. At her peak flew the horizontally striped ensign of the Honourable East India Company.

"A John Company ship," said Griffiths, relaxing. *Hellebore* foamed up to the stranger and came to the wind as the snow lowered a boat.

"He's all for co-operation," said Griffiths to Drinkwater.

"Well I'm damned . . . those ain't gunports, they're slatted blinds."

"Jalousies, Mr. Drinkwater, she's a dispatch vessel for the Company, a country ship they use for conveying their officials about and carrying dispatches. I'll wager it's that he wishes to see us about."

Griffiths proved right. While the Hellebores, relaxing from action stations and eagerly salving what remained of their lukewarm dinner, chaffed incomprehensibly with the grinning lascars in the boat, a handsome sun-bronzed officer in the crisp well-laundered uniform of the Company's Bombay Marine told them the news.

"Lieutenant Lawrence, gentlemen, at your service." They exchanged formal greetings and withdrew to Griffiths's cabin.

"Lieutenant Thomas Duval of His Majesty's ship *Zealous* arrived at Bombay on 21st October, sir, with the news from Admiral Nelson." Griffiths and Drinkwater exchanged glances. *Hellebore* had been at the Cape then. "Please go on, Lieutenant."

"It seems that on 1st August last the British fleet under Rear-Admiral Nelson annihilated the French at Aboukir Bay. The attack was made at sunset while the French fleet lay at anchor. I understand that, despite the shoaling of the bay and the grounding of *Culloden*, the British engaged the French on both sides and the victory was a most complete one. The flagship, *L'Orient*, blew up." He finished with a smile, as though the disintegration of a thousand humans was a matter for personal satisfaction.

"Do you have sercial in Bombay, Lieutenant?" asked Griffiths ironically, motioning Drinkwater to open a bottle. He called through into the pantry for Meyrick to bring in some glasses.

"We do not want for much in Bombay," said Lawrence, "but I have not tasted such excellent Madeira for a good while." From his appearance Lawrence wanted for absolutely nothing. They toasted the victory.

"And where are you from now, Lieutenant, what is your purpose?"

"I am from Mocha, sir, where we left dispatches for Commodore Blankett. Captain Ball of *Daedalus* was daily expected. The Red Sea Squadron uses Mocha as a watering place, sir. Mr. Wrinch is the agent there," he paused, then added, "a man of considerable parts, sir, you would find calling upon him most profitable." Lawrence's eyes fell to Griffiths's gouty foot, then he rattled on, "unfortunately we could not delay as the north-east monsoon in the Arabian Sea makes a lengthy passage for us back to Bombay."

"And your dispatches conveyed the news of the victory at Aboukir to Blankett I assume?"

Lawrence nodded over the rim of his glass.

"And was there mention of a French army in those dispatches? Of a force landed in Egypt?"

"Oh that! Yes sir, there are indications of such a thing. Duval suggested that they might attempt a descent on India but the idea is quite preposterous: their force in the Red Sea is totally inadequate. It gave us a nasty shock, though," he laughed gaily, "quite unexpected!"

"What?" snapped Griffiths, "d'you mean there are already French ships in the Red Sea?"

"Oh yes, one of them, a smart little sloop, call 'em corvettes I recollect, attempted to chase us off Perim two days ago. We led him a merry dance through the reefs and soon shook him off."

"*Myndiawl,*" growled Griffiths while Drinkwater asked, "How many ships have the French got out there, sir?"

"I've really no idea, sir, two or three. The Arabs don't view their arrival with much enthusiasm since they seem to be taking dhows. God knows what for. It might be the will of Allah but the faithful don't take too kindly to it."

"A true corsair by the sound of him," said Griffiths pondering.

"Tell me sir, could you oblige us with a modern chart of the Red Sea? Ours is most fearfully wanting in detail." Drinkwater pulled the appropriate chart from the drawer beneath the settee. He showed Lawrence. The lieutenant laughed. "Good God, gentlemen, I believe Noah had a better. Yes, I am sure I can furnish your wants there, send a midshipman back with me."

"There's a further thing," said Griffiths, "we've a woman on board and I want her given passage to Bombay."

Lawrence's face clouded. "Who is she?"

"Oh, some convict scum we found floating in a ship's boat in the South Atlantic. She got amongst the men with her damned fornicating."

Lawrence was indignant: "I'm sorry sir, but I cannot help you with convicts."

"Damn it man, I order you to, I hold a commission in the King's Service . . ."

"You say you picked her up in the South Atlantic?" temporised Lawrence.

"Yes."

"But you come from the Cape. Could you not have landed her there?" Lawrence frowned. He supposed these naval officers had tired of the jade and now wished to be rid of her. "You must understand, sir, that I have a crew of lascars, their notion of Englishwomen is not such that they would readily comprehend the nature of a whore and a convict." He picked up his hat and bowed. "But the chart you shall have with pleasure. Good morning gentlemen, my thanks for your hospitality . . ."

"Wait, Mr. Lawrence," snapped Griffiths. The man's refusal to take Mistress Best had not surprised him. Other things were crowding the mind of Madoc Griffiths. "A moment more. I desire you to inform the Governor at Bombay and the General Officer commanding the Company's troops that there *is* substantial risk of the French descending upon India. It is most important that you carry Admiral Nelson's apprehen-

sions upon this matter with more conviction than did Lieutenant Duval. To this end I shall have the matter in writing . . ." The commander turned to his desk. Lawrence's face
was a picture of scepticism; he seemed unable to take such a
threat seriously. Drinkwater was not surprised; he had heard
that prolonged service in India induced a euphoria in Euro-
peans that was a consequence of their exalted position.
Lawrence's lofty dismissal of Catherine Best amply demonstrated this attitude.

"See Mr. Lawrence over the side, Mr. Drinkwater," Griffiths handed the Company officer a letter. Lawrence bowed,
took the packet and left the cabin. As the two men climbed
into the brilliant sunshine of the deck Drinkwater called Quilhampton to accompany the officer to his ship.

"I'll send my boat back with him, sir," smiled Lawrence,
"lest it be said that I refused a woman but took a boy, eh?"

Drinkwater found the jest distasteful and dismissed
Lawrence as a sybarite. But he managed a thin smile out of
courtesy.

"You be careful of those Frogs," Lawrence said lightly,
"you don't have the local knowledge that we do and even my
chart is not a great deal of use above Jabal Zuqar, but it'll get
you to Mocha. Good day, sir."

"Good day, and thank you. I suppose you know no more of
the French force?"

Lawrence shrugged. "A frigate and one or two corvettes
. . . commodore's name was unusual," he paused with one elegant calf over the rail. "I remember Tom Duval sounded
more Frog than this villain. Something like Santon . . .
Santa . . ."

"Santhonax?"

"You have it exactly sir, Santhonax. Good day, sir."

"God's bones!" Nathaniel turned swiftly away and scrambled below while Lawrence returned to his ship. Drinkwater burst in upon Griffiths. "I just asked that popinjay who commanded the French squadron, sir!"

Griffiths looked up: "Well?"

"Santhonax!"

For a second Griffiths sat silent, then a torrent of Welsh oaths rolled from him in a spate of invective that terminated in the pouring of two further glasses of sercial. Both men sat staring before them. Both thought of the long duel they had fought with Santhonax in the Channel and the North Sea. They had put an end to his depredations by capture at Camperdown. Now, by some twist of fate, Santhonax had beaten them, arrived ahead of them in the Red Sea.

"It is not coincidence, Nathaniel, if that is what you are thinking. *Du*, it is Providence . . . *myndiawl*, it is more than that, it is *proof* of Providence!"

"There is one thing, sir."

"Eh? And what is that?" asked Griffiths, pouring a third glass of the wine.

"He does not know it is us that are in pursuit."

"Huh! That is something like cold comfort, indeed it is."

The bump of a boat alongside told where Quilhampton had been returned. A minute later the boy knocked and came in. He handed Drinkwater the rolled chart. "Beg pardon sir, but it *was* a snow, sir, name of *Dart*, sir and . . ."

"Mr. Quilhampton!" snapped Griffiths.

"Sir?" said the boy blushing.

"Do you tell the master that I desire him to brace up and lay a course for the Straits of Bab el Mandeb."

"B . . . Bab el . . ."

"Mandeb."

"Aye aye, sir."

CHAPTER NINE

Mocha Road

December 1798—May 1799

Lieutenant Drinkwater slowly paced *Hellebore*'s tiny quarterdeck. The almost constant southerly wind that blew hot from the Horn of Africa tended to ease at nightfall and Drinkwater, in breeches and shirt, had come to regard his sunset walks as an indispensable highlight to the tedium of these weeks. Now, as the sun sank blood-red and huge, its reflection glowing on the sea, he felt a bitter-sweet sadness familiar to seamen at the close of the day when far from home. He turned aft and strode evenly, measuring the deck. His eyes were caught by the rose-coloured walls and towers of Mocha to the east, a mile distant. The mud brick of the town's buildings also reflected the setting glory of the sun. The slender minaret pointed skywards like a sliver of gold and beside it the dome of the mosque blazed. Behind the town the Tihamah plain stretched eastward, already shadowing and cooling until, like a fantastic backcloth it merged with the crags and fissures of the Yemeni mountains that rose into a sky velvet with approaching night. It was not the first time that the beauty of a tropical night had moved him, provoking thoughts of home and Elizabeth and the worry of her accouchement. Then he chid himself for a fool, reminding himself that although he knew a good deal about the ship beneath his feet he knew precious little about the fundamentals of human life. Elizabeth would have been long since brought to bed. He wondered whether the child had lived and tore his mind from the prospect of having lost Elizabeth.

Mr. Brundell approached him and reported the sighting of the captain's boat. Drinkwater hurried below for his coat and hat, then met Griffiths at the entry.

After the exchange of routine remarks Griffiths beckoned Drinkwater into the cabin, and throwing his hat onto the settee he indicated the first lieutenant should pour them both a glass of wine. Flinging himself onto his chair the commander covered his face with his hands.

"No news, sir?" enquired Drinkwater, pushing the wine across the table.

"Aye, *bach*, but of a negative kind, damn it. It *is* Santhonax. Wrinch is certain of it." Griffiths's frequent visits ashore to the delightful residence of Mr. Strangford Wrinch had almost assumed the character of a holiday, so regular a thing had they become in the last month. But it was not pleasure that drove Griffiths to the table of the British "resident".

Wrinch was a coffee merchant with consular powers, an "agent" for British interests, not all of them commercial. Drinkwater had dined with him several times and formed the impression that he was one of those strange expatriate Britons who inhabit remote parts of the world, exercising almost imperial powers and writing the pages of history anonymously. It had become apparent to Griffiths and Drinkwater that the man sat spider-like at the centre of a web that strung its invisible threads beside the old caravan routes of Arabia, extended to the ancient Yemeni dependencies in the Sudan and the uncharted tracks of the dhows that traded and plundered upon the Red Sea.

Griffiths had long been involved with the gleaning of intelligence, had spent the latter part of his life working for greater men whose names history would record as the conductors of foreign policy. Yet it was a war within war that occupied Griffiths and Wrinch, a personal involvement which gave them both their motivation. And for Griffiths the personal element had reached an apogee of urgency. Santhonax had been their old adversary in the Channel and the North Sea in the anxious months before Camperdown. Santhonax had been responsible for the barbaric execution of Major Brown, a fact that stirred all Griffiths's latent Celtic hatred. Griffiths was an old, infirm man. Santhonax's presence in the Red Sea mocked him as a task unfinished.

So Griffiths sat patiently in the cool, whitewashed courtyard, brushing off the flies that plagued the town, and waited for news of Santhonax. What Drinkwater did not share with his commander was the latter's patience.

In the weeks they had swung at anchor Drinkwater had concluded that Admiral Nelson had sent them on a wild goose chase; that Lieutenant Duval's overland journey to Bombay was sufficient. They had strained every sinew to reach the Red Sea only to find Admiral Blankett was not at Mocha, that he had gone in search of the French squadron and might have by now destroyed Santhonax. The admiral had been told by Wrinch that a French force was loose in the area. Wrinch affirmed the accuracy of his intelligence without moving from his rug where he would sit in his *galabiya* and *fadhl* with his fellow merchants, with the Emirs el Hadj that led the caravans, with the commanders of dhows who swapped news for gold, pearls or hashish, or fondled the pretty boys Wrinch was said to prefer to women.

Whatever the truth of the gossip about himself, Wrinch was shrewd enough to know when an Arab invoked the one true God to verify his lies, and when he reported facts. And Griffiths was not interested in the moral qualities of his sources; for him the world was as it was.

Blankett too, had taken alarm. Red-faced and damning Wrinch roundly he had set off north while the season of southerly winds lasted. After his departure Lawrence had arrived, only to be chased by one of Santhonax's ships, appearing mysteriously in Blankett's rear. Despite this intelligence Wrinch urged Griffiths not to cruise in search of either party. He should simply wait. For Wrinch, waiting and "fadhling" were part of the charm of Arab life. For Griffiths they were a tolerable way of passing the time, enduring the heat and sharpening his appetite for revenge. For Drinkwater the delay was intolerable.

"So we continue to wait, sir?"

Griffiths nodded. "I know, *bach*, idleness is bad for the people forrard but, *du*, we have no choice. Wrinch is right," Griffiths soothed, brushing the flies away from his face. "Damned flies have the impertinence of Arabs . . . No, Mocha Road is the rendezvous." His white-haired head sank in thought. "Hmmm, *Yr Aifft* . . ."

"Sir?"

"Egypt, Nathaniel, Egypt. There is great activity in Egypt. Bonaparte has made himself master of Cairo. A general named Desaix is blazing a trail through Upper Egypt with the assistance of a Copt called Moallem Jacob." He paused. "I think Nelson may be right and with that devil Santhonax to reckon with . . ." He raised his white eyebrows and clamped his mouth tight shut. Then he blew out his cheeks. "I wish to God you'd shot him."

*   *   *

naction, like the heat, seemed to have settled permanently upon the brig. The pitch bubbled in the seams and Drinkwater had the duty watch keep the decks wet during daylight. They listed the ship with the guns and scrubbed the waterline, they overhauled the rigging and painted ship. Griffiths forbade exercising the guns with powder and a silent ritual was meaningless to the men. To divert them Drinkwater sent Lestock, his mates and the midshipmen off in the boats to survey the road. Although this stimulated a competitiveness among the junior officers and promoted a certain amount of professional interest, once again highlighting Mr. Quilhampton's potential talents, it was limited in its appeal to the hands and soon became unpopular as the boats roamed further afield. Lethargy began to spread its tentacles through the brig, bearing out Appleby's maxim that war was mostly a waste of time, a waste of money and a waste of energy.

As week succeeded week Drinkwater's frustration mounted. He was tormented by worry over Elizabeth, worry that could not easily be set aside in favour of more pressing duties because there were none to demand his attention beyond the routine of daily life at anchor. The myriads of flies that visited them drove them to distraction and the lack of shore leave for the hands exacerbated their own cramped lives.

Strangford Wrinch passed them alarming intelligence, gathered from a certain Hadji Yusuf ben Ibrahim, commander of a *sambuk*. In December of the old year a French division under General Bon had occupied Suez. Bonaparte himself had accepted tribute from the Arabs of Tor in Sinai and reached an accommodation with the monks of the mysterious monastery of St. Catherine at the southern extremity of that peninsula. General Desaix was scattering the mamelukes to the four winds in an energetic sweep up the

Nile Valley. Egypt had become a province of France and it was clear that, despite Nelson's victory at Aboukir and the subsequent blockade of the Mediterranean coast under Sir Samuel Hood, the French were far from beaten. They might yet move further east and in the absence of Blankett *Hellebore* would be no more than a straw under the hooves of the conqueror.

At the end of January Griffiths ordered them to sea. For a fortnight they cruised between Perim and Jabal Zuqar, exercising the guns and sails. Then they returned to Mocha Road and the shallow bight of its bay, to the heat and flies and the deceptive, fairy-tale wonder of its minaret. Again Griffiths departed daily, smilingly ordering them to submit to the will of Allah, to learn to *keyf*, to sit in suspended animation after the manner of the Arabs.

"Holy Jesus Christ," blasphemed the intemperate Rogers in sweating exasperation, "the stupid old bastard has gone senile."

"Mr. Drinkwater!" The knocking at the door was violently urgent. The face of Quilhampton peered round it, white with worry. "Mr. Drinkwater!"

Drinkwater swam stickily into consciousness. "Eh? What is it?"

"Two ships standing in from the south, sir!"

Drinkwater was instantly awake. "Inform the captain! General Quarters and clear for action!"

The midshipman fled and Drinkwater heard the brig come alive, heard the boy's treble taken up by the duty bosun's mate piping at the hatchways. He reached for his breeches, buckled on his sword and snatched up the loaded pistol he habitually kept ready. He rushed on deck.

It was just light and the waist was all confusion with the

slap of two hundred bare feet and the whispered exertions of five score of sleep-befuddled seamen driven by training and fear to their stations.

Drinkwater picked up the night glass from its box and did the required mental gymnastics with its inverted image. He swept the horizon and steadied it on the two shapes standing into the road. The larger vessel might be a frigate. Some of the new French frigates were big vessels, yet she seemed too high and not long enough to be a French thoroughbred. The smaller ship was clearly a brig of their own size.

Griffiths appeared. "Hoist the private signal, Mr. Drinkwater!"

Rogers reported the batteries cleared for action. "Very well, Mr. Rogers. Man the starboard. Mr. Drinkwater, set tight the spring. Traverse three points to larboard!"

"Aye, aye, sir." Drinkwater cast a final glance at Quilhampton's party hoisting the private signal to the lee foretopsail yardarm where the wind spread it for the approaching ships to see. "Mr. Grey, waisters to the capstan!"

Hellebore trembled slightly as the spring came tight and she turned off the wind, bringing her starboard broadside to bear upon the strangers. Drinkwater watched apprehensively. There was no reply to the private signal.

"Starboard battery made ready, sir," Rogers reported. All activity had ceased now, the gun crews squatting expectantly around their pieces, the captains kneeling off to one side of the recoil tracks, the lanyards tight in their hands.

Hellebore was a sitting duck, silhouetted against the sunrise while the newcomers approached out of the night shadows.

"Mr. Rogers! Fire Number One gun astern of her if you please."

Drinkwater raised his glass and watched the bigger of the two ships. Forward the gun barked. Daylight grew rapidly, distinct rays from the rising sun fanned out from behind the crags of the Yemeni mountains. As the muezzin called the faithful to prayer from the distant minaret of Mocha, Drinkwater saw the British ensign hoisted to the peak of the approaching ships and an answering puff of smoke from the off-bow of the bigger one.

"British ensign, sir."

"Then answer at the dip."

An hour later he was anxiously waiting for Griffiths to return from the fifty gun *Centurion*, commanded by Captain Rainier.

Drinkwater ran a surreptitious finger round the inside of his stock. He could not understand why, in the heat of the Red Sea, the Royal Navy could not relax its formality sufficiently to allow officers to remove their broadcloth coats when dining with their seniors. After all, this moment, when the humidor of cheroots followed the decanter of port round the table, was tacitly licensed for informality.

They were listening to an anecdote concerning the social life of Bombay told by *Centurion*'s first lieutenant. It was an irreverent story and concerned a general officer in the East India Company's service whose appetite for women was preserved within strictly formal bounds: ". . . and then, sir, when the nautch-girl threw her legs round him and displayed a certain amount of enthusiasm for the old boy, d'you see, he ceased his exertions and glared down at her; 'any more of this familiarity,' the old bastard said, 'and this coupling's off'!"

The easy laughter of *Centurion*'s officers was joined by that of the young commander of the eighteen-gun brig *Albatross*, a man more than ten years Drinkwater's junior. It seemed that all these officers from the India station led a life of voluptuous ease and licence. It suddenly rankled Nathaniel that their partners with Duncan in the grey North Sea, with St. Vincent off Cadiz and with Nelson in the Mediterranean led a different life. He thought of the rock off Ushant and of the storm-lashed squadron that kept a ceaseless watch on Brest and, in the smoky heat of Captain Rainier's cabin, had a sudden poignant urge to be part of that windy scene, where the rain squalls swept like curtains across the sky, obscuring the reefs that waited impassively to leeward of the lumbering divisions of British watchdogs. This effete bunch of well-laundered, red-faced hedonists made Drinkwater feel uncomfortable, offended his puritan sensibilities. It was as if over-long exposure to the heady tropical beauty of Indian nights had affected them with moon-madness.

Neither had Griffiths forgotten his duty, as the slight edge of sarcasm in his voice implied.

"*Du*, sir, 'tis a wonder you sallied so far from home with such delights to keep you at Bombay. May one enquire of your intentions?"

"Of course, Captain," said Rainier, a large fleshy man with an expansive manner who appeared like an Indian Buddha surrounded by blue cheroot smoke. "The news we had from Nelson, both from Duval and yourself, is what brings me to carry out the present reconnaissance of the Red Sea."

"And effecting a junction with Admiral Blankett, sir?"

The captain shrugged. He did not seem eager to combine his force with Blankett's. Yet if he did the Red Sea squadron would almost certainly be sufficient to bottle up the Straits of Bab el Mandeb, locate and destroy whatever ship Santhonax had at his command.

"Blankett's whereabouts are somewhat unknown. My own instructions are clear. I am to determine the extent of French military action in Egypt relative to a descent upon India. That is all." It was clear to Drinkwater that the nautch-girls of Bombay sang a sweeter song than the sirens lurking on the imperfectly known reefs of the Red Sea.

Rainier exhaled elaborately, indolently watching the three concentric smoke rings waft slowly towards the deckhead with obvious satisfaction.

"Oh bravo, sir," breathed Adams sycophantically, giving Drinkwater a clue to his early promotion. Rainier raised his fingers in a gesture of unconcern that seemed not to warrant a shrug of the shoulders. "I think the matter of little moment, 'tis but in the nature of an excursion." He caught sight of Griffiths's frown. "Oh, I know, Captain Griffiths, you come panting from the battlefields of Europe, lathered with the sweat of your own efforts, your energy is not the plague, you know. It is not contagious. We have our own way of attending to the King's business out here. We are not unaware that Tippoo Sahib, the Sultan of Mysore," he added for the benefit of the new arrivals from England, "is raising rebellion against us. We even have information that Bonaparte himself has been in contact with him. But I am not of the opinion any great risk attends the matter."

Rainier drew heavily upon the cheroot and a comfortable little ripple of self-satisfaction went round the table amongst the officers of the two ships.

"I wish I shared your confidence, sir," Griffiths said.

"Oh, come, sir," put in Adams, "the French are not here in force. Why, how many ships does Blankett have, eh?" Adams turned to the only non-uniformed figure at the table, strange in civilian clothing a decade out of fashion.

"He has three sixty-fours," said Wrinch, "*America*, *Stately* and *Ruby*. The two first named were due home, the third on a cruise. He has two frigates, *Daedalus* and *Fox* with the sloop *Echo*. She too is due home."

"You see, Griffiths," said Adams, "that is a sizeable squadron."

"If it is all together," growled Griffiths, unconvinced.

Rainier seemed to want to terminate the argument.

"Come Griffiths, it is not as though we are up against Suffren, is it?" The captain muttered through his fist as he picked at a sliver of mutton lodged irritatingly in his molars, "Eh?"

"The French commander is a pupil of Suffren, sir. He is well-known to my first lieutenant and myself, sir. A true corsair, cunning as a fox, dangerous and resourceful. Not a man to underestimate." Griffiths's voice was low and penetrating.

"How come that you know him, sir?" enquired *Centurion*'s captain of marines.

Griffiths outlined the tasks assigned to the twelve-gun cutter *Kestrel* during her special service on the coasts of France and Holland. He spoke of how they had come into conflict with the machinations of Capitaine Edouard Santhonax, how they had tracked him from the coves of France to the sandy beaches of Noord Holland and how Drinkwater had finally captured him during the bloody afternoon of Camperdown. He told them of the brutal murder of the British agent, Major Brown, taken in civilian clothing and strung up on a gibbet above the battery at Kijkduin in full view of the blockading squadron. As his voice rose and fell, assembling the sentences of his account, he compelled them all to listen, straightening the supercilious mouth of Commander Charles Adams. ". . . And so gentlemen, Santhonax contrived to escape, devil take him, by what means I do not know, and if this French army in Egypt is as powerful and as dangerous as Admiral Nelson seemed to think, then, *myndiawl*, you should be cautioned against this man." A silence followed, broken at last by Rainier.

"That was bardic, captain, truly bardic," said Rainier dismissively, taking snuff.

"Captain Griffiths is right, sir," put in Wrinch at a moment when Drinkwater sensed Rainier wished to conclude matters. "Santhonax is taking native craft, perhaps to use as transports to India, perhaps to prevent the transfer of the faithful from the Hejaz across the Red Sea to Kosseir. These 'Meccan' reinforcements have been told they have but to shake a Frenchman to dislodge the gold dust from his clothes. They are flocking to join Murad Bey by way of the caravan route to Qena. Murad," he added with the same condescension as had been used to explain Tippoo Sahib to the uninitiated, "is a Circassian who commands the Mameluke forces in Upper Egypt. Now, although Desaix has beaten him and scattered his forces, Murad is, in reality, undefeated. To bring him to his knees Desaix must strangle his reinforcements from Arabia either by taking the dhows at sea, or by taking Kosseir. If this is done then additional tarrifs will be levied on trade from Arabia, as Bon is already doing at Suez on the trade from Yambo and Jeddah. Bonaparte's government in Cairo is already said to be much pressed for cash and driven to all manner of expeditions to raise it."

"And do you think Santhonax and Desaix could concert their actions to the necessary degree?" asked Rainier at last, disquieted despite himself by the turn the conversation had taken.

"Indeed, sir. Men have done such things. Egypt is ungovernable, of course. It may well be that the French will push on to India. That would be more prestigious for them than ultimate retreat."

"Do you think prestige would outweigh military sense?" sneered Adams.

"In France," retorted Wrinch coolly, "they have just undergone a revolution caused by inferiors revolting that they may be equal. Equals, like Bonaparte and Desaix, Captain Adams, revolt in order that they may be superior. Such is the state of mind that creates, and is created by, revolutions."

"That is sophistry, sir," bridled the commander, flushing.

"That is Aristotle, sir," replied Wrinch icily.

An uncomfortable silence fell on the table. Then Wrinch went on.

"By June the wind in the Red Sea will be predominantly from the north. Often this northerly wind reaches as far south as Perim and lasts until August. A *sambuk* goes excellent well down wind, a *baghala* could carry a battery of horse artillery or three companies of infantry. In the Arabian Sea from May to September the monsoon is favourable for a fast passage, if an uncomfortable one."

"Ah," interjected Adams, at last able to put a technical obstacle in front of Wrinch, "but you cannot land at Bombay or on the Malabar coast during the south west monsoon."

Wrinch raised an eyebrow. "Even a Frenchman may round Cape Comorin, Captain. They may still have friends in Pondicherry and it is not many miles from there to Mysore."

Rainier had had enough. He rose. "We sail in two days, gentlemen."

"Am I to join you, sir?" asked Griffiths.

"No, Griffiths. Do you stay here and wait for Blankett. You are possessed of all the facts and can best acquaint the admiral of 'em. Your orders from Nelson were explicit. You have managed to convince me that perhaps I must look a little further into the matter, damn you."

So *Hellebore* continued to wait. Having, as Appleby put it, sped with the wings of Hermes half way round the world, they had now to acquire the patience of Job. Griffiths spent less time ashore, apparently happier now that Rainier had gone north. But it was not only this that had relaxed the man. The true reason was revealed one night over a more frugal and less formal meal than that enjoyed aboard *Centurion*. In the cabin of *Hellebore* the brig's officers dined off mutton, of which there was a good supply in Mocha, and drank their madeira with dark coffee and sweet dates, listening to the reason for Griffiths's change.

"To be without pain, gentlemen, is like a rebirth. Mr. Strangford Wrinch is a man of many parts. You have seen only one side of him; that of a gossiping coffee merchant who keeps a kind of court in Mocha. In fact he is much more than that. He has journeyed into the interior and tells of mysterious cities long deserted by their inhabitants. He is a hadji who has twice been where it is not permitted for an infidel to go. He has fought in three Arab wars, is an expert in mathematics, astronomy and Arab literature, writes verse in Arabic and keeps a flight of sakers worthy of a prince . . ." He paused and Drinkwater heard Rogers mutter a reference to boys. If Griffiths heard it he ignored it, fixing Appleby with a stare. "And he has some medical knowledge."

As if on cue Appleby snorted. "You are going to tell me he knows a few nostrums, sir," the surgeon said archly.

"Indeed not. I am going to tell you he knows a great deal. That he can cauterize a wound with hot oil, or sear the back with hot irons to cure rheumatism. Furthermore for open wounds an application of rancid butter or cow dung . . ."

"Cow dung?" Appleby's head shot up in disbelief, his chins quivering. Rogers was laughing silently as if this revelation proved his private theory that Griffiths was mad. Griffiths ignored him, obviously enjoying Appleby's scepticism.

"Just so, Mr. Appleby. An application of cow dung, see, possesses certain properties which enable a wound to heal cleanly."

Behind his hand Rogers muttered, "No wonder there are so many flies . . . good-damned cow shit, for Christ's sake." Mr. Dalziell began to giggle and even the loyal Quilhampton found it impossible to resist. The sniggers spread to uncontrollable open laughter to which Appleby succumbed.

Drinkwater coughed loudly, mindful of a first lieutenant's duty. "And this cure for your pain, sir, was that one of these, h'hm extreme and, er . . . h'hm unusual remedies?"

Griffiths turned towards Drinkwater, a mildly benevolent smile on his face. He shook his head, his eyes twinkling beneath their bushy eyebrows. "For the gout, Mr. Drinkwater, an affliction long considered by the best *English* brains as incurable, Mr. Wrinch prescribed crocus bulbs and seeds . . ."

"Crocus bulbs . . . !" guffawed Rogers, whose mirth was past rational control. The tears streamed down the faces of the midshipmen and even Appleby was too stunned to offer resistance to this challenge to *English* medicine.

"And you are quite without pain?" asked Drinkwater, controlling himself with difficulty.

"Quite, my dear Nathaniel. Fit enough to finish the task that brought us here."

At the beginning of May Blankett arrived at Mocha having exchanged his flag into the *Leopard*, newly arrived from England. He had with him *Daedalus* and *Fox*. They had swept the Red Sea and the Gulf of Aden without discovering Santhonax. Off Guardafui Blankett had transferred into *Leopard* and sent the fourth-rates home. He was disinclined to listen to the dire warnings of Griffiths, not admitting the argument that he had not only failed to find the French but had missed Rainier. Annoyed, Griffiths returned to *Hellebore* and fumed like Achilles in his tent. Then, a week later Rainier returned. He had penetrated as far as Suez and bombarded the place. Although the French army was there no ships were to be seen and it was said that *Centurion* was the first ship of force seen before the town.

"That," said Appleby, "is a piece of conceit I mislike. I daresay Egyptian ships of force were off Suez while Rainier's ancestors were farting in caves."

"Ah, but not with eighteen-pounders in their batteries," said Drinkwater, laughing, "cannon are a powerful argument to revise history."

"Pah! A matter of mere comparisons."

"Like the ingredients of medicines, eh?" grinned Drinkwater at the surgeon.

Convinced that the French threat was illusory, Rainier departed for India, leaving *Hellebore* to the mercies of Blankett. After his exertions the rear-admiral was not inclined to cruise further. He took himself to Wrinch's house to *keyf* and dally with a seraglio of houris while his squadron settled down to wait. Though for what, no one seemed quite certain.

"Boat approaching, sir. Looks like that fellow Sinbad." Quilhampton interrupted the first lieutenant who had had the carpenter make a small portable desk for him on deck where, beneath the quarterdeck awning, the breeze ruffled his shirt and made the intolerable paperwork that was part of his duty a trifle more bearable.

"Sinbad?"

"That damned Arab Yusuf ben Ibrahim, sir!" Drinkwater

looked up. It was a great pity this idleness was affecting Mr. Quilhampton. The contempt the meanest of *Hellebore*'s people felt for the local population struck Drinkwater as quite incomprehensible. Perhaps it was a result of their being cooped up on board, but there was little contemptible about Yusuf ben Ibrahim. A striking figure with the hawk-like good looks of his race who could handle his rakish *sambuk* with a skill that compelled admiration.

"Go and inform the captain, Mr. Q." Ben Ibrahim had assumed the duty of chief messenger between Wrinch and Griffiths now that Blankett's residence precluded Griffiths's presence. The Arab clambered over the rail. He salaamed at Drinkwater and handed over a sealed letter. Drinkwater bowed as he took it, straightening up to see three men turning sheepishly back to their work while Mr. Dalziell insolently essayed a bow himself.

"Bosun's mate," Drinkwater called sharply, "I desire you to keep those men at their duty or I will be obliged to teach 'em better manners. Mr. Dalziell you will be mastheaded until sunset." He turned away and went below. Griffiths read the letter then handed it back to Drinkwater. "Read it," he said, transferring his attention to the chart before him.

My Dear Madoc, [Drinkwater read] I am writing to you as I doubt that blockhead Blankett will take alarm from what I have learned. It occurs to me that since you have no written instructions from the admiral you might still consider yourself under Nelson's orders. Although my official powers are limited, my influence is not. I can offer a considerable measure of protection in case of trouble with your superior.

I have received news from Upper Egypt that Desaix is everywhere and Murad's force is scattered. This is confusing. What is certain is that General Belliard has occupied Kosseir and Murad's reinforcements from the Hejaz are choked. Also the bearer, Ben Ibrahim, has sighted French ships in the Gulf of Aqaba and at Kosseir. I am certain our quarry is accumulating dhows at Kosseir for Bonaparte or Desaix to proceed against India.

I shall exert pressure upon the admiral but, I beg you my dear Madoc, to go and cruise northwards with your brig. Even now Blankett snores upon my divan but I purpose to wake him to his duty. I know his ships have yet still to water and anticipate he will yet delay. If you regard this Santhonax as dangerous, now is the time to locate him.

[The letter was signed] Strangford W.

Drinkwater looked up at Griffiths. "I warned them both, damn them." Griffiths beckoned Drinkwater over to the chart. The long sleeve of the Red Sea ran almost north to south. At its head, in a gesture of vulgar contempt as if refusing to link up with the Mediterranean at the last minute, the two fingers of the Gulfs of Aqaba and Suez were divided by the mountains of Sinai.

Griffiths moved his finger up the Gulf of Aqaba. "Those two numbskulls scoured the Egyptian coast while Santhonax hid round the corner and snapped up potential transports like a fox does chickens. *Du bach*, what fools these Englishmen are . . ."

Drinkwater smiled ruefully. "Not quite all, sir. Nelson's an Englishman, he could see clearly enough."

Drinkwater put down the letter, seeing the postscript.

Take Yusuf and his dhow with you. I have instructed him to go as your eyes and ears. Though he does not speak English he understands the situation.

"Send that Arab down and pass word to get the spring off the cable. We'll slip out an hour after dark. Send Lestock to me and have the water casks topped off."

"With the greatest of pleasure, sir." Drinkwater left the cabin eagerly.

CHAPTER TEN

Winging the Eagle

June–July 1799

The favourable southerly breeze left them in the region of sixteen degrees north and they worked patiently through the belt of variables for a hundred miles before picking up the northern wind. Their passage became a long beat to windward with Yusuf ben Ibrahim laughing at their clumsy progress from his graceful and weatherly sambuk. But the wind, though foul, was fresh and cooling while the spray that swept over the weather bow sparkled in the sunshine and gave the occasion a yachting atmosphere. North of Jeddah they encountered several large dhows which Yusuf investigated, shepherding them alongside the brig. They were seen to be full of green-turbanned "Meccans" who waved enthusiastically, having proclaimed a *jihad* against the infidel army of Desaix and Moallem Jacob.

"They say," said Griffiths, watching them through his glass, "that Murad Bey deploys them in front of his Mameluke cavalry as a breastwork. Have the men give the poor devils three cheers."

Sheepishly the Hellebores on deck raised a cheer for their expendable allies. The warlike enthusiasm of the "Meccans"

left an indelible impression of great events taking place over
the horizon to the west; of the strength of Islam that could
summon up such zealous cannon fodder and of the energy of
French republicanism that it could raise such a ferment in this
remote corner of the world.

They beat on to the north, passing the reef discovered for
the Royal Navy by the frigate *Daedalus*, but they saw no sign
of the tricolour of France. Griffiths declined to put into Kosseir until their southward passage, assuming Santhonax and
his frigate might be there in overwhelming force.

"No, Mr. Drinkwater, first we will reconnoitre the Gulf of
Aqaba then cross from Ras Muhammad to the west coast and
pass Kosseir with a favourable wind. I have no desire to meet
our friend at anything but an advantage."

Both of them wondered what would be the outcome if Santhonax was elsewhere.

Two days later they were off Ras Muhammad at the southern extremity of the Sinai peninsula. The land closed in upon
them, the dun coloured landscape rising in row upon row of
peaks that lay impassive under the blue skies and sunshine of
noon and were transferred at sunrise and sunset into ruddy
spines and deep purple gullies. Between this forbidding bar-
rier the Gulf opened up, a deep blue channel of white-capped
sea over which the wind funnelled with gale force.

Regarding this cradle of religions, Appleby observed wondering, "You can imagine Moses striking those rocks and
Almighty God handing down the commandments from such a
place . . ." Robbed of his usual pomposity Appleby seemed
reduced to a state of awe.

But if this grim landscape failed to impress the majority of
Hellebore's people, daylight the following morning had a different impact. From the masthead the news of several ships to
windward included the intelligence that one was the square

sail of a European vessel. There was no doubt that there was a French warship in the offing, though of what force they had yet to discover.

"Get aloft Nathaniel," growled Griffiths anxiously and Drinkwater went forward and swung himself into the foremast shrouds. Around him *Hellebore*'s deck swarmed with activity as the men prepared for action.

At the topgallant doubling the wind was distinctly chilly. Stokeley was the lookout and he pointed the newcomers out. Settling himself against the exaggerated motion of the brig Drinkwater levelled his glass to larboard and caught the image of a dhow in the lens. There were five such craft being convoyed south by the warship. He searched the latter for details to determine her size. He counted her mastheads: there were three. A ship rigged corvette or a frigate? He transferred his attention to the hull. At this angle it was difficult to say as the enemy approached them, yawing slightly, a bone of white water in her teeth, but there was a simplicity about her bow that inclined Drinkwater to dismiss his worst fears. He descended to the deck.

"I believe her to be a ship-sloop, sir, say about twenty guns."

"Very well." Griffiths paused and studied the approaching dhows. "D'you think they're fitted with teeth or are they under convoy for Kosseir or Suez?" He did not wait for an answer, glancing astern at the supporting sambuk of Ben Ibrahim. "We'll engage, Mr. Drinkwater, take the topgallants off her and hoist French colours." Drinkwater acknowledged the order and turned away while Griffiths bellowed forward for all to hear. "Mr. Rogers! Load canister on ball, run your larboard guns to the sills and secure them! Keep your ports closed and all the larbowlines to cheer as we pass the Frenchman, all except the gun captains who are to lay their pieces at the horizon and fire on command." He lowered his voice. "Mr. Lestock, have a quartermaster ready to hoist British colours the moment I say, and men at the braces below the bulwarks. I shall wear to starboard then cross his stern." Griffiths stood beside the men at the wheel. Drinkwater returned from amidships, casting his eyes aloft where the topgallants flogged impotently in their buntlines. The topmen were spreading out along the yards. Already *Hellebore* began her deception, peacefully clewing up her topgallants as she waited for her "friend" to approach. "*Du*, Nathaniel, tell them not to be so damned fast aloft."

Drinkwater grinned and raised the speaking trumpet.

"Fore t'gallant there, take your time, you are supposed to be Frenchmen!" He could see from the attitudes of the men aloft who shouted remarks to their mates on the main topgallant that the business amused them. The obvious high spirits and exaggerated pantomime that followed this order spoke of a soaring morale amongst the hands at the prospect of action. Battle, conducted in such a spirit in such a breeze and in such brilliant sunshine could not fail to be exhilarating.

"That's better," nodded Griffiths approvingly. "Take station on the poop, Mr. Drinkwater, when he is abeam I shall open fire then wear downwind. It means exposing the stern but I doubt he'll take advantage of it. Wave your hat as we pass, *bach*, do your best to look French."

Rogers came aft and reported the larboard battery ready as directed.

Drinkwater wondered if the French squadron included a brig like themselves. If not then they were going to look decidedly foolish in a quarter of an hour. Astern of them Yusuf ben Ibrahim was dropping into *Hellebore*'s wake. He would be mystified as to their intentions unless he guessed from the tricolour now snapping out over the quarter. Yusuf might ruin their deception but then he might also enhance it, appearing to the approaching Frenchman like his own captured dhows. Drinkwater shivered slightly in his shirtsleeves. He waited impatiently for the order to open fire. Drinkwater motioned to the men at the after starboard guns. "Stand by to brail in the spanker there!"

He saw them grin, glad of something to do while their mates in the larboard battery went into action.

The dhows ahead had dropped back while the French corvette came on suspiciously, a private signal flying from her foremast. Drinkwater saw Mr. Quilhampton instructed to hoist a string of meaningless bunting. As the enemy signal flew almost directly towards them a little confusion might be permitted. The two vessels were a mile apart now, the Frenchman broad on *Hellebore*'s larboard bow. The brig had slowed without her topgallants and she lay in wait for her opponent, her guns still hidden and several of the larbowlines hanging casually in the rigging waving.

To the Frenchman the brig lay off his bow, supinely furling her upper sails, men congregating about her decks while he came down before the wind to pass close under the stranger's stern where he could rake her if she ultimately proved to be an enemy. But no enemy, least of all a British captain, would lay so passively before a windward foe. It was a deception lent piquancy by the remoteness of their location, and the belief, briefly true, that Egypt was a possession of France.

Drinkwater saw the corvette take in her own topgallants, as if about to round to and hail her "compatriot". His heart was thumping with excitement. He knew in a moment the weeks of waiting, of struggling off the Cape, of listening to the sweaty moanings of the members of the gunroom, of solving the problem of the hands, of Dalziell and of Catherine Best, would all dissolve in the drug-like excitement of action. There was also the possibility that they might find a permanent solution in death. He felt dreadfully exposed as fear and exhilation fought for possession of him. He remembered an old promise to Elizabeth that he would be circumspect and run no needless risk. The recollection brought a rueful smile to his face.

The gun crew waiting at the mainmast fiferails for his order nudged one another and grinned too, taking encouragement from Drinkwater's apparent eagerness, seeing in his introspection their own relief at imminent action. For them action meant an interruption of the endless round of drudgery, of hauling and pumping that was their life, an opportunity to throw off the fear of the lash, to swear and kill to their heart's content.

"Brail in the spanker!" Drinkwater nodded to the men watching him. The outhaul was started and the huge sail billowed, flapped and was drawn to the mast. By the helm, Griffiths corrected the rudder for that loss of pressure aft. Drinkwater took off his hat and waved it with assumed Gallic enthusiasm about his head.

"Dip the ensign," he ordered and the quartermaster at the peak halliards lowered the tricolour a fathom. Perhaps, by such a refinement, if the enemy captain did not expect to see a French brig hereabouts, he might be fooled into thinking it was a new arrival paying her respects to an old Red Sea hand.

The enemy ship was very close now. Men could be seen on her topgallant yards looking curiously across at them and Drinkwater heard a thin cry of *"Bonjour mes enfants."*

From the main topgallant he heard the ever resourceful Tregembo yell back *"Vive la Republique!"*

The cheer that erupted from the enemy was echoed by the Hellebores whose joy at achieving such a complete deception lent their mad excitement a true imitation of revolutionary fervour.

"Braces there," growled Griffiths in a low and penetrating voice. Drinkwater saw a French officer on the quarter-rail bowing. He swept his own hat across his chest in response. "*Bon chance!*" he yelled across the diminishing gap between them. An angle of sixty degrees lay between the ships, with everyone of *Hellebore*'s guns levelled at that crowded rail.

"Colours!"

Griffiths threw aside the mask.

Above their heads Old Glory replaced the half lowered tricolour. The gunports snapped open.

"Fire!"

The gun captains jerked their lanyards as the crews leapt back to the deck and grabbed rammers, swabs and buckets. The charring of the port lintels was quickly extinguished as the men toiled to reload.

"Up helm! Braces there! Wear ship!"

Hellebore turned, pointing her vulnerable stern at the Frenchman but avoiding the ignominious possibility of failing to tack. Griffiths had gambled on his plan working and, had it not done so, he had only to stand on and carry himself swiftly out of range. But a single glance astern told the ruse had been complete. Details were obscure but amidships the corvette's rail was a splintered and jagged shambles. The human wreckage behind that smashed timber could be imagined.

"Aloft there, left fall! Let fall!" Tregembo and his mates slipped the topgallant gaskets and the sails fell in folds.

"Leggo bunt and clewlines there! Sheet home!"

Hellebore was before the wind and still turning, bringing the wind first astern and then round, broad on the starboard quarter. Drinkwater descended from the tiny poop. "The advantage of surprise sir," he said.

Griffiths nodded, his mouth suppressing a grim smile of self-congratulation. "Do unto others, Mr. Drinkwater, before they do unto you . . . clew up the foresail, I intend to rake."

"Aye, aye, sir. D'you intend boarding?" Griffiths shook his head.

"Too great a risk of heavy casualties. Flesh wounds'll be the very devil to heal in this climate. No, we'll stand off and pound him." Griffiths nodded to the distant Ben Yusuf. "He's playing a waiting game."

They clewed up the forecourse as they made to cut across the corvette's stern. She was still running before the wind though many ropes had been severed at the pin rails on deck. Smoke appeared from her guns now as she attempted to halt the Nemesis that bore relentlessly down upon her. Then they were suddenly very close to her, surging across her stern, masking her from the wind. Rogers was shouting and running aft, commanding each gun to fire as it bore into the corvette's stern. Drinkwater read *La Torride* a split second before it was blown to atoms, saw the crown glass windows of her cabin shatter and the neat carvings about her quarters disintegrate into splinters. A row of men with pistols and muskets fired at the British ship as she rushed past and the hat that he had so insouciantly waved but a few moments ago was torn from his head. He aimed his own pistols, his mouth pulled back in a grimace. Then Griffiths was putting *Hellebore* on a parallel course with the Frenchman.

"Starbowlines to larboard!" Drinkwater roared. As if eagerly awaiting the call the frustrated men from the starboard guns hopped nimbly across the deck to fling their weight on the tackles of the larboard six pounders.

La Torride fired her starboard battery as the brig overtook and a storm of shot poured across *Hellebore*'s deck. Men were flung back clutching their heads and bellies. One stood staring at a vacant arm socket and from aloft a body fell on the deck with an obscene impact.

But the surprise of *Hellebore*'s manoeuvre had robbed the French of their greater weight of metal. The sudden appearance of a British cruiser had utterly surprised them, the more particularly as they had known Blankett's squadron did not include a brig. To this psychological advantage the British had added that first devastating broadside. The lethal spray of canister combined with the round shot to produce an appalling effect. The destructive power of the shot was augmented by the splinters it caused while the range concentrated its effect. French resistance was robbed of its edge. Half of *La Torride*'s gun crews were already dead or wounded, her wheel was shot away, her rudder stock split and her commander mortally wounded in the space of a few minutes.

Hellebore ran past her adversary as *La Torride* swung to starboard, broaching into the trough of the sea, out of control. *Hellebore* also swung to avoid being raked and came round to starboard, tacking through the wind and, once on the larboard tack, running back onto her victim. As the yards were secured there was a mad rush across the deck where the starbowlines returned to the their guns.

"Maximum elevation there!" yelled Drinkwater, judging the angle of heel as the brig lay over to the wind. "Cripple her, Rogers!" roared Griffiths and Drinkwater leapt at the after guns to pull out the quoins. Spinning round, he grabbed a tiny powder monkey. "Boy! Get Mr. Trussel to send up some bar shot."

But *La Torride* had recovered slightly, her men were not yet finished. Under her first lieutenant she had had the time to prepare another broadside for the British.

"Heel's too much, sir," shouted Drinkwater, straightening up from sighting along a gun barrel. "Leggo t'gallant sheets!"

The pressure at her mastheads eased slightly and the brig came nearer the vertical as she sped past *La Torride*. Both ships fired their broadsides simultaneously. Amidships a gun was dismounted at the moment of discharge with a huge crash. Men fell back and blood spurted from a dozen wounds while splinters of wood flew about. Griffiths was spun round by a musket ball that left his single epaulette hanging drunkenly from his shoulder. Drinkwater was hit by a splinter which lanced across his face, missing his eye and cheek and nicking his right ear. Then *Hellebore* was past and preparing to tack again. In the temporary respite Drinkwater supervised clearing the deck of wounded, while Lestock hauled the yards. He was aware of a large number of casualties, of blood staining the sanded planks in the waist but also of an unshaken band of men who toiled to make their lethal and brutish artillery ready for another broadside.

La Torride had had enough. A cheer from first one gun's crew spread along *Hellebore*'s deck. Looking up Drinkwater saw the tricolour that lay over the corvette's shattered rail. Her foremast had gone by the board.

"Take possession, Mr. Drinkwater; Mr. Lestock, heave to." Drinkwater went to inspect the boats and found the cutter serviceable. Griffiths came up to him.

"I want neither prisoners nor prize, Nathaniel. Toss her guns overboard and order an officer aboard her as hostage against her good conduct. They may proceed to Suez if they are able."

"Aye, aye, sir."

"I think we have winged the eagle, Nathaniel," he added confidentially. Drinkwater grinned back. "Indeed sir, I believe you are right."

Drinkwater threw a leg over the rail to descend to the cutter bobbing alongside.

"Knocked the bollocks of that Froggie, eh, Drinkwater?" said Rogers, smiling broadly, his tendency to criticise temporarily quiescent.

"Then perhaps you will consider our commander less senile than you are wont to assert."

Drinkwater and his party scrambled over the side of the corvette to the disquieting crackle of musketry and the shouts and screams of intense fighting. The sight that met their eyes was astonishing. Amid the ruin of her upper deck, covered as it was by the wreckage of her foremast, broken spars and torn sails, amid the tangled festoons of rope, amid the bodies of her dead and the writhing tortures of her wounded *La Torride*'s survivors fought a furious hand to hand action with Yusuf ben Ibrahim and his men. The Arab's sambuk had held off, awaiting the outcome, but was now alongside the defeated corvette her men were boarding in search of loot. Catching sight of the British a young *aspirant* waved frantically at the folds of the tricolour lying over the stern.

"*M'sieur . . . J'implore . . . m'aider . . .*" The boy looked wildly round, seeing Drinkwater's bare sword blade, drawn in self defence at what he might find aboard the prize. The young officer had fallen at his feet in terror and Drinkwater put a calming hand upon his shoulder, but even so it was several minutes before the combined bullying of Drinkwater and his men had beaten off the fury of the Arabs.

Yusuf himself seemed angry at Drinkwater's refusal to allow his men to butcher the French. "*In'sh Allah,*" he said shrugging, his eyes wild with the effects of hashish: "It is the will of Allah."

Drinkwater shook his head "*Bism' Allah,*" he said in the only Arabic he knew, "In the name of God, Emir Yusuf, the dhows . . ." he conveyed the gift of the captured dhows with dramatic gestures, knowing Griffiths was not interested in prizes so far from home. God knew there were enough Frenchmen aboard them to satisfy Yusuf's bloodlust without putting the corvette's crew to the sword. "You," he said pointing at Yusuf's chest, "take dhows. This," he said stabbing a finger at the deck of *La Torride* and to the French cadet, "this belong me . . ." he waved his arm in a circular motion ending up pointing at his own chest.

To Drinkwater's surprise Yusuf rocked back on his heels and roared with laughter. Several members of his crew that had come menacingly to his support during the argument joined the laughter, after Yusuf had addressed a stream of Arabic at them. Yusuf made an aggressively sexual gesture with his forearm, tousled the cadet's hair and slapped the amazed Drinkwater upon the back. Then, still laughing, he took himself off, followed by his men who made a series of good naturedly obscene gestures in Drinkwater's direction.

Beneath his tan Nathaniel flushed at the implication. "Dirty bastards, zur," muttered Tregembo loyally but Drinkwater was not to escape so lightly. To his further embarrassment the young Frenchman, who was trying to smile while tears made furrows through the powder grime upon his face, embraced him.

Drinkwater shook the youth off. "*Vôtre capitaine? Où est vôtre capitaine?*" he asked. The reply was a torrent of French, incomprehensible to Drinkwater but containing what he took to be names, each succeeded by the word *mort*, from which he deduced that most of *La Torride*'s officers were either dead or dying. Certainly no other uniformed figure appeared. Leaving the *aspirant* to muster his crew and draw up a list of the casualties Drinkwater made a brief inspection of the ship before returning to *Hellebore*.

"She's the ship corvette *La Torride* of the Rochefort

squadron, sir, hulled in several places and unmanageable with her steering destroyed . . ." He went on to outline the shambles he had found. When he had finished Griffiths pursed his lips and thought for a moment.

"If we can get a dhow back from Ben Ibrahim we'll let them go, *bach*, on parole for Suez. Take out of her powder, any useful shot, stores, water and rope, I recollect you want rope. In fact ransack her, though no man is to touch an item of personal belongings, we'll leave looting to our Arab friends. Go on, get back to her, quick now. I'll send Rogers and the other boat to requisition a dhow if that pirate has already grabbed them all. Bring back the cadet, he may be more forthcoming than a recalcitrant officer with ideas of his honour."

There followed a day of back-breaking endeavour in which Drinkwater, with an enthusiasm engendered in first lieutenants when storehouses are thrown open to them, replenished almost every want of the *Hellebore*. On the basis that there were no officers surviving to lay claim to her cabin stores, he judiciously appropriated a quantity of wine which brought a gleam to Trussel's eye comparable to that bestowed on the French powder. Trussel begged Drinkwater for a pair of fine brass chase guns but the condition of the boats and the state of the sea prevented their removal. The operation was carried out despite the sharks that were congregating astern, round the flotilla.

By nightfall, when Drinkwater's weary party finally returned to *Hellebore*, *La Torride* was stripped of useful moveables, an empty shell with smoke issuing from her hatchways and sufficient powder left aboard to dismember her. She blew up and sank an hour later but by then *Hellebore* with her attendant dhows was five miles to the southward, standing towards the Strait of Tiran and the Red Sea.

Leaving the deck of Lestock, Drinkwater stumbled wearily below, calling for Meyrick to pour him a glass of grog. He was relaxing as Dalziell entered, thrusting the French cadet before him with a vicious shove. He seemed slightly discomfitted to find Drinkwater in the gunroom.

"Er, Mr. Rogers's orders sir, the captain wants to interview him." He jerked his head at the dishevelled French youth who looked terrified.

"You may leave him here, Mr. Dalziell, and on your return to the deck acquaint Mr. Rogers with my desire that he draws up a list of our casualties and brings it to me on completion."

Dalziell took the muster book from Drinkwater's outstretched hand. Drinkwater motioned the French cadet to a seat and poured him some grog. He saw the boy gag on the spirit then swallow more. Gradually a little colour came to his cheeks.

"*Nom, m'sieur?*" asked Drinkwater in his barbarous French as kindly as he could manage.

"*Je m'appelle Gaston, m'sieur, Gaston Bruilhac, Aspirant de la première classe.*"

"*Comprenez-vous anglais, Gaston?*"

Bruilhac shook his head. Drinkwater grunted, finished the grog and made up his mind. He leaned across the table. "*Mon Capitaine, Gaston, il est très intrepide, n'est pas?*"

Bruilhac nodded. Drinkwater went on, "*Bon. Mon Capitaine . . .*" he struggled, failing to find the words for what he wished to convey. He picked up the pistol he had removed earlier from his belt and pulled back the hammer. Taking Bruilhac's hand, he placed it palm down on the table and spread the fingers. "Bang!" he said suddenly, pointing the weapon at the index finger. He repeated the melodrama for the other three. The colour drained from Bruilhac's face and Drinkwater refilled his grog. "Courage, mon brave," he said, then, as the boy stared wide eyed over the shaking rim of the beaker, "*Ecoutez-moi, Gaston: vous parlez, eh? Vous parlez beaucoup.*"

As if on cue Griffiths entered with Rogers behind him, bearing the muster book. Drinkwater stood up and snapped "Attention!" Bruilhac sprang to his feet, rigidly obedient. "I think he'll talk, sir," said Drinkwater, quietly handing the pistol to Griffiths. "Rum will loosen his tongue and I said you'd shoot each of his fingers off in turn if he did not speak."

Griffiths's white eyebrows shot upwards and a wicked twinkle appeared in his eyes as he turned to the cadet, and the swinging lantern light caught his seamed face. To Bruilhac he seemed the very personification of Drinkwater's imminent threats.

Drinkwater motioned the boy to follow Griffiths into the after cabin. As he closed the door he heard Griffiths begin the interrogation. Words began to pour from the hapless boy. Drinkwater smiled; sometimes it was necessary to be cruel to be kind. He turned to Rogers.

"Well Rogers, what kind of a butcher's bill do we have?"

"Oh, not too bad, bloody shame we blew the prize up. I'd have made a comfortable purse from her."

Drinkwater withheld a lecture on the impracticability of such a task as getting La Torride in order, and contented himself with saying, "She was a wreck. Now, how many did we lose?"

"Only eleven dead."

Drinkwater whistled. "Only? For the love of God . . . what about the wounded?"

"Eighteen slight: flesh wounds, splinters, the usual. I caught a splinter in the cheek." He turned so that the light caught the ugly jagged line, half bruise, half laceration, that was scabbing in a thick crust. "You escaped unscathed, I see."

Drinkwater looked Rogers full in the face, feeling again a strong dislike for the man. He found himself rubbing at a rough congealed mess in his right ear. "Almost," he said quietly, "I was lucky. What about the serious cases?"

Rogers looked down at the muster book. "Seven, six seamen and Quilhampton."

"Quilhampton?" asked Drinkwater, a vision of the boy's pretty mother swimming accusingly into his mind's eye. "What's the matter with him?"

"Oh, a ball took off his hand . . . hey, what's the matter?"

Drinkwater scrambled below to where Appleby had his cockpit at the after end of the hold. Already the stench was noisome. To the creak of the hull and the turbid swirl of bilgewater were added the groans of the wounded and the ramblings of delirium. But it was not only this that made Drinkwater wish to void his stomach. There seemed some sickness in his fate that Providence could pull such an appalling jest upon him.

He paused to allow his eyes to become adjusted to the gloom. He could see the pale figure of Catherine Best straighten up, a beaker in her hand. She came aft, catching sight of the first lieutenant. "Mr. Drinkwater?" she said softly, and in the guttering lamplight her face was once again transfigured. But it was not a beauty that stirred him. He saw for the first time that whatever life had done to this woman, her eyes showed a quality of compassion caused by her suffering.

"Where is Mr. Q?" he asked hoarsely. Catherine led him past Tyson who was bent over a man Drinkwater recognised as Gregory, the helmsman who had held the brig before the wind the night they struggled with the broken foreyard. Tyson was easing a tourniquet with a regretful shake of his head.

The woman stepped delicately over the bodies that lay grotesquely about the small, low space.

Quilhampton lay on his cloak, his head pillowed on his broadcloth coat. His breeches stained dark with blood and urine. His left arm extended nine inches below his elbow and terminated in a clumsy swathe of bloodstained bandages. His eyelids fluttered and he moved his head distressingly in a shallow delirium. Catherine Best bent to feel the pale sweating forehead. Drinkwater knelt beside the boy and put his hand on the maimed stump. It was very hot. He looked across the twitching body. Catherine's eyes were large with accusation.

Drinkwater rose and stumbled aft, suddenly desperate for the fresh air of the deck. At the ladder he ran into Appleby. The surgeon's apron was stiff with congealed blood. He was wiping his hands on a rag and he reeked of rum. He was quite sober.

"Another glorious victory for His Majesty's arms . . . you will have been to see Quilhampton?" Drinkwater nodded dumbly. "I think he will live, if it does not rot." Appleby spat the last word out, as if the words "putrefy" or "mortify" were too sophisticated to waste on a butcher like Drinkwater.

Nathaniel made to push past but Appleby stood his ground. "Send two men to remove that . . . sir," he said, pointing. Drinkwater turned. A large wooden tub lay in the shadows at the bottom of the ladder. Within it Drinkwater could see the mangled stumps and limbs amputated from Appleby's patients.

"Very well, Mr. Appleby, I will attend to the matter."

Appleby expelled his breath slowly. "There's a bottle in the gunroom, I'll join you in a moment." Drinkwater nodded and ascended the ladder.

Griffiths sat in the gunroom, while Rogers poured for both

of them. "The teat of consolation, *annwyl*," said Griffiths gently, seeing the look in Drinkwater's eyes. "Santhonax is at Kosseir."

"Ah," Drinkwater replied listlessly. The rum reached his belly, uncoiling the tension in him. He stretched his legs and felt them encounter something soft. Looking under the table he saw Bruilhac curled like a puppy and fast asleep.

"He still has all his fingers."

Drinkwater looked at Griffiths and wondered if the commander knew in what appalling taste his jest was. Griffiths could not yet have seen the casualty list.

"He's lucky," was all he said in reply.

CHAPTER ELEVEN

Kosseir Bay

August 1799

On the afternoon of 10th August it seemed that Santhonax had surprised them. Anxious glasses trained astern at the two ships foaming up from the southward while *Hellebore* staggered under a press of canvas in a desperate claw to windward and safety. The leading pursuer was indisputably a frigate. Optimists claimed it was *Fox*, the more cautious Griffiths assumed the worst. Bruilhac had told them of a third ship in Santhonax's squadron, for whom *Hellebore* had been taken by the officers of *La Torride*. He was not to be caught by the same ruse. "Let the wrecks of others be your seamarks, Mr. Drinkwater," he said without removing his eye from the long glass.

"She's tacking." They watched the leading ship come up into the wind, saw her foresails flatten and the swing of the mainyards. As she paid off, the foreyards followed suit and the bright spots of bunting showed from her mastheads.

"British colours and Admiral Blankett's private signal, sir," reported Rogers. Her exposed side revealed her as *Fox*.

"It seems you were right, Mr. Drinkwater," said Griffiths drily. Keeping his men at quarters, the commander put *Helle-*

bore before the wind and ran down towards his pursuers. They proved to be *Fox* and *Daedalus*, sent north by Rear-Admiral Blankett who had taken sufficient alarm from Strangford Wrinch to despatch Captains Stuart and Ball without seeing the necessity to come himself and thus forgo the carnal delights of Mr. Wrinch's hospitality.

Griffiths was summoned on board for a council of war, the outcome of which was to attack Kosseir, destroy Santhonax and open the port to traffic from the Hejaz. French defeat would not only result in an improvement to the Meccans able to join Murad Bey, but would enable the British to pre-empt any French attempt upon India the following year. Returning from the meeting, Griffiths also brought back personal news.

A replacement for *Echo* had joined the squadron. The ship-sloop *Hotspur* had brought out mail, news and orders. The latter included a tersely worded instruction that *Hellebore* was to be returned at once to England. Nelson, the author of her present predicament was, it seemed, in disgrace. His euphoric languishing at Naples after Aboukir had been tarnished by the Caraccioli affair and followed by a leisurely return home by way of a circuitous route through Europe during which his conduct with the wife of the British Ambassador to the court of the Two Sicilies was scandalous.

Drinkwater paid scant attention to this gossip, depressed by the realisation that *Hotspur* had brought no letters from Elizabeth. Then Griffiths swiftly recalled him to the present.

"Oh, by the way, Nathaniel, *Hotspur* brought two lieutenants to the station. One is appointed to *Daedalus* and he wished to be remembered to you. He was insistent I convey his felicitations to you."

An image of the ruddy and diminutive White formed in his mind. Perhaps White had news of Elizabeth! But he checked his sudden hope on the recollection that White would not ex-

change the quarterdeck of *Victory* for an obscure frigate in a
even more obscure corner of the world without an epaulett
on his shoulder.

"The gentleman's name sir?"

"A Welsh one, *bach*. Morris if I recollect right."

A strong presentiment swept over Drinkwater. From th
moment he had jestingly suggested shooting off Bruilhac'
fingers and found Quilhampton handless, Providence seeme
to have deserted him. The strain of weary months of servic
manifested itself in this feeling. His worries for Elizabet
stirred his own loneliness. It was a disease endemic amon
seamen and fate lent it a further twist when he recalled th
words Morris had uttered to him years earlier.

Drinkwater had been instrumental in having Mr. Midship
man Morris turned out of the frigate *Cyclops* where he ha
dominated a coterie of bullying sodomites. Morris had threat
ened revenge even at the earth's extremities. Suddenl
Drinkwater seemed engulfed in a web from which he coul
not escape. The revelation that Dalziell was related to Morri
made months earlier seemed now to preface his present ap
prehension.

On the morning of 14th August 1799 in light airs the brig o
war *Hellebore* led Captain Henry Lidgbird Ball's squadro
slowly into Kosseir Bay. The indentation of the coast wa
formed by a headland, a small fort and a mole which pro
tected a large number of native craft gathered inside. Mo
dhows lay anchored in the inner roadstead. Above the fort th
tricolour floated listlessly. Of the frigate of Edouard San
thonax there was no sign.

Griffiths swore as he paced up and down the quarterdec
one ear cocked to hear the leadsman's chant from the chair
Whilst the taking of the dhows and fort were of importance

Ball, only the destruction of Santhonax would satisfy Griffiths.

The men waited round the guns, the sail-trimmers at their stations. Lestock fussed over a rudimentary chart he had copied from *Fox*'s as *Hellebore* picked her way slowly inshore. Drinkwater stared at the town through his glass. It was past noon with the sun burning down on them from almost overhead. Drinkwater indicated the dhows.

"Santhonax's fleet of transports, I believe sir." He handed the glass to Griffiths. The commander swept the yellow shoreline shimmering under the glare. He nodded. "But that *cythral* Santhonax is nowhere to be seen." Griffiths cast a glance about him. "Strike number five the instant the leadsman finds six fathoms, the closer in we get the greater the risk of coral outcrops."

As if to justify Griffiths's concern *Hellebore* trembled slightly. Griffiths and Drinkwater exchanged glances but even the jittery Lestock seemed not to have noticed the tremor. The leadsman allayed their fears: "By the mark seven . . . by the deep eight . . . a quarter less eight!"

Hellebore crept onward. "By the deep six!"

"Strike number five! Braces there! Main topsail to the mast!" The red and white chequered numeral flag fluttered to the deck and the brig lost way as the main yards braced round to back their sails. She ceased her forward motion.

"Let go!" The anchor dropped with a splash as the first gun boomed out from the fort. Unhurriedly the three British ships clapped springs on their cables and traversed to bring their full broadsides on the wretched town. The fire from the fort ceased, as though the gunners, having tried the range, paused to see what the British would do.

Aboard *Hellebore* they waited for Ball's signal to open fire, their own capstan catching a final turn on the spring to align the guns to Griffiths's satisfaction. Drinkwater listened to the stage whispers of the gun crew nearest him.

"Why don't the bastards open fire at us, Jim?"

"'Cos they're shit-scared, laddy. Froggies is all the same."

"Don't be bleeding stupid. They want to save their sodding powder until the brass have stopped pissing about and decide where to station us sitting ducks."

"It's only a piddling little fort, mates. Bugger all to worry about."

"But you still save your powder an' bleeding shot, Tosher, you stupid sod."

"How the hell d'you know?"

"Look if you had to carry the fucking stuff over them mountains behind this dunghill you wouldn't throw the stuff away, now would you, my old cock?"

This debate was interrupted by *Daedalus* opening fire. Her consorts followed suit. The bombardment of Kosseir had begun.

For an hour the men toiled at the guns under a burning sun. The constant concussions killed the wind and when Ball hoisted the signal to cease fire the men slumped exhausted at their pieces or scrabbled for the chained ladle at the scuttle-butt. They tore off their headbands and shook their heads to clear the ringing from their ears, wiping the grimy sweat from their foreheads. In his berth two feet below the now silent cannon, Midshipman Quilhampton writhed, tortured by heat, inflammation and fever. From time to time Catherine Best wiped the heavy perspiration from his brow and desultorily fanned his naked body. Appleby waited for casualties in the cockpit, cooling himself with rum and ignoring the groans of the wounded that had survived their earlier action and now twisted in the stifling, stinking heat of *Hellebore*'s bowels.

Stripped to his shirt sleeves Drinkwater scanned the dur

coloured shore, watching for a response to the flag of truce
now at *Daedalus*'s foremasthead. But although the fort's guns
had fallen silent the tricolour still hung limply from its staff.
No movement could be discerned in the town after a first terrified evacuation of the dhows in the harbour. Drinkwater felt
a strong sense of anti-climax. The fort seemed weak, no more
than half-a-dozen cannon.

"Old guns installed by the Turks," observed Lestock.

"Place looks like a heap of camel-shit," muttered Rogers.
They all suffered from a sense of being engaged in an unwor-
thy activity, not least Griffiths.

"A most inglorious proceeding indeed," he said, disgust
filling his dry mouth. And Drinkwater knew the old man considered this a side-show compared with the task of destroying
Santhonax himself.

"Commodore's signalling for an officer, sir." Dalziell reported.

"*Du* . . . see to it Mr. Drinkwater."

Clambering in at the entry of *Daedalus* Drinkwater was es-
corted by a cool-looking midshipman to the quarterdeck. He
found a lieutenant from *Fox* already there, together with a figure he knew well.

Time had not been kind to Augustus Morris. The years had
ravaged his body, the skin drawn over prematurely withered
flesh, his stance flaccid, listless in a manner that could not entirely be attributed to the heat. His face bore the marks of a
heavy drinker, a tic twitching beneath his right eye. But although time might be remarked in his person and emphasised
by his long worn lieutenant's uniform, his eyes, beneath their
heavy lids, glittered with a potent malevolence.

There was no time for formalities. Captain Ball turned from
a consultation with his sailing master and addressed the three
lieutenants.

"Gentlemen, I propose in an hour to hoist the Union at the foremasthead. Upon that signal I require you to take the boats from your ships and attack the native craft exposed in the outer roadstead. You should direct your respective boats to the nearest craft and thereafter concert your efforts as seems best to you. That is all." Ball turned away dismissively.

"What's the date of your commission, Drinkwater?" asked Hetherington of *Fox*, a small, pinch-faced man with prominent ears.

"October '97."

"That makes you senior, Morris."

"It does indeed," said Morris with relish, never taking his eyes off Drinkwater. "Mr. Drinkwater once outranked me Hetherington. A temporary matter, d'you know. It is only just that I should have the whip hand now."

"Well what are we going to do?" enquired the anxious Hetherington who was not much interested in Morris's autobiography. Morris took his eyes reluctantly off his old enemy and fixed Hetherington with an opaque look that Drinkwater remembered from twenty years earlier. "Why, just what we have been told, Hetherington. Take the dhows of course. Mr Drinkwater will lead the attack . . ." Drinkwater met his gaze again, reading Morris's intentions quite clearly. Morris turned to Hetherington. "You may return to your ship." His hand shot out and restrained Drinkwater who had thought to leave

"Not you, my dear Nathaniel," said Morris with heavy sarcasm, his hand gripping viciously upon Drinkwater's right upper arm, twisting the muscle maimed two years earlier by Edouard Santhonax, "we have an old acquaintance to revive."

"I think not, Morris," said Drinkwater coolly as the other dropped his hand.

"Ah, but I order you to stay, there is so much to discuss. Your wife for instance . . ."

Drinkwater froze, suddenly anxious and searching Morris's face for the truth.

"Oh, yes, I have seen her, Nathaniel. Heavy with child too. You have overcome your prudery I see. Unless it was another." Morris broke out into low laughter as Drinkwater's hand reached for his hanger. Morris shook his head. "That would be most imprudent." Drinkwater clenched his fist impotently. "She looked unwell."

Drinkwater saw in Morris's expression a cruel delight, such as Yusuf ben Ibrahim had worn as he butchered the Frenchmen of *La Torride*.

Drinkwater opened his mouth to reply but the words were lost in the sudden roar of *Daedalus*'s guns. Ball had hauled down the flag of truce and resumed the bombardment. Spinning on his heel, Drinkwater returned to his boat and *Hellebore*.

"Bear off forrard! Give way together!" Drinkwater took the tiller and swung the cutter away under *Hellebore*'s stern. Passing across *Daedalus*'s bow, he steadied for the nearest dhow. Looking to starboard he saw Hetherington's boat shoot ahead of *Fox*, then Morris came out from the shelter of *Daedalus*.

"Pull, you lubbers. Let's get this business finished quickly!" The boat's crew were already grimed and sweat-seamed from working the guns in relays, but they lay back on their oars willingly enough. Over their heads shot whined through the sullen air. Drinkwater looked ahead at Kosseir. The town was passing into shadow, purple and umber as the sun westered behind the mountains of the Sharqiya.

They reached the first vessel, a large *baghala*, deserted by her crew. Drinkwater led his men aboard and it was the work of only a few minutes to set her on fire. As they tumbled back into the cutter *Daedalus*'s boat came alongside, a midshipman in charge of her.

"Mr. Morris orders you to attack yon dhow, sir." The youth pointed to a vessel anchored just off the ramshackle mole. Drinkwater swung around to look at the dhow next astern of them. He could see Morris on its deck. No smoke as yet issued from her, though their own target was well ablaze. A dark suspicion crossed Drinkwater's mind as he nodded to the midshipman. "Very well."

"Give way . . ." Rounding the burning *baghala*'s bow, Drinkwater headed for the mole. They were no more than two hundred yards from the decaying breakwater, their new victim lying midway between.

"Is that match all right?" The gunner's mate in charge of the combustibles blew on the slow match and nodded. "Aye, sir."

"Pull, damn you!" growled Drinkwater, seeing for the first time men in blue uniforms running out along the mole and dropping to their knees. They were French sharpshooters, the tirailleurs of the 21st Demi-Brigade. The oar looms bent under redoubled effort.

The cutter ran alongside the dhow and the seamen jumped aboard. At the instant they stood on the deck the sharpshooters opened fire. It was long musket range but Drinkwater immediately felt a searing pain across his thigh and looked down to see where a ball had galled him, reddening his breeches. Beside him a man was bowled over as though dead but sat up a few moments later, nursing bruised ribs from a spent musket ball. Drinkwater and his men crawled about the deck, assembling enough combustibles to ignite the dhow, wriggling backwards with the small keg of black powder leaving a trail across the deck. Drinkwater nodded and the gunner's mate blew on his match and touched it to the powder train. The flame sputtered and tracked across the deck, over the coaming and below. Smoke began to writhe out of the dhow's hold.

"Back to the boat!" he called sharply over his shoulder, venturing one last look at the crumbling mud brick of Kosseir's pitiful defences. Overhead the whirr of cannon shot told where the squadron were thundering away, while puffs of dust and little settling disturbances of masonry showed the process of reduction. He scanned the beach that curved away to the left of the town. A few small fishing boats were drawn up on it and the dull green of vegetation showed where a hardy and pitiful cultivation was carried on. Some taller palms grew in a clump by a waterhole. As he ducked again and was about to crawl back to the boat Drinkwater noticed something else, something that brought him to his feet in a wild leap for the cutter. Round the end of the mole a boat was pulling vigorously towards them.

The cutter was shoved off from the burning dhow and pulled clear of its shelter. Shot dropped round them and a brief glance astern showed the enemy boat no more than thirty yards astern.

"She's closin' on us, sir," muttered the man at stroke oar nodding astern. Drinkwater's back felt vulnerable. He looked over his shoulder and stared down the muzzle of a swivel gun. The puff of smoke that followed made his heart skip and he felt the ball hit the transom. Drinkwater looked down to see the dark swirl of water beneath him.

Twilight was increasing by the minute and they had no hope of reaching the brig before being overtaken or sinking. They had a single chance.

"Hold water all! Oars and cutlasses!"

The enemy boat came on and Drinkwater pulled a pistol from his belt. He laid the weapon on one of the gunners and saw the man stagger, a hand to his shoulder. A second later the two boats ground together.

Lent coolness by desperation, Drinkwater grabbed the gunwale of the enemy boat. Beneath his feet *Hellebore*'s cutter felt sluggish and low as behind him the crew stumbled aft. Swiping upwards with his hanger, Drinkwater leapt aboard the French boat. Manning the swivel were three artillerymen from Desaix's army. Their eyes were pus-filled from ophthalmia and one already clasped a wounded shoulder. A second had recovered from Drinkwater's sword swipe as he straightened up. Drinkwater lunged his shoulder into the man, knocking him backwards and banging the pommel of his sword into the side of the man's head.

The impetus of the approaching French boat had slewed the cutter round so that her crew could leap the easier from their sinking craft. Drinkwater was aware of a stumbling, swearing mêlée of men to his right as, over the fork of the swivel gun, the third gunner faced him, a heavy sword bayonet in his hand.

Drinkwater saw the matter in his eyes, and the mouth set hard beneath the black moustache. He stumbled as the boat rocked violently under the assault. A man, thrown overboard in the scuffle, screamed as the first shark, attracted by the blood, found him. His frenzied cries lent a sudden fury to them all.

The artilleryman struck down at Drinkwater as he recovered. Desperately Nathaniel caught the impact of the heavy blade on the forte of his sword and twisted upwards, carrying the big bayonet with him. Then, in a clumsy manoeuvre, he executed a bind, riding over the blade and forcing it across to the right. He made the movement in instinctive desperation, with every ounce of his strength. In this he had the advantage. The gunner, weakened by disease and malnutrition, only half able to see and unused to boats, lost his balance as he tried to avoid the Englishman's much longer blade. Drinkwater felt the pressure stop and saw, with a curious mixture of relief and pity, a pair of tattered bootsoles as the man fell overboard.

This emotion was swiftly replaced by a savage gratification as he swung half right to plunge amongst the fighting still raging in the boat. Then it was all over, suddenly the boat was theirs and men were grabbing oars and tossing Frenchmen callously overboard. In perhaps three minutes the British had destroyed their pursuers and had begun to pull the boat offshore to where the three British warships still cannonaded the town. It was almost dark. The gun flashes of the squadron were reflected on the oily surface of the sea, the burning dhows flamed like torches. There were only four of them; so neither Morris nor Hetherington had burned more than one dhow and two still remained unscathed. It was clear to Nathaniel that he had run more than the gauntlet of death from the French. The events of less than an hour seemed at that moment to have lasted a lifetime. He felt very tired.

After reporting to Griffiths, Drinkwater went in search of rest. The British remained at quarters during the night, snatching what sleep they could beside their cannon as the chill of the desert night cooled them. From time to time a gun was discharged to intimidate the French. Rolling himself in his boat cloak Drinkwater settled down under the little poop to sleep. He had barely closed his eyes when someone shook him.

"Zur," Tregembo whispered softly, "Mr. Drinkwater, zur."

"Eh? What is it, Tregembo?"

"Did you know that bugger Morris was aboard *Daed'lus*, zur?"

"Of course I did. He commanded her boat in the raid." A sudden desire to communicate his fears seized him. There was between the two of them a bond that stretched beyond the bulwarks of the brig to the small Hampshire town of Petersfield. This bond underran the social barriers that divided them. "I think he tried to kill me this evening."

Drinkwater heard Tregembo whistle. "That explains it, zur. We saw *Fox*'s boat pull towards you when you was attacked. As it passed *Daed'lus*'s cutter it were turned back. Then the signal for recall was hoisted I heard say, zur. I also heard Mr. Dalziell mention he knew the lieutenant just joined *Daed'lus*, and when I heard him tell Mr. Lestock it was a Mr. Morris . . . well I guessed, zur."

Drinkwater's mind flew back to a day twenty years earlier when this same man had given a nervous midshipman the courage to challenge Morris.

"If anything happens to you, zur, I'll swing for the bastard."

"No Tregembo," said Drinkwater sharply. "If anything happens to me do you get yourself home to your Susan and tell Lord Dungarth. Appleby'll help you. That's an order man."

Tregembo hesitated. "Damn it Tregembo, I'll rest easier if I thought he'd die by due process of law."

Tregembo sighed. Such niceties were the penalty he paid for his contacts with "the quality". "Aye, zur. I will. And I'll keep a weather eye out for your lady."

A wave of pure fear swept over Drinkwater but he suppressed it beneath a rough gratitude for Tregembo's loyalty. "Aye, you do that Tregembo. My thanks to you. The sooner we are away out of this accursed bay the better. We have orders for England once . . ." he checked himself. He had been about to say "once the captain has rid himself of his present obsession." But that was too much of a confidence even for Tregembo. The recollection steadied him and Tregembo left, silently swearing to himself that Lieutenant Drinkwater need have no fear if it was left to him.

But sleep would not now come to Drinkwater. He rose and went below. The scratches of his wounds throbbed and in the gunroom he cleaned them with the remains of a bottle of rum. Above his head a guntruck squealed and the boom of the six-pounder split the night. Mr. Rogers was clearly going to let the French know that he was on deck, middle watch or no. Drinkwater went forward to look at Quilhampton.

The apparently indefatigable Catherine Best still minis-tered to him, washing the small white body with wine and water so that evaporation might cool the boy.

"How is he?"

"A little cooler, but still fevered. You have been wounded, sir?"

"It is nothing at all."

"But it will mortify in this climate."

"No. I have washed it with rum. I shall survive." He took the rag off her and gently pushed her aside. "Get some rest. I shall sit with him a while."

He eased himself down beside the midshipman and sniffed the bandages on the stump. Thank God there was no offensive taint to it, as yet. Presently his head drooped forward and he slept.

At five o'clock in the morning the three British cruisers re-opened their cannonade on Kosseir. It was to last seven hours.

At noon when the bombardment halted, anxious gunners reported the serious depletion of their stocks of ammunition and Ball summoned his fellow captains. At four in the after-noon the boats of *Daedalus* succeeded in burning the two dhows that remained anchored in the inner roadstead.

As the day drew to a close a swell rolled into Kosseir Bay,

setting the boats of the squadron bobbing and grinding one another as they assembled alongside *Hellebore*. The brig was the most southerly of the three British ships and a convenient starting place for the next phase of Captain Ball's questionable strategy. All the boats had their carronades mounted, those in the frigate's launches of eighteen pound calibre. The expedition was to land south of the town. Its object was to destroy the wells used by the French, located in the miserable oasis observed by Drinkwater earlier. About eighty seamen and marines were mustered for this purpose under the command of Captain Stuart of *Fox*. Seconding him were Lieutenants Morris, Hetherington and Drinkwater.

"Watch this swell upon the beach, *bach*," said Griffiths at parting and Drinkwater nodded. Service in *Kestrel* and the buoy yachts of Trinity House had rendered him acutely conscious of sea state.

Night was again falling as they pulled away from the brig. Stuart's boat led, the others following. At the last moment Drinkwater had ordered Tregembo back on board with a message for Lestock. As soon as the Cornishman had disappeared Drinkwater pushed off.

Already the sun was touching the distant peaks of the Sharqiya, but in the gathering shadows troops could be seen hurrying along the road to the oasis. Drinkwater turned his boat, that captured from the French when the cutter had been lost, in the wake of Stuart's launch. As they approached the beach they could feel the swell humping up beneath them, see it rolling ahead of them to break in a heavy surf.

"Mr. Brundell!" Drinkwater hailed the master's mate commanding the gig next astern. "There's a surf. Do you use your anchor from forward, let go abreast of me!"

He saw Brundell wave acknowledgement. The gig did not mount a gun, was too light for the six-pounders lent to the boats that had no carronades. Thankful that there were old Kestrels in *Hellebore*'s company who would appreciate the technique, Drinkwater watched with misgiving where, ahead of them, he saw Stuart's boat anchor by the stern.

"Forrard there!" He stood up to command attention. The gunner's mate looked astern. "Sir?"

"You will have time for only a single discharge. Make sure you fire on the upward pitch. Make ready!"

Drinkwater could see the beach, becoming monochromatic in the dusk. Troops were deploying on it, well back from the water's edge. Drinkwater put the tiller over and cast a single glance astern. The build up of the breakers was very noticeable. He straightened the boat for the beach. "Oars!" The men ceased rowing. "Fire!" The carronade barked. "Hold water starboard!" The boat slewed. "Let go!" The anchor splashed overboard and the boat drifted broadside. "Backwater starboard! Backwater all!" The boat turned and from the corner of his eye he saw Brundell bring the gig round.

"Drinkwater! What the hell d'you think you're playing at?" Morris's voice cut across the roar of the breakers. Drinkwater ignored it. "Check her forrard!" A twitch on the anchor warp told the anchor held. "Backwater all!" Drinkwater repeated, his back to the beach, watching the boat's head rise to the surf which increased in sharpness as they drove into shallow water. They were surrounded by tumbling wave crests. He cast a single glance astern. "Hold on! Boat Oars!"

He nodded to the corporal of the marine detachment from *Fox*. Together the two men led the boat's crew over the transom. For a minute they floundered, found their footing and scrambled ashore. Drinkwater cast a single glance back at the boat to see the boat-keepers at their stations.

To right and left the British were coming ashore. Stuart's

men were already deploying, the marines in the centre, but his boat was in trouble, her forefoot pounding on the hard sand, her flat transom presenting a greater impediment to the breakers than the sharp bows of the *Hellebore*'s.

The marines had opened fire, a rolling volley designed to pin down any interference from the town while the seamen attacked the wells. The party began to advance up the beach as the last boats came in. Two had followed Drinkwater's example, the remainder had anchored by the stern, their carronades or borrowed long guns theoretically covering the landing. In the event the violence of the surf prevented more than an occasional lucky shot, while the gunners were bounced and shaken by the motion.

Drinkwater waved his detachment up on the flank of the marines. The men ran forward, their bare feet slapping on the sand, the cutlasses gleaming dully in their brawny hands.

The buzz of a thousand bees halted them. A company of French infantry occupied low scrub ahead of them, galling them with a furious musket fire. The seamen were in soft sand now. Several fired pistols while the officers cheered them forward. They could hardly see the enemy's dark uniform blending with the thorn scrub, the flashes of their muskets too brief to lay a pistol on. Men were falling and the forward rush was checked.

Then the French charged and a stumbling fight ensued, the seamen hacking with their clumsy weapons, glad of the proximity of their enemy, shaken by the earlier fire they had received on the open beach. Drinkwater thought they had a chance. He looked round hoping to find Morris's men coming up behind them. Morris and his men had halted seventy yards away. To his left Stuart was equally hard pressed. Hetherington's men seemed to be in support of the marines. Drinkwater's eye was caught by a movement at the water's edge. The stern line of one of the boats had parted. He saw her broach and roll over in the surf, saw her split like a melon. The moment's inattention was paid for as a Frenchman drove his musket butt into Drinkwater's guts. He gasped and retched, vaguely aware that Brundell's pistol butt caught the man's face, then he was on his knees fighting for breath.

He did not hear Stuart's order to retreat. A kind of obscurity was clouding his mind. He was not even aware that he was half crouched in a kind of stumbling run, with Brundell on one side of him and a seaman on the other. He did not feel the seaman fall, a musket ball in his heart, did not feel another's arm bear him up, nor hear the shouted instruction from Morris.

"I have him, Mister, he's an old friend. You take charge of the brig's detachment now."

"Aye, aye, sir," Brundell turned uncertainly away. There was nasty gossip in the squadron about Lieutenant Morris.

Everywhere men ran to the boats, the seamen first to man the oars and haul in the anchors. In a wavering line the marines retreated, holding the advancing French just far enough away to permit the embarkation of the British.

It was as well the French garrison was both sickly and small. The commandant, Adjutant Donzelot, could not afford to lose men. To drive the British back to their boats and to preserve his wells was enough. Desert war had taught him not to attempt the impossible.

In the dark confusion of the embarkation Morris found it a matter of ease to spin the semi-conscious Drinkwater round as they waded into the water, to bring his knee up into Drinkwater's groin and to drop him as though shot. Morris spared a single glance at his enemy. In falling Drinkwater had cut his leg upon the blade of the sword that had all the while dangled on its martingale from his wrist.

Morris was smiling as he scrambled over the bow of his boat. In the final surge of the sea as it washed the beach of Kosseir Bay lay the body of Nathaniel Drinkwater.

CHAPTER TWELVE

A Stink of Fish

August 1799

Adjutant Donzelot's caution did not prevent him allowing his men to bayonet the wounded and dying British. Those that did not die during the night would be killed the following morning by Arabs and eaten by the yellow-necked vultures that wheeled above the town. That Drinkwater was not one of these unfortunates was the merest whim of fortune. He was washed all a-tumble among the wreckage of the smashed boat, one more black hummock upon the pale sand beneath the stars. Those of Donzelot's men who ventured to the edge of the sea were content to find the groaning body of an eighteen-year-old boy, an ordinary seaman from *Fox* whose task of tending the launch's anchor warp had resulted in his being rolled on by the heavy boat. The bayonets of the infantrymen only added to the perforation in the boy's lungs.

Drinkwater knew nothing of this. He came to long after the French had returned to their billets, long after the young seaman was dead. He was already missed by Griffiths and Appleby, already being revenged in the mind of Tregembo. And while Brundell puzzled over his disappearance, Morris was already half-drunk over it. Even aboard *Hellebore* it had its element of satisfaction. To Lestock it justified a certain mean pleasure that "Mr. Drinkwater was too clever for his own good," while Rogers's career could only benefit from Nathaniel's death.

Whatever agency ensured his survival, be it fortune, the Providence he believed in, or the prayer Elizabeth daily offered for his preservation, it was pain not life that he was first aware of.

Waves of it spread upwards from the bruises in his lower abdomen where his legs terminated in huge, unnatural swellings. It was an hour before the pain had subsided sufficiently for him to command his faculties. An hour before his mind, registering facts from casual observation, gave them the meaning of cause and effect. It penetrated his mind that it was the hog of a boat that blotted out his vision of the stars, that he lay on sand shivering and soaking wet, an occasional wave still washing up around him. Fear of a terrible loneliness slowly replaced that of death. And that comparative condition was the first awakening of his mental will to live. He became aware that he was sheltered from observation by the boat's wreckage, that he could not move his right arm only because its wrist was fast to the martingale of the sword upon which the inert weight of his body lay. He moved, this time by conscious effort, fighting the pain from his swollen testicles. The pain in his gut he could account for, that in his loins was a mystery.

He muttered a string of meaningless filth as he drew his knees up and tried to rise. Just as the distraction of the smashing boat had caused his incapacity yet saved his body, now the cold numbed him and revived him to make an effort. The North Sea had taught him the dangers of succumbing to cold. Cold was an enemy and the thought of it brought him unsteadily to his feet.

As he stood panting with shallow respirations, waiting for the nausea to wane, the necessity of a plan presented itself to him. He remembered where he was. Slowly he turned his head. The occasional flame and thump from seaward showed where the squadron fired its minute guns as it had the night before. Less than two miles away was all he held sacred. His career, the talisman of his love, his duty; the brig *Hellebore*. Like a vision of the Holy City beckoning Pilgrim on, that gunfire cauterised his despair.

Aware that the moving chiaroscuro of the sea's edge facilitated his own movement he began to crawl north, along the curve of the bay towards Kosseir itself.

At first it was easy. He developed a simian lope that accommodated his hurt, but as he approached the town his senses urged caution and progress slowed. He had no idea where the French posted their vedettes. They *must* have someone watching the beach. He rested in the protection of a small fishing boat drawn up above the high water line. The sharp stink of fish assailed him and from its offensive odour he had an idea. Wriggling round the boat he discovered a net lying nearby. Carefully, trying to prevent the slightest gleam of starlight on its blade, he used the hanger to cut off a section the size of a blanket, pulling it round his shoulders like a cloak. If a sentry should challenge he could pull it round him, humping his body so that in the darkness he might look like an old pile of net such as may be found on any beach in the world used by fishermen.

Encouraged, he continued his painful and patient advance towards the little harbour that lay behind the mole. He could not risk swimming to the squadron. The presence of sharks made that a suicidal choice. But he could steal a boat. He came to the first building and heard the dull clink of accoutrements. Upon the flat roof a sentry yawned, the smell of his tobacco mingling with the stink that filled Drinkwater's offended nostrils as he struggled beneath his net.

It was after midnight when the prospect of the harbour was exposed to him. He was warm with exertion and his pain had subsided to inhabit only those parts of him that were worst affected. Hope had given him the courage to make the journey, now success this far spurred him on. He sat and caught his breath. The occasional crash told where the balls from the British guns landed. Once he heard a scream and shouts. The scream was a woman's and the shouts unmistakably French oaths.

The harbour presented a fantastic sight. It was crammed with native craft of all sizes. In the centre the large hulls of a group of *baghalas* were to be dimly perceived, rising above the lower decks of *sambuks* and fishing dhows. It was a testimony to the energy of Edouard Santhonax. But it was also a testimony to British seapower. For though it seemed to observers on board the squadron off-shore that Kosseir was capable of absorbing an infinity of round-shot, Drinkwater's seaman's eye saw immediately the irregularities in that close-packed wedge of ships. The broken masts, the jagged lines of their rails, the dark holes in their decks and the lower ones, already resting on the bottom, spoke of the results of cannon fire.

Drinkwater moved forward, sure that somewhere a dinghy or small boat existed to carry him back to *Hellebore*.

That hope was nearly his undoing. From nowhere a dog appeared. Both parties shared surprise but the dog barked, not once, but with the persistent yapping of the pariah. Above him Drinkwater heard an oath and curled like a woodlouse. The dog snuffled round him, its hunger almost audible. Then it began to bark again. The stone hit the ground an inch from his head and the dog yelped and ran off. Drinkwater froze, imagining the sentry looking down. Had he scanned the ground earlier? Would the presence of an old net excite his suspicion? For as long as his nerves could stand it Drinkwater remained immobile. Then he began to move forward, eager to reach a downward slope onto the crumbling quay that ran along the inside of the harbour. He made it without mishap, moving swiftly across the open quay when he heard a fortuitous disturbance within the town.

He knew it instinctively for what it was, an argument that would engage the interest of any sentries in the vicinity. A woman's shrill voice screamed outrage at some demand made on her by one of the "moustaches", the man bellowed back. Thus did a Frenchman's passion cover his escape. Once on the first craft the shadows and fittings provided cover. All the craft were deserted and he moved across them cautiously, anxiously searching for a small boat. He found several but none could be moved to the outer limit of the moored craft and the open sea. He lay panting and cursing after a protracted and final attempt to dislodge one for his use.

He must have dozed, for he sensed the passage of time when he next had a conscious thought. If no boat were available he might, just might, be able to attract attention at dawn from the extremity of the mole. He knew Griffiths scanned the town at first light and he remembered loose stonework at the end where he might remain unobserved from the town. He reached the mole half an hour later and found himself a hiding place among a pile of nets and pots. He fell asleep.

He woke at dawn but it was not daylight that startled him. The pounding of feet was accompanied by the crackle of musketry, shouts and orders. He recognised Stuart's voice and peered out to see a file of marines trot past him. Then Stuart appeared, leading a band of armed seamen ashore. He saw Mr. Brundell and the gig's crew from *Hellebore* and it was as if he had been absent a hundred years. "Mr. Drinkwater!" He stood unsteadily and bowed at Brundell's smile, aware that he still clasped the fishnet about his shoulders.

"Have the goodness to direct a boat to convey me back to the ship, Mr. Brundell."

"Of course. Here you! Support the first lieutenant back to the gig. And go handsomely with him."

Drinkwater accepted the rough arm, aware that a face appeared in front of him that was aghast with astonishment.

"Mornin' Morris," he said, stumbling past as *Daedalus*'s landing party stormed the mole.

"How are you, sir?"

"Eh?" Drinkwater stared round him in the darkness. The stink of the orlop finally identified his whereabouts. He turned. Quilhampton lay next to him, a Quilhampton sitting up on his good elbow. "I believe I am quite well," he sat up and stopped abruptly. His bruises, severe at the outset, had been strained by the exertions of the night and the cut on his leg had gone septic from contact with the filthy fishnet.

"I am exceeding glad to see you sir, notwithstanding the stink of fish hereabouts." Safety and the impertinent cheek of the youngster blew the shadows of fear from Drinkwater's spirit. He was no longer alone.

"I am glad to hear it, Mr. Q. I apologise for my malodorous condition."

"That is all right, sir. The captain and Mr. Appleby were glad you survived."

"I am glad to hear that too," observed Drinkwater drily.

"I wish the same could be said of Lieutenant Rogers."

"Ahhh." Drinkwater could imagine Rogers's rapid assumption of his own duties. "You should not gossip, Mr. Q. I understand Mr. Rogers's motives as you will do one day. I trust he was the only one."

"The only one I know of, sir. Except of course Gaston."

"Gaston? Oh yes, I recollect. The French boy. What of him? How have I offended to warrant such a return?"

"For some reason that I cannot fathom, sir, he is of the opinion that either the captain or yourself shot off my hand. Leastways that is what I think he meant, unless I mistook his sense." The boy shrugged and smiled with a puzzled expression.

"It's damned good to see you smiling. Mr. Q. One day I'll tell you the whole story."

As if from nowhere Catherine Best appeared, a bowl of water in her hands. Simultaneously the concussion of *Hellebore*'s broadside roared overhead.

"What has happened?" Drinkwater asked, making to get up and suddenly guiltily aware that the silence had driven all thoughts of duty from his mind.

He felt Catherine's hand firm on his breast. "Lie back, sir. Mr. Appleby's orders are that you are not to move, that your cut leg needs cleaning or you may yet lose it."

He lay back while the vibration of the brig's cannon reached down through the hull. He closed his eyes, the dull throbbing in his lower parts reasserting itself.

"The attack on the town has been beaten off, sir." Catherine's voice seemed to come from a great way off. So; the fight for Kosseir was over.

And Catherine's hands were unbelievably cool on his burning flesh.

CHAPTER THIRTEEN

Y Môr Coch

August 1799

"How much, damn it?"

"Three feet, sir," replied Johnson, screwing up his eyes against the glare of the newly risen sun.

"God's bones!" Drinkwater cursed with quiet venom, suddenly remembering something. "Take a look forrard, larboard bow, low down." He dismissed the carpenter who turned away with a puzzled look. The lieutenant fell to a limping pacing of the deck, his left leg still stiff from Appleby's ruthless cauterisation, his abdomen and loins still bruised and sore. But his mind no longer dwelt upon these matters. He thrashed over a score of problems that fluttered round in his head like so many bats seeking anchorage. He was aware of being bad tempered, for the gnawing presence of Augustus Morris on board clouded every issue. Morris was amongst the squadron's wounded, all bundled aboard *Hellebore* after Ball's withdrawal from Kosseir.

Morris had been wounded in the attack on the mole, a stone chipping driving into his shoulder, breaking his collar bone.

"'Tis to disencumber himself of the evidence of defeat more than from compassion," Appleby had said, referring to

Captain Ball with a bitterness born of the prospect of additional duty as the two officers watched the silent procession out of the boats.

In compliance with the orders brought from England, Ball was sending *Hellebore* south, to call at Mocha and land the sick or carry them homewards at the behest of Rear-Admiral Blankett. And the admiral was not pleased with *Hellebore*'s unsanctioned departure from Mocha, a fact that had led Ball to take fifteen of her crew as replacements for losses sustained by the frigates. That loss was only one of the consequences of the sorry affair at Kosseir. Now the matter of the leak demanded Drinkwater's attention. He remembered the slight tremble *Hellebore* had given when standing into Kosseir Bay. She had probably caught a coral head and torn her copper sheathing. The damage was undoubtedly slight and had produced no significant inflow of water while they sat and pounded Kosseir. A few hours of working in a seaway would have torn off loose copper and strained any sprung planks.

Drinkwater swore again as the first of the wounded emerged on deck for their morning airing. The watch were just completing the ritual of washdeck routine and he noticed one or two of them wrinkle their noses. He realised that a faintly repulsive smell had been pervading the ship since the night before, overlaying the indigent stink of bilge and crowded humanity. He knew what it was: gangrene.

For a moment he worried that it might be Quilhampton, simultaneously wishing it were Morris and that Providence might twist a little in his favour. But Appleby's features were no more animated than usual as he appeared on deck and touched his hat to Drinkwater. "Morning."

"Mornin' Harry. Who's succumbed to gangrene?"

"Gregory. I cannot amputate again, the shock will kill him. They will be bringing him up now."

Even with a following wind the stench was offensive, causing an involuntary contraction of the nostrils. The men lifting Gregory on deck performed the duty with a mixture of peremptory haste and rough solicitude. Appleby strode forward to direct a hammock slung on the fo'c's'le, where the unfortunate man was hastily suspended. He came aft again, tired and old, Drinkwater thought, but a sudden surprising light spread across the surgeon's features as Catherine Best emerged on deck, wiping a lock of greasy hair off her forehead and clearly as weary as Appleby himself.

Drinkwater smiled as the surgeon made to step forward then, as if recollecting himself, drew back. "Mistress Best has surprised us all, eh Harry?" he said quietly. Catching his eye, Appleby blushed and Drinkwater smiled again. Something was stirring old Harry Appleby and it was not his usual outrage at the bloody waste of action or the follies of mankind.

"How is Mr. Quilhampton today, Catherine?" Drinkwater asked in a louder voice.

She refocused tired eyes upon the first lieutenant, dragging them away from a distant horizon. "He's on his feet this morning, Mr. Drinkwater, I believe he is breaking his fast in the gunroom." She looked shyly at Appleby. "I think Mr. Appleby intends to try the ligatures this morning . . ."

Appleby nodded. "He's a healthy boy and healing well, thanks to Catherine's ministrations. Would that all my patients could have such treatment."

"It's not your fault . . ." began the woman, breaking off with a look at Drinkwater. It was clear even to Nathaniel's preoccupied mind that there was an intimacy here, professional and ripeningly personal. It was curiously touching and he felt oddly embarrassed and strode across to the wheel where the helmsmen were half a point off course. Catherine Best influenced them all, he reflected, suddenly irritable again.

"Quartermaster, you're half a point off your course. I'll have the hide off you for neglect if you don't pay more attention."

"Aye, aye, sir." Drinkwater strode forward and cast his eyes aloft at the foremast, spun on his heel and surveyed the mainmast. "It'll be t'gallant buntlines next, my cockers," muttered the quartermaster to his helmsmen, shifting a quid surreptitiously over his tongue.

"Mr. Brundell!"

"Sir?" The master's mate came aft.

"D'you not know your damned business, sir? Those t'gallant buntlines are in need of overhauling. Get about it on the instant!" He missed Brundell's wounded look.

Drinkwater came aft again, scowling at the men at the wheel whose downcast eyes were attentively following the lubber's line.

The pale form of Lieutenant Morris emerged from the companionway. Morris wore his uniform coat over his shoulders and his left arm was slung across his chest. Mild fever sharpened the malevolent glitter in his curiously hooded eyes and Drinkwater was once again disturbed by the almost tangible menace of the man.

"Good morning, my dear Drinkwater," he hissed, little agglomerations of spittle in the corners of his mouth.

"Mornin' Morris," Drinkwater managed out of courtesy and passed aft.

Drinkwater judged the sun high enough to take an observation for longitude, ignoring Morris leaning negligently on the companionway, never taking his eyes off Drinkwater. In the middle of the calculation, hurriedly tabulated on a slate, a worried looking carpenter returned to the quarterdeck.

"Well, Mr. Johnson?" said Drinkwater as he flicked the table of versines over.

"You was right, sir. Shifted two tiers of barricoes under the sail locker to larboard o' the cables an' found a bleeding split, sir. Reckon the copper's off outside."

"H'm, can you do anything with it?"

Johnson rubbed his chin which was blue with a fast growing stubble. "Reckon if I shift a few more o' the casks I can tingle it from the inside, temp'r'y like, sir."

Drinkwater nodded. "See to it after breakfast, Mr. Johnson. I'll have Mr. Rogers send the mate of the day below at eight bells to shift the casks for you."

He bent again to his figures.

"Beg pardon, sir?"

"Yes, what is it?"

"How did you know it was the larboard bow?"

Drinkwater smiled. "I thought she touched when we were entering Kosseir Bay, Mr. Johnson. Probably hit a coral head and broke it off."

Johnson nodded. "Reckon that's the size of it, sir."

Drinkwater watched him waddle off, saw him hop up onto the fo'c's'le and look into Gregory's hammock, then turn away shaking his head.

"Still a deuced clever and knowing dog are you not, my dear Drinkwater," insinuated Morris. Drinkwater flicked a glance at the helmsmen. Their fixed expressions showed they had heard and Drinkwater was filled with a sudden anger.

"Don't presume upon our *friendship*, Morris, and mind your tongue upon *my* deck."

But Morris did not react, merely smiled with his mouth, then turned away below. Drinkwater stared ahead. Mocha was eight hundred miles to the southward and the brig could not fly over the distance fast enough.

"Mr. Brundell!"

"Sir?"

"At eight bells have both watches hoist studdin' sails."

"Aye, aye, sir."

He waited impatiently for the quadruple double ring and the arrival of Mr. Lestock to relieve him.

The gunroom was crowded when he went below. Cots had been constructed in each of the two after corners, one for Dalziell, displaced by Catherine Best from his own cabin, the other, a hasty addition, for Morris. Gaston Bruilhac still slept beneath the table. Appleby was just emerging from the after cabin when Drinkwater sat for his bowl of burgoo.

The surgeon jerked his head over his shoulder as he caught Drinkwater's interrogative eye. "Taken to his bed," explained Appleby, "the Gambia trouble again."

Drinkwater sighed. Griffiths had taken the Kosseir débâcle very badly. He was never prodigal with the lives of his men, many of whom were old Kestrels, volunteers from the almost forgotten days of peace. The butcher's bill for the action with *La Torride* and the attack on Kosseir had been excessive. With the thunder of the silent guns ringing in his ears as they withdrew from before the battered but defiant town, Griffiths had succumbed to an onslaught of his malaria.

Finishing his breakfast, Drinkwater went into the after cabin. The sweet smell of perspiration filled the stuffy space. Griffiths lay in his cot, his eyes closed, but he opened them as Drinkwater leaned over the twisted sheets.

"How are you sir?"

"Bad, Nathaniel, *bach . . . du*, but get me a drink, get me a drink . . ."

Drinkwater found a bottle and poured the wine.

"Watch them all, Nathaniel, watch them all. You were the only one I ever trusted." There was a frantic quality about him, a desperation that Drinkwater suddenly found frightening, reminding him of Griffiths's fragile mortality. The idea of being left without him was unthinkable. As if divining Drinkwater's sense of abandonment Griffiths suddenly asked, "Where are we? What the devil's our position?"

"Latitude . . ."

"No *where? Where* for God's sake?" Griffiths had half sat up and was clawing at Drinkwater's sleeve, like a man who had laid down to sleep in a strange place and, on waking, is unable to recall his whereabouts.

"The Red Sea, sir," Drinkwater soothed.

Griffiths lay back as though satisfied. "Ah, *Y Môr Coch, Y Môr Coch,* is it . . ." His voice trailed off in a murmur of incomprehensible Welsh. For a while Drinkwater sat with him as he seemed to drift off into sleep.

Then Griffiths struggled up, an abrupt frown seaming his gleaming forehead. "The Red Sea, d'you say? Yes, yes, of course . . . and we head south, eh?"

"Aye sir."

"Don't forget the sun's ahead of you, neglect the lookout at your peril . . ." He fell back from this vehement warning. Drinkwater left the cabin and went to find Johnson and his party in the forehold.

Griffiths's warning was timely. The central part of the Red Sea ran deep but the approach to Mocha was made dangerous by many coral reefs. Sailing north they had always had the sun behind them, facilitating the spotting of reefs from the foremasthead. Now the reverse was true and the force of a favourable wind lent a southerly course the quality of impetuosity. Drinkwater remembered his order to hoist the studding sails with a pang of cautionary misgivings, then allayed his fears with the reflection that this portion of the Red Sea was free of reefs except for the low islet of Daedalus Shoal some sixty leagues south-east of them.

He found Johnson busy crouched in the darkness between two timbers, the gleam of incoming water lit by lanterns held by ship's boys, burning weakly in the bad air. Johnson had a pad of picked oakum pressed against the leak to batten over with timber and tarred canvas. Drinkwater looked round him in the gloom.

"The devil's task moving the casks, eh, Mr. Johnson?"

"Aye, sir. I reckon Josh Kirby's ruptured himself, like, beggin' your pardon."

Drinkwater sighed. Another customer for one of Appleby's trusses. The hard physical labour of working His Majesty's ships of war resulted in frequent hernias, a debilitating condition for any man, let alone a seaman. Drinkwater knew of many officers who suffered from them too, and next to addiction to alcohol it was the commonest form of affliction suffered by seamen of all stations.

Returning aft he called on Mr. Quilhampton. Opening the flimsy cabin door he found the boy sitting in a chair, reading aloud from *Falconer's Marine Dictionary*. Drinkwater was aware of a sudden thrusting movement as Gaston Bruilhac shoved past him in apparent panic.

"Good mornin', Mr. Q. What the deuce has that puppy been up to to look so damned guilty?"

"Morning sir." Quilhampton frowned. "Damned if I know, sir. It's rather queer, but despite my assurances to the contrary he's still terrified of all the officers sir, especially the captain, you and your friend Mr. Morris."

Drinkwater snorted. "Mr. Morris, Mr. Q, is an old 'Admiralty acquaintance' with whom I never saw eye to eye. You may disabuse yourself of ideas of intimacy."

Quilhampton appeared pleased.

"What are you reading?" asked Drinkwater, aware that he should not discuss even Morris with a midshipman. "Are you communicating with the French boy?"

"Yes, sir," said Quilhampton enthusiastically, "Falconer has a French lexicon appended to his dictionary, as you know, sir, and we're making some progress. If only he wasn't so damned nervous."

"Well I'm glad to see you so cheerful, Mr. Q." He forebore mentioning the ligatures. If Appleby was premature in drawing them Quilhampton would suffer agony. That was the surgeon's province.

At noon Drinkwater and Lestock observed their latitude. Both expressed their surprise that the brig was not more to the south but their ponderings were interrupted by a strange cry from the masthead.

"Deck there! Red Sea ahead!"

Such an unusual hail brought all on deck to the rail. The sea had lost its brilliant blue and white appearance and at first seemed the colour of mud, then suddenly *Hellebore* was ploughing her way through vermillion waves. This strange novelty caused expressions of naïve wonder to cross the faces of the men and Drinkwater remembered Griffiths's muttered "*Y Môr Coch*". They dropped a bucket over and brought up a sample. It was, in detail, a disappointing phenomena, a reddish dust lay upon the water, the corpses of millions of tiny organisms which, in dying, turned a brilliant hue. In less than an hour they had passed out of the area and the men went laughing to their dinners.

The sight, the subject of a long entry in Drinkwater's journal, drove all thoughts of the suspect latitude from their minds.

When he came on the deck again at eight bells in the afternoon he based his longitude observation on the latitude observed at noon. He was not to know that refraction of the horizon made nonsense of the day's calculations. They were well to the south and east of their assumed position and for some it was to be a fatal error.

But it was Lieutenant Rogers whose greater mistake spelled disaster for the brig. They had experienced the magically disturbing phenomena of a "milk sea" many times since that first eruption of phosphorescence in the southern Indian Ocean. Conversations with officers at Mocha, experienced in the navigation of the eastern seas, had led them to remit their instinctive fear of shoaling which was often occasioned by this circumstance. They had heard from Blankett's men how captains and all hands had been called and precious anchors lost on several occasions when an officer apprehended the immediate loss of the ship on a shoal in the middle of the night. Subsequent soundings had shown a depth greater than the leadline could determine and the "foaming breakers" were discovered to be no more than the phosphorescent tumbling of the open sea.

But such arcane knowledge bestowed on a man of Rogers's temperament was apt to blunt his natural fears and he disallowed the report from the masthead with a contemptuous sneer.

And so, at ten minutes after three on the morning of the 19th August 1799, His Britannic Majesty's Brig of War *Hellebore* ran hard ashore on the outlying spurs of Abu al Kizan, ironically known to the Royal Navy as Daedalus Reef.

CHAPTER FOURTEEN

The Will of Allah

August 1799

Drinkwater was flung from his cot by the impact. In the darkness he was aware of shouts, curses and screams. The entire hull seemed to flex once as a loud crack was followed by the crash of falling spars and blocks, the muffling slump of canvas and the peculiar whirring slap of ropes falling slack across the deck. In his drawers he pushed his way through the confused press of men making for the upper deck. As he emerged he was aware that the lofty spread of the brig's masts, rigging and sails were gone, that the mighty arch of the heavens spread overhead uninterrupted. Lieutenant Rogers stood open-mouthed in shock, refusing to believe the evidence of his eyes.

Drinkwater leapt for the rail and in an instant saw the fringe of white water breaking round the low islet to larboard, lifeless patches of blackness in the night marked the presence of rock outcrops. All around *Hellebore* the surge and welter of water breaking over shallows confirmed what his nerves were already telling him. Beneath his feet the brig's hull was dead.

He turned to Rogers. It was pointless remonstrating with the man. Rogers would be needed in the coming hours and in any case Drinkwater's acute sense of responsibility was already aware that he himself was not without blame. The reef was undoubtedly Daedalus Reef; their assumed position had been woefully in error and, although he did not yet know why, his conscience nagged him.

"Well sir," he said to Rogers in as steady a voice as he could muster, "it seems that *we* have wrecked the ship . . . and for God's sake close your mouth."

Drinkwater was suddenly aware of many faces in the night, all clamouring for attention. There was fear too, revealed by panicky movements to and from the rails. He saw Catherine Best, her face white, a shawl made of sennit-work round her shoulders. Undercurrents of disorder swept the deck.

"Silence there!" bawled Drinkwater, leaping onto a gun breech, forgetful of his near-nakedness. "We ain't going to sink, damn it, come away from those boats. Mr. Rogers! A roll call if you please. Mr. Lestock! Sound round the hull; Mr. Johnson the well. Mr. Trussel examine the extent of damage to the hull . . . take parties with you . . ." His voice trailed away. Rising from the companionway like an apparition, a tall nightcap falling to one side of his face, the wind whipping a voluminous nightshirt about him, came Commander Griffiths. Men fell silent and drew aside from his path.

"*Myndiawl!* What in the name of Almighty God have you done to my ship?"

Griffiths's mighty voice rolled in anguish across the shambles of the deck which had the appearance of a scene from hell. The jagged ends of the masts stuck upwards, their remains grinding alongside, worked by the surge of the sea. Forward of the galley funnel the ship was buried under spars, rigging and canvas which lifted like the obscene death-throes of a gigantic bird. By some fluke the mainmast had tottered over to larboard, leaving a clear path of deck amidships which seethed with the brig's people.

Drinkwater felt a sharp contraction in his guts, a sudden sense, awful in its intensity, that he had betrayed Griffiths. His nakedness seemed at once shameful and penitent. He was robbed of speech before Griffiths's agony, then a brief anger spurred him to denounce Rogers. But his own underlying sense of culpability checked such a mean outburst. He looked at Griffiths, whose eyes glittered with tears and fever, then slipped sideways to another face, staring at him out of the gloom with amused satisfaction. Drinkwater's nakedness was reflected in Morris's expression. Real anger came to his aid; he found his voice.

"Carry on with my orders, gentlemen. Mr. Grey . . ." The boatswain pushed forward, "get a party to start raising provisions out of the storerooms. Master's mate, do you put a guard on the spirit room and if I find a man the worse for liquor I'll have him at the gratings calling for his mother before the sun's up." He turned to Griffiths. "Sir . . . I . . . we are lost, sir . . . Daedalus Reef . . . our reckoning was out sir, I, er . . ." He felt close to tears himself, a weak desire to capitulate to the overwhelming feeling of frustration that laid siege to his spirit. But then Griffiths tottered forward and Drinkwater caught him. Already the period of shocked lucidity had passed, the ague had reclaimed him and he muttered deliriously to himself in his native tongue. The sudden urgent need to get the captain below reassured Drinkwater. All round them the men were bustling to their new tasks. Catherine Best's hair brushed his face. "Get him below, hey, you there, lend a hand . . ."

"Sir, can I . . .?" It was Mr. Quilhampton, his stump across his chest, his right hand held protectively over it. Appleby had tried the ligatures without success. Mr. Quilhampton had not flinched. "Get the surgeon! And round up some men to carry the captain below." Then he added in a lower voice, "Look after him Catherine, we have great need of him now." Two seamen arrived to relieve them of their burden. The woman straightened up. In the darkness he could see her smile of reassurance.

"I will sir," she said, and her hand closed for a second on his arm. Then Appleby appeared and Drinkwater turned to attend to Johnson.

"Five feet o' water in the well, sir, but the line's short. I think we've lost the bottom, sir." Lestock arrived. "Two fathoms aft, barely one forrard, both masts gone by the board . . ."

"Twenty barrels of powder spoiled and we've lost some water. Deal of the dry stores spoiled and judging by the top tier of casks in the hold we've stove in the bottom . . ." Trussel reported.

Drinkwater forced his mind to assimilate the details. Already a plan for their immediate survival was forming in his mind. He already knew there was no chance of saving the ship.

"Well, Mr. Rogers?"

Rogers had recovered his composure. "Three men killed, sir. Gregory, the foremast fell across his hammock; Stock, foremast lookout, killed when the mast fell, and Jeavons, he was forrard and was struck by a block. There are quite a number of injuries . . ."

"Right," Drinkwater cut him short, "all the unfit to go below. Is that all?"

"Two missing," added Rogers.

Drinkwater could imagine that, men on duty swept overboard in the chaos of falling gear. He thought for a moment.

"We must get the galley stove lit and all hands fed well at daylight. Use broached stores to conserve stocks. I've put the master's mates in charge of the spirit store until we get things sorted out. Keep a watch for drunkenness, Rogers, if this lot get out of hand there will be the devil to pay."

"And then what d'you propose?" a voice sneered. Lieutenant Morris intruded into the little group.

"We wait until daylight Morris," replied Drinkwater coolly, "unless you have any better suggestions, then we will move the wounded to the reef and salvage what we can. The boats, Mr. Grey, must be preserved at all costs. About your duties gentlemen." The officers dispersed and Drinkwater was left alone with Morris. He was again uncomfortably aware of his lack of clothing.

"I think, my *dear* Nathaniel, that this time even you have bitten off more than you can chew."

Drinkwater moved towards the companionway to find a shirt and his breeches. He turned sharply towards his enemy and retraced his steps. For one delicious moment he wished he had had his sword for he would have had no compunction in trusting it deep into Morris's belly. The satisfaction, like that of lancing a boil, would have been cathartic. Instead he was reduced to a venomous retort.

"Go to the devil!"

"Careful Nathaniel, remember that old Welsh goat is a sick man and I am far senior to you . . ." The insinuation was plain enough and it choked Drinkwater with his own rising bile.

"Go to hell, Morris!"

"Witness that remark, Mr. Dalziell," snapped Morris in a sudden change of tone as the midshipman hurried up. Drinkwater turned away in search of his breeches.

It was late afternoon before Drinkwater paused to take stock of their situation on the tiny island. In the hours that succeeded the brush with Morris he had worked ceaselessly. It

was only as he stood staring westwards that he realised why
the brig had been lost. As the sun sank the mountain peaks of
Upper Egypt were clear on the horizon. Drinkwater knew
they were sixty to seventy miles away, far over the sea horizon. It had been the unusual refraction of that very horizon
that had caused their errors and he walked tiredly over to Lestock to point it out. But Mr. Lestock, who had long ago been
prejudiced against Mr. Drinkwater's methods of navigation,
especially that of determining longitude by chronometer,
merely curled his lip.

"Perhaps, Mr. Drinkwater, it would have been more prudent to have observed the phenomena before the loss of the
ship . . ." Lestock rose and cut him, leaving Drinkwater isolated as he stared after the retreating back of the retrospec-
tively wise master whose fussing indecision seemed justified.

Mr. Quilhampton appeared at his elbow. "Beg pardon, sir,
Miss Best says you are to drink this and take some rest, sir."
He took the tankard of blackstrap and felt it ease the tension
from him. "I'm keeping the log going, sir, and the ship's
name, sir." Drinkwater looked at the boy. "Eh? Oh, oh, yes,
quite, Mr. Q, very well."

Drinkwater looked at the sandy, scrub-covered island upon
the flat top of which a dozen crude tents had been erected.
Piles of casks of pork, powder and water were under guard of
the master's mates. So too were those of spirits and biscuit.

They had toiled to heave as much of the ship's stores
ashore as were available, rigging a stay from the stump of the
mainmast to an anchorage ashore upon which rode a block to
convey load after load. They had rigged shelter from spars
and remnants of *Hellebore*'s sails; they had constructed a galley; they had tended the wounded and buried the dead; they
had got the boats safely away from the wreck and into a small
inlet that made a passable boat harbour on the lee side of the

islet, and Drinkwater was pleased with their efforts and achievements. Perhaps he ought to be more charitable toward Lestock.

"It is a little like Petersfield market, ain't it, Mr. Q?" he said, managing a grin. The boy smiled back. "Aye sir. A little."

"How's your arm, Mr. Q?"

"Oh, well enough, sir. I can write, sir," he added eagerly, "so I'm keeping the logs, sir, and I saw the chronometer ashore safe, together with your quadrant and your books."

"You're a capital fellow, Mr. Q, I had not thought of them at all."

"Tregembo got your sword and uniforms." Drinkwater realised that he was surrounded by good fellows. Lestock could go hang. "Thank you, Mr. Q."

"They're all in the gunroom tent, sir."

Drinkwater suppressed a smile. It was inconceivable that it should be otherwise, but every space on the islet already had its nautical name. The hold was where the stores were stowed, the gunroom tent where the officers were quartered, the berth deck where the forecourse was draped over its yard to accommodate the hands.

Drinkwater drained the blackstrap and handed the empty tankard back to Quilhampton. "I had better do as Mistress Best directed me," he said wrily.

"Very well, sir. She's a most remarkable woman," the boy added precociously.

"She is indeed, Mr. Q, she is indeed."

In the two days that followed they added a quarterdeck to His Majesty's stone sloop *Hellebore*, hoisting the ensign from a topgallant yard set and stayed vertically. They blasted a few coral heads out of the boat channel and surveyed another haven for the boats in case the wind changed. They tore the brig's rails to pieces to provide firewood for cooking and built a beacon on the low summit of the reef to ignite if any passing ship was sighted, and they built a lookout tower from where a proper watch was maintained, with an officer, mate and petty officer in continual attendance. They dragged three guns ashore with plans to construct a proper battery in due course, for Drinkwater realised that the men must be kept busy, although he was equally worried about drinking water and the demand on their stocks that such a policy would entail. But morale was good, for *Daedalus* and *Fox* were expected south within the month. Drinkwater's greatest worry was for Griffiths. The commander had suffered a severe shock over the loss of the brig. His malarial attack was, as he himself had predicted, a bad one, exacerbated by the wrecking. Appleby worried over him, but consoled Drinkwater, aware that the lieutenant had other things to worry about. That the old man was very ill was obvious, and the indisposed presence of Lieutenant Morris, who refused to exert himself beyond the self-preservation of his person and belongings, had all the appearance of a vulture waiting for his prey to die.

On the morning of the fourth day they saw a large dhow. The vessel sailed slowly in towards the reef, clearly curious as to the islet's new inhabitants. But despite the firing of a gun and the friendly waves of a hundred arms it stood off to the eastwards. Spirits remained reasonably high, however, since it was confidently asserted that neither *Fox* nor *Daedalus* would miss them.

Then, at dawn, twelve days later, away to the south-east the square topsails of two frigates were discerned. Summoned from his bedroll, Drinkwater ordered the beacon lit and climbed the lookout post. At the top he levelled his glass. He was looking at the after sides of mizzen topsails: *Daedalus* and *Fox* had passed them in the night.

*   *   *

For twenty-eight hours the Hellebores and their guests from
the two now far distant frigates wallowed in the depths of despair. Even Drinkwater seemed exhausted of ideas but he
eventually determined to fit out the Arab boat they had captured at Kosseir for a passage. The boat, too large to hoist
aboard *Hellebore*, had been towing astern of the brig when
she grounded. Although damaged she was repairable and the
following morning Drinkwater had her beached and over-
turned for repairs. The wrecked hull of *Hellebore* was once
again resorted to for materials and by mid-afternoon a de-
tectable lightening of spirits swept the camp.

As the men went to their evening meal a dhow was seen to
the eastward. The beacon was lit and the dhow was still in
sight as the sun set. At dawn the next day it stood purpose-
fully inshore and Drinkwater put off in *Hellebore*'s gig. An
hour later Mr. Strangford Wrinch stood upon the sandy soil of
Abu al Kizan.

He looked curiously about him, resplendent in yellow
boots, a green *galabiya* and white head-dress. He smiled. "I
learned of the presence of infidels upon this reef from a dhow
that sighted you a fortnight ago. They spoke of many men
waving and the wreck of a ship close by." He paused, his face
more hawk-like than ever. "I also learned of another ship. A
French ship . . ."

"Santhonax?" asked Drinkwater eagerly. Wrinch nodded.

"*In'sh Allah*, my dear fellow, it is the will of Allah."

CHAPTER FIFTEEN

Santhonax

September 1799

Drinkwater moved forward on the heeling deck of the *sambuk*, cursing the restrictions of the *galabiya*. The head-dress he found even less easy to handle as it masked his vision. He resolved to dispense with it the instant he could and turned his attention to the men cleaning small arms and sharpening cutlasses. Yusuf ben Ibrahim's Arab crew watched them with interest, shaking their heads over the crudity of the naval pattern sword.

The sambuk sliced across the sea, heading east with the wind on the larboard quarter, the great curved yards of the lateen sails straining to drag the slender hull along, as if as impatient as Drinkwater to put the present matter to the test. Strangford Wrinch came on deck, his green robe fluttering in the wind. He nodded to Drinkwater, then opened his hand in invitation as he squatted down on a square of carpet. Drinkwater joined him.

"Relax, Nathaniel," said Wrinch, his dark eyes fixed on the face of the lieutenant and it occurred to Drinkwater that this strange man was not much older than himself. They fell to discussing the events of the previous weeks that had brought Wrinch so timely to their rescue.

A day or two after Blankett had sent *Daedalus* and *Fox* to follow *Hellebore* north, a report had reached Wrinch that a mysterious ship had appeared off the coast of the Hejaz. It was soon identified as the frigate commanded by Santhonax who had apparently left off molesting the native craft. On the contrary the captain was now known to have distributed large sums of *baksheesh* for assistance in piloting his ship through the reefs off Rayikhah and Umm Uruma islands. When Wrinch had passed this information to Blankett the rear-admiral had waved Wrinch's apprehensions aside, assuring the agent that if the "poxed frog" were dangerous Ball and Stuart would "trounce him". In the meantime his escape from the Red Sea was sealed off by *Leopard*'s blockade of the Straits of Bab el Mandeb. Blankett did not apparently see the anomaly in this assertion, seeing that *Leopard* was comfortably anchored off Mocha and His Excellency was ashore seeking to board nothing more belligerent than a small seraglio of willing houris.

Wrinch, however, did not suffer from the admiral's lethargy. He had in any event been supine for too long and set out north with a small entourage. After an overland journey of six hundred miles which he passed off with an inconsequential shrug, Wrinch and his *mehari* camels reached Jeddah. Here he found Yusuf ben Ibrahim, luxuriating after the sale of the prizes taken for him by the *Hellebore* in the action with *La Torride*. Wrinch kicked him out of bed and in the sambuk both men sailed north to Al Wejh, where positive news awaited them of a great French ship, lying a few leagues to the northward in a *sharm*, with her guns ashore. Santhonax was careening his ship, preparing her for the next stage of his campaign.

"But what I don't comprehend, Strangford, is why a careenage on the Hejaz? Surely the Egyptian coast was more sensible, where he could contact Desaix."

"Ah, my dear fellow," said Wrinch, putting an intimate hand briefly upon Drinkwater's knee, "You profess to know the man without quite comprehending the depths of his cunning. Certainly the Egyptian coast would appear the best, but he would be harried continuously by mamelukes. Murad Bey would never suffer him to be left in peace for long enough to cast a timenoguy over a bobstay or whatever he does," concluded Wrinch in mock ignorance.

"But Kosseir was held by the French. He could have done it there."

"Not so. You yourself went a-looking for him there. Certainly he could have defended himself at Kosseir but not left his ship defenceless while he carried out the necessary maintenance. No, Santhonax needed the last place you'd look, so he found an isolated careenage on the Arabian side. The *sharms* of the Hejaz are ideal for the purpose being the flooded ends of *wadis*, dry river beds that run into these shallow bays, often well protected by coral and intricate approaches to foil a surprise attack and break up the sea. The usual small village can provide some comforts for his men and the local headmen may be bribed with ease. Santhonax could lie for a month before taking alarm." He paused, reaching for a paper beneath his *galabiya*. "Now, this is my intention."

Drinkwater bent over the sketch-map. He listened to Wrinch's words, feeling excitement coiling inside him, remembering the drawn-out council of war that had been held in the gunroom tent of "HM sloop *Hellebore*", a rocky islet in the middle of the Red Sea. Most he remembered its dramatic termination.

Griffiths had been there, half conscious and lying in his cot. The worst of the fever was over and he had slept peacefully for some hours. Wrinch had presided with Drinkwater, Rogers, Lestock and Appleby in attendance. Morris had also insinuated his presence.

Lestock was against the venture from the beginning. He was unable to see the strategic consequences of allowing Santhonax to refit and escape from his careenage. Appleby would embrace almost any expedient that got his precious patients to Mocha, a point that he made at considerable length, urging that the sambuk would more properly be employed in chasing Ball and Stuart and recalling them to attack the French frigate. "For," concluded the surgeon, "it is patently obvious to even a non-combatant like myself that the presence of two frigates is decidedly superior to one."

"They were of damn-all use at Kosseir, Appleby," said Rogers with a trace of recurring impatience.

Drinkwater agreed. "Besides," he added cogently, "virtually any delay will almost inevitably result in our losing this elusive Frenchman. And I for one, have not come all this way to lose the game to Edouard Santhonax."

"Bravo, Nathaniel," said Wrinch. "I think we may accommodate the dissenters," he said urbanely. "If, gentlemen, after say seven days we have not made our reappearance you could send Mr. Lestock off in the boat you were preparing on my arrival. I will leave you a man capable of seeing you into Mocha."

Rogers accepted the idea of an attack on Santhonax with enthusiasm, while Lestock shook his head and mumbled his misgivings to Appleby. Morris remained silent, fitter than hitherto, but still with that predatory look of a man biding his time. Then, as they fell into groups and discussed the matter Griffiths sat up, fully conscious for the first time in days. He

looked haggard and old beyond his years, the flesh hanging
loosely about his face. But his eyes were bright with intelligence, like those of a child, instantly awake after a refreshing
nap.

"Wrinch? Good God man, is it you? What . . . where the
devil are we? Nathaniel? Where the deuce . . ." Drinkwater
detached himself and came over to the commander while Appleby called for water. He knelt down beside Griffiths and patiently began the long explanation. The questions Griffiths
shot at him from time to time made it plain that the old man's
senses had returned to him and at the end of Nathaniel's
speech he threw off his sheets and rose unsteadily to his feet.
"Gentlemen, this is no longer a matter for debate. Make
preparations at once. I shall command you myself, Nathaniel,
pick forty able men, Mr. Rogers prepare small arms . . . Mr.
Lestock, you may take charge in our absence. Mr. Appleby
will second you." He swayed a trifle but by an effort held
himself upright.

"Perhaps I might remind you, Commander Griffiths, that I
am now fit enough to take command in your absence." Morris spoke for the first time. Drinkwater opened his mouth to
protest but Morris quickly added, "After yourself I'm the senior officer." His eyes met those of Drinkwater and the latter
read the satisfaction of a small scoring over his enemy.

"Oh, very well, Mr. Morris, you may command the invalids
and cripples. The rest of us will prepare ourselves to catch
Reynard in his den."

Drinkwater did not let his mind dwell on the possible consequences of leaving Morris in charge of the island. He already had the amusing company of Dalziell, now perhaps he
would exert his influence upon the scared rabbit Bruilhac or
worse, the convalescing Quilhampton. There were also the
ship's boys and, for added diversion, Catherine Best. Through

her he might gain an advantage over Appleby, also a party to his former disgrace. Foreboding clouded Drinkwater's mind as he fought to concentrate on Wrinch's words. There had been a strange quiescence in Dalziell since Mr. Morris came aboard. Drinkwater watched Wrinch's face, aware that he shared some of Morris's tastes, though to a less perverse degree. But what he found offensive in one, Nathaniel scarcely thought of in the other, associating Wrinch's peccadillo with his way of life.

"So you see, Nathaniel, we shall observe the three basic principles of warfare. First simplicity of purpose, second detail in preparations, hence the *galabiya* with which I perceive you are not yet familiar, and thirdly the advantage of surprise in execution."

They reached Al Wejh after nightfall and anchored. A small boat was hauled over the side and Wrinch and Yusuf slipped ashore. Yusuf's men sat in a huddle and smoked hashish while Drinkwater briefed the Hellebores, explaining in detail what was to happen. Among the forty men selected for the enterprise were Tregembo and Kellett, together with most of the topmen, Mr. Trussel and a party of the best gun captains. Mr. Rogers was also there. Quilhampton had begged to come but Drinkwater had forbidden it. Instead he had entrusted a bundle of letters to the midshipman, "in case of contingencies not, at this moment, envisaged."

He went below and found Griffiths sleeping quietly in a hammock. At the moment of the final attack he hoped Griffiths would remain aboard the *sambuk* for he would be little use for anything else, weakened by the fever as he was. In the interim Drinkwater was glad to see him sleeping so peacefully. He returned to the deck and lay down. But he was restless and sat up, leaning against the bulwarks while the stars wheeled slowly overhead, aware that the smells of Al Wejh were unrelievedly noxious. He thought of Elizabeth and her child, curiously he could not think of it as his until he had seen it. He wondered if it were a boy or a girl and what Elizabeth had called it. In the darkness he whispered her name, very low, but loud enough to give it substance, to convince himself that somewhere a lady of this murmured name actually lived, and that reality was not Nathaniel Drinkwater sitting on the deck of a dhow dressed like an Arab horsethief, but a brown-haired woman with a child at her breast. Thinking thus he dozed.

He woke at the sound of a boat bumping alongside. Wrinch had returned and they weighed anchor. In the calm of the night four sweeps propelled the dhow closer inshore and soon they secured alongside a stone pier. Striking the hold open they swung the great lateen yards round and laboured to gingerly lift each of the three six-pounders out of the hold and onto the waiting carts. It was dawn before the last gun had gone, followed by Mr. Trussel and his gunners who departed with their powder and shot on a fourth cart.

Wrinch came to say his farewells. He addressed Griffiths who was still in his huge nightshirt. "It is all arranged Madoc. I had sufficient gold. Your artillery was a powerful persuader. Nathaniel is fully aware of the precise nature of my intentions. As for yourself, Madoc, I entreat you not to be quixotic. That you have come is sufficient. Let Nathaniel here lead the attack."

"I am a naval officer, not a mawkish schoolgirl to be cozened," growled Griffiths. In a milder tone he added, "Be off with you. Give us your blue light when y're ready and you'll not find us wanting." He held out his hand.

"Let us hope that we may toast our success in this Santhonax's cabin stores before long." Wrinch extended his hand to Drinkwater.

"Good luck, Strangford. I hope Allah wills our little enterprise."

Wrinch had hardly disappeared before the Hellebores were bundled below and Yusuf ben Ibraham called his drugged crew to order. With no apparent ill effects the *sambuk* slipped seawards and two hours after sunrise was beating northwards through sparkling seas. Aware that for the moment he was a passenger, Drinkwater slept like a child.

By mid-morning they had left Rayikhah Island well astern and turned north-east to raise Ras Murabit. They began to fish as they closed the shore again and by the afternoon were in company with two other native craft similarly employed. At about four o'clock with the mountains of the Hejaz well defined against a sky of perfect blue and the low, paler dun-coloured coastal plain still shimmering in the heat, they made out the frigate, tiny at first, but growing larger as they sailed closer, in company with the other boats returning after their day's fishing to the *sharm* Al Mukhra. As they approached they could see the vessel was upright and lying head to wind with her yards crossed. They must have completed their maintenance work, for the ship had all the appearance of being ready for sea.

As the wind died towards evening their pace slackened. Once again the Hellebores were sent below, only the officers with Arab dress being permitted to keep the deck. Looking pale and drawn, Commander Griffiths remained, his eyes fixed upon the enemy frigate.

The French ship lay in a *sharm* which formed a spoon-shaped indentation in the coastline. A few scrubby mangroves were visible on the foreshore and the square shapes of low, mud-brick houses squatted among palms. At the head of the *sharm* the dried up water-course wound inland, the *wadi* that Wrinch would use to cover his own approach.

Boldly, and with the setting sun silhouetting them, the *sambuk* of Yusuf ben Ibrahim accompanied the boats from Al Mukhra, his crew exchanging shouted comments about the paucity of fish off Rayikhah and blaming it upon the anger of Allah that the infidel had overrun Egypt. The men from Al Mukhra were clearly of the same opinion. They pointed to the French frigate and made obscene gestures. Their women, they said, were being contaminated by the heathen French who had been anchored too long and were hornier than goats with their drunkenness and their lusting. Indeed Allah must have turned his face from the faithful of Al Mukhra who were among the most wretched of men. All this was perfectly comprehensible to Drinkwater, accompanied as it was by universally accepted gestures. It was clear that though Santhonax might have bought the local headmen with gifts and gold, the humbler people who dwelt here had no love for the French.

Drinkwater tried to concentrate on the approach to the *sharm*, storing up knowledge for later use but it seemed to be well chosen, for the approach was wide and deep and clearly Santhonax relied upon the fear of reefs more than their actual presence. Drinkwater found himself thinking more of Santhonax himself and knew intuitively that that was what preoccupied Griffiths. The tall, handsome Frenchman with the livid scar, whom they had chased the length and breadth of the English Channel and pursued along the sandy coast of Holland, seemed drawn towards them by a curious fate. Drinkwater thought of the extraordinary circumstances that had led them to the grey afternoon off Camperdown when, in a Dutch yacht, they had taken him prisoner. And there had been his mistress too, the beautiful auburn-haired Hortense, who had fooled the British authorities for months, living as an émigrée in England. He wondered what had become of her, whether Santhonax knew that he, Drinkwater, had released her, turned her loose on a French beach like an unwanted bitch.

He shook his head and drew his glass from under his robe. Careful not to catch the sun upon its lens he levelled it at the French frigate. Half an hour later they anchored off the beach and settled to wait for nightfall.

The fish-hold of the *sambuk* presented a bizarre spectacle. Crammed into its odoriferous space the Hellebores, faces blackened with soot, prepared for battle. The two lieutenants checked the men and struggled aft to where Griffiths waited, sitting on a coil of rope. He had hardly spoken since they had left Daedalus Reef.

"We are prepared sir. I am almost certain that she is not fully armed yet, her draft is too light and there is still a large encampment ashore. A boat came off just after we anchored but pulled ashore again. The land breeze is already stirring and we will need only a little sail to cover the two cables 'twixt us and the enemy."

"*Da iawn*, Mr. Drinkwater, well done. You will want to be leaving soon, is it?"

"Aye, sir, in a moment or two."

"Did you observe our friend at all?"

"Santhonax? No sir."

Griffiths grunted. "Very well, good luck. I hope Wrinch told this blackamoor not to move till he saw the signal."

"Yes sir. I do not think Yusuf will move without a fair chance of victory. He is not the kind to embark on forlorn hopes."

"Off you go then, *bach*, and be careful."

Drinkwater went on deck. The small dinghy was bobbing alongside and Rogers waited to see him off. Yusuf ben Ibrahim was also on deck, smoking hashish with his wild-eyed crew. The moon was up, a slender crescent, an omen of singular aptness thought Drinkwater pointing it out to the Arab. Yusuf grinned comprehendingly. "*In'sh Allah,*" he breathed fervently, drawing a wickedly curved sabre that gleamed dully in the starlight.

"Good luck, Drinkwater," said Rogers offering his hand. "'Tis a damned desperate measure but if it don't succeed . . ." he left the sentence unfinished.

"If it don't succeed, Samuel, we can all kiss farewell to a prosperous future." Nathaniel took the man's hand, searching for the blackened face in the night. Rogers was much chastened since wrecking the brig and Drinkwater found himself liking the man for the first time since leaving home. "Good luck, Samuel."

He descended into the little boat. Drinkwater squatted aft and saw where Kellett and Tregembo each took an oar. The third topman, named Barnes, settled himself in the bow. Drinkwater struggled out of his *galabiya* as they pulled away from the dhow and made a wide detour round the stern of the frigate as she pointed landwards, head to the offshore breeze. When they had worked round to a position on her starboard bow they began to pull quietly in towards her and, three quarters of an hour after leaving, Barnes caught the boat's painter round the heavy hemp cable of the frigate. Kellett and Tregembo brought their oars inboard and all four men sat in silence under the stem and figurehead of the ship. They had achieved total surprise. Perfection of the plan now depended upon Wrinch.

Faint sounds came to them; the myriad creaks of a ship at rest, a whistled snatch of the *Ça Ira* ended in mid-phrase. A muted burst of laughter and the low tone of conversation indicated where the watch on deck spun yarns and played cards. Once the coarse noise of hawking and a loud expectoration was followed by a plop in the water close to them.

The minutes dragged by and a man came forward to use the heads. The four men maintained a stoic silence beneath the arc of urine that pattered down beside them accompanied by the quiet humming of a man on his own.

As the man returned inboard Mr. Trussel's rocket soared into the night and burst over Al Mukhra with a baleful blue light.

For what seemed an age total silence greeted the appearance of this spectral flare then above their heads the fo'c's'le of the frigate was crowded with men. They jabbered together and pointed ashore while Drinkwater made a motion of his hand to Barnes. They eased the dinghy further under the round bow of the frigate, slackening the long painter until level with the tack bumpkin. Now they would have to wait for Griffiths and the *sambuk* to divert the attention of the men above.

Drinkwater turned his attention ashore. A flash and bang told where Mr. Trussel's six-pounders on their improvised carriages were going into action. The concussions increased the speculation and excitement on the deck above them and now the noise of whooping Arab horsemen could be heard, mingling with the shouts of surprised Frenchmen and the commands of officers. Flickering movements around the fires told their own story and on the fo'c's'le above them someone was giving orders too.

A terrific explosion shook the air, making Drinkwater's ears ring. The wave of reeking powder smoke that engulfed them a second later told that those on board had at least one gun mounted, a long bow chaser fired more for effect than anything, for no one could say where the fall of shot was. Two minutes later it boomed out again and Drinkwater wished he had a kerchief to wrap around his ears like the seamen were doing. But then there came another cry. A sharp *"Qui va là?"* of alarm from amidships and suddenly the fo'c's'le was empty as the Frenchmen streamed away to repel the threat from the approaching dhow.

"Now lads!" Caution did not matter any more. With an effort Drinkwater swung himself upwards at the bumpkin, dangled a moment then felt Tregembo heave him upwards. The dinghy bobbed dangerously beneath the topman but Drinkwater scrambled upwards reaching the stinking gratings of the heads and covering himself with more filth. He wiped his hands on the gammoning of the bowsprit as his men joined him then they went over the bow onto the now deserted fo'c's'le.

"Is the boat all right?"

"Aye zur," answered Tregembo's offended tone. Tregembo had been offended since the evening Drinkwater had left him behind at Kosseir, but that was of little moment now.

Coming round the foremast they could see the whole of the waist filling with men from the lower deck. The masts of the *sambuk* were visible alongside and already Drinkwater could see several Hellebores on the rail. Lieutenant Rogers was there, hacking downwards, one hand grasping a mainmast shroud. He saw the squat shapes of quarterdeck carronades then there were more figures on the rail, British and Arab. Drinkwater recognised Yusuf and his wicked scimitar.

"Up we go!" he called to the men behind him and flung himself in the larboard foremast rigging. He felt Tregembo beside him; Barnes and Kellett made for the opposite side. Drinkwater looked down once. The *sambuk* could be seen now, its deck empty. The waist of the frigate was a mass of heaving bodies, of dully flashing blades and the yellow spurts of pistol fire. Then, as he swung back downwards into the futtocks, he heard above the grunting, swearing, shouting men below the thunder of cannon and the blood curdling screams of Arab horsemen as they decimated the French camp at the head of the *sharm.*

Drinkwater reached the foretopsail yard and moved out along the footrope. He felt for the seaman's knife on its lanyard and began to slit the ties. At the bunt, having done the same thing, Tregembo was busy severing the bunt and clew lines. In heavy folds, flopping downwards by degrees the huge topsail fell from its stowed position and flattened itself against the mast, all aback.

Out on the other yardarm Kellett and Barnes completed their half of the task. In a few minutes they were in the top. Kellett and Tregembo ran out along the foreyard, whipping yarns from their belts and seizing the topsail clews to the sheet blocks. The sail secured, the four men scrambled to the deck. Amidships the struggle raged with unabated fury.

"Below lads!" he snapped, pushing them towards the forward companionway. They descended to the gundeck. It was deserted and in the glimmering light of the lantern at the after companionway sixty feet astern of them, they could see the six guns that had been mounted. The empty gun carriages at the remaining gunports along the deck and the untidy raffle of ropes, blocks, tackles, spikes and ropeyarns bespoke a busy day tomorrow. "Untidy bastards," volunteered Barnes as he followed Drinkwater to where the lieutenant had already begun work on the cable.

"Not too much, Barnes," Drinkwater said, "there will be a fair weight on it with that topsail aback. It mustn't part before we're ready." Drinkwater ran aft with Tregembo and Kellett in his wake. It was obvious now why the boarding nettings

were down. The encumbrance caused by them when hoisting
in the guns would have combined with Santhonax's feeling of
security to persuade him that they were unnecessary. Besides
a further day's labour and the frigate would be ready for sea,
ready to challenge any other vessel on the Red Sea. They had
arrived only just in time. Above their heads the fight for the
deck went on, a scuffling, stamping shouting mêlée of men.
The legs and waists of several Frenchmen below the level of
the deck were temptingly exposed but the three men trotted
past their undefended posteriors. Drinkwater swung below
into the berth deck.

There was a whimpering and stifled cry from the dense
shadows and Drinkwater picked up the single lantern allowed
near the companionway after dark. Holding it before him, he
continued aft. They found the rudder and tiller lines abaft the
cadet's cockpit. Sudden reminders of the hell-hole aboard *Cyclops* flooded his mind. He dreaded finding the tiller lines un-
rove but no, Santhonax had obligingly rigged new ones.

They cut them by the lead blocks to the deck above and
hauled the tiller across to starboard, forcing the rudder over to
port. "You two remain here!" Leaving the lantern with Kellett
and Tregembo, Drinkwater ran forward and up onto the gun
deck, finally reaching Barnes after pushing through a number
of wounded Frenchmen who stumbled about the gun-deck
tripping over their own breechings.

"Cut the bloody thing, Barnes!"

"Aye, aye, sir!" Drinkwater reached the upper deck via the
forward companionway only to blunder into more Frenchmen. He drew his hanger and yelled, slashing wildly out to
right and left. Like butter they parted before him and he was
aware of the last remnants of French resistance crumbling.
Against Griffiths, Rogers and their two score men the French
had had an anchor watch of thirty-six under a lieutenant. The

officer lay mortally wounded, having surrendered his sword to Commander Griffiths. Griffiths stood panting with his exertions, his white hair plastered to his skull by sweat, his sword blade dark. Behind Griffiths stood Yusuf ben Ibrahim, arms akimbo like a harem guard, his men about him daring the surprised Frenchmen to lift a further finger against their conquerors while their frigate was raped.

Barnes yelled triumphantly as the cable parted.

"Foretopsail halliards!" shouted Drinkwater, "Forebraces there!" The special details of men ran to the pinrails.

The sheeted topsail rose into the night, its bunt pressed against the foremast. He looked over the side. The frigate was gathering sternway.

"Mr. Rogers, secure the prisoners!" Griffiths ordered.

"We've the tiller lines cut and men manning it, sir. As soon as this lot is under control I'll splice 'em, in the meantime we've sternway on and men at the forrard braces," Drinkwater reported.

"*Da iawn*. Foredeck there! Heave larboard braces!" The frigate's head swung slowly to starboard as she gathered sternway. The foreyards came round against the catharpings and she increased the speed of her swing. Already the noise and flames of the battle ashore were on the beam. The weather leech of the foretopsail was a-flutter.

"Leggo and haul!" shouted Griffiths and then, turning to Drinkwater and in a quieter voice. "Very well, put your helm over and restore steering to the wheel."

Drinkwater dashed below and ordered Tregembo and Kellett to haul the huge tiller hard across to the other extremity, then he directed the shortening and resecuring of the tiller lines. In the meantime he stationed several men in a chain for passing orders. With the foretopsail yard braced square the frigate stood seawards.

"D'you have the blue light, Mr. Rogers?"

After a search the rocket was found, still in the *sambuk* bobbing and grinding alongside. It was leaned against the taffrail and, after more delays, finally ignited. It whooshed skywards and burst in a blue light over the *sharm* and was answered by a second that soared up from the hand of Mr. Trussel somewhere ashore.

"So that's why they call the gunner 'Old Blue Lights'," quipped Rogers flippantly, and Drinkwater chuckled, moving over to the compass to watch the steering. It had all gone very smoothly, very smoothly indeed. He saw the Frenchmen had been herded forward and one of the quarterdeck carronades spiked round to cover them. Topman Barnes sat negligently on its breech, a slow match in one hand while the other was employed to pick his nose. Tregembo also stood guard, watching Yusuf ben Ibrahim with patent distrust.

Drinkwater wiped his sword and sheathed it, walking aft to stand by Griffiths.

"Congratulations, sir."

"Thank you, Nathaniel. Your party played their part to perfection."

"Thank you, sir . . ." He was about to say more but took sudden alarm from the expression on Griffiths's face. "Behind you, *bach!*"

Spinning round, he saw a man standing on the rail, some six feet from him. As the pistol he held flashed Drinkwater saw who it was. The light from the priming pan flared momentarily on the disfigured features of Edouard Santhonax, contorted with fury and recognition.

CHAPTER SIXTEEN

The Price of Admiralty

September 1799

It was supremely ironic that it should have been Santhonax's astute intelligence that saved Drinkwater's life. For that brilliant officer, so swift in resource and quick in perception, instantly recognised Nathaniel Drinkwater, even in the dark. And that second of distraction from the purpose of discharging his pistol made him miss his aim. Even as the priming sparkled, Drinkwater threw up his left arm to cover his face and the ball passed his ribs with an inch to spare.

"*Vous!*" howled the Frenchman in exasperated fury, flinging the pistol from him and leaping to the deck to draw his sword. Drinkwater's epée rasped from its scabbard. Other figures came over the rail behind Santhonax. Forward there was an ugly movement as the huddle of Frenchmen recognised their commander. Drinkwater heard Griffiths's voice steady the men on the tiller ropes as he and Santhonax circled each other warily.

Suddenly the carronade roared as the captured French seamen surged aft. Barnes had applied his match and as several of them fell screaming to the deck Drinkwater felt the jar of steel on steel. Yusuf ben Ibrahim was alongside him, advancing on the three officers and half dozen armed seamen that had boarded with Santhonax. He was aware of a white-haired figure on his other flank, a pistol extended towards Santhonax. Then Drinkwater was savagely parrying Santhonax's cut, lunging and riposting as Yusuf's whirring scimitar swung pitilessly to his right. He did not know what happened, but suddenly Santhonax was falling back against the rail, his sword hanging uselessly by its martingale, his left arm clutching his shoulder. Drinkwater turned in time to see Griffiths too falling, a dark stain on his breast. Six feet from him a French officer stood with the pistol still smoking in his hand. Cheated of Santhonax and in the full fury of his cold battle lust, Drinkwater swung half left, the French sword singing in his hand. The blade bit down on the officer's shoulder, bumping over clavicle and ribs, opening a huge bloody wound across the chest. Drinkwater pressed the blade savagely, all around him men were closing on Santhonax's party: battle was to become massacre for already in his heart he knew Griffiths was dying. But in that moment this knowledge was refined into a mere lunge, an increase of pressure on the sword-blade that reached the lower limits of the officer's ribs and, slashing through the muscles of his stomach, eviscerated him.

Drinkwater turned from his act of vengeance to see Yusuf ben Ibrahim stretched on the planking, his head and chest laid open by the blades of three Frenchmen, men who had soon succumbed to the overwhelming numbers of Ben Ibrahim's supporters. The whole incident had taken perhaps five minutes, five minutes in which the slashed tiller lines had been temporarily repaired and the frigate drew offshore, steered from her wheel.

"*Attendez votre capitaine!*" snapped Drinkwater to one of the cowering Frenchmen and turned away to discover the extent of Griffiths's injuries.

Tregembo had already loosened the commander's shirt and they found the hole above the heart. Blood issued darkly from the old man's mouth and breathing was accomplished only with an immense effort. Struggling, they propped him up against the breech of a carronade. Rogers came up.

"Is he bad?" Drinkwater nodded. "What course d'you want, Nathaniel?"

"West, steer due west. Get the main topsail on her and then the foretopmast staysail . . . and for God's sake get those bloody Frogs mewed up below."

"There aren't many left after Barnes blew them to hell." Rogers hurried off and checked the course then bellowed for the hands to gather at the foot of the mainmast. Drinkwater turned back to Griffiths. The old man's eyes were wide open and his lips formed the name "Santhonax?"

Drinkwater flicked a glance in the direction of the French captain. He was still slumped in a faint against the bulwarks. Drinkwater jerked his head in the wounded man's direction. "Tregembo, make arrangements to secure yonder fellow when he comes round."

"Does I recognise him as that cap'n we took before, zur?"

Drinkwater nodded wearily. "You do, Tregembo." He called for water but Griffiths only choked on it, feebly waving it aside.

"No good, *annwyl*," he whispered with an effort, "too late for all that . . . done my duty . . ." One of the seamen approached him with a boat cloak found below and they made Griffiths comfortable, but as they moved him he choked on more blood. His eyes were closed again now and the sweat poured from him like water wrung from a sponge.

Nathaniel put an arm round him, hauling him upright to ease the strain on his chest muscles. He felt the final paroxysm as Griffiths choked, drowning on his own blood, felt the will to live finally wither. Griffiths opened his eyes once more. In the darkness they were black holes in the pallor of his face, black holes that gradually lost their intensity and at the end were no more than marks in the gloom.

They recovered Mr. Trussel and his party off Al Wejh that afternoon. By the time Wrinch rejoined them the frigate was well in hand. The Frenchmen had been turned-to securing the gun deck and stowing the loose gear, while the slashed rigging was made good aloft. Trussel cast his eyes about the frigate with gnomish amusement.

"This *is* an improvement, Mr. Drinkwater."

"Indeed, Mr. Trussel," said Drinkwater gravely. "We have paid a heavy price for it by losing the captain."

"I beg your pardon, sir, I had no idea . . ."

"No matter, Mr. Trussel. What about your guns?"

The cloud on the wrinkled face further deepened. "All gone sir, all of my beauties gone, but surely we have some replacements here?"

"No, we are only armed *en flûte*, Mr. Trussel, these carronades and half a dozen main deck guns below. The Frogs had 'em all ashore. But yours, what happened to *Hellebore*'s sixes?"

"Those damned Arab carts fell apart after half a dozen discharges, though we moved 'em up like regular flying artillery." He checked his flight of fancy, remembering the circumstances of his report. "Left my black beauties in the desert, sir, and damned sorry I am for it."

"Very well, Mr. Trussel," Drinkwater lowered his voice, "you will find a bottle of claret in the great cabin. Use it sparingly."

Trussel's eyes gleamed with anticipation. Drinkwater turned his attention to Wrinch. "A moment, Mr. Wrinch, if you please. Forrard there! Hands to the braces! Hard a-starboard, steer nor'west by west!"

"Nor'west by west, aye, aye, sir."

They braced the yards and set more sail, hoisting the topgallants and lowering the forecourse. The frigate slipped through the water with increasing speed. It ought to have given Drinkwater the feeling of keenest triumph. He turned to Wrinch.

"I went to report to Griffiths . . . I'm sorry. What happened?"

"He took a pistol ball in the lungs. He was trying to save me from Santhonax."

"You took this Frenchman then?"

Drinkwater nodded. "Yes, Griffiths shot him and shattered his shoulder. He's very weak but still alive. He chased us in a boat. Boarded us after we had taken the ship. Ben Ibrahim was killed in the scuffle."

"I know, his men told me."

"But what of your part? The plan worked to perfection."

Wrinch managed a wry little laugh. "Well almost, the guns were more terrifying to us than to the enemy in fact, though their reports in the dark confused them. The two sheiks whose horsemen I led had a blood feud with the very man whom Santhonax had brought to protect his immunity at Al Mukhra. When I offered gold, guns and the distraction of yourselves it was more tempting than a pair of thoroughbreds. Although those damned guns cost us a deal of labour, we had them in position without the French knowing. The ride had strained the carts and they flew to pieces, but I doubt, despite Mr. Trussel's excellently contrived lashings, they would have managed much more. My cavalry, however, were superb. You have never seen Arab horsemen, eh? They are fluid, restless as sand itself. The enemy rushed from their miserable tents and the hovels in which they were quartered and we chased them through the thorn scrub . . ." he paused, apparently forgetful of their dead friend, reliving the moment of pure excitement as a man reflecting on a passionate memory. Drinkwater remembered the feeling of panic that had engulfed the men of *Cyclops* when caught on land by enemy cavalry.

"We lost four men, Nathaniel, four men that walk now with Allah in paradise. We killed God knows how many. There will not now be a Frenchman alive in the Wadi Al Mukhra."

There was an alien, pitiless gleam in Wrinch's eye as he described the murder of a defeated enemy as a scouring of the sacred earth of the Hejaz after the defiling of the infidel. It occurred to Drinkwater that Wrinch was a believer in the one true faith. It was Islam and patriotism that kept this curious man in self-imposed exile among the wild horsemen and their strangely civilised brand of barbarity. And as he listened, it occurred to him that his own life was beset by paradoxes and anomalies; brutality and honour, death and duty. As if to emphasise these disturbing contradictions Wrinch ended on a note of compassion: "Do you wish me to attend this Santhonax?"

Drinkwater nodded. "If you please. Would that your skills had arrived early enough to have been of use to Griffiths."

"Death, my dear Nathaniel," said Wrinch, putting his hand familiarly upon Drinkwater's shoulder, "is the price of Admiralty."

CHAPTER SEVENTEEN

A Conspiracy of Circumstances

September–October 1799

Drinkwater stared astern to where Daedalus Reef formed a small blemish on the horizon. He felt empty and emotionless over the loss of Griffiths, aware that the impact would be felt later. They had buried him among the roots of the scrubby grass on the islet, a few yards from the burnt out shell of his brig. During the brief interment several of the hands had wept openly. An odd circumstance that, Drinkwater thought, considering that he himself, who of all the brig's company had been closest to the commander, could feel nothing. Catherine Best had cried too, and it had been Harry Appleby's shoulder that supported her.

Drinkwater sighed. The blemish on the horizon had gone. Griffiths and *Hellebore* had slipped from the present into the past. Such change, abrupt and cruel as it was, nevertheless formed a part of the sea-life. The Lord gave and took away as surely as day followed night, mused Drinkwater as he turned forward and paced the frigate's spacious deck. The wind shifted and you hauled your braces; that was the way of it and now, in the wake of Griffiths came Morris.

It had taken two days to get the stores off Daedalus Reef, two days of hard labour and relentless driving of the hands, of standing the big unfamiliar frigate on and offshore while they rowed the boats, splashed out with casks and bundles and hauled them aboard. The paucity of numbers had been acutely felt and officers had doffed coats and turned-to with the hands.

Morris had taken command by virtue of his seniority. It was an incontravertible fact. Drinkwater did not resent it, though he cursed his ill-luck. It happened to sea-officers daily, but he dearly hoped that at Mocha Morris would return to his own ship.

Drinkwater took consolation in his profession, for there was much to do. As he paced up and down, the sinking sun lit the frigate's starboard side, setting the bright-work gleaming. She was a beautiful ship whose name they had at last discovered to be *Antigone*. She was identical to the *Pomone*, taken by Sir John Warren's frigate squadron in the St. George's Day action of 1794. Although she had only six of her big main-deck guns mounted, her fo'c's'le and quarterdeck carronades were in place, as were a number of swivels mounted along her gangways. With the remnants of the brig's crew it would be as much as they could manage.

Drinkwater clasped his hands behind his back, stretched his shoulders and looked aloft at the pyramids of sail reddening in the sunset. She would undoubtedly be purchased into the service. All they had to do was get her home in one piece. Inevitably his mind slid sideways to the subject of prize money. He should do well from the sale of such a splendid ship. Griffiths would . . . he caught himself. Griffiths was dead. As the sun disappeared and the green flash showed briefly upon the horizon Drinkwater suddenly missed Madoc Griffiths.

That passage to Mocha in the strange ship, so large after the *Hellebore*, had a curious flavour to it. As though the tight-knit community that had so perfectly fitted and worked the brig now rattled in too large a space, subject too suddenly to new influences. The change of command, with the nature of Morris's character common knowledge, served to undermine discipline. Men obeyed their new commander's orders with a perceptible lack of alacrity, displaying for Drinkwater a partiality that was obvious. The presence on board of Santhonax and Bruilhac was also unsettling, although the one was still weak from his wound and the other too terrified to pose a threat.

But it was Morris who exerted the most sinister influence upon them, as was his new prerogative. Two days after leaving the reef the wind had freshened and Rogers had the topgallants taken off. Morris had gone on deck. During the evolution a clew line had snagged in a block, the result of carelessness, of few men doing a heavy job in a hurry. Rogers had roared abuse at the master's mate in the top while the sail flogged, whipping the yard and setting the mainmast a-trembling.

"Take that man's name, Mr. Rogers, by God, I'll have him screaming for his mother yet damn it!" Morris came forward shaking with rage, the stink of rum upon him. "Where's the first lieutenant? Pass word for the first lieutenant!"

A smirking Dalziell brought Drinkwater hurriedly on deck to where Morris was fuming. The rope had been cleared and the topmen were already working out along the yard, securing the sail.

"Sir?" said Drinkwater, touching his hat to the acting commander.

"What the hell have you been doing with these men, Mr. Drinkwater? Eh? The damned lubbers cannot furl a God-damned t'gallant without fouling the gear!"

Morris stared at him. "What d'you say, sir? What d'you say?"

Drinkwater looked at Rogers and then aloft. "I expect they are still unfamiliar with the gear sir, I . . ." He faltered at the gleam of triumph in Morris's eye.

"In that case, Mr. Drinkwater, you may call all hands and exercise them. Aloft there! Let fall! Let fall!" He turned to Rogers. "There sir, set 'em again, sheet 'em home properly then furl 'em again. And this time do it properly, damn your eyes!"

Morris stumped off below and Rogers met Drinkwater's eyes. Rogers too had a temper and was clearly containing himself with difficulty.

"Steady Samuel," said Drinkwater in a low voice. "He *is* the senior lieutenant . . ."

Rogers expelled his breath. "And two weeks bloody seniority is enough to hang a man . . . I know." He turned away and roared at the waisters. "A touch more on that lee t'garn brace you damned lubbers, or you'll all feel the cat scratching . . ."

It was only a trivial thing that happened daily on many ships but it had its sequel below when Drinkwater was summoned to the large cabin lately occupied by Edouard Santhonax. It was now filled with the reek of rum and the person of Morris slumped in a chair, his shirt undone, a glass in his hand.

"I will have everything done properly, Drinkwater. Now I command, and by God, I've waited a long time for it, been cheated out of it by you and your ilk too many times to let go now, and I'll not tolerate one inch of slip-shod seamanship. Try and prejudice my chances of confirmation at Mocha, Drinkwater, and I'll ruin you . . ."

"Sir, if you think I deliberately . . ."

"Shut your mouth and obey orders. Don't try to be clever or to play the innocent for by God you will not thwart me now. If you so much as cross me I'll take a pretty revenge upon you. Now get out!"

Drinkwater left and shunned the company of Appleby and Wrinch that evening while he thought over their circumstances.

"Well, well, my dear Wrinch, a most brilliant little affair by all accounts and the loss of the *Hellebore* more than compensated by the acquisition of so fine a frigate as the *Antigone*. Pity *Daedalus* and *Fox* knocked the brig *Annette* about so much that she's not worth burning for her damned fastenings, eh?" Blankett sniffed, referring to the capture made by the two frigates on their way south of the third vessel in Santhonax's squadron.

"I think the frigate the better bargain, Your Excellency," said Wrinch drily. Admiral Blankett dabbed at his lips then belched discreetly behind the napkin. "A rather ironic outcome, don't you know, considering the *Hellebore* ain't under my command. I suppose I may represent that in this affair she was operating under my orders even though you exceeded your damned authority in sending her."

Wrinch merely smiled while the admiral weighed Wrinch's impertinence against the gains to be made upon the fulcrum of his own dignity. He appeared to make up his mind.

"Well her damned commander's dead and so it seems I owe that popinjay Nelson a favour after all, eh?"

Wrinch nodded. "French power is no longer a factor in the Red Sea, sir."

"What did you make of that damned cove Santhonax?" asked the admiral, recollecting his duty together with the fact that Wrinch had interrogated the French officer.

"He was quite frank. Had no option as we had captured his papers entire. He was to have carried a division to India this year, then Bonaparte invaded Syria and Murad Bey tied down Desaix in Upper Egypt and he was ordered to wait. He decided to careen on the coast of the Hejaz, as we know, and was in the process of collecting his squadron before seeking out Your Excellency. Had we arrived two days later he might have achieved his aim. After all he *had* secured Kosseir and Ball's attempt to dislodge his men failed somewhat abysmally, I believe . . ." Wrinch went no further, aware that the admiral had had the Kosseir affair represented in a somewhat more flattering light.

"Ha h'm. Well we have a handsome prize to show for our labours, eh Strangford?" Wrinch smiled again. The admiral would make a tidy amount in prize money, despite the loss of *Annette*. He would receive one-eighth of the *Antigone*'s value if she were purchased into the Royal Navy.

"We had better get *Antigone* home without delay, eh?" Wrinch inclined his head in agreement. "And we'll disburse a little more than you claim to those Arabs, they're well-known for their rapacity." The admiral grinned boyishly. "You and I to split the difference, what d'you say, eh?"

Wrinch shrugged as though helpless. "Whatever you say, Your Excellency."

"Good." Blankett looked pleased and Wrinch reflected he had good reason. Without stirring from his anchorage at Mocha he had enriched himself considerably by the capture of the *Antigone* and the embezzlement of public money that would be officially disbursed to contingent expenses. Furthermore his subordinates had removed all threat of French expansion to India and, at least from Captain Lidgbird Ball's account of it, his squadron had taken part in a highly creditable bombardment of Kosseir. That this had been rendered significant more by the capture of Santhonax and his ship than the six thousand rounds of shot picked up by the French upon the foreshore was of no consequence to the admiral. While all this excitement had been going on he had been enjoying the voluptuous pleasure of two willing women. All in all Blankett's circumstances were most satisfactory.

"Whom will you appoint to command the prize home, sir?" enquired Wrinch.

The admiral screwed his face up. "Well there's young what's his name on the Bombay station to be given a step in rank, but I think one of my own officers . . . er, Grace, the commander of *Hotspur* could be posted into the ship; but ain't she only *en flûte?*"

Wrinch nodded, "Only six main-deck guns mounted, sir."

"Hmmm, I doubt Grace'd thank me if I posted him into a sitting duck for a Frog cruiser . . ." Blankett rubbed his chin which rasped in the still, hot air. "No, we'll give a deserving lieutenant a step to commander. If he loses the prize on the way home then there's one less indigent on the navy list. Now let me see . . ."

"Surely the honour should go to the officer whose exertions secured the prize? Isn't that the tradition?"

Blankett waved the assumption aside. "Well 'tis a tradition, to be sure, but sometimes a little done for one's friends . . . you know well enough, Strangford."

"True sir, but I thought *myself*," Wrinch laid a little emphasis on the pronoun to indicate his was a position of some influence, "that the officer most deserving was Drinkwater.

His efforts have been indefatigable." Wrinch met the eyes of the admiral. "I am sure you agree with me, sir, now that Griffiths is dead, that you will see eye to eye in the matter." Wrinch's voice had an edge to it which changed abruptly to a tone of complicit bonhomie, "As of course we have over so much lately: your accommodation at my house with its attendant comforts, the matter of the disbursement to my Arab friends at Al Wejh . . ." He trailed off, allowing the significance of his meaning to sink in.

But Blankett was unabashed and shrugged urbanely. "Perhaps Strangford, but Mr. Morris is a pressing candidate, he has some clout with their Lordships though why he is only a lieutenant I cannot guess. I shall consult Ball upon the matter. At all events I am obliged to hold an enquiry into the loss of the *Hellebore*, the more now that their Lordships are screaming out for her speedy return home."

The court was convened aboard *Leopard* on 1st October 1799 under the chairmanship of the rear-admiral. The members of the court were Captain Surridge of the *Leopard*, Ball and Stuart of *Daedalus* and *Fox*, and Commander Grace of the *Hotspur*, the sloop that had brought Morris out from England.

In his capacity as British consular agent Strangford Wrinch, having some formal knowledge of the law, sat as judge advocate. He wore European clothes for the purpose.

In the absence of her commander, Drinkwater was called first. His deposition as to the brig's loss was read out. In it he outlined his own misgivings about the accuracy of their assumed position. It was followed by that of Mr. Lestock, a cautiously worded and prolix document which said a great deal about Mr. Lestock's character and little in favour of his abilities. It called forth a *sotto voce* comment from the admiral that the master seemed very like his "damned namesake", referring to an Admiral Lestock who had failed to support his principal in battle half a century earlier.

Rogers's statement was then read out to the court who were by this time finding the heat in *Leopard*'s cabin excessive, packed as it was by so many officers in blue broadcloth coats. Rogers was called to the stand.

"Well, Mr., er . . ."

"Rogers, sir."

". . . Rogers," said the admiral, whose wig was awry above his florid face, "this ain't a hanging offence but it does seem that you presumed a great deal, eh?" On either side of him three post-captains and the commander nodded sagely, as if men of their eminence never made errors of judgement.

"It was hardly 'a misfortune' that breakers turned out to be over a reef, sir, is it, eh? Stap me, where else d'you expect to find 'em? Had you hove-to and found two hundred fathoms and made yourself the laughing stock of the whole damned squadron you could hardly have been blamed. It would certainly have made more sense."

Drinkwater watched the colour mount to Rogers's face and felt sorry for him. He knew the loss of the brig had been acutely felt by Rogers. It had tempered his fiery self-conceit into an altogether different metal. Blankett whispered to the officers on either side of him. Drinkwater noted Commander Grace seemed to be making a point and looking in his direction. Blankett passed a napkin across his streaming face and addressed the court.

"Very well gentlemen, I see there are mitigating factors. Captain Grace reminds me of Mr. Drinkwater's observations about refraction and adds he has been making a study of the phenomena. In the circumstances the court take cognizance of these factors, though these do not relate directly to Mr., er, er the lieutenant's conduct on the night in question." He looked round at his fellow judges and they each nodded agreement.

"It is the opinion of this court of enquiry that the loss of His Britannic Majesty's Brig-of-War *Hellebore* upon the night of 19th August last was due to circumstances of misadventure. But it wishes to record a motion of censure upon Lieutenant . . ."

"Rogers," put in Wrinch helpfully.

"Rogers, as to the degree of care he employs while in charge of a watch aboard one of His Majesty's ships of war." The sweat was pouring down Blankett's face and he wiped it solemnly. "That I think concludes our business."

The admiral rose heavily and withdrew as the court broke up. Drinkwater found himself approached by Grace who wished to see his figures on refraction while Rogers hovered uncomfortably. When Grace had been satisfied Drinkwater turned to Rogers. "Well Sam, 'twasn't too bad, eh?"

"Is that it? Does that mean there will be no formal court-martial?"

"I think not. Griffiths is dead and the navigation of the Red Sea intricate enough to mollify this court. By the time the admiral's secretary has dressed up the minutes of these proceedings for the consumption of a London quill-pusher, and by the time it takes for the mills of Admiralty to grind, I wager you'll not hear another word about it."

They went out into the blinding sunshine of the quarterdeck to bid Wrinch farewell.

"I doubt we will meet again, Nathaniel," said Wrinch, extending his hand which emerged from an over lavish profusion of cuff extending from a sober black sleeve. "Now that the matter of the brig's loss is concluded Blankett will be anxious to have you on your way. I have done you a little service. I think by sunset you will have an epaulette." Wrinch smiled while Drinkwater stammered his thanks. "Do not mention it, my dear fellow. God go with you and do you mind that sot Morris, there's no love for him in the squadron and I think he'll accompany you home."

They watched him descend into the admiral's barge and were on the point of calling their own boat when a midshipman approached Drinkwater.

"The admiral desires that you attend him in the cabin, sir."

Drinkwater returned to the admiral's presence. The green baize covered table was swept clear of papers and a bottle and glass had replaced them. The admiral sat in his shirt-sleeves with his stock loosened.

"Ah, Mr. er, Mr. . . ."

"Drinkwater, sir."

"Ah, yes, quite so. Prefer wine myself," chuckled the admiral pouring himself a glass. He swallowed half of it and looked up. "The matter of the *Antigone*. I have it in mind to promote you, subject of course to their lordships' ratification. You will receive your commission and your orders to proceed without delay to Spithead. You will also carry my dispatches. Have the goodness to send an officer an hour before sunset. I understand the frigate is adequately supplied?"

Drinkwater expressed his gratitude. "As to provisions, sir, she was wanting only her guns when we took her. The French had salted a quantity of mutton looted from the Arabs and we were able to salvage much from the *Hellebore*."

"Good, good. Now, Mr., er, Mr. Drinkwater, as to the conduct of the prize, I understand that Commander Griffiths had no prize money arrangements with Stuart or Ball, is that so?" Blankett's voice was suddenly confidential.

"I believe that to be the case, sir."

"Good. Well you stand to profit from the venture if you

bring her home in one piece." The admiral fixed Drinkwater with a steely eye.

"I think your eighth will be safe, sir," he volunteered, forming the shrewd and accurate suspicion that the rear-admiral had some designs on Griffiths's share of the head money on the action with *La Torride* as well as his portion of the condemned value of the *Antigone*. Blankett scratched his head beneath his wig.

"You will need an additional officer; best keep that fellow Morris with you. Ball don't want him aboard *Daedalus*. Damned fellow's got some petticoat influence but Ball says he's a sodomite. I'll send the bugger home before I have to hang him."

Drinkwater's mouth fell open. It was clear Blankett would not want Morris left on his hands, even that he knew all about him to the point of remembering his name.

"That will do, Mr., er . . . yes that will do, now be damned sure you look after that frigate. Use caution in the Soundings, I don't want my prize money ending up as firewood in some poxy Cornish wrecker's hovel."

Drinkwater withdrew, mixed feelings raging within him. He stopped outside the admiral's cabin to trim his hat. "Commander Nathaniel Drinkwater," he muttered experimentally beneath his breath. Then he flushed as the rigid marine sentry, bull-necked and bright red in the heat, coughed discreetly. He strode out onto *Leopard*'s quarterdeck.

"Nothing serious I hope?" asked Rogers anxiously, still smarting over the censuring of the court. Drinkwater smiled.

"Depends on your point of view, Samuel."

"I'm sorry, I don't follow."

"That venal old reprobate," Drinkwater checked his wild exuberance at having his step in rank at last, "His Excellency

Rear-Admiral John Blankett has had the goodness to promote me to commander."

"Well I'm damned! I mean, damn it, congratulations, Mr. Drinkwater."

"That's very decent of you, Samuel. But don't let us count our chickens just yet. This news will poison Morris."

"Isn't he to return to *Daedalus* . . . sir?"

"No, I regret he is not. By a wonderful irony he is to be my first lieutenant. I'm sorry it ain't you, Samuel, but there we are."

They hailed their boat, resolving to remain silent upon the matter until Drinkwater had the commission in his hand and could read himself in.

He waited impatiently for the interminable afternoon to draw to a close. At two bells in the first dog watch he quietly desired Rogers to send a boat to *Leopard* for their orders. Rogers sent Mr. Dalziell.

Drinkwater sat in his cabin and took out his journal and began to write. *It was with great satisfaction that I attended the R.Ad this morning and was acquainted with the fact that I am to be made Master and Commander. This in my thirty-sixth year, after twenty years sea service. This step in rank removes many apprehensions and vain imaginings from my mind.* He paused then added: *I thank God for it.*

It was both pious and pompous but he felt his moment of vanity, though it might earn a rebuke from Elizabeth, could be allowed expression in the privacy of his journal. He fell into a brown study dreaming of home.

Aboard *Leopard* Mr. Dalziell waited in the admiral's secretary's cabin while that worthy, a man named Wishart, inscribed with painful slowness upon a packet.

"There are your orders." He carefully handed over a sealed

bundle and being a proper man insisted Dalziell signed the receipt before receiving a second. "And there are the admiral's dispatches. See that your commander puts them in a secure place." Again they performed the ritual of signature and exchange. "And now," said Mr. Wishart drawing a paper towards him, "the admiral has a dreadful memory for names, what is the name of your senior lieutenant, eh?"

He dipped his pen and held it expectantly. "Morris, sir, Mr. Augustus Morris, related by marriage to the Earl of Dungarth, not unknown to the Earl of Sandwich sir," Dalziell wheedled ingratiatingly.

"Is that so? In that case," said Mr. Wishart, sprinkling sand over the recipient's name, "he seems admirably fitted to sail so fine a frigate home. Here is Mr. Morris's commission as Commander."

CHAPTER EIGHTEEN

Morris

October 1799

Drinkwater was not listening to the garbled words of divine service as Morris mumbled his way through them. Morris's voice had not the resonant conviction of Griffiths's splendid diction and Drinkwater's loathing of Morris's too-obvious feet of clay made parody of the Book of Common Prayer. Instead Drinkwater looked forward, beyond the semi-circle of commissioned and warrant officers in full uniform with their left hands upon their sword hilts and cocked hats beneath their elbows, at the hands massed in the waist. There were about eighty men left to take the big frigate home, not many to work her, not enough to fight her.

But it was not the quality of the number that concerned Drinkwater. His acute senses were tuned to their mood, and in the present calm as the Indian Ocean lay quiet waiting for the first breath of the north-east monsoon, there was an ugliness about it. It was as though the expectant oiliness of the sea exerted some influence upon the minds of the men like that of the moon upon the sea itself.

Drinkwater discarded the over-ripe metaphor, aware that his own chronic disappointment was souring him. Their hur-

ried departure from Mocha, the stunned disbelief as he had
stood as he did now and listened to Morris confidently reading his commission to the ship's company had triggered his
depression and sent him miserable to his cabin, to grieve
over his own ill-fortune and, at last, the loss of Griffiths.

In reality that onset of depression had saved him from
rashness. Later Rogers had accosted him over the matter,
only to reveal that he had himself sent Mr. Dalziell to obtain
the commission. Now Rogers, already shaken in his confidence over the loss of the brig and the censure of the admiral, had retreated into his own resentment. With the two
lieutenants nursing their private grievances Morris had tri-
umphed and *Antigone* was out of the Gulf of Aden before
Drinkwater cast aside his "blue devils" and resolved to
make the best of things.

But he knew it was already too late. While the officers
had sulked the men had been scourged. Morris flogged savagely for every small offence that was brought to his notice
by his toadies. Among these was a man named Rattray,
Morris's servant sent over from *Daedalus,* a thin seedy man
who padded silently about the ship and swiftly became
known, predictably, as "the Rat." There was Dalziell, of
course, promoted acting lieutenant by Morris, who terrorised the hands to Drinkwater's fury; and there was Lestock, whose fussing temperament seemed seduced by
Morris's brand of command by terror. It was these men who
formed the Praetorian Guard round their new commander, a
little coterie of self-seekers and survivors who wielded enormous influence and filled the punishment book with trivial
entries.

Drinkwater's mouth set in a hard line as he thought of the
increased number of times he had had to make entries in that
book. The binding no longer cracked as it had done when

Griffiths commanded them. Of course the entries read well. Insolence for a man laughing too loudly when the captain was on deck; Defiling the Deck for a man who spilled his mess kid by accident; Improper Conduct when a rope was untidily belayed on the fife-rails, all trivial matters ending up with the culprit being seized to the gratings.

Morris closed the Prayer Book with a snap, recalling Drinkwater to his duty.

"On hats!" Routinely Drinkwater touched his hat brim as Morris went below.

"Bosun! Pipe the hands to dinner!" He turned away to find Rattray alongside him, as though he had been there all the time, silently listening to Drinkwater's thoughts.

"Cap'n's compliments, sir, and he'd be obleeged if you'd join him for dinner at four bells."

Drinkwater searched the man's face for some reason for this unexpected courtesy. He found nothing except a pair of shifty eyes and replied. "Very well. My thanks to the captain."

He looked forward again to see Appleby and Catherine Best crossing the deck. They had become very close since Morris took command and Drinkwater thought that the presence of the woman even exerted some restraining influence upon Morris himself. Drinkwater uncovered to her. "Mornin' Mistress Best. I see Mr. Wrinch's promise of something more suitable to wear was no vain boast."

Catherine smiled at him, a shy kind of happiness lighting her eyes while her right hand swirled the skirt of Arab cotton in a small coquettish movement.

"Indeed, Mr. Drinkwater, it was not." Drinkwater looked at Appleby, who was blushing furiously. He smiled, touched his hat again and turned to the quartermaster.

"Well bless my soul," he muttered to himself, then, in a

louder tone, "call me if there's any wind." The quartermaster acknowledged the first lieutenant and Drinkwater went below to change his shirt.

The meal, at which no others were present, was conducted in silence. Rattray padded behind their chairs and even with the after sashes lowered the air in the large cabin was stale and hot. When the dishes were cleared away a bottle of port was decanted in Santhonax's personal crystal and, Drinkwater noticed, circulation was slow. The decanter did duty at Morris's glass three times before being shoved reluctantly in his direction. Drinkwater drank sparingly, aware that Morris's appetite was gross.

"Have you seen that?" Morris pointed to where, half hidden behind the cabin door a woman's portrait hung on the white bulkhead. Already his voice was slurred. "I presume it to be the Frog's whore." Drinkwater found the portrait amazing. Hortense's grey eyes stared out of the canvas, her long neck bared and her flaming hair piled up above her head, wound with pearls. A wisp of gauze covered the swell of her breasts. He remembered the woman in the cabin of *Kestrel* and stumbling on the beach at Criel where they had let her go free. He found the portrait disquieting and turned back to Morris. The man was watching him from beneath his hooded eyelids.

"She's his wife," said Drinkwater, returning Morris's stare.

"And what of Appleby's whore, Nathaniel? Is she what I am told she is, a convict?"

It was pointless to deny it, but then it was unnecessary to confirm it. "I believe she has redeemed herself by her services to the ship. As to her status, I think you are mistaken."

Morris waved aside Drinkwater's compassion, to him the

pompous assertion of a liberal. "Pah! She is Appleby's whore," repeated Morris, slumping back into his chair.

Drinkwater shrugged, aware that Morris was wary, beating about the bush of his intention in asking Drinkwater to dine. He wished they might reach a truce, unaware that Morris had left him upon the beach at Kosseir. Their enmity aboard *Cyclops* was long past, they were grown men now. Whatever Morris's private desires were, they were not overt.

"You are wondering why I have asked you to dine with me, eh? You, who crossed me years ago, who saw to it that I was dismissed out of *Cyclops* . . ."

"I did no such thing, sir."

"Don't haze me, damn you!" Morris restrained himself and Drinkwater was increasingly worried about the reason for this cosy chat. Drinkwater had played a small part in Morris's disgrace, which had largely been accomplished by his own character. The captain of the frigate was long dead; the first lieutenant, now Lord Dungarth, beyond Morris's vengeance. But Drinkwater was again at his mercy and Morris had intended his ruin, for he had nursed a longing for revenge for twenty years; twenty years that had twisted rejected desire into an obsession.

The pure, vindictive hatred that had made Morris drop the fainting Drinkwater on the beach at Kosseir had been thwarted in the latter's survival, but was now complicated by his reliance on the man he had tried to kill.

"I have my own command now, Drinkwater," he said, his mouth slack, his chin on his chest, a sinister cartoon by Rowlandson. "Do anything to prejudice me again and I'll see you in hell . . ."

"I shall do my duty, sir," said Drinkwater cautiously, but too primly for Morris's liking.

"Aye, by God you will!" Spittle shot from Morris's mouth. "Then why should you suppose . . ."

"Because there is a damned rumour persisting in this ship that I have the swab," he gestured at the damaged epaulette on his shoulders that he had rifled from Griffiths's belongings, "that should have gone to you." It was not the only reason but one on which Morris might draw a reaction from Drinkwater whom he now watched closely, his mind concentrated by alcohol on the focus of his obsession.

But Drinkwater did not perceive this, merely saw the matter as something to be raised between them, another ghost to be laid. "I *was* given to understand Admiral Blankett desired I should command the prize, certainly. Whatever made him change his mind is no longer any concern of mine." He paused, sitting up, hoping to terminate the interview. "But in the meantime I shall do my duty as first lieutenant as I did for Commander Griffiths, sir." Then he added, irritated at being catechised: "Unless you have a notion to promote Mr. Dalziell over my head."

"What the hell d'you mean by that?" flared Morris, and Drinkwater sensed he had touched a nerve. Dalziell. The relative, quiescent of late. A catamite? Drinkwater looked sharply at Morris. The commander's glare was unchanged but a sheen of sweat had erupted across his face.

All was suddenly clear to Drinkwater. Morris had obtained his command at last. Unable to earn it by his own merits, a twist of fate had delivered it unexpectedly into his lap. A further helix in that turn of circumstances had made Drinkwater both his unwitting benefactor and first lieutenant on whose abilities he must rely to take advantage of this new opportunity. He would not sacrifice the possibility of a post-captaincy even for revenge on Drinkwater, but Drinkwater knew of his past and might know of his present.

Morris, long driven by vengeance, could not imagine another dismissing such an opportunity with contempt. Even a sanctimonious liberal like Drinkwater. And Morris was guilty of unnatural crimes specifically proscribed by the Articles of War.

But this potential nemesis was of small apparent consolation to Nathaniel. He merely found it odd that that usurped tangle of gold wire could tame so disturbed a spirit as Augustus Morris's.

"It was a poor jest, sir. I am sure you will know how to keep Mr. Dalziell in his proper place." Drinkwater rose. It had not been a deliberate innuendo but Morris continued to stare suspiciously at him. "Thank you for the courtesy of your invitation." He turned for the door, his eye falling on the picture of Hortense. "By the way sir, the surgeon tells me Santhonax would benefit from some fresh air. May I have permission to exercise him on deck tomorrow?"

"Solicitude for prisoners, eh?" slurred Morris, his eyes clouding, turning inwards. "Do as you see fit . . ." He dismissed Drinkwater with a flick of his wrist, then reached for the decanter. Alone, he saw, with the perception of the drunk, the pair of level grey eyes staring at him from the bulkhead. They seemed to accuse him with the whole mess of his life. Viciously his hand found a fork left on the table by the careless Rattray. With sudden venom he flung it at the canvas. The tines vibrated in the creamy shoulder, reminding Morris of the past, good old days when the senior midshipmen drove a fork into a deck beam as a signal to send their juniors to bed while they "sported." The euphemism covered many sins. Things had changed in His Majesty's navy since the mutinies of 1797. Now canting bastards like Drinkwater with their liberal ideas were ruining the Service, God damn them. He flung his head back and roared, "Rattray!"

"Sir?"

"Pass word for Mr. Dalziell."

Drinkwater drew the air into his lungs. After the calm the strengthening north-easter was like champagne. Above his head the watch had just taken in the royals and were descending via the backstays. Those to windward were taut and harping gently as a patter of spray came over the windward rail. He walked over to the binnacle. "Steer small now, a good course will bring us home the sooner."

He resumed his pacing, free of the effects of his bruising and the cauterised cut on his leg that would not even leave a scar worth mentioning. He passed along the squat black breeches of the quarterdeck carronades, as near content as his circumstances would permit. After the dinner with Morris he sensed an easing of tension between them, aware that his own duties preoccupied him while Morris, isolated in command, would brood in his cabin. Despite the promotion of Dalziell to acting lieutenant, Drinkwater had not relinquished his watch. He might have availed himself of big-ship tradition, had not the notion with so small a crew been a piece of conceit that ran contrary to his nature. In Dalziell's abilities he had no confidence whatsoever, regarding his elevation as a shameful abuse of the system, a blatant piece of influence that he thought unlikely to last long after their return home. For himself he kept the privacy of his morning and evening watches while the poor devils forward were compelled to work watch and watch. It could not be helped. It was the way of the world and the naval service in particular.

Unfamiliar figures emerged on deck and Drinkwater remembered his own orders. Gaston Bruilhac assisted the tall figure of Edouard Santhonax whose arm was still slung beneath his coat. The hands idled curiously as Santhonax cast his eyes aloft, noting the set of the sails.

"Good mornin', sir." Drinkwater touched his hat out of formal courtesy. Long enmity had bred a respect for the Frenchman and Drinkwater hoped his presence as a prisoner satisfied the shade of Madoc Griffiths.

"Good morning, Boireleau . . ." He winced, adjusting himself against the motion of the ship. "Perhaps I should call you Drinkwater, now the ship is yours."

"I should be honoured, sir. She is a fine ship."

"That is a compliment, yes?"

"It was intended so, sir, and the only one I can offer, under the circumstances."

Santhonax narrowed his eyes. "You do not have many men to work her."

"Sufficient, sir."

"You are pleased with your success, *hein?*" He bit his lip as a wave of pain swept over him, "pleased that I am your prisoner?"

"*C'est la guerre,* sir, the fortune of war. I would rather Griffiths lived, you have the advantage over him there."

"He saved your life." Santhonax looked down at his shoulder.

"But you are not dead, Capitaine."

Santhonax smiled. "He intended to kill me."

"He was intent upon revenge."

"Revenge? *Pourquoi?*"

"Major Brown," Drinkwater said icily, "rotting on a gibbet over the guns of Kijkduin."

Santhonax frowned. "Ah, the English spy we caught . . ." Drinkwater remembered the jolly brevet-major Santhonax had captured in Holland. He and Griffiths had been friends, brothers-in-arms.

Santhonax shrugged. "Most assuredly, Lieutenant, we are all of us mortal. My wife has not yet forgiven you this . . ." His finger reached up and indicated the disfigurement of his face. "I doubt she ever will."

For a moment it occurred to Drinkwater to roll up his sleeve and reveal the twisted flesh of his own right arm, but the childishness of such an action suddenly struck him. He remained silent.

"You are bound for England, yes?" Santhonax went on. Drinkwater nodded. "It is a long way yet, eh?" Santhonax turned and began to pace the deck, leaning on Bruilhac's shoulder.

"Mr. Drinkwater!" Morris's voice cut across the quarterdeck as he emerged from the companionway.

"Mornin' sir," Drinkwater uncovered again.

"Mr. Drinkwater, hands are to witness punishment at four bells."

"Punishment, sir? Nothing has been reported to me . . ."

"Insolence, Mr. Drinkwater, insolence was reported to me at six bells in the first watch, Mr. Dalziell's watch."

"And the offender sir?"

"Your lackey, Drinkwater," said Morris with evident pleasure, "Tregembo."

Drinkwater forced himself to watch Tregembo's face. The eyes were tight shut and the teeth bit into the leather pad that prevented the Cornishman from biting through his own tongue as each stroke of the cat made him flinch. At the twelfth stripe the bosun's mates changed. The second man ran the bloody tails of the cat through his hand as he braced his feet. He hesitated.

"Lay on there, damn you!" Morris snapped and Drinkwater sensed the wave of resentment that ran through the people assembled in the waist. Tregembo's "insolence," Drinkwater had learned in the roundabout way that a good first lieutenant might determine the true course of events, had consisted of no more than being last back on deck after working aloft during Dalziell's watch. When accused of idleness Tregembo had mumbled that one must always be last on deck and it was usually the first aloft who had been working on the yard-arm.

For this piece of logic Tregembo was now being flayed. The bosun's mates changed again. Drinkwater recollected Dalziell's earlier attempt to have Tregembo flogged and the smirk on the young man's face fully confirmed his present satisfaction. Morris too had a reason for flogging Tregembo. The Cornishman had been a witness to his disgrace aboard *Cyclops,* indeed Tregembo had had a hand in the disappearance one night of one of Morris's cabal.

Drinkwater was pleased to note that Lieutenant Rogers appeared most unhappy over an issue that previously might have pleased him, while Quilhampton, Appleby and the rest stood mutely averting their eyes. At the conclusion of the third dozen Tregembo was cut down. Drinkwater dismissed the hands in a dispassionate voice.

That evening it fell calm again, the sea smooth on its surface with the ship rolling on a lazy swell. The sun had set blood-red, leaving an after glow of scarlet reaching almost to the zenith, through which the cold pin pricks of stars were beginning to break. Venus blazed above Africa eighty leagues to the west. Drinkwater paced the deck, an hour and a half of his watch to go. His uniform coat stuck to his back, a prickling example of Morris's tyranny, for the commander had refused to allow his officers to appear on the quarterdeck in their shirt-sleeves as they had done under Griffiths.

Already shadows were deepening about the deck. The second dog-watch idled about restlessly. Drinkwater picked up the quadrant Quilhampton had brought up.

"Ready, Mr. Q?"

"All ready, sir," replied the midshipman, squatting down on the deck next to the chronometer box and jamming the slate between his crossed knees in the position he had found most suitable, minus one hand, for jotting down the first lieutenant's observations. Drinkwater smiled at the small, crouched figure. The boy frowned in concentration as he watched the second hand jerk round, the slate pencil poised in his only fist.

"Very well then, Venus first." Drinkwater set the index to zero and caught the planet in the mirrors, twisting his wrist and rotating the instrument about its index. His long fingers twiddled the vernier screw and he settled the planet's disc precisely on the horizon, his fingers turning slowly as he followed the mensurable descent of it, rocking the whole so that the disc oscillated on the tangent of the horizon. "On!"

Quilhampton noted the time as Drinkwater read the altitude off the arc and called the figures to the midshipman. Quilhampton dutifully repeated them.

Drinkwater took a second observation of Venus then crossed the deck. "Canopus next!"

"Get up, brat!" Drinkwater turned at the intrusion. Morris stood over the midshipman who, in his concentration, had not seen the commander arrive on the quarterdeck. "Have you never been taught respect, you damned whoreson?"

Quilhampton put out his left arm to push himself to his feet, forgetting he had no hand. The still soft stump gave under him and he slipped onto his knees, the colour draining from his face. "I, I'm sorry sir, I was watching the chronometer . . ." Morris's foot came back and sent the chronometer box spinning across the deck. It caught against a ring bolt, tipped and the glass shattered.

Drinkwater swiftly crossed the deck. "Turn a glass," he snapped at the quartermaster by the binnacle. Perhaps there was not too much damage and any stopping of the timepiece might be allowed for, "then go below and get the precise time from Mr. Appleby's hunter." Morris had begun to rail at the terrified midshipman. It was clear that he was drunk.

"I think, sir," intervened Drinkwater, "that you are mistaken in supposing Mr. Quilhampton intended any disrespect. The loss of his hand necessitates that he . . ."

"Be silent, Mr. Drinkwater," slurred Morris, "and have this scum at the foremasthead at once."

Drinkwater took one look at the swaying figure of Morris. "Up you go, Mr. Q," he said quietly, lowering the quadrant into its case. Quilhampton's eyes were filling with tears. Drinkwater jerked his head imperceptibly and the boy turned forward. Drinkwater bent over the chronometer case.

"Mr. Drinkwater! I am addressing you!" Drinkwater picked up the case.

"Sir?" He was looking down at the bent gimbals. The second hand no longer moved. "I don't expect that sort of disrespect on my quarterdeck . . ." Morris was very drunk. It was clear that he had not yet realised what it was he had kicked across the deck.

"I doubt that it will occur again, sir," said Drinkwater, looking down at the ruined chronometer.

"It had better bloody not." Suddenly Morris heaved, swallowed and staggered below. Darkness stole over the ship. The time to take stellar observations had passed. Drinkwater did not know precisely where they were and, in truth, he did not greatly care.

"Don't worry, Mr. Drinkwater," said Lestock, apparently pleased at the destruction of the timepiece. "Your theoretical navigation lost us a brig and the captain has had the sense to deprive you of your toy before you cause more damage."

"Go to the devil, you addle-brained old fool!" snapped Drinkwater.

They got Quilhampton down at dawn, calling the surgeon to roll him in warmed blankets and chafe him with spirits. The inside of his left elbow was raw from where the laborious climb had caused him to use it as a hook. At the conclusion of his watch Drinkwater sought out the surgeon and found him still attending the boy in the company of Catherine Best.

"How is he?"

"He'll live, but he's chilled to the marrow and cramped."

"Aye the damned wind got up during the middle watch and it's already half a gale. This is the monsoon all right."

"Damn your monsoon, Nat, have we to put up with that vicious bastard aft all the way home? Oh, don't worry about Catherine," he added, seeing Drinkwater's covert glance at the woman, "she well knows all my sentiments on Mister festering Morris."

"You know the answer to your own question, Harry."

"So it's shorten canvas and ride out the gale even if it lasts another three or four months, eh?"

"Your metaphor is good enough."

"Pity he can't be ill like poor old Griffiths, then he could let you run the blasted ship."

"I doubt he would allow that," smiled Drinkwater resignedly.

"Well if he goes on swilling rum at the present rate he'll either destroy his intestines or drink us out of the damned stuff and be raving from delirium tremens!" Appleby stood up as Quilhampton opened his eyes. "Then you would have to take over, eh?"

"That talk from another I would take as sedition, Harry," said Drinkwater seriously. "I beg you do not be so free with your opinions."

"Bah!" said Appleby contemptuously while Catherine Best gave both the men an odd look.

CHAPTER NINETEEN

A Woman's Touch

October–November 1799

Appleby regarded his new patient with distaste. Commander Morris lay exhausted in his cot, the sweat pouring from him, the seat lid of his cabin commode lifted and a bucket swilling with vomit by his side. Appleby moved nearer the open stern window for some fresh air. *Antigone* slipped south, her clean hull slicing the blue waters of the Indian Ocean, her towering pyramids of canvas expanding laterally as studding sails increased the speed. Beneath her elegant bowsprit and white figurehead the bottlenosed dolphins leapt and cavorted, effortlessly outstripping the ship as she threw up scores of flying fish on either hand. October was passing to November and the high summer of the southern hemisphere.

The hiss of the sea, upwelling green and white from under the frigate's plunging stern, the creak of the rudder chains and tiller ropes a deck below and the chasing seas seemed a cleansing antidote to the stink of the cabin. Appleby turned back into it.

"The diaphoresis is very severe, sir, and the flux abnormal. How many times did you purge yourself during the night?"

"Don't bandy your medical quackery here Appleby, I was

up shitting most of the night and when I was not doing that I was puking my guts into that bucket. I tell you someone is poisoning me!"

"Come, come, sir. Don't be ridiculous. These are not the symptoms of poison. Where would one obtain poison on a ship? My chest is locked and I wear the keys, here," he jingled the bunch on his fob.

"Appleby, you damned fool, you can poison a man . . ."

"Sir," cut in Appleby sharply, "I assure you that you are *not* being poisoned. Such a notion is preposterous. You are exhibiting symptoms of chronic gastritis. Your dependence upon alcohol has ulcerated the mucous membrane of the stomach as a result of which you are unable to retain nourishment in your belly. The natural reaction of the body is to void itself. If you do not trust my diagnosis sir, I would be only too happy to transfer to another ship at the Cape. In the meantime I shall send Tyson in to attend you and clean up some of this mess. Good morning."

Appleby left the commander to attend to Santhonax. His wound was healing badly, a continuing process of exfoliation preventing the tissues from knitting properly. An easy familiarity had developed between the Frenchman and the surgeon as commonly exists between a man and his physician.

"Where did you learn to speak English, sir?" asked Appleby, removing the dressing.

"I was the son of a half-English mother, Mr. Appleby, the daughter of a wild-goose Englishman who supported King James III."

"Ah, the Old Pretender, eh?" said Appleby wryly, "but you are not so partial to kings since the Revolution?"

"They are not noted for their gratitude to even their most loyal adherents."

"We notice that in King George's navy."

"Treason, Mr. Appleby?"

"Truth, Captain Santhonax."

"You would make a most excellent revolutionary."

"Perhaps, if the material was worth the saving, but I doubt even your brand will materially alter this tired old world. Were you not yourself about to enslave the Hindoos?"

Santhonax smiled, a bleak, wolfish smile. "Had that damned combination of Drinkwater and Griffiths not been at my tail I might have succeeded."

"You forget, captain, I too was on *Kestrel* . . ."

"*Diable,* I had forgot . . . yes, it was you sutured my face. It is a strange coincidence, is it not, that we should find ourselves fighting a private war?"

Appleby finished binding the new dressing over a clean pledget. "Griffiths called it proof of Providence, Captain. What would your new religion of Reason call it?"

"Much the same, Mr. Appleby . . . thank you."

"You will be well enough soon. I think the exfoliation almost complete. It will be a whole man we return to the hulks at Portsmouth."

"You have yet to get your stolen vessel past Ile de France, Appleby. Perhaps it may yet be me who will be visiting you."

"Well what *is* the matter with him?" asked Drinkwater, straightening up from the chart spread on the gunroom table, "he tells me he is of the opinion that he is being poisoned. Damn it, I think he half thought I might have instigated it! What Morris surmises he believes, God help us all, and if there is a shred of truth behind such an apparently monstrous allegation . . ."

"Oh for the love of heaven don't you start, Nat. Permit me the luxury of knowing my own business yet. You would take exception to my advice upon the reduction of altitudes. I tell you the man is suffering from alcohol induced gastritis."

"Very well, Harry, I trust your judgement." Drinkwater cut short the long dissertation that he knew would follow once Appleby was allowed to start expanding on Morris's symptoms.

Rattray scratched at the gunroom door. "Cap'n's compliments, Mr. Drinkwater, and would you join him in the cabin." Drinkwater cast a significant glance at the surgeon, picked up his hat and followed "the Rat."

Drinkwater bridled at the stench in the cabin. Morris looked ghastly, weak and pale, his face covered with perspiration, his cot sheets twisted. He spoke with the economy of effort.

"Would you poison me, Drinkwater?" The man was clearly desperate.

"Certainly not!" Drinkwater's outrage was unfeigned. He recollected himself. Whatever Morris was, he was a sick man now. "Please rest assured that the surgeon is quite confident that you are suffering from a gastric disorder, sir. I have no doubt that if you modify your diet, sir . . ."

"Get out, Drinkwater, get out . . . Rattray! Where the devil is that blagskite?"

As he left Drinkwater noticed the tear in the portrait of Hortense.

The bottle Rattray brought to Drinkwater's cabin that evening for him to take with his biscuits in the gunroom was a surprise. Drinkwater removed the cork and sniffed suspiciously. He was alone in the room, Rogers having turned in and Appleby gone to change Santhonax's dressing. He poured the Oporto that had arrived, uncharacteristically, with the captain's compliments and held the glass against the light of the lantern. He sniffed it then, shrugging, he sipped.

If it was supposed that this was poisoned wine, Drinkwater mused, then it was indeed nonsense and Morris's generosity was but a manifestation of his phobia. He finished the glass and felt nothing more than a comfortable warmth radiating in his guts. Dismissing the matter he sat down, pulled his stores ledger towards him and unsnapped the ink-well. Meyrick brought him a new quill from his cabin and he dismissed the messman for the night and stretched his legs.

The water biscuits were in quite good condition, he thought, picking up a third. He settled to his work. And poured a second glass of wine.

Dawn found Nathaniel Drinkwater violently sick, a pale sheen of perspiration upon his face. He sent for Appleby who came on deck expecting he had been summoned to attend the captain.

"What is it, Nat?" Drinkwater beckoned the surgeon to windward, out of earshot of the helmsmen and the quartermaster at the con.

"What d'you make of my complexion, Harry?"

"Eh?" Appleby paused then peered at the lieutenant. "Why a mild diaphoresis."

"And I've been violently sick for an hour past. Also I purged myself during the middle watch . . ."

Appleby frowned. "But that's not possible . . . no, I mean . . ."

"It means that Morris may indeed be being poisoned, man. Last night he sent me a bottle of Oporto . . . he must have meant me to try it, to see if it had any effect upon me! I drank it entire!"

"For God's sake, Nat, of course he's being poisoned. Rum and fortified wines addle the brain, corrode the guts. Try cleaning brass with them." Appleby's exasperation was total.

Then he calmed, looking again at his friend. "Forgive me, that was unpardonable. Your own condition I would ascribe to a tainted bottle. Maybe Morris had been consuming a case of bad wine. That would produce such symptoms and aggravate the peptic ulcer I am certain he suffers from."

"But the wine tasted well, seemed not to be bad."

Appleby was not listening. Even in the vehemence of his diagnostic defence a tiny doubt had crept into his mind. The symptoms were those produced by sudorifics, used by himself to promote the sweating agues that eased Griffiths's malaria. And though the key to his dispensary never left his side he was wondering who possessed knowledge enough to incapacitate Morris.

". . . 'tis commonly supposed a woman's weapon," he muttered to himself.

"I beg your pardon?"

Appleby shook his head. " 'Tis nothing," he turned away then came back, having thought of something. "Nat, would you oblige me by concealing your indisposition . . . at least for the time being."

Puzzled, Drinkwater nodded wanly. "As you wish, Harry." He fought down a spasm of nausea and stared seawards. Whatever the cause it was not lethal. Just bloody uncomfortable.

"Deck there!" The hail broke from the masthead: "Ship on the lee beam!"

"God's bones!" swore Drinkwater beneath his breath, fishing in his tail pocket for his Dollond glass.

CHAPTER TWENTY

The Fortune of War

November 1799

In the mizen top Drinkwater fought down a bout of nausea with the feeling that the effect of the bad wine was weakening. In reality the bluish square on the horizon distracted him. He levelled the glass, crouched and trimmed it against a topmast shroud. It was difficult to see at this angle, although the sail was dark against the dawn, but it appeared to be a ship on the wind like themselves. Not that there was a great deal of wind, and the day promised little better. He wiped his eye, looked again and then, still uncertain, he determined to do what any prudent officer could do in a ship as ill-armed as *Antigone*: assume the worst.

Descending to the deck, he addressed Quilhampton. "You have the deck, Mr. Q." Such an errand as he was bound on was not to be left to a midshipman. Mr. Quilhampton's astonishment changed to pride and then to determination.

"Aye, aye, sir!" Despite his preoccupation Drinkwater could not resist a smile. Quilhampton had turned into a real asset, competent and with a touch of loyalty that marked him for a good subordinate. Drinkwater recollected how it had been Mr. Q that had brought his effects off Abu al Kizan. It had been touching to discover his books and journals neatly shelved, his quadrant box lashed and the little watercolour done for him by Elizabeth all in place in the cabin aboard *Antigone*. That had been a long time ago. There were more pressing matters now.

Drinkwater knocked perfunctorily and entered Morris's stateroom. Automatically his eyes flicked over the portrait of Hortense Santhonax.

"What the hell d'you want? What brings you from the deck?"

"An enemy, sir. To loo'ard," Drinkwater fought back the desire to vomit. He had forgotten his own sickness and retched on the stink of Morris's. "I believe her to be a French cruiser out of Ile de France."

Morris absorbed the news. He swallowed then frowned. "But, I . . . a French cruiser d'you say? What makes you so sure?"

"Does it matter, sir? If she's British and we run there's nothing lost, if she's French and we don't we may be."

"May be what?" Morris frowned again, his obtuseness a symptom of his feeble state. Drinkwater was suddenly sorry for him.

"May be lost, sir. I recommend we make our escape, sir, put the ship on the wind another half point and see what she will do." He paused. "We are without a main battery, sir," he reminded Morris.

The responsibility of command stirred something in Morris. He nodded. "Very well."

Drinkwater made for the door.

"Drinkwater!"

Nathaniel paused and peered back into the cabin. Dragging his soiled bedding behind him, Morris was straining to see the enemy through the stern windows. "Yes, sir?" Morris turned, his face grey and fleshless beneath the skin.

"I . . . nothing, damn it." Morris looked hideously alone. And frightened.

"Truly sir, you will be better if you abstrain from all strong and spirituous liquors." He hurried off, almost glad to fasten his mind on the problem of escape.

"Hands to the braces!" The cry was taken up.

"All hands sir?" Quilhampton asked eagerly, "Beat to quarters?"

"Not yet, Mr. Q," said Drinkwater, looking aloft, "we have no marine drummer to do the honours. Besides, one runs away with less ceremony." It occurred to Drinkwater that he had said something shaming to the boy, as if, occasionally, even British tars may not run when probably outgunned and certainly outnumbered.

"Trice her up a little, there! Half a point to windward, damn you!" He looked aloft as the watch hauled the yards against the catharpings, each successively higher yard braced at a slightly more acute angle to the wind.

"Royals, sir?"

"Royals, Mr. Q."

The chase wore on into the afternoon and the wind became increasingly fluky. The quality of drama was absent from the desperate business with such a light breeze but it was replaced by a sense of the sinister. Drinkwater kept the deck, amazed at the dark looks of outrage cast by Acting Lieutenant Dalziell. Morris made several appearances on deck, borrowing Drinkwater's glass and mumbling approval at his conduct before slipping below to continue his debilitating flux.

Drinkwater wondered what Appleby had done with the news that he too had been sick, then realised that he was no longer so, merely hungry and that there was another matter to occupy his brain.

"Mr. Dalziell, be so kind as to fetch my quadrant from my cabin."

"Mr. Drinkwater, may I remind you that I hold an acting . . ."

"You may stand upon the quarterdeck, devil take you, but not upon your festerin' dignity! Go sir, at once!" Dalziell fled. For the next half hour he carefully measured the angle subtended by the enemy's uppermost yard and the horizon. In that time it increased by some twelve minutes of arc.

"I do not know if I might do that, sir." He heard Quilhampton's voice and looked up to see the midshipman clasping the watch glass behind his back. He was withholding it from the outstretched hand of Capitaine Santhonax.

"Do you allow the captain the loan of your glass, Mr. Q. Perhaps he will be courteous enough to oblige us with his opinion." Santhonax grinned his predatory smile over Mr. Quilhampton's head. "Ah, Drinkwater, you would not neglect any opportunity to gain information, eh?"

"Your opinion, sir." Santhonax took the glass and hoisted himself carefully into the lee mizen rigging. His wound had much improved in recent days and Drinkwater saw from the set of his mouth that his own fears were confirmed. Santhonax regained the deck. "It is a French vessel, is it not, captain?"

Santhonax favoured Drinkwater with a long penetrating look. "Yes," he said quietly, "she is French. And from Ile de France."

Drinkwater nodded. "Thank you, sir. Mr. Quilhampton, pass word for the gunner." He turned to Santhonax. "Captain I regret the necessity that compels me to confine you but . . ." he shrugged.

"You will revoke my parole, please?"

Drinkwater nodded as the gunner arrived. "Mr. Trussel, Captain Santhonax and Cadet Bruilhac are to be confined in irons . . ."

"*Merde!*"

"My pardon, sir, but your character is too well-known." He spun on his heel. "Pipe all hands, Mr. Dalziell, and take the deck while I confer with the captain."

Morris listened to what Drinkwater had to say, aware that he was powerless. A man who had never been troubled by moral constraints, who had managed his profession by a bullying authoritarianism and sought to excuse his failures upon others, found it easy to delegate to Drinkwater's competence. Although a bitter irony filled his mind it was not caused by the chance that Drinkwater might steal his thunder and fight a brilliant action. Whatever happened, a victory would be attributed to him as commander. What wormed in Morris's mind was that Drinkwater might botch it, perhaps deliberately.

"If you desert me, or disgrace me, as God is my witness I shall shoot you."

There was no dissembling in Drinkwater's reply, uttered as it was over his shoulder. "I should never do that, not in the face of the enemy."

Drinkwater ran back on deck. One glance to leeward confirmed his worst fears. He could see the enemy hull now. *Antigone* was losing the race. He began to shout orders.

The burst of activity on deck was barely audible in the orlop. Inside the tiny dispensary, by the light of a guttering candle end, Appleby looked from book to pot and back again. At last he sat back and stared at the jar, its glass greenish and clouded, and holding something given apparent life by the flame that flickered uncertainly in the foetid air.

He pulled the stopper from the jar and poured a trickle of white crystals into the palm of his hand. The potassium antimonyl tartrate twinkled dully from the candle flame.

Appleby poured them back. A few adhered to his perspiring skin. He sighed. "Tartar emetic," he muttered to himself, replacing the jar in its rack, "a sudorific promoting diaphoresis." He sighed.

The sudden glare of a lantern through the louvred door made his hand shoot out and nip the candlewick. In the sudden close darkness he almost prayed that he might be mistaken, but he heard her indrawn and alarmed breath as she discovered the padlock hanging unlocked in the staple and the hasp free. She paused and he knew she was wondering whether anyone was within. Making up her mind, she drew back the door and thrust her lantern into the tiny hutch.

He sat immobile, the trembling lantern throwing his face into sharp relief, its smooth rotundities lit, the shadows of his falling cheeks and dewlap etched black. She drew back a hand at her throat.

"Oh! Mr. Appleby! Sir, how you did frighten me, sitting in the dark like that . . ."

"Come in and close the door."

He watched her with such an intensity that she thought it was lust, not displeased. Indeed she began to compose herself for his first embrace as he stood, stooped under the deckhead beams.

"What in the name of heaven are you up to?" Appleby's breath was hot with the passion of anger. She drew back. He picked up the lantern from where she had placed it on the bench and held it over the jar of Tartar Emetic.

"You are giving this to the captain," he said it slowly, as a matter of fact.

"You know then . . ."

"I do. In his wine, though I have not yet discovered how you do it."

For a long moment she said nothing. Appleby put the lantern down and sat again. He looked up at her. "I am disappointed . . . I had hoped . . ."

She knelt at his knees and took his hands, her huge eyes staring up at him.

"I did not . . . I wished only to make him indisposed, too ill to command. You yourself suggested it in conversation with Mr. Drinkwater . . ."

"I . . . ?"

"Yes sir," she had sown the seed of doubt now, caught him between her suppliant posture and her rapid city-bred quick wittedness. "You see what he has done to the men, how he has flogged them without mercy or reason. Why, look at the way he sent poor little Mr. Q to the top of the mast, and him with one hand missing . . ." She appealed to his inherent kindness and felt him relax. "We all know what Mr. Rogers said about what happened at Mocha, how Mr. Drinkwater should've been in command."

"That is no reason to . . ."

"And the kind of man he is, sir . . ." But Appleby rallied.

"That is not for *you* to say," he said vehemently, a trace of misogyny emerging "it does not justify poisoning . . ."

"But I gave him only a little, sir, enough to purge himself with a flux. Why, 'twas little more than you gave the old Captain for his ague, sir. 'Twas not a lethal dose."

Appleby knitted his brows in concentration. His professional sense warred with his curious regard for his woman kneeling in the stinking darkness. He would not call it love for he thought of himself as too old, too ugly and too much a man of science to be moved by love. This wish to defend her was aided by his dislike of Morris. He found he was no longer angry with her. He could understand her motives much as one does a child who misbehaves. It did not condone the crime.

"You poisoned Mr. Drinkwater, Catherine," he said, unknowingly reproving her most effectively.

"Mr. Drinkwater, my God! How?"

"Morris sent him in a bottle last night."

"Oh!" It was Catherine's turn to deflate. She had not meant to harm any other person, especially he who offered her almost her only chance of avoiding a convict transport. "H . . . how is he?"

"He will be all right." He paused. "Are you sorry?"

She could read him now. She had won. Flipping open the lantern she blew it out. And sealed her advantage.

On the gun deck every man who could be spared was at work. Drinkwater had relinquished the upper deck to Dalziell with an admonition to the quartermaster that if he was a degree off the wind more than was necessary he would be flayed. The man grinned cheerfully and the first lieutenant went below to orchestrate the idea that was already causing a buzz of comment, much of it unfavourable.

"Belay that damned Dover court and take heed of what I have to say . . ."

The wind eased by the minute but it continued to blow down to leeward, conferring an advantage on the pursuer. She could be plainly seen from the deck now but Drinkwater no longer fretted over her approach. Instead he sweated and swore, admonished and encouraged, belaboured and bullied the tired Hellebores as they lugged the six larboard eighteen pounders across the deck to assemble a battery of twelve in the vacant gun-ports on the starboard side.

The deck was criss-crossed with tackles, bull ropes and preventers. After several hours employed in hauling first one and then another, of casting stoppers on and off, of wracking seizings and heaving on handspikes Rogers, stripped to his shirt and mopping his florid face with a handkerchief, fought his way over the network of lines.

"Christ alive, Drinkwater, this is a confounded risky trick, ain't it. Damn me if I can see the logic of putting all your eggs in one basket." There was a murmur of agreement from several of the men.

"Why, Mr. Rogers," said Drinkwater cheerfully, suddenly realising that his flux and nausea had vanished, and pitching his voice loud enough for all to hear, "the easier to hurl 'em at the French!"

"So's they can make bleeding hommelettes . . ."

"To go with their fucking frog's legs . . ." A burst of laughter greeted this sally while Mr. Lestock, peering down from the deck, tut-tutted and went aft.

"The captain is aware of our doin's, Mr. Lestock," called Drinkwater and another burst of laughter came from the men. It might be a dangerous indication of indiscipline but what the hell? They might all be dead in the coming hours. Or exchanging places with Santhonax. "Right; a touch more on that tackle, Mr. Brundell, if you please."

"Come then, lads," roared the master's mate. The men spat on their hands and lay back. They broke out into the spontaneous cry they had evolved for concerted effort: "Helleeee-bores . . . Bellee-ee-whores . . . !" The eighteen-pounder moved across the deck and Drinkwater thought Griffiths would have approved of that cry.

*   *   *

Night found them almost becalmed but the whisper of wind remained constant in direction and Drinkwater held to his belief that they must not throw away their position to windward, that to attempt to run down past their enemy and escape only put the French between them and the Cape. But dawn found them to leeward, the wind backing and rising as, in growing daylight they were able to see the wind fill the enemy's sails before their own.

But Drinkwater's chagrin was swiftly replaced by hope an hour after dawn. Without warning the wind chopped round to the south-west again and began to freshen, both ships leaned to it, *Antigone* less than usual since she carried all her artillery on her starboard, windward side.

But the fluky quality of the wind had overnight brought their opponent almost within gunshot. At last Drinkwater was compelled to order his men to quarters.

He had not done so earlier to preserve their energy but, hardly had he taken the decision and the watch below came tumbling sleepily on deck, then the first shot fell short upon their larboard quarter.

The four-score Hellebores ran to their stations. Rogers came aft and received his instructions. When Drinkwater explained what he intended to do Rogers held out his hand.

"I've misjudged you in the past, Nathaniel, and I'm sorry for it. I only hope my new-found confidence is not misplaced."

"Amen to that, Samuel," replied Drinkwater, smiling ruefully. Appleby came on deck.

"D'you have your saws and daviers at the ready, Harry?" jested Drinkwater hollowly, shuddering at the thought of being rendered limbless by such instruments.

"Aye, Nat, and God help me," he added with a significant stare at Drinkwater, "Kate Best assists me." He disappeared below, followed by Rogers en route to command the battery of eighteen-pounders. Lestock coughed beside him, affecting to study the enemy and remarking upon his shooting as the French bowchaser barked away at them. The tricolour could be seen trailing astern from her peak and mainmasthead. As yet no colours flew from *Antigone*'s spars. Mr. Dalziell strutted nervously along the line of larboard quarterdeck carronades. To starboard Mr. Quilhampton was quietly pacing up and down, his stump behind his back, doing his best to ape Mr. Drinkwater. At the mainmast Mr. Brundell commanded the waisters to board or trim sail as the need arose while, legs apart on the fo'c's'le Mr. Grey, his silver whistle about his neck, commanded the head party.

The person of Rattray appeared carrying a chair. He placed it upon the quarterdeck and Morris, pale and shaking, slumped into it. Drinkwater approached him.

"I am glad to see you, sir, your presence will encourage the hands." Under the circumstances he could say no more. Morris's courage had surely been misjudged, perhaps the responsibility of command could yet temper the man just as culpability had changed Rogers.

Morris stared up at Drinkwater and moved his hand from beneath the blanket. The lock of a pistol was visible in his lap.

"Stuff your sanctimonious cant, Drinkwater. Fight my bloody ship or I'll blow you to hell."

Drinkwater opened his mouth in astonishment. Then he closed it as a thump hit the ship and a spatter of splinters flew from the larboard quarter rail. The action had begun.

All on deck stared astern. In the full daylight the frigate foaming up looked glorious, her hull a rich brown, her gunstrake cream. She was a point upon their larboard quarter. Thank God for a strengthening wind, thought Drinkwater as he spoke to Lestock. "Mr. Lestock! Do you let her fall off a little, contrive it to look a trifle careless."

"D'you give away weather gauge, Mr. Drinkwater?" contradicted Lestock with a look in Morris's direction.

"Do as you are told, sir!" The quartermaster eased the helm up a couple of spokes and *Antigone* paid off the wind a few degrees. The gunfire ceased. Relative motion showed the Frenchman slowly crossing *Antigone*'s stern. For the moment his bow chasers would not bear.

"British colours, Mr. Q." Old Glory snapped out over their heads and almost immediately the enemy's larboard bow chaser opened fire. She had crossed their stern. Drinkwater had surrendered the weather gauge and still the *Antigone* had not fired a shot.

Drinkwater walked forward and gripped the rail. "Mr. Brundell! Ease your foremast lee sheets a little!" A tiny tremble could be felt through the palms of his damp hands as he clasped the rail tightly. *Antigone* was losing power through those trembling foresails. He hoped the enemy could not see those fluttering clews behind the sails of the mainmast. The French ship began to draw ahead, overtaking them on their starboard side, a fine big ship, almost, now, they could see her in profile, identical to themselves. "Are you ready, Mr. Rogers?" Drinkwater hailed and the word was passed back that Samuel Rogers was ready. To vindicate his honour, Drinkwater guessed.

"I hope you know what you are about Mr. Drinkwater." Morris's voice sounded stronger. "So do I, sir," replied Drinkwater swept by a sudden mood of exhilaration. If only the Frog would hold his broadside until all his guns would bear.

"Stand by mizen braces, Mr. Brundell," he called in a sharp, clear voice.

"What the bloody hell . . . ?"

"For what we are about to receive . . ."

"Holy Mary, Mother of God . . ."

A puff of smoke erupted from the forward larboard gun of the French frigate. They were her lee guns, pointing downwards on a deck sloping towards the enemy. So much for the weather gauge once the manoeuvring was over.

But it was not over: "Mizen braces! Mr. Rogers!"

The lee mizen braces were flung from their pins, a man at each to see them free, with orders to cut them if a single turn jammed in a block. The faked ropes ran true as the weather braces were hauled under the vociferous direction of Brundell. All along the starboard side the smoke and flame of the main-deck battery opened fire, the twelve eighteen-pounders rumbling back on their trucks to be sponged and reloaded. Drinkwater did not think they would manage more than a single shot at their adversary as, under the thundering backing of the mizen sails, *Antigone* slowed in the water, appeared to stop dead as the enemy stormed past, suddenly firing ahead of the British prize. Quilhampton was hauling the carronade slides round to get off a second shot, screaming at his gun crews like a regular Tarpaulin officer.

"Come you sons of whores, move it up, lively with that sponge, God damn you . . ."

Drinkwater looked for the fall of shot. At maximum elevation with the ship heeling *away* from the enemy they must have done some damage. Christ, they had hurled all the damned bar shot and chain shot they could cram in the guns, all the French dismasting projectiles to give the Frogs a taste of their own medicine.

And they had missed her. Mortified, Drinkwater's ever observant eye could already read the name of the passing frigate: *Romaine*. And now, by heaven, they *must* run.

A cheer was breaking out on the fo'c's'le and he looked again. The enemy's maintopmast was tottering to leeward. It formed a graceful curve then fell in a splintering of spars and erratic descent as stays arrested it and parted under the weight.

Relief flooded Drinkwater. There was cheering all along the upper deck and from down below. Rogers had come up and was pumping his hand. Even Lestock's face wore a sickly, condescending grin.

"Sir! Sir!" Quilhampton was pointing.

"God's bones!"

The wreckage was slewing the *Romaine* sharply to larboard, across *Antigone*'s bow. In the perfect position to rake. And men were working furiously at the wreckage with axes. Forward a man screamed as his leg flew off. It was Mr. Brundell. "Mr. Grey! Back the yards on the foremast!" He turned. "Mr. Dalziell, back the yards on the main, lively now."

He waited impatiently. *Antigone* had hove herself to. Now they must make a stern board, to get out of trouble before . . .

The raking broadside hit them, the balls whirling the length of the deck. Mr. Quilhampton fell and beside Drinkwater Lestock went "Urgh!" and a gout of blood appeared all over Drinkwater's breeches. Drinkwater stood stock still. On the fo'c's'le, legs still apart, stood Mr. Grey. The two men stood numbed, one hundred feet apart, regarding each other over a human shambles. As if by magic figures stood up and the main yards groaned round in their parrels. They were followed by those on the foremast. *Antigone* began to gather sternway. The next broadside roared out. It had been fired on an upward roll. *Antigone*'s foretopgallant mast went overboard.

"Helm a weather! Hard a-starboard!" But Drinkwater's order was too late. The frigate was already paying off, her bow coming up into the wind, across the wind, until finally she wallowed with her unarmed larboard side facing the enemy.

"Lee forebrace!" If he could trim the yards to the larboard tack they might yet escape. The third broadside brought the main topmast down, the mizen topgallant with it. No one stood alive at the wheel.

Drinkwater looked at the *Romaine*. French cruisers, he knew, carried large crews. Now the advantages thus conferred upon them became apparent. Already the wreckage was cleared away and she was under control, setting down towards them.

"Mr. Dalziell, prepare your larboard carronades. Mr. Grey! Larboard fo'c's'le carronades." Bitterly Drinkwater strode forward and jerked one of the brass gangway swivels. He lined it up on the approaching frigate.

"Mr. Drinkwater!" He turned to find Morris pointing the pistol at him. "You failed, Drinkwater . . ."

"Not yet, by God, Morris, not yet!"

"What else can you do, dog's turd, your cleverness has destroyed you." Drinkwater's brain bridled at Morris's suggestion. True, a second earlier he himself had been on the verge of despair but the human mind trips and locks onto odd things under stress. It did not occur at that moment that Morris's action in pointing the gun at him was irrational; that Morris's apparent delight at his failure would also result in Morris's own capture. It was that old cockpit epithet that sparked his brain to greater endeavours.

"No, sir. By God there's one card yet to play!" he shouted below for Mr. Rogers even as Dalziell approached with a coloured bundle in his arms.

"What the hell is that?" screamed Drinkwater.

"I was ordered to strike," said Dalziell.

CHAPTER TWENTY-ONE

A Matter of Luck

November–December 1799

Drinkwater snatched the ensign from Dalziell's grasp. The red bunting spilled onto the deck. He turned to Morris, the question unasked on his lips. Morris inclined his head, implying his authority lay behind the surrender.

The belief that he was dying had taken so sharp a hold upon his mind that he was sure surrender offered him survival. The enemy cruiser was from Ile de France. As commander of such a well-fought prize he would be treated with respect, and removed from the source of his poisoning he would recover. Into Morris's mind came another reason, adding its own weight in favour of surrender. While he enjoyed an easy house arrest at Port Louis his officers would be incarcerated. Drinkwater would be mewed up for the duration of the war. It would finish the work he had failed to do at Kosseir.

In the electric atmosphere that charged the quarterdeck all this was plain to them both. Their mutual antipathy had reached its crisis.

"The French are sending a boat, sir," said Dalziell, eyes darting from one to the other. Drinkwater turned and shoved the ensign back at Dalziell.

"That is *Hellebore*'s ensign, by God! I'll not see it struck yet!"

Rogers arrived on the quarterdeck. He saw the ensign. "Surely we haven't . . . ?"

"No, by Christ, we have not!" Dalziell was pushed towards the halliards as Drinkwater snapped to Rogers, "Get Santhonax up here, and Bruilhac! Quick!"

Drinkwater looked at the approaching boat, a launch packed with men, a cable from them.

"I command, damn you!" Morris hissed furiously. Drinkwater turned and looked down the barrel of the pistol.

He crossed the deck in two strides and wrenched the gun from his grasp. "You may rot, Morris, but I am not through yet . . . get that ensign up, Dalziell, you lubber . . ."

Drinkwater was aware that he was holding the pistol at the young man. Dalziell threw a final, failing glance at Morris then did as he was bid. He belayed the halliards as Santhonax came on deck. The Frenchman looked curiously about him, took in the fallen spars, the broken bodies and blood spattered across the deck. He saw too the ensign being belayed and his quick mind understood. A glance to windward showed him his countrymen, the gun-ports of *Romaine*, and the boat, almost alongside.

"Get 'em up on the rail, Rogers, that Frog won't fire on his own boat."

But a gun did fire, the ball whistling overhead, a single discharge to recall the British to the etiquette of war.

Drinkwater pointed the pistol at Santhonax. "Captain, tell that boat to pull off. This ship has not surrendered. The ensign halliards were shot through. If the officer in the boat pulls off I will not open fire until he has regained his ship, otherwise I shall destroy him," he paused, "and you also, Captain."

The French boat was ten yards off, the officer standing in

the stern, looking up in astonishment at the apparition of a Republican naval officer standing beneath the British ensign like Hector on the walls of Troy.

Santhonax looked at Drinkwater. "No," he said simply. "I leave it to the desperation of your plight and your conscience to shoot me."

Drinkwater's heart was thumping painfully and he could feel the sweat pouring out of him. He sensed Morris awaiting events. He swore beneath his breath.

"Get up, Bruilhac!" The terrified boy climbed trembling on the rail as Drinkwater jerked his head at Rogers to pull Santhonax off the rail. Rogers leapt forward, together with Tregembo. But they were too late.

Drinkwater was about to threaten Bruilhac with instant death if he did not do his bidding but he was spared this cruel necessity. A sudden eruption of cannon fire to the east of them swung the focus of attention abruptly away from the wretched little drama on *Antigone*'s rails. At first it seemed *Romaine* had fired a final shattering broadside to compel *Antigone* to strike. In their boat the French thought the same. There was a simultaneous ducking of heads. Bruilhac fainted through sheer terror while a similar reflex caused Santhonax to dive outboard.

Even as Drinkwater registered Santhonax's escape and heard the howl of rage from Morris he had noticed there was no flame from *Romaine*'s larboard broadside. The sun beat down through the clearing smoke of their earlier discharges as the wind shredded the last of it to leeward and there, in the bright path laid by the sun upon the sea, they saw the newcomer.

"A British frigate, by all that's wonderful!" shouted Rogers, suddenly releasing them all from their suspended animation. Tregembo picked up two round-shot from the carronade garlands and tried to lob them into the French boat. The French-men suddenly laid on their oars and spun her round just as Captain Santhonax's hand reached up for help. Drinkwater had a brief glimpse of his face, disfigured and distorted by the pain in his shoulder, his left arm trailing, his long legs kick-ing powerfully.

Another thundering broadside, this time from *Romaine*, caused a second's pause. There was no fall of shot near *Antigone*; *Romaine* was bracing her yards round to fill her sails with wind.

Drinkwater leapt to the deck. "Rogers! Tregembo!"

He picked up a cartridge and rammed it into the nearest carronade. Tregembo rolled a shot into the muzzle and joined Rogers on the tackles. Drinkwater spun the screw and watched the blunt barrel depress. He leant against the slide and felt it slew on its heavy caster. "Secure!"

Through the gunport he could see the boat, see the officer and a man hauling Santhonax over the transom. Rogers drove the priming quill into the touch-hole and blew powder into the groove. Still sighting along the barrel, Drinkwater's right hand cocked the lock and his long fingers wound round the lanyard. The boat traversed the back-sight.

It occurred to him that it was easier to kill at a distance, re-moved from the confrontation from which Santhonax had just escaped. He had only to jerk the lanyard and Santhonax would die. He thought of the grey eyes staring from the por-trait below, and of how he and Dungarth had let her go. From Hortense he thought of Elizabeth. The boat's transom crossed the end of the barrel. He jerked the lanyard.

The carronade roared back on its slide. Drinkwater leapt up to mark the fall of shot. He saw the spout of water a foot off the boat's quarter. He was surprised at the relief he felt.

"Let's try for the frigate." Drinkwater spun the elevating

screw again, bringing the retreating *Romaine* into his sights as, with crippled masts, she moved sluggishly away. The wind was falling light, the concussion of their guns having killed it. They fired six shots before giving up. *Romaine* was out of range.

They craned their necks to see what was happening. They saw their rescuer begin to turn, trying to work across *Romaine*'s stern to rake. The French captain put his helm over and followed the British ship so they circled one another like dogs, nose to tail. A shattering broadside crashed from *Romaine,* a lighter response from the other. Another came from the Britisher. The *Romaine* began to draw off to the southeast. The stranger wore in pursuit, her mizen topmast going by the board as she did so.

"*Telemachus,*" Drinkwater spelled out, peering through his glass. The two ships moved slowly away, leaving *Antigone* rolling easily. The boat had vanished.

Drinkwater turned inboard. He and Morris exchanged a glance. Beneath his hooded lids Morris bore a whipped look. He went below.

Without any feeling of triumph Drinkwater's eyes fell upon the body of Quilhampton. Tregembo joined him.

"There's not a mark on him. Hold, he's not gone . . . Mr. Q! Mr. Q! D'you hear me?" Drinkwater began to chafe the boy's wrists. His eyes fluttered and opened. Rogers bent over them. "Winded by a passing shot. He'll live," said Rogers.

It took three days to re-rig the frigate, three days of strenuous labour during which the much depleted crew struggled and cursed, ate and slept between the guns. But although they swore they laboured willingly. They were not Antigones but Hellebores and the big frigate was their prize, the concrete proof of their corporate endeavours. She was also the source of prize money, and their shrinking numbers increased each individual's share.

By dint of their efforts they sent up new or improvised topmasts and could cross courses and topsails on all three masts. Later, Drinkwater thought, after they had carried out some additional modifications to the salvaged broken spars they might manage a main topgallant.

For Drinkwater the need to bring the frigate under command over-rode everything else. Morris retired to his cabin from whence came the news that he was keeping food down at last. From the cockpit came the hammock-shrouded corpses that failed to survive Appleby's surgery, the bravely smiling wounded and the empty rum bottles that sustained Appleby during the long hours he spent attending his grim profession.

Johnson reported they had been struck in the hull by twenty-one shot, but only two low enough to cause serious leakage.

The pumps clanked regularly even as the remaining men toiled to slew those half-dozen eighteen-pounders back into their larboard ports. They had lost sixteen men killed and twenty wounded in the action. Rank had almost ceased to exist as Drinkwater urged them on, officers tailing on to ropes and leading by example. Mr. Lestock shook his head disapprovingly and Drinkwater left the deck watch to him and his precious sense of honour, deriving great comfort from the loyal support of Tregembo and even poor, handless Mr. Quilhampton, who did what he could. Samuel Rogers emerged as a man who, given a task to do, performed it with that intemperate energy that so characterised him.

Late in the afternoon of the third day after the action with *Romaine* a sail was seen to leeward. Nervously glasses were trained on her, lest she proved the re-rigged *Romaine* come to finish off her late adversary. The last anyone aboard *Antigone* had seen of the two ships had been the *Telemachus* in pursuit of the *Romaine*. There had been no sign of Santhonax and the French boat and it was supposed that he had made the shelter of *Romaine*.

Drinkwater put *Antigone* on the wind and informed Morris. He was favoured with a grunt of acknowledgement.

"I think she's the *Telemachus*, sir," Quilhampton informed Drinkwater when he returned to the deck.

"Hoist the interrogative, Mr. Q. Mr. Rogers! General quarters, if you please!"

The pipes squealed at the hatchways and the pitifully small crew tumbled up, augmenting the watch on deck. The stranger was coming up fast, pointing much higher than the wounded frigate. The recognition signal streamed from her foremasthead. "She's British, then," said Lestock unnecessarily.

Drinkwater kept the men at their stations as the ship closed them. At a mile distance she fired a gun to leeward and hoisted the signal to heave to.

Drinkwater gave the order to back the maintopsail. In her present state *Antigone* could neither outsail nor outfight the ship to leeward.

"Sending a boat, sir," Quilhampton reported.

Drinkwater went below to inform Morris. He found the commander watching the newcomer from the larboard quarter gallery.

"A twenty-eight, eh? A post ship. D'you know who commands her?"

"No, sir."

"I'll come up."

The boat bobbed over the wave-crests between them. "There's a midshipman in her, sir," reported Mr. Quilhampton, his eyes bright with excitement. It occurred to Drinkwater that Mr. Q was suddenly proud of his lost hand. It was little enough compensation, he thought. "Do you meet the young gentleman, Mr. Q."

The men were peering curiously at the approaching boat, those at the guns through the ports. "Let 'em," said Drinkwater to himself. They had earned a little tolerance.

His uniform awry, Morris came on deck, holding out his hand for a glass. Lestock beat Dalziell in the matter. The midshipman swung himself over the side. There were catcalls from the lower gunports and Rogers's voice snapped, "Silence there!" The boat's crew were tricked out in blue and white striped shirts and trousers of white jean. They wore glazed hats with ribbons of blue and white and their oars were picked out in the same colours. Such a display amused the Hellebores and led Drinkwater to the conclusion that her captain was a wealthy man. An officer with interest of the "Parliamentary" kind, probably young and probably half his own age. He was almost right.

Quilhampton approached the quarterdeck, saw Morris and diverted his approach from Drinkwater to the commander. "Mr. Mole, sir."

The midshipman bowed. His tall gangling fair haired appearance was in marked contrast with his name. His accent was rural Norfolk, though mannered.

"My respects, sir, Commander Morris, I believe." Morris stiffened.

"Captain to you, you damned brat. Who commands your vessel, eh?"

The lad was not abashed. "Captain White, sir, Captain Richard White, he desires me to offer whatever services you require, though I perceive," he swept his hand aloft, "that you have little need of them. My congratulations."

Drinkwater smiled grimly. The young gentleman's affront

could only be but admired, particularly as he appeared impervious to Morris's forbidding aspect.

Morris's mouth fell open. He closed it and turned contemptuously away, crossing the deck towards the companionway. "Mr. Drinkwater, I expect the nob who commands yonder will want us to obey his orders. Tell this dog's turd what we want, then kick his perfumed arse off my ship." He disappeared below.

"Aye, aye, sir." Drinkwater regarded the midshipman. "Well, Mr. Mole, are you commonly addressing senior officers in that vein?"

The boy blinked and Drinkwater went on, "Your captain; is that Richard White from Norfolk, a small man with fair hair?"

"Captain White is of small stature, sir," Mole said primly.

"Very well, Mr. Mole, I desire you to inform Captain White that we are short of men but able to make the Cape. We carry despatches from Admiral Blankett and are armed *en flûte*. We are the prize of a brig and most damnably grateful for your arrival the other day."

Mole smirked as though he had been personally responsible for the timely arrival of *Telemachus*.

"Oh, and Mr. Mole, I desire that you inform him that the captain's name is Augustus Morris and my name is Drinkwater. I urge that you give him those particulars."

Mole repeated the names. "By the way, Mr. Mole, what became of the Frenchman?"

"He slipped us in the night, sir."

"Tut tut," said Drinkwater, catching Quilhampton's eye. "That would never have happened to us, eh, Mr. Q?"

"No, sir," grinned Quilhampton.

"See what happened to Mr. Quilhampton the last time we had an engagement . . ."

Quilhampton held up his stump. "Mr. Quilhampton

stopped the enemy from running by taking hold of her bowsprit . . ." Laughter echoed round *Antigone*'s scarred quarterdeck and Mole, aware the joke was on him, touched his forehead and fled.

"Boat ahoy!" Lestock hailed the returning boat.

"*Telemachus!*" That hail confirmed that she bore the frigate's captain.

"How d'you propose we man the side, Mr. Drinkwater?" Lestock asked sarcastically. Drinkwater lowered his glass, having recognised the little figure in the stern.

"Oh, I'd say you and Mr. Dalziell will do for decoration, Mr. Grey with his mates for sideboys. This ain't the time for punctiliousness. Mr. Q!"

"Sir?"

"Inform the captain that Captain White is coming aboard."

"Aye, aye, sir." Drinkwater went forward to join the side party. Lestock was furious.

Grey's pipe twittered and Drinkwater swept his battered hat from his head.

"Stap me, but it *is* you!" Richard White, gold lace about his sleeve and upon his shoulder, held out his hand in informal greeting, "Deuced glad to see you, Nat . . ." He looked round the deck expectantly. "What's it that imp of Satan Mole said about . . . ?" He paused and Drinkwater turned to see Morris emerging on deck.

"Well damn my eyes, if it isn't that bugger Morris!"

CHAPTER TWENTY-TWO

The Cape of Good Hope

November 1799–January 1800

Captain Richard White had many years earlier suffered from the sadistic bullying of Morris when he and Drinkwater served on the frigate *Cyclops* as midshipmen. Since that time, when the frightened White had been protected by Drinkwater, service under the punctilious St. Vincent followed by absolute command of his own ship had turned White into an irascible, forthright character. Beneath this exterior his friends might perceive the boyish charm and occasional uncertainty of a still young man, but the accustomed authority that he was now used to, combined with an irresistible urge to thus publicly humiliate his former tormentor.

There was for a moment a silence between the three men that was pregnant with suppressed emotions. Drinkwater, caught like a shuttlecock between two seniors, prudently waited, watching Morris's reaction, aware that White had committed a gross impropriety. Unaccountably Drinkwater felt a momentary sympathy for Morris. If the commander called for satisfaction at the Cape he would have been justified, whatever the naval regulations said about duelling. For his own part White was belligerently unrepentant, weeks of adolescent misery springing into his mind as he confronted his old tormentor.

Morris stood stock still, colour draining from his face as the insult on his own quarterdeck outraged him. Brought up in the old school of naval viciousness, protected by petticoat influence from the consequences of his vice, his brutal nature protected by the privileges of rank for so long, Morris now found himself confronted by a moral superiority undeterred by the baser motives of naval intrigue. White's impetuous candour had disarmed him.

Morris shot White a look of pure venom, but his new-found accession to command caused him to hold his tongue. He turned and made for the companionway below, half jostling Drinkwater as he did so, his mouth twisted with rage and humiliation.

White ignored Drinkwater's embarrassed glance after the retreating figure of Morris. "Well, Nat, I'm damned sorry we lost the Frog, gave me the slip during the night. Blasted wind fell light under a threatening overcast. Black as the Earl of Hell's riding boots, by God. A damned shame." He cast his eyes over *Antigone*'s spars and rigging. By comparison with when he had last seen them they had all the hallmarks of Drinkwater's diligence. "You've been busy, I perceive. But come, tell me what the deuce became of that brig I last saw you on, heard you'd been sent to the Red Sea. St. Vincent was damned annoyed. I do believe if Nelson had not blown Brueys to hell at Aboukir he might have been called to account." White grinned his boyish smile. "I wrote to Elizabeth and told her. Didn't think you'd get word off until you reached the Cape . . ." Drinkwater tried to express his thanks but White rattled on, all the while pacing the deck and staring curiously about him. "By the devil but you've a fine frigate here, and no mistake. Mole said you were *en flûte*."

"Aye, sir. Twelve eighteens on the main deck."

"And you fought the *Romaine* with a broadside of six, eh?"

"Not quite. We had 'em all mounted to starboard." White's eyebrows went up and then came down with comprehension. "So your larboard battery was empty?"

"Yes, sir."

"Well stap me. You're becoming as unorthodox as Nelson. But we thought you'd struck."

"Ensign halliards shot through," Drinkwater said obscurely.

"Ahhh." White gave Drinkwater a quizzical look. "We had been looking for a French cruiser ever since *Jupiter* was mauled by *Preneuse* in October. We thought *Romaine* was the *Preneuse*, damn it." He rubbed his hands. "Still, we will see you to the Cape, eh? Table Bay for orders, you may tell Morris that. What d'you say to dinner on the *Telemachus*, eh?"

Drinkwater cast a rueful glance at the cabin skylight. "I shall be honoured to accept, sir. And I am indebted to you for writing to Elizabeth. She was with child, d'you see."

White made a deprecating gesture with his hand, pregnant women being outside his experience. He had caught the significance of Drinkwater's concern for the smouldering Morris beneath them. "Haven't made it too hard for you, have I? Between you and Morris, I mean?"

"It couldn't be much worse, sir."

White cocked a shrewd eye at Drinkwater. "Had you struck?"

"*I* hadn't sir." Drinkwater returned the stare and emphasised the personal pronoun.

"I'll see you at the Cape, Nat." Drinkwater watched

White's gig pull smartly away. The Cape of Good Hope was still a thousand miles distant and seamen called it the Cape of Storms. It had been that on their outward voyage, he hoped it might live up to its other name on the homeward. Drinkwater put his hat on.

"Brace her sharp up, Mr. Lestock. A course of south-west if she'll take it."

He went below to confront Morris.

The commander sat bolt upright in his chair, his hands gripping the arms. He was paralysed by the judicial implications of White's remark and fear of the noose warred with a sense of outrage at being humiliated on his own quarterdeck. The timid White had become a choleric, devil-may-care captain, a coming man and recognisably dangerous to Morris's low cunning.

Drinkwater had the distinct impression that Morris would spring at his throat even while he sat rigid with shock. Perhaps Nathaniel saw in his mind's eye the intent of Morris's spirit.

"I am sorry for Captain White's remark sir, I was not a party to . . ."

"God damn you, Drinkwater! God damn you to hell!" Morris spat the words from between clenched teeth, but so great was his fury as it burst through his self restraint that his words became an incomprehensible torrent of filth and invective.

Drinkwater spun on his heel. Later Rattray came in search of Dalziell.

Two weeks passed during which Morris made no appearance on deck. Appleby paid him daily visits, announcing that though there was some improvement in his condition it was not as rapid as he himself had hoped. He did not amplify the remark but it was made with a significant gravity that was not lost on Drinkwater.

*   *   *

They were not to come to the shelter of Table Bay without leave of the sea. *Antigone* carried the favourable current round the southern tip of Africa ignorant of the fact that somewhere off the Agulhas Bank, where the continental shelf declines into the depths of the Southern Ocean, a combination of the prevailing westerlies opposing the force of the current produces some of the most monstrous seas encountered by man.

As the frigate beat laboriously to windward, her small crew wet through, tired and hungry, the westerly gales blew furiously. Even the bad jokes about the southern summer faded giving way to hissed oaths as men struggled to haul the third earings out to the topsail yardarms.

In the screaming madness of an early morning Lieutenant Drinkwater clung onto a mizen backstay. The decks were shiny with water, pools of it still running out through the lee ports from the last inundation. Every rope ran with water, the sails were stiff with it. To windward *Telemachus* buttered into the seas.

Amidships he heard a cry and saw the seaman's pointing arm.

"Oh, my God," whispered Drinkwater, his voice filled with awe. He reached for the speaking trumpet: "Hold fast! Hold fast there!"

At the cry Mr. Quilhampton looked up from the coil of log line in its basket. His gaze fell stupidly on his left arm. He had a hook there now, cunningly fashioned from a cannon worm by Mr. Trussel. He flung himself down behind the aftermost carronade slide and hooked its point round a slewing eye, throwing a bight of the train tackle round his waist and catching a turn on the gun's cascabel. It was his very vulnerability that saved him.

At the main deck companionway Dalziell emerged on deck unbidden, dismissed by Morris in the dawn. The wave was three-quarters of a mile away when they had seen it, looming huge over the crests before it, a combination of forces far beyond the imagination. Its crest was reaching that critical state of instability that would induce its collapse in a rolling avalanche of water.

The frigate fell into the trough and her sails cracked from loss of wind. Even in the depths of her hull, where Appleby was doing his morning rounds this momentary hiatus was felt. Then the mass of solid water thundered over the ship.

Drinkwater was smashed to his knees and swept along the deck like flotsam. He was washed beneath a gun, the air squeezed from his lungs as his mind filled with a red and roaring struggle for breath. Mr. Quilhampton too, lay gasping as the seemingly endless mass of water poured green across the deck. Forward a tremble and a shudder told where the frigate's long jib-boom detached itself from the bowsprit. A body bumped past Drinkwater and then *Antigone* began to rise, the water sluicing from her decks. The succeeding waves were much lower, giving men time to catch their breath. They staggered to their feet, stumbling among the shot, dislodged from the garlands and rolling menacingly from side to side, ready to trip or cripple the unwary.

Drinkwater coughed the last of the sea water from him and helped Mr. Quilhampton to his feet. "Get below, see Meyrick for a flask of rum!" He raised his voice.

"Quartermaster! Up helm! Ease the ship before the wind." He picked up the speaking trumpet rolling fortuitously past him across a deck that was still inches deep in water. "Mr. Grey! Have your men at the braces! Rise foretacks and sheets, get the ship before the wind! Have Johnson sound the well!"

Already the ship was turning, gathering way from her broached position, supine in the huge wave troughs and rolling abominably, sluggish from the water washing about below.

"Spanker brails there! Douse the spanker, Mr. Q!" He grabbed the flask from the midshipman and drew on its contents.

He looked forward as the spirit warmed him. They might have lost the jib-boom but they could still set a fore topmast staysail. He would get everything off her in a minute, leaving only the clews of the forecourse to goosewing her before the wind while they sorted out the shambles and pumped her dry. They must not run off too much easting for they would have to claw every inch back again.

Slowly they fought the ship before the wind, cutting away the raffle forward, unjamming the blocks aloft where parted ropes had fouled, and laboriously pumping the Southern Ocean from their bilges. It was four hours before they brought the ship to the wind again. *Telemachus* had disappeared.

It was only then they found Dalziell was missing.

"Permission to make the signal, sir?" Drinkwater requested. Morris did not turn, merely nodded. Drinkwater looked up at the peak of the gaff. Old Glory, the British red ensign they had salvaged from *Hellebore* and that had fluttered briefly over a tiny islet in the Red Sea, now cracked, tattered, in the sharp breeze blowing into Table Bay. Beneath it flew the much larger ensign of France, its brilliant scarlet fly snapping viciously, as though resenting its inferior position.

"Hoist away, Mr. Q." The little bundles rose to break out in the sunshine and stream colourfully to leeward. Mr. Quilhampton looked aloft with evident pride.

"Beg pardon, zur," said Tregembo, belaying the halliards, "but what do it say?"

"It says, Tregembo," explained Quilhampton expansively, "that this ship is the prize of the brig-sloop *Hellebore*."

Not one of the most memorable of signals, Drinkwater concluded, levelling his glass at the fifty-gun two-decker *Jupiter* with a broad pendant at her masthead. But given the limitations of the code an apt description of *Antigone*. He wished it was old Griffiths who occupied the weather side of her quarterdeck.

Morris turned, as if aware of Drinkwater's thoughts. There was a calmness about the commander that had come with returning health. It pleased Appleby but worried Drinkwater. There was a triumph in those hooded eyes.

"Have the ship brought to the wind, Mr. Lestock," ordered Morris. There was a new authority about Morris too, a confidence which disturbed Drinkwater. The sailing master obeyed the order with obsequious alacrity. Morris had exploited the dislike between his master and first lieutenant to make Lestock a creature of his own. Lestock now wore a permanently prim expression, anticipating Drinkwater's imminent downfall. It occurred to Drinkwater as he observed this new and unholy alliance that Dalziell had gone unmourned.

Drinkwater touched the letter in his pocket. If he could have it delivered to White all might yet be set right, provided it did not fall into the wrong hands or was misconstrued. That thought set doubts whirling in his brain and to steady himself he raised his glass again.

Antigone was turning into the wind, her sails backing. At an order from the quarterdeck Johnson let the anchor go. The splash was followed by the rumble of the cable snaking up from the tiers.

"Topsail halliards!"

"Aloft and stow! Aloft and stow!"

"Commence the salute, Mr. Rogers!"

Drinkwater could see six vessels in the anchorage. Three flew the blue pendant of the Transport Board and partially obscured what appeared to be two frigates and a sloop. He stared hard, satisfying himself that one of the frigates was *Telemachus*. White had beaten them to the Cape after their separation in the gale. He felt a sensation of relief at the sight of the distant frigate.

"Hoist the boat out." Morris addressed the perfunctory order to Drinkwater who ignored the implied discourtesy. They had repaired a single boat for use at the Cape and Drinkwater watched it swung up from the waist and over the side by the yardarm tackles. The crew tumbled down into it. A sight of the land had cheered the hands at least, he mused, wondering if he dared dispatch the letter in the boat.

He decided against it and joined the side party waiting to see Commander Morris ashore. He knew Morris would keep them all waiting. Rogers joined him, having secured his signal guns.

"I suppose we must wait for that dropsical pig like a pair of whores at a wedding, eh?" Rogers muttered into Drinkwater's ear. Drinkwater found himself oddly sympathetic to Rogers's crude wit. From a positive dislike of each other the two men had formed a mutual respect, acknowledging their individual virtues. In the difficulties they had shared since the loss of the brig and assumption of command by Morris this had ripened to friendship. Drinkwater grinned his agreement.

Morris emerged at last in full dress. He paused in front of Drinkwater, swaying slightly, the stink of rum on his breath.

"And now," said Morris with quiet purpose, "we will see about you."

As he stared into Morris's eyes Drinkwater understood. The death of Dalziell removed substantial evidence of any possible case against Morris. Dalziell was a used vessel, the breaking of which liberated Morris from his past. The action which *Antigone* had fought with *Romaine* had been creditable and, as commander, Morris would benefit from that credit. A feeling almost of reform animated Morris, consonant with his new opportunities and encouraged by his reinvigoration after his illness. The huge irony that Morris had obtained his step in rank thanks to Drinkwater's efforts was enlarged by the reflection that he might yet found a professional reputation based upon his lieutenant's handling of the *Antigone* during the action with the *Romaine*. All these facts were suddenly clear to Nathaniel as he returned Morris's drunken stare.

He took his hat off as Morris turned to the rail. Another thought struck him. To succeed in his manipulation of events Morris must now utterly discredit Drinkwater. And Nathaniel had no doubt that was what he was about to do.

The problem of conveying the letter to *Telemachus* solved itself an hour later when Drinkwater renewed his acquaintance with Mr. Mole. Drinkwater had viewed the approaching boat with some misgivings but was relieved when Mole's mission was revealed to be the bearing of an invitation to the promised dinner aboard White's frigate.

"Would you oblige me, Mr. Mole," Drinkwater had said after accepting the kindness and privately hoping he was still at liberty to enjoy it, "by delivering this note to Captain White when you return to your ship. It is somewhat urgent."

"Captain White attends the commodore aboard *Jupiter*, sir."

Drinkwater thought for a second. "Be so kind to see he receives it there, Mr. Mole, if you please." The departure of Mr. Mole sent Drinkwater into an anxious pacing during which Appleby tried to interrupt him. But Appleby was snubbed. Drinkwater knew of the surgeon's apprehensions, knew he was worried about the possible discovery of Catherine Best's activities and guessed that the future of Harry Appleby himself figured largely in those fears. But Drinkwater's anxiety excluded the worries of others. That pendant at the masthead of *Jupiter* meant the formal and sometimes summary justice of naval regulation. The Cape might be an outpost, a salient held in the Crown's fist at the tip of Africa but it was within the boundaries of Admiralty. Nathaniel shivered.

When nemesis appeared a little later it was in the person of a midshipman even more supercilious than Mr. Mole. Mr. Pierce was conducted to Drinkwater by Quilhampton.

"The commodore, desires, sah, that you be so kind as to accompany me to the *Jupiter* without unnecessary delay, sah," he drawled. Pierce's manner was so exaggerated that it struck Drinkwater that all these spriggish midshipmen must see him as an old tarpaulin lieutenant, every hair a rope-yarn, every finger a marline spike. The thought steadied him, sent him below for his sword with something approaching dignity. When he emerged in his best coat, now threadbare and shiny, the battered French hangar at his side and his hat fresh glazed with some preparation concocted by Meyrick from God knew what, only the violent beating of his heart betrayed him.

"Very well, Mr. Pierce, let us be off."

Watching from forward Tregembo muttered his "good luck," aware that his own future was allied to Drinkwater's. Further aft Mr. Quilhampton saw him go. The midshipman had watched the furious pacing of the last hour, knew the

Antigone's open secret and shared his shipmates' hatred of their commander. He had also once taken a most ungentlemanly look at Mr. Drinkwater's journals. He too muttered his good wishes which mingled with a quixotic vision of shooting Morris dead in a duel if anything happened to Mr. Drinkwater.

Captain George Losack, commodore of the naval forces then at the Cape, leaned back in his chair and looked up at Captain White. The cabin of *Jupiter* had an air of relief in it, as though something unpleasant had just occurred and both men wished to re-establish normality as quickly as possible; to divert their minds from contemplating the recently vacated chair and the papers surrounding it. Commander Morris's hat still lay on the side table where he had laid it earlier.

"Well, by God, what d'you make of that?"

"He did not want me here, sir," replied White, "it was clear he considered I prejudiced his case."

"Because you are an acquaintance of this fellow Drinkwater?"

"That sir, and the fact that the baser side of his nature is known to me . . ."

Losack looked up sharply. "Be advised and drop that, Richard. A court-martial under that Article would be politically risky for us both. Though Jemmy Twitcher no longer rules the Admiralty and addresses blasphemous sermons to a congregation of cats he is still powerful. To antagonise the brother of his lordship's mistress would not only move the earl's malice it might invite the enmity of his whore."

White shut his mouth. He did not subscribe to the older man's fear of the Earl of Sandwich. Petticoat interference in the affairs of the navy had affected men of his generation deeply. The disasters of the American War could in part be attributed to this form of malign influence. "Nevertheless," he said, "Morris terrorised the cockpit and lower deck of the *Cyclops* in the last war. Sometimes a man is called to account for that."

"Rarely," replied Losack drily, ringing the bell on his deck, "though 'tis a fine, pious thought." His man appeared. "Wine Jacklin, directly if you please."

White watched Losack as the commodore once again scanned the papers before him. The allegations that Morris had made against Drinkwater looked serious for the lieutenant. But the circumstances that had followed White's own questions had thrown a doubt over the whole and Losack was too diligent an officer to take refuge in his isolation from London and dismiss the affair. And the matter of Morris's influence could not be ignored. It behove Losack to tread carefully. He had seen something of one party. What of the other?"

"You say Drinkwater had a commission years ago?"

"He had a commission as acting lieutenant back in eighty-one. He passed over Morris."

"Ah. Then Morris was appointed over him at Mocha, eh? The first action turns his head, the second overturns his senses. The consequence is bad blood . . ." Losack paused as the wine arrived. Jacklin placed the salver and decanters. He turned to White.

"Mr. Mole's compliments sir, and I was to give you this at once." White took the letter. Losack went on: "There would be a case to answer if I was sure . . ." he stopped indecisively, worried about Morris's wild allegations.

"I do not think Drinkwater was greatly disappointed in eighty-one, sir. His commission dates from ninety-seven. . . ."

"Well, what manner of man is he, White?" snapped Losack exasperated. "You seem damned eager to befriend him."

"Damn it, sir," said White, flushing with anger, "'tis a devilish difficult business serving under a . . . a . . ." He recovered himself. "Drinkwater, sir, is a thoroughly professional officer. He commands little or no influence. I doubt he gave Morris grounds for his allegations beyond an excess of zeal and surely it has not come to an officer suffering for that?"

Losack stood and turned to stare through the cabin windows, his hands clasped behind his back. He found his command at the Cape a tiresome business. His force was inadequate to police the converging trade routes that made his post so important and such a rich hunting ground for French corsairs. The parochial problems of passing ships were a confounded nuisance. The present one was no exception; bad feeling between the officers of a prize, a woman convict mixed up in some unholy cabal. He felt irritated by the demands of his rank, envying White who sat on the table edge, his leg swinging while he read the letter Jacklin had brought in.

"It was the remark you made about the striking of the flag that caused our late visitor to fly into a passion. What was behind that, eh?"

White looked up from the letter. "May I suggest you ask Drinkwater, sir. I have here a letter from him. It would appear that at Mocha some error was committed. Morris's commission should have gone to him!"

"Good God!" Losack looked up sharply. "An excess of zeal, d'you say? By God, it looks to me more like bloody-minded madness! '*Quos deus vult perdere, prius dementat.*'"

"I do not think for a moment that he is mad, sir. Overwrought, perhaps. Angry even. As Horace has it, '*Ira furor brevis est*'."

"Hmmm. Let us send for this friend of yours."

* * *

Appleby too had been summoned. He sat on a bench in the bare anteroom of the hospital and looked down at the chequered Dutch floor tiles. Despite the cool of the room he was sweating profusely, his mind a confusion of counteracting thoughts in which his professional detachment was knocked all awry by the depth of his feeling for Catherine Best. "They have sent for me," he had told her shakily, "I am too old to dissemble, Catherine, I am fearful there may be consequences . . ."

She had been silent, having said all she had to say days before. Now her opportunist nature waited upon events. She was not a maker of circumstances, simply a manipulator of their outcome. But she kissed him as he left, puffing up the ladders, fat, ungainly, ageing and kind. Now he sweated like a man under sentence.

"You seem to be suffering from diaphoresis yourself, Mr. Appleby," said the physician, surprising him. Appleby rose to his feet. "Shall we take a turn in the garden, my dear sir?"

Mr. Macphadden was a dry, bent little Scot who exuded an air of erudition, the garden a cloistered square of trimmed lawn suitable for the exchange of medical confidences. "From the message that ran ahead of the patient I fully expected to find I had a derangement on my hands. Indeed I had effected the precaution of preparing a jacket for the fellow. But I was misinformed. The ravings were no more than those of a drunk, far gone in his cups and overcome by an exaggeration of the choleric humour, so my anticipation was a little out of kilter with the facts." The doctor chuckled wheezily to himself while Appleby held his breath. "The effects of rum are well-known. I don't doubt but that you know Haslar is full of men for whom rum has been a consolation, men for whom responsibility is too great, whose expectations have been disap pointed, whose abilities are inadequate. Why, the chemical effect of rum upon the brain itself . . ."

"But his sickness, doctor. The diaphoresis, the purging and vomiting . . ." Appleby could restrain himself no longer, though he checked himself sufficiently to adopt a tone of deference, not daring to suggest a diagnosis lest such presumption invited contradiction.

"Oh, you are worried about his wild allegations about being poisoned, eh? Well he is, in a manner of speaking, but I think we may consider that he is effecting his own ruin. No, he has chronic gastric inflammation, undoubtedly due to a peptic ulcer of some inveteracy. You see, my dear sir, his temperament seems to vacillate between the choleric and the melancholic humours. The man who depends upon drink hides both an acknowledged weakness and an inability to accept his own culpability for self-destruction. The consequence of such a vicious spiral can have but one result. That of the unhappy man now lying in his bed yonder."

Macphadden turned and they began pacing back to the white walled hospital. A flood of relief began to wash over Appleby and he nodded at the physician's words: "I doubt you will want a commanding officer in the throes of a delirium tremens."

Drinkwater returned to *Antigone* after the frustrations of an hour-long interview with Losack. It was clear from the manner of the commodore's questions that the contents of his letter to White had made known. A sense of betrayal that the information had been made available to Losack was heightened by White's silence during Drinkwater's ordeal. The letter had been a private document between friends. Now it seemed a court-martial might be pending against him.

The knock at his cabin door announced the arrival of Ap-

pleby for whom he had sent as soon as the surgeon arrive
from the shore.

"Things have turned out well, Nat. A didactic Scot name
Macphadden has diagnosed gastritis . . ."

"Things are *not* well, Harry . . ."

"What the devil is it?"

"Catherine, Harry. She is known to be a convict. She is t
be transported. I did my best," he paused at the unintende
pun, "my uttermost, but Morris has revealed her real status t
Losack."

The colour drained from Appleby's face. "Why the un
charitable whoreson bastard!"

"Calm yourself. There is nothing either of us can do here
Perhaps when we reach home . . ." It was a straw held out t
a drowning man. It was doubtful if he would reach home wit
a reputation untarnished enough to secure a convict's pardon
no matter how meritorious her services.

"But Nat, I cannot let her go."

"She is to take passage in the *Lord Moira* without delay.
am so very sorry."

In silence Appleby left the cabin. Opening his des
Drinkwater took out inkwell and pen and began to write th
report Losack had requested.

Drinkwater sat in silence while Losack read his report, occa
sionally referring to the corroborative evidence of the dec
and signal logs and what remained of Griffiths's papers. A
last the commodore looked up and removed his spectacle
For a moment he regarded the man sitting anxiously befor
him.

"Mr. Drinkwater," he said after this pause, "it seems that
have been unnecessarily suspicious of you." He waved th
spectacles over the books and papers spread out upon th

table. "I am persuaded that your services merit some recognition, but you will understand it is a difficult matter to resolve. I am not empowered to restitute your commission and it may be some consolation to you that in any event it would have required their Lordships' ratification. There the matter must rest."

Drinkwater inclined his head. "I understand, sir."

Losack smiled. "The only reparation I can offer you is command of the prize home. Do you attend to her refit. A convoy sails in some three weeks. You should be ready to join it. Your devoted friend Captain White will command the escort."

"Thank you, sir. And Commander Morris?"

"Is sick, Mr. Drinkwater. A peptic ulcer, I understand." Losack closed the subject.

Drinkwater rose and Losack tossed a bundle across the table. "My secretary recognised your name, this letter has been here for months wainting for you."

With a beating heart he picked up Elizabeth's letter.

The air of the quarterdeck of the *Jupiter* was undeniably sweet and in an unoccupied corner he tore open the packet, catching the enclosure for Quilhampton and stuffing it in his pocket. Impatiently he began to read.

My Dearest Nathaniel,

At long last I have received news of you, that you were sent round Africa in accordance with some notion of Ad. Nelson's. I write in great anxiety about you and pray nightly for your well-being and that, if God wills it, you will return whole and safe.

But you will not wish to hear of me now that another claims your affections, my dearest. Your daughter Charlotte Amelia is past a twelve-month now and has her fa ther's nose, poor lamb . . ."

Drinkwater handed the letter with the thin feminine super scription to Quilhampton. "Pass word for Tregembo, Mr. Q." When the boy had gone he peered into the mirror let into the lid of his cabin chest. What the devil was the matter with his nose?

Tregembo coughed respectfully at the open door and Drinkwater started, aware that for several minutes he had been staring vacantly at his reflection contemplating his new role as a father.

"Ah, Tregembo. Your Susan is quite well. Mrs. Drinkwa ter writes to tell me the news. She had a little quinsy some months past but was in good spirits. The letter is some months old I am afraid."

"An' your baby, zur?"

"A daughter, Tregembo."

"Ahhh." The awkward, almost embarrassed monosyllable was full of hidden pleasure. Tregembo flushed and Drinkwa ter swallowed. "And the commission, zur?"

"No commission, not yet."

"'Tis nought but a matter of time, zur."

Drinkwater smiled as Tregembo resumed his duties. It oc curred to him that he was smiling a lot this morning. He turned again to the letter and re-read it.

Appleby burst in upon him. "Nat, a word, do I hear cor rectly that you command the ship home?"

Drinkwater looked up. The surgeon was agitated, his hands fluttering, his jowls wobbling. "Yes I do."

"Then I beg you will permit me to leave the ship."

"What the devil d'you mean?"

"The *Lord Moira* has a vacancy for a surgeon's assistant.

have made enquiries, there are precious few surgeons in the colony . . . I have taken the vacancy for the passage." Appleby swallowed hard. He had crossed his Rubicon.

"Harry, you sly dog, do you purpose to become an emigrant?"

Appleby ran a finger round his collar. "She'd hardly be fit company for me at Bath, would she?"

Drinkwater began to laugh but was interrupted by Appleby. "Come Nat, I pray your attention for a moment, I have little time. Here are some papers giving you powers to act on my behalf in the matter of prize money. I beg you consent and purchase for me the quantities of medicines here listed. Any apothecary will comprehend these zodiacal signs. I am also in need of new instruments, doubtless I will need become a man-midwife and I am without forceps . . ."

Drinkwater nodded at Appleby's instructions, taking the bundle of papers, thinking of Catherine Best, of Elizabeth and of Charlotte Amelia and the power of the hand that rocks the cradle.

Drinkwater returned the decanter to White and leaned forward to light the cheroot from the candle flame. "I think now that the others have left we might forget the divisions of rank, eh?" White chuckled. "Young Quilhampton is something of an imp of Satan, is he not? Did you hear his assertion that young Bruilhac considers you eat human limbs? No, don't protest, my dear fellow, I heard quite clearly."

"Mr. Quilhampton is given to exaggeration, I regret to say," said Drinkwater with some affection. Then he frowned. "There's something I want to ask you, Richard. Something I don't understand. What exactly happened the other day when Morris reported to Losack? You *were* there, were you not?"

White puffed out his florid cheeks. "Yes, I was there and

my presence seemed to infuriate Morris. I suppose he thought I was going to mention his unpleasant habits. He began to complain about you. Minor matters; the way you did not always refer to him when shortening sail, you know the sort of thing. He kept looking at me as if I might contradict him. I could smell rum on his breath and could see he was enunciating his words with care. He began some cock and bull allegations that you were poisoning him. I didn't like the sound of that! I could tell Losack was taking an interest and I asked Morris why he struck to the *Romaine*." White laughed.

"By heaven, that threw him flat aback! He looked at me with his jaw hanging like a scandalised gaff. Then he began a stream of meaningless abuse, interspersed with occasional references to you and poison. He was beside himself and in the middle of this outburst he had what I took at first to be a fit. In fact I understand it to have been a gastric spasm."

White paused, refilled his glass and continued. "Although it was obvious that Morris was ill, or drunk, or both, Losack fretted over the allegations of poisoning. I'm certain he had it in mind to put the matter to a court-martial, he had sufficient ships here to convene one. While I thought Morris had gone off his head he thought you were mad."

"Me?"

"Aye, you. I showed him the letter in which you claimed the commission granted Morris had been intended for you."

"Oh, my God . . . I thought you had. But that was a private letter, Richard, I had no idea . . ."

"I know, I know, my dear fellow, but it did the trick. Losack wanted to see you, and once he had the doctor's diagnosis and had studied your report he knew the truth as well as I did. But for a while I thought he would have you examined! He quoted Euripides at me. Er, 'Whom God destroys he first makes mad.'"

"That might more readily be applied to Morris."

"To which," White pressed on, not to be deterred, "I managed to reply with a snippet of Horace, to wit '*Ira furor brevis est*.'"

"I'm sorry, you have the advantage of me."

"'Anger is a brief madness.'"

"Ahhh." Drinkwater leaned back in his chair. He had had a narrow escape from a dangerous vindictiveness. "I am greatly indebted to you, Richard."

White waved his thanks aside. "I owed you for your support on the *Cyclops* against that unsavoury rakehell."

"Well, the score is even now," said Drinkwater. "I suppose I had better see Morris. Try to make my peace with him before we leave."

White looked at him sharply. "See Morris? What the devil for? Let the bastard rot."

"But he is ill, Richard . . ."

"Stap me, Nat, you are a soft-hearted fool. But 'tis why we love you, Bruilhac's limbs notwithstanding. Besides, Morris would not thank you for it. He would misconstrue your motives, assume you had come to gloat. There is no point in seeing Morris. Ever again." The remark seemed final and White tossed off his glass. Refilling it, he too eased back in his chair. The cabin filled with a companionable silence, broken only by the creak of the hull, the groaning of the rudder chains and the occasional muffled noise from the people forward. Drinkwater felt a massive weight lift from him. White's explanation had cleared the air of lingering doubts, images of Elizabeth and the yet unseen Charlotte Amelia floated in the blue cheroot smoke. He felt a great contentment spread through him.

"I recollect another piece of Horace that is perhaps more apposite to the case," said White at last. " "*Caelum non ani-*

mum mutant qui trans mare currunt.' Which rendered into English is, 'They change their skies but not their souls who run across the sea.'"

And looking across the table at his flushed friend Drinkwater nodded his agreement.

Author's Note

Detractors of Napoleon have insinuated that his Indian project was a fantasy of St. Helena. There is evidence, however, to suggest there was a possibility that he contemplated such an expedition in 1798 or 1799. Certainly Nelson regarded it seriously enough to send Lieutenant Duval overland to Bombay *after* his victory at the Nile, and as late as November 1798 the dissembling Talleyrand suggested it.

The British attack on Kosseir is rather obscure. Even that most partial of historians, William James, admits that *Daedalus* and *Fox* shot off three quarters of their ammunition to little effect. He finds it less easy to explain how about a hundred diseased French soldiers, the remnants of two companies of the 21st Demi-brigade under Donzelot, could drive off a British squadron of overwhelming power. Perhaps this is why he makes no mention of *Hellebore*'s presence, since Captain Ball did not do so in his report, thus saving a little credit for the British.

The senior officers who appear in these pages actually existed. Rear Admiral Blankett commanded the Red Sea squadron at this time, though his character is my own invention. So too is Mr. Wrinch, though a British "agent" appears to have resided at Mocha at about his period.

The part played by Edouard Santhonax is not verified by history, but the consequences of his daring are the only testimony we have to Nathaniel Drinkwater's part in this small campaign. Napoleon later complained that the British had a ship wherever there was water to float one. The brig *Hellebore* was one such ship.

As to sources of other parts of the story, the mutiny on the *Mistress Shore* is based on the near contemporary uprising on the transport *Lady Shore*, while the presence of women on British men-of-war was not unknown.

For proof of drunkenness and homosexuality in the navy of this time I refer the curious to the contemporary evidence of Hall, Gardner and Beaufort, amongst others. Much may also be inferred from other diarists.